A NOVEL

Saturday Morning

LAURAINE SNELLING

WaterBrook
PRESS

SATURDAY MORNING
PUBLISHED BY WATERBROOK PRESS
12265 Oracle Boulevard, Suite 200
Colorado Springs, Colorado 80921
A division of Random House Inc.

The characters and events in this book are fictional, and any resemblance to actual persons or events is coincidental.

ISBN 1-57856-788-2

Library of Congress Cataloging-in-Publication Data
Snelling, Lauraine.
    Saturday morning / Lauraine Snelling.— 1st ed.
        p. cm.
    ISBN 1-57856-788-2
    1. Women's shelters—Fiction. 2. Female friendship—Fiction. 3. Abused women—Fiction. I. Title.
    PS3569.N39S28 2005
    813'.54—dc22

                                                                2005012228

Printed in the United States of America
2005—First Edition

10 9 8 7 6 5 4 3 2 1

Years ago, I belonged to a study/prayer group at Saint Andrew's Lutheran Church in Vancouver, Washington. We decided to take God at His Word and see what happened. Ever since then I have truly believed in miracles, the power of prayer, and our Father who loves and listens and still acts today. Someday I'll see you all again. I wish everyone a "Girl Squad."

Acknowledgments

How grateful I am for friends who give their time and expertise to help a book become. Chelley Kitzmiller went far beyond the norm in helping me rewrite this book and make it work. Thanks, my friend, I will be forever in your debt. Kathleen Wright can ask questions like no other in order to help me understand who the characters really are and what they want and need. This is no little gift that she shares so generously. Chelley, Nanci, and Karen, thanks for reading and commenting to help me pull out the best for this book. I am convinced I have the best support group possible. Thanks to all of you for your prayers, wise counsel, and constant encouragement. Oh yes, and the brainstorming, too. Bonnie Line is my tea and scone expert. Thanks, Bonnie.

Thank you, Cecile, who hired on as an assistant and did not know, nor did I, how your editorial skills would grow and blossom. You do the work of three people, and I know my editors appreciate you too.

Dudley Delffs and all those at WaterBrook Press, thanks for believing and pursuing excellence. What a team you are. Thanks for being part of my life. Thanks, Laura Barker, for encouraging me to write this book.

Thanks to Brian and Brian and for your stories and information about San Francisco and encouragement; to Rose Liggon who gave me the idea for Hope; to Woodeene for taking me to the Lavender farm in Eugene; to Brian at Speedy's, best wishes for all success at your store. I love farmers' markets and shop there whenever I can. I think that comes out in this book, so thanks to all those who've made markets so enjoyable. You get an A+ for sharing recipes and knowledge.

Mark Bittner wrote a book of his experiences with the Wild Parrots of San Francisco. Thanks, Mark, for all you shared, and the movie was pure pleasure. One of the highlights of research for this book was seeing the flock of parrots fly overhead and watching them land and chatter in the trees of Mrs. Marchant's Garden. What a delight.

And always, husband, partner, researcher, and best friend, Wayne, the research trips on this one were wonderful fun. You were so patient as we figured out exactly where and why things should happen for this story. We do enjoy San Francisco, but like Andy, we find visiting good, and we're glad to go home again to our mountain valley and to all the critters who make our life complete.

Thanks, God, for letting me write and tell stories that I pray bring You glory.

Chapter One

Lavender Meadows
Medford, Oregon

"We did it! We did it!"

Andy Taylor threw the purchase order in the air, leaped from her chair, and whirlwind dance-stepped around the workshop barn of Lavender Meadows. "We finally made it." She switched from shouting to singing, making up words as she went. "We're in the money. From now on every day will be sunny. Give lavender sachets to your honey. Yeah, yeah, yeah, yeah."

After two turns around the twenty-by-twenty workspace, Andy stopped, caught her breath, then retrieved the purchase order from the plank floor where it had landed. Her hands trembled as she read it again, this time committing each word to memory, beginning with the Nordstrom store letterhead. When she got to the signature, she squealed in delight. She hadn't imagined it. It was real. Mike Johnson, the head buyer, wanted the entire line of lavender-based products: soaps, hand and body lotions, sachets, tea—even the cookbook—for all his California stores.

Andy sank into the closest chair and stared at the paper. She felt tears gather in her eyes. All the hard work was finally starting to pay off. It had been a long, hard transition from the apple and pear orchards, which had been her parents' livelihood until the competition had beaten them out, to the fields of lavender, which had no competition at all because nobody thought it was a crop worth growing.

She focused on the quantity column and whistled. This was just the beginning. She knew how retail worked. Once the products were in the store and the other chains got wind of them, there would be calls from other buyers and more orders. Now that was the kind of competition she welcomed.

She tried to mentally calculate the profit on this first order. Numbers flashed in front of her eyes like a calculator gone berserk. She would have to put pencil to paper, but she was sure there would be enough profit to stash a few thousand into her parents' retirement account as well as to buy or lease the equipment she needed to produce essential oil of lavender.

Andy wrapped her arms around her middle and squeezed herself. She could hardly wait to give her parents the good news.

From the day she'd begged them to become her business partners, telling them that she really needed their experience and help, they had been behind her with encouragement and support. If they had ever seen through her intentions, they never let on.

She wished her husband was half as encouraging and supportive as her parents. He loved her and admired her, of that she had no doubt. He often told her she had "many fine qualities." But as far as he was concerned, Lavender Meadows was and always would be just a "nice little hobby." Why last year's balance sheet hadn't made him see Lavender Meadows' potential, she didn't know, but surely this order would wake him up, make him see now what the rest of them saw.

Andy's thoughts raced. Martin. How would she tell him? What would she say? "Dear, I have something to tell you." She shook her

head. Not enough punch. "Martin, I think you should sit down."
Scratch that. Too dramatic. "Martin, you know how you've always
called Lavender Meadows my *little hobby?*" She mentally handed him
the purchase order and imagined his eyes widening and the corners of
his mouth teasing into a smile.

"Andy, dear, where are you?" Her mother's voice came from the
walk between the house and the barn.

Martin's stunned face faded into nothingness. While the idea of
flaunting the order in his face was fun to think about, she would never
do it. Not in a million years. Instead, she would tell him the news via
e-mail, with words carefully chosen so they wouldn't sound like she
was saying, "I told you so."

"In here," Andy called back, putting Martin to the back of her
mind. She knew her mother always stopped at the sundial garden
where the flagstone path divided in a Y, one arm to Andy's house, the
other to the refurbished barn-turned-studio, office, production, and
shipping center. A half-dozen roses surrounded the sundial, the only
roses on the farm. Her mother's favorite was the tea rose named
Double Delight. It had a creamy center with petals tipped with the
pinks and reds of a brilliant sunrise. She didn't have to see her mother
to know she was bending over and inhaling the rose's potent fragrance.

"That rose is blooming more this year than ever before," Alice
said from the doorway, where she paused until her eyes could adjust.
Ever since her cataract surgery, she was more careful about going from
the bright daylight into the dimness of the refurbished barn. At length
she moved away from the door, walking as gracefully as she had
twenty years ago. It was all in her posture, Andy reminded herself, a
posture her mother had learned and practiced faithfully throughout
her years as a dancer.

"You say that every year."

"I know, but here it is September, and the meadows are covered with blossoms." Alice closed her eyes and sniffed the air. "Between roses and lavender, I always feel like I'm on a scent-sational high."

Andy smiled at her mother's unique use of their advertising slogan. "Clever. Very clever."

"Yes, I thought so too," Alice said with a laugh.

In years past, Andy and her mother had more than once been accused of being sisters, not only because they sounded so much alike but also because they looked alike, with straight hair cut just below their ears, broad brows, strong chins, and clear hazel eyes.

Once Andy had turned fifty, however, she refused to let her hair show any gray, and she always plucked her eyebrows to some semblance of order.

Andy could barely contain her excitement, but she'd decided to wait for the right moment to give her mother the good news. She wanted that moment to be one they would both savor for years to come. "You always make me feel good," she said instead.

Alice picked up the raffia-tied clump of lavender on her worktable. "Why, thank you. What a nice compliment."

Something I don't do often enough. Andy promised to rectify that failing and held out the purchase order. "I got a fax a few minutes ago from a new customer. It's the biggest order we've had yet." Andy handed her mother the purchase order and watched her read it.

Alice's face underwent a series of expressions: disbelief, shock, and finally jubilation. "This is— Oh, my. This is wonderful, I mean fabulous, I mean— Oh, honey." She glanced up, her eyes sparkling. Clearly, she was incapable of expressing herself further.

"This is just the beginning, Mom. Just the beginning." Andy surged to her feet and flung herself into her mother's arms. "We're a team, Mom. You, me, and Dad." She glanced around the workshop: bunches of drying lavender hanging from the lattice attached by chains to the aging beams, dried lavender blossoms piled in bins, toiletries and sachets displayed on a table. Cubbyholes with various sizes of plastic bags lined the wall above the worktable, where she and her father, Walt, spent hours preparing the various products for shipping.

Alice pulled back, concern wrinkling her brow. "Do we have enough product on hand for an order this size?"

Andy nodded. "It'll be tight, but we'll make it."

Alice breathed a sigh of relief, but the look of concern stayed with her. A moment later she asked, half under her breath, "Have you told Martin?"

Andy knew what her mother was thinking, the same thing Andy had been thinking a few minutes ago. "No. I'll e-mail him tonight after dinner. I'm sure he's in a meeting right now and wouldn't appreciate being interrupted." Martin, her husband of thirty-two years, spent all his afternoons in meetings, selling product for Advanced Electronic Systems, or AES as it was commonly known. When he wasn't in a meeting, he was on the road traveling to the next meeting. It was a never-ending cycle that had kept him absent from their home most of their married life. Andy had learned to cope because travel was what Martin did, what he'd always done. She contented herself with having him home at least two weekends a month, and she planned her schedule accordingly.

Alice laid the purchase order down on the worktable. "If we get any more orders like this, we'll have to hire more help."

"What do you mean *if*?"

"Don't be too cocky now," her mother warned, then turned toward the window that looked out over the south field. She had a faraway look in her eyes. "Who'd have thought that that lavender sachet I gave you way back when would come to…this?" She looked over her shoulder at her daughter. "You were right on, honey. About everything."

"I did a lot of praying, Mom."

"Well, it looks like your prayers and ours have been answered." Alice glanced heavenward, then turned back to Andy.

Now it was Andy's turn to gaze out the window. The south field, three acres lovingly planted with French lavender and cared for solely by her father, was the newest. Andy knew she'd inherited her love of growing things from her father and her love of cooking from her mother. From both of them came her love of Medford, Oregon, where she'd grown up and where she'd learned her faith at her parents' sides.

As newlyweds, she and Martin had purchased a corner of the family farm, making them the third generation to live on the land, and their three children, the fourth. Andy had insisted that they build the house close to her grandfather's old milking barn so the children could have all the animals their hearts desired. Over the decades, the barn had served as a home for her grandfather's milk cows, then as a shelter for the kids' beef cattle, sheep, and barn cats, and now as the center of business for Lavender Meadows.

"You know, it's funny," Alice said. "Your dad and I were talking over lunch about working up that stretch of pasture behind the barn. Do we have enough starts for that?"

Andy mentally counted her nursery rows of lavender cuttings rooted in four-inch plastic pots. "No, but it's not a problem. I'll have to order some Hidcote from one of the other nurseries." She raised her hands over her head in a stretch and inhaled the fragrance of lavender, underlain with old barn scents of hay, cattle, and manure.

With the excitement over, at least for the moment, Alice flipped through the in-box, looking through the rest of the mail. She pulled out a sheaf of paper-clipped order forms and laid them out on the worktable. "My goodness. That last ad we put in the *Rogue Valley News* has really paid off. There must be thirty orders here."

"I ran another one in the classifieds for this weekend, and now I wish I hadn't," Andy said. "Martin e-mailed and said that he has a long weekend at home and that I should plan something, but…"

"Dad and I can handle things here," Alice volunteered as she always did.

"Are you sure? That would be great." Andy turned her thoughts to the weekend ahead. "I wonder what he'd like to do. He always says that when he's home, he just wants to be home, but I'd sure like to go out to dinner on Saturday night. Maybe we could even take in a movie. I'll have to check what's playing."

Alice sat down and began to make order of the paperwork. "Have you heard from Morgan?"

"She's homesick. That hasn't changed. You'd think that she'd be thrilled to be there, what with all the years she dreamed of following in Bria's and Cam's footsteps in the hallowed halls of Pacific Lutheran University."

"Being happy to be someplace has no bearing on homesickness. I remember the first year you went to Bible camp." Alice chuckled softly.

Andy heard her mother's soft laughter and pretended an indignation she was far from feeling. "Mother, I was only eight. Besides all our family vacations, Morgan's been to 4-H camp, to Bible camp, and to Washington DC with her senior class, and she stayed with Bria in Seattle. I didn't really expect this of her."

"Just because three children are reared in the same family doesn't mean they will be anything like each other." Finished with her sorting, Alice picked up a one-pound plastic bag and set it on the digital scale.

"You don't need to weigh every one of those."

"I know. Just checking to make sure the machine is working right."

Andy's father had invented a machine, similar to a grocery store coffee grinder, with a dial that could be set to release dried lavender by ounces or pounds. One needed only to hold a bag under the spout, press the foot pedal, and wait until the bag was full. Both Andy and her mother had tried to talk him into patenting the invention, but he said it really wasn't that ingenious.

Andy noted how efficiently her mother worked. How good it was when parents and children could work together and still remain best friends. Not for the first time, Andy thought about how much she was like her mother. Besides looking like sisters, they had similar work ethics and morals. There was one similarity, however, that Andy wished were different. Both of them had given up promising careers for love. Alice had been the lead female dancer in a prestigious dance troupe in Los Angeles, and Andy had been halfway up the corporate ladder in a clothing store chain.

Sadly, the only dancing Alice had done since her wedding day was at church socials and the occasional evening out on the town. Until a couple of years ago, Andy had thought her own talent as a business-woman would be wasted as well. For thirty-two years there hadn't been much to apply it to, other than comparing rates for insurance com-panies and long-distance phone carriers. With extra time of her own, once the older children had started off to college, she found herself working outside more. She'd always loved lavender, and before she knew it, she had herself a lavender garden. One thing led to another, and soon the lavender blossoms were finding their way into her bath, under her pillow, and even into her cooking.

The making of lavender products for sale had seemed a natural transition, although she hadn't anticipated such a big demand. And what a delightful surprise that her "little hobby" had grown into a thriving home-based business.

When she accidentally stumbled across her parents' Merrill Lynch statement and saw that they had lost more than half of their retire-ment savings in bad stocks and wouldn't have enough to see them through their golden years, she knew she would have to do something to help them get back their nest egg. She prayed for a solution that would give them the money they needed without hurting their pride.

"You want to help me with the lavender wands?" Her mother's voice broke into her thoughts.

The woven lavender wands were her personal favorite. "Sure." Though the most labor-intensive of all their products, the ribbon-laced wands were also their bestsellers. The week before, Andy had offered two different classes in making them, but more people were still on the waiting list, eager for her call. "Hey, Mom, you want to teach the next round of classes?"

Alice snorted loudly. "No! I'll do whatever you need, except teach. You know that."

"Never hurts to ask." Andy shrugged and turned to the ringing phone. "Lavender Meadows. This is Andy. May I help you?" Picking up a pen, she poised it over a blank invoice. "I can ship that out FedEx tomorrow." She jotted down the customer's name, mailing address, and credit-card information. "May I ask how you heard about us?" She smiled when she heard the source. "Thank you for calling." She hung up and put the invoice in the in-box, then turned to her mother. "Word of mouth. The best advertising ever. Thank You, Lord." She glanced heavenward, as if adding an *amen* to her praise. "Is Dad at the house?"

In the midst of making a wand, Alice answered without taking her eyes off her work. "I think so. He was fixing the leak under the bathroom sink when I left."

"Ow! That probably means he's going to be in a bad mood all night." Plumbing was not her father's favorite thing.

"Probably. But once the blue smoke clears, he'll be fine again."

"I want to tell him our news and ask how soon he wants to start digging holes." She picked up the phone again and dialed her parents' number. She waited until the answering machine was ready to click on, then hung up. "He must be outside."

"Or still under the sink."

"I hope not." Andy gave a shudder that made them both smile. "You should have hired a plumber."

"He refused. He said there was no reason to pay fifty dollars for a plumber to do what he could do for free. Then he went out to the garage for his wrenches, and that was that."

Andy laughed. "I guess I don't have to wonder where I got my stubbornness, do I?"

That evening, after she and her mother had closed up shop, Andy went around the side of the barn to the lean-to that served as the chicken house and put the "girls" to bed. The evening ritual of counting hens and closing the door prevented marauding skunks and foxes from raiding the henhouse. Andy had raised chickens since she was in preschool. She had never eaten store-bought eggs, and she refused to start at her advanced age of fifty-two. Whistling for her dog, Comet, who was part Border collie and part traveling salesman, she gazed over at the pond. A stately white egret waited there for a last fish to swim near enough for a snack before flying to the trio of tall trees at the end of the lavender fields, where he roosted every night along with other egrets from miles around. Comet bounded over the lavender plants and wriggled her joy at being summoned. With her black ear flopped half forward and her white one standing erect, Comet doggy-grinned up at Andy.

"Good girl." Andy leaned over and rubbed the dog's ears. "Have you been helping Dad with the plumbing?"

More wriggles and a happy yip. The dog was watching the original farmhouse, which was shaded by a hundred-year-old maple. Comet patrolled the entire forty acres, taking care of both houses and those who lived in them. She and Chai Lai, the Siamese cat who ruled

Andy's house, had developed a truce over the years, growling at each other once in a while to lay to rest any thought that they might have become friends.

"I suppose you're hungry too."

Comet cocked her head up at Andy, her white muzzle and black nose bright in the fading light. If it weren't for her animals and the lavender business that kept her at a dead run, Andy might have been lonesome like her best friend, Shari, who couldn't seem to get out from under the empty-nest pangs and start enjoying herself and her freedom.

Andy headed toward the house, her joy making her steps light. With a few more customers like Nordstrom and steady orders coming in, one of these years Lavender Meadows might be so profitable that Martin would consider leaving his pressure-cooker job and helping her manage it.

A lovely thought, but not very realistic.

Chapter Two

Andy

"You want us to *what?*"

"To move to San Francisco."

Andy gasped. Move? Was this her husband talking, or an imposter? Physically, this man looked like Martin: six feet tall, dark hair silvered at the temples, and slender but packing a stubborn paunch that refused to submit to diet or the weight bench. It was Martin all right, but there was something very different about him—his eyes were full of anticipation. He leaned against the doorframe to her workshop; he tried to look nonchalant, but the knots of his hands in his pockets gave him away.

"Remember that I told you AES moved our headquarters there last year?" Martin, never Marty, smiled, a real smile that stretched his cheeks and brought out an oh-so-rare dimple.

Stunned by its appearance, Andy could only stare. How she loved that dimple. When had it gone into hiding? Worse, when had she failed to notice its absence?

"Andy?"

"Hmm? What?" She blinked and lifted her gaze up to his eyes. "Of course I remember. But you never said anything about having to move."

Martin took in a deep breath and nodded. For a normally poker-faced man, he was showing an amazing amount of enthusiasm. "It's not just a move," he added, excitement building with each word. "I've finally been offered the promotion I've always wanted—vice president of sales."

Andy sat back, clear now as to the reason for his enthusiasm. For years he'd been hoping he would be offered the vice presidency, but getting it meant that somebody had to either step up or be let go. Andy decided not to ask which it was. "Oh, Martin. That's wonderful." The words tumbled out of her mouth. "It's about time! I'm happy for you, honey. Really happy." She got up, crossed the room, threw her arms around him, and hugged him. "You'll do a wonderful job. I just know it."

He squeezed her tight and brushed his lips across hers, reminding her of the romantic Martin she'd fallen in love with years ago. "I know it won't be an easy move, honey, but we'll figure it all out. We always do."

Andy stiffened in his embrace. There was that word again—*move.* So she hadn't imagined it. Her mouth went dry. She pulled out of his arms, turned to go to the fridge to get an iced tea, only to find her knees had turned to jelly. The tea could wait. What she needed was a chair.

She sat back down at her desk and tried to look as relaxed and interested as possible, despite the turmoil tumbling in her middle like laundry in the washing machine.

Martin followed her across the room, grabbed her mother's desk chair, and turned it around so he could straddle it. The dimple was still there. Now she remembered the last time she'd seen it—when he'd told her they were going on a company cruise. Then, like now, he had thought she would be as excited as he was. She would have been, if she'd thought it would be a real vacation and not a test to see if she could play well with the other executives' wives.

Fighting the sudden constriction in her chest, Andy kept her gaze from wandering over to the neat stacks of boxes her parents had packed for the Nordstrom order. UPS would be by on Monday to pick them up, and they would arrive at their destination by Wednesday, Thursday at the latest.

"Just think," Martin went on, seemingly oblivious to the effect his sudden news was having on her, "we'll get to live in San Francisco." His smile widened, deepening his dimple.

Unable to help herself, Andy grimaced. *Get to live in San Francisco?* He acted like living in San Francisco was a privilege only bestowed on a rare few.

She had to say something, do something, now, before things got out of hand. She swiveled her chair around and got the copy of the Nordstrom invoice out of its file folder. "Martin, did you get my e-mail about the Nordstrom order?"

"Yeah," he said with a chuckle. "Funny how things always work out, isn't it? That ought to just about wipe you out of inventory, which means you won't have to have a big going-out-of-business sale." His gaze swept the nearly empty shelves and the boxes. "Everything else, the equipment and office stuff, we can just put into storage."

Andy's first thought was whether to ask if he was really so oblivious to the significance of the order or whether to chalk his lack of an appropriate response up to his being clueless about the opportunity with Lavender Meadows. For safe measure, she clamped her teeth down on her tongue. Often throughout their married life, her tongue had suffered the wounds of self-control. Painful, yes, but peace was worth a few wounds.

Taking a deep breath, she decided to give him the benefit of the doubt a little longer while she gathered more information. Maybe he was just so excited that he wasn't thinking about the ramifications of a move. "So why would we have to, er, *get* to live there?" Even swallowing took concentration.

"They're taking me off the road and settling me into the home office. No more waiting in airports and eating restaurant food, honey. And better yet, I'll be working a regular nine-to-five just like normal people."

His smile reminded her of the cat who dreamed of the canary.

Right, Martin. "Officially, it'll be nine to five, but I know you. You'll bring your work home with you, because you can't bear to leave anything undone. You have to dot every *i* and cross every *t* before you call it a day. The weekends will be the same as they've always been. You'll be at home, but you'll be in your office, up to your hairline in work for AES. And I'll be alone. At least here, I have plenty to keep myself busy, and I'm surrounded by people I know and love. If we move to San Francisco, I won't have anything to do except keep house, and I won't know anyone." She shook her head. "I'm sorry, Martin. I'm not understanding why we need to move. What's the difference between you coming home on weekends here or in San Francisco?"

"Living in San Francisco is a requirement of the position."

Andy felt herself pull back as if she'd been struck. *A requirement of the position.* It took her a moment to absorb the news. When she could think again, she asked, "Did they tell you that, or are you just assuming that's what they want?"

"It's part of the package, honey. That and a big raise, a key man insurance policy, a new company car, stock options, and semiannual bonuses. Big bonuses. We'll finally have the financial freedom we've always dreamed about."

"I see." She nodded. "So the powers-that-be have spoken," she said, her thoughts still focused on the news that living in San Francisco was a requirement of the position.

He leaned forward, his expression alive with fire. "I know the moving part is a big surprise. I couldn't believe it at first either, but I can't say I'm not happy about it. I've always wanted to live in a city. Especially San Francisco. There's so much to see and do: art galleries, the theater, Fisherman's Wharf with good—no, great restaurants, interesting people." He clasped her hands between his, crushing the invoice. "The truth is, I've dreamed about it, lusted for it—for years."

Her eyes narrowed. *How could you have felt this way without my knowing?* She glanced down at her hands, at the paper sticking out of the hole between her thumb and her index finger. "I understand that you're happy about the raise, the bonuses, and all that—but moving? You've always told me you loved it here on the farm, with the animals and the wide open spaces. You never said anything about wanting to live in a city. And you hate the theater, Martin. At least that's what you've said every time I've asked you to go with me." She could feel her self-control start to founder. Had their life together, the life she'd thought to be near perfect, been a sham?

His expression softened, and he looked almost bashful. "I hate *community* theater, Andy. And you're right. I never said anything about wanting to live in a city. First, because I felt that our children would benefit from smaller schools, away from crime, drugs, and all the stuff city kids have to face. And second, because I never thought I'd have the opportunity."

Andy took her hands back and straightened her spine. "Martin, there's something you're forgetting here—Lavender Meadows." She showed him the wrinkled invoice. "My parents and I are running a business—a business that is growing by leaps and bounds. I can't just close the doors and say good-bye to all the hard work we've put in. And I can't believe that you're asking me to, either." She watchfully awaited his reply. In the last five years, she'd gone from a woman who had planted two lavender plants on the berm of their water lily pond for personal use, to a well-known lavender grower who had acres of lavender beds that bloomed from early summer until late fall.

He scooted his chair back a few inches. "I don't know what to say, Andy. I thought you would want this as much as I do."

That was not the reply she'd hoped for. Andy looked heavenward and prayed she wouldn't blow up before she said everything she needed to say. "Don't make it sound like I'm against your promotion, Martin, because I'm not. I couldn't be happier for you, and certainly no one deserves it more. But you should have asked me before you included me in the deal. Have you forgotten what Lavender Meadows means to my parents?" She saw his eyebrow arch. "You know as well as I do that without the income from Lavender Meadows they would have to sell the farm, because they wouldn't be able to afford to live here."

He sucked in a breath. "Well, what's wrong with that? Most people, when they reach a certain age, start to downsize. This is a big place to take care of. I'll bet your dad would be glad not to have so much to do."

Lord, give me patience. "You're wrong, Martin. If Dad didn't have this place to take care of, he'd die. But that's beside the point. This isn't just a *place.* It's the Coulter family farm. My grandparents are buried here along with Uncle Seamus and Aunt Millie. The kids' pony is buried behind the wellhouse. Have you talked to the kids and asked them what they think about selling the farm? I can't imagine that Morgan would want that. She loves it here."

Martin appeared to give her little speech serious thought. But a moment later, she knew that appearances were deceiving.

"All right, so you don't quit the business and sell the farm. But there's nothing that says you can't move to San Francisco. Your parents are perfectly capable of running things. How many times have I heard you say what a tireless worker your dad is and what a born business-woman your mom is?"

Andy felt her face grow hot with anger. He was so bent on getting what he wanted that he was ignoring everything she had just said. "They are perfectly capable of running things for a few hours a day, but Mom turns seventy-five this year, and Dad will be seventy-seven. There is only so much physical labor people their age can do." She shook the invoice to make her point. "If any more orders come in like this Nordstrom order—and they will, Martin, you can count on it—" She broke off, her anger getting the better of her. "I can't believe we're having this conversation."

Seemingly unruffled by her display of anger, Martin took the invoice from her hand and gave it a quick once-over. "Well, since you're swimming in money, why not hire an employee or two?"

"At some point in time, I'm sure that can happen, but not yet. There isn't enough cash flow to pay for all the things associated with having an employee. Besides that—I don't want to quit. I love this business, and I love this farm. I have no desire to move to San Francisco. I hate cities. Always have." She almost laughed at the absurdity of the situation, but this was no laughing matter. This was a praying matter. *Father, help me. Help Martin to see that there is more to consider than just what he wants.*

Are you going to trust Me, Andy?

The inner nudge Andy knew to be her Father's voice caught her by surprise. Did it mean that Martin's eyes would be opened, or that she was supposed to move to San Francisco?

His excitement dimming, Martin shook his head. "I'm between a rock and a hard place, Andy. If I don't move to San Francisco, I won't lose my job, but I will lose the vice president position. I've worked too long and too hard to let that happen." He leaned forward, arms wide, hands open as if pleading. Beseeching? "I want to be AES's next vice president, Andy. Don't ask me to give it up."

Her stomach tied itself in a knot. When had she ever known

Martin to beseech her for anything? *Oh, God. Please, please, please help us find a resolution.* "Do you think you can go back to them and tell them our situation here?"

"Sure, but that isn't going to change anything."

"How do you know when you haven't tried?"

He got up and turned away from her. "It's always about you, Andy," he shot back over his shoulder, "you and Lavender Meadows." At the door he stopped, reached up and pulled a bunch of lavender down from the drying rack, and threw it across the room. "I'm so sick of this stuff, I could choke."

Andy was speechless. Who was this man stomping away from her? Where was the sensitive, caring, unselfish man she'd married?

Something told her there was more going on with him than she realized, maybe more than he realized. But what?

Lord, I feel like I'm on a bumper car, getting banged from all sides, with no way to get off. And I don't like it!

Chapter Three

Andy

"I guess you could say we're at a standoff. He won't give up the move to San Francisco, and I won't give up Lavender Meadows or my home."

Shari Griffeth, long-time friend and faithful prayer partner, stared at Andy over the rim of her china teacup, which was filled with Andy's trademark lavender tea. "I'm glad you're not moving, but I sure hate to see you and Martin at odds with each other."

Andy sighed. "Me too."

"You've always gotten along so well. I can't ever remember a time when a problem came along that the two of you couldn't resolve."

"I guess we've just never had a problem this big before."

"I've lost count of the number of times we've moved. It's never been a really big deal for either of us. But it's different with you. You have roots and issues we never had."

"I tried everything I could think of to make him see what was at stake, but he ignored every point I tried to make." She glanced around her kitchen-cum-family-room, her favorite room in the house. Drying lavender hung from an old clothes rack, giving the house the same heady fragrance as the workshop in the barn. A brushed-steel rack above the center island held her collection of cookware, including several cast-iron skillets that had belonged to her grandmother and matched the teakettle she used as a steamer in the winter. Blue half-gallon jars filled with a variety of dried beans caught the sunlight from the east-facing bay window. Cushions in green and lavender plaid lined the built-in benches, a favorite place for kids doing homework and cats taking naps.

"I can forgive him for not understanding what Lavender Meadows means to me and why I don't want to sell a farm that's been in my family for generations. His parents moved around a lot, so he never lived in one place very long. I can safely say he never formed an attachment to a house or a piece of land, not even to our house or our land. He liked it all well enough, but he didn't love it like me and the kids. And I suppose, if I dig real deep, I can forgive him for not taking my parents' financial problem into consideration. His parents were losers, always sponging off other people to get what they wanted. I don't even know if he knew any of his grandparents; he's never mentioned them." She gasped at her own realization. "Isn't that terrible that I don't know that? I should know. I wonder if the kids know." A stab of guilt sliced straight to her gut. Not for the first time in the last few days, she realized she didn't know her husband as well as she'd thought she did.

Shari drew circles on the plaid tablecloth, which matched the seat covers. "Speaking of the kids, what do they say about all this?"

"I haven't told them yet. No sense getting them all upset until I know more. Everything is kind of up in the air right now, at least as far as I'm concerned." Andy held up her cup. "Need a refill?" She poured more tea into her cup, topped off Shari's, then sat and stared off into space. "But I can't forgive him for acting like my business was nothing," she said, picking up where she'd left off before the segue into guilt and the kids. "After all our hard work! I am so angry at him that if he were here, I-I'd—" She clenched her fist and huffed. "Arsenic in his tea perhaps, or rather his coffee. He never has liked tea much, especially my lavender tea."

"It occurs to me that he doesn't like anything to do with lavender," Shari observed. "Could he be jealous?"

Andy squinched her face. "Of what?"

"Of you. Of your success. I mean…you are a success, Andy. You turned a hobby into a moneymaking business, and you gave your parents the means to keep their home and support themselves throughout their later years." She nodded, obviously sure of herself.

Andy tipped her head back and stared up at the ceiling. "I never thought of that. I suppose he could be, but…"

"Look at Meredith Robinson," Shari said, pointing her index finger. "She started out selling cosmetics at home parties, earning one or two hundred a party. Little by little she worked her way up to regional manager, then district manager, then to general manger of the company. Ted Robinson couldn't take his wife not always being home to fix dinner or tuck him in bed at night, so he left her and went to live with his brother. And remember Jill Evans? She started out writing romance novels, which her husband thought was very funny and teased her about constantly. But when she got an advance that was more than Ralph made in a year, he asked for a divorce. A lot of men can't handle it when their wives become successful. It does something to their ego."

Andy stared into her tea. She had never looked at herself that way—a success—but she could see where some people might think so. Obviously, Shari thought so. If Martin thought so, he'd never told her. For that matter, he'd never given an indication that he considered her work more than just her "little hobby." That he had never acknowledged her accomplishments irked her, but she'd never said anything. It wasn't worth getting upset with him. *Blessed are the peacemakers.* That had always been her life verse. She wondered now if she'd made a mistake. Maybe if she had gotten upset with him, he

would have seen Lavender Meadows for what it was—successful. Not
something you just threw away.

Not much later Shari headed for home, promising to keep praying about Andy's situation.

Andy spent the evening writing up orders that had come in from
her Web site and answering e-mails from friends and family. Just before
ten, she glanced at the clock, then closed by sending her nightly message to her kids. She had no sooner mentioned that she'd spent the
morning cleaning closets than Bria instant-messaged her back.

<All right, Mom, what's up with the closet cleaning?>

<Just a little fall housecleaning.>

<You've never done fall housecleaning or spring housecleaning,
either, for that matter. You only clean closets when you're angry.>

<Can't I turn over a new leaf?>

<Not when you're in the middle of harvest.>

*Why do I have to have such a perceptive daughter? I should have kept
my mouth, er, rather my fingers shut, er, still.*

Camden bleeped in. <What's going on?> Daughters were not the
only perceptive ones.

Camden was going for his master's in geology at Montana State,
thanks to Bria's encouragement.

Andy blew out a full-cheeked breath and sent the same message
to both. <I'm working some stuff out, and I'm not going to talk about
it until I know more.>

<M-o-m!>

They both still did it, turned *Mom* into a three-syllable word,
even on the computer screen.

<Is Dad all right?>

Bria, her eldest daughter, had always known she was her father's
favorite, even more so now that she was pursuing corporate life on the

fast track. She was barely twenty-nine and already an executive in a communications company. Andy often wondered if Martin was vicariously reliving his life through Bria.

She mentally stopped herself from going there. <As far as I know. Why?> She glanced at her calendar. Martin would be in St. Louis tonight, and tomorrow morning he would have breakfast with his new client. *Should I have asked how his trip was going?* Andy pondered the thought. How long had it been since her husband discussed his travels with her? Or more to the point, how long since she'd asked him about them, other than the perfunctory "How was your trip?"

<He seemed abrupt when we chatted on IM last> Bria wrote.

Knowing that Martin kept in regular e-mail contact with his kids had always cheered Andy. They had more contact with him through the Internet than actual face-to-face talking time, but they didn't seem to mind. Of the three, Morgan, their youngest, was the only telephone addict.

Speak of the angels. Ten thirty and the phone rang.

"Hi sweetie." Andy tucked the phone between shoulder and ear and typed <good-bye> to the two online.

"Mom, do you miss me as much as I miss you?"

Andy could hear the sob behind the words and knew Morgan was still suffering from acute homesickness. It had been three weeks since Andy had taken her youngest to college. Thank God for cell phones and long-distance family-calling plans.

"Of course I do. Why?" What was happening with her little chick now?

"I don't know. I just feel like I'd rather be home. I should have gone to school in Medford."

"But you always dreamed of PLU." She pronounced it as one word. Sometimes Andy felt like they were paying for a new science wing, what with all the money they'd sent north to Pacific Lutheran University in Tacoma, Washington, over the years.

"You know, Mom, all my life I've been the third Taylor, behind an overachiever and a Mensa candidate. Then there is me-of-little-brains."

"Sorry, can't do much about the birth order now," Andy joked as she clicked Check Mail to see if there was a message from her husband. Nothing. Before this weekend, he had always e-mailed her last thing before heading for bed. And bed was earlier back in St. Louis. She signed off the computer. "What brought on this, um, attack?" she asked into the phone.

"The profs expect me to do as well as B and C." Morgan called her sister and brother B and C whenever speaking of the two of them. At one time she'd gone on a short-term revolt to make sure that she wasn't known as a goody two shoes like they had been.

"So?"

"So, Mother, I want to have a life."

"Far as I can tell, you are still breathing." Andy knew she would receive the long, sighed-out "Mother!" but couldn't resist. Morgan did not like to be teased. A silence grew louder for its length. "All right, I'm sorry for the smart remarks. What is it?"

The answer came stiffly. "I'm just warning you in advance not to expect straight As."

She'd heard this before, like at the beginning of every school year, with this youngest child. But having said that, Morgan would dig in and work herself into a frenzy to make sure she measured up.

"I mean it."

"Sweetie, I'm sure you do, but now you have to listen to me. I have never required straight As from you. I know what you are capable of, but I also know how hard you work. I want you to enjoy college, to get a great education, but that doesn't mean you have to be on the dean's list every semester."

"What if I'm never on the dean's list? What if I am the only Taylor sibling to never make the list?"

"So?" Andy knew her shrug wouldn't be heard, but this child always worried needlessly.

"So what will Dad say?"

"Perhaps you should ask him."

"I can't wait until Thanksgiving." Morgan ignored her mother's remark. "I want to come home so bad. How're Henny and Chai Lai?"

Andy glanced over to the rocking chair. "Chai Lai is sound asleep in her chair as usual, and Henny is out on her roost with her head tucked under her wing." She chanted the latter like an old camp song they used to sing, about some ghoul with his head tucked underneath his arm.

Morgan didn't acknowledge her mother's attempt at humor. "Mom, what if I don't want to come back here next semester?"

"I'd say it's too early to make a judgment call like that yet. Did you know that Bria felt the same as you for the first couple of months she was at college?"

"No way!" she said, obviously surprised by the news.

"Yes, she did. All she could think about was missing home and Comet and her family and Comet..." There, she'd brought a slight giggle to her daughter's voice. "It'll be okay, Morgan, really it will."

"Thanks, Mom. I gotta go."

Andy could now hear what sounded like relief in her daughter's voice. "God loves you, and so do I."

"I know, just you both feel so far away right now."

"Good night, little one." Andy clung to the phone after Morgan hung up until the buzz came on the line. *Lord, please go to her in a real way. This is breaking my heart, and yet I know she is where You want her to be. Father, she is the prettiest one, the one who looks most like her father, so why does she have the problem with…with being shy, with not being sure of herself? Is it because the other two are so sure? Please, if it is something I—we—said or did…* This sigh came from the very bottom of her heart. "Please, please make up for any mistakes we—I made." She leaned back in the chair and closed her eyes. "God, I don't want to move to San Francisco. And I don't want to live my life without my husband at my side."

Are you going to trust Me?

"Yes, of course I trust You." She caught her breath and thought about what she'd just said. *What are You asking of me?* No wonder Peter got a bit put out when Jesus asked him three times, "Do you love me?" Tears welled up in her throat, a hot, hard lump of them. The back of her eyes and nose burned, so hot was the moisture. "I am sick and tired of crying too. You know that?"

Chai Lai, her seven-year-old, cross-eyed Siamese cat, purred from her chair, stood up, and arched her back, stretching every muscle as only felines do. She leaped to the floor and, tail like a question mark, minced her way between the buckets of cut lavender stems. When the cat got close enough, Andy reached out, scooped her up in her arms, and buried a tear-streaked face in the warm fur.

The week went by, and Andy and Martin communicated only through the Internet. His e-mails came first thing in the morning and never at night before he went to bed as they used to. He never mentioned the new job, moving, or whether or not he'd spoken with the powers-that-be about her circumstances. Instead of the newsy, interesting e-mails he used to send, the morning messages were short and to the point: <I'll be in Baltimore tomorrow> or <I heard from Morgan today, and she needs a new textbook. Her account was low, so I made a deposit.>

Only hard work drove the demons from Andy's mind. But even

harvesting lavender—much as she enjoyed gathering in the purple blossoms, stems, and seeds—left too much freedom to think about things, about her and Martin. She kept hearing *Are you going to trust Me?* in her heart, and a particular scripture kept circling in her head, *"For wherever you go, I will go; and wherever you lodge, I will lodge."* If she lived by that scripture or the message in the country-western songs, she thought, she should stand by her man and move to San Francisco.

When the weekend came and went without Martin making an appearance, she called him on his cell phone. She fought to appear unconcerned as to where he was or who he might be with. "Martin, we have to talk. I don't want to live my life without you. I love you." Handset to ear, she sat down in the kitchen and spooned honey into her teacup. Maybe the tea would help keep her calm. And maybe the honey would help sweeten her tongue.

He heaved a sigh that echoed through the phone lines. "Me too. I don't know what the solution is for all this. I have a week left before I have to give them my answer."

"Honey, I know that if we put our heads together, we can figure out a workable solution. Did you talk to them about our, I mean, my situation here?"

"No. I haven't had a chance, but it won't do any good. It's their way or no way."

Andy bit back the retort that popped into her head. *Make nice, Andy. Use your motherly coaxing skills.* "Come on now, honey. Surely once you explain, they'll understand. You can tell them we're working toward the time when I can hire someone."

"As if *that* would ever happen," he was quick to reply.

Shari's words came back to her like a slap in the face. *Could he be jealous?* "What do you mean by that? I told you before that there isn't enough cash flow right now to hire someone, but as soon as there is, I will."

"You'll move here, to San Francisco?"

"Yes. And no. If moving there means giving up our home here, no. But I would certainly consider staying there a few weeks at a time. We could have two homes. Would that work for you?" She put all her love and encouragement into her voice.

"We can't afford two homes, Andy. Are you nuts?"

Against all the screaming going on in her head, she kept her voice even. "But you said they offered a big raise and *big* semiannual bonuses. Maybe you should tell me just how big *big* is."

Silence met her outburst. Then, "We'll talk about this later, when I get home next weekend."

"Martin, listen to me—" But all she heard was the dial tone. She pulled the handset away from her head and glared at it, as if it were to blame for his hanging up on her. "Martin J. Taylor, you're a coward!" she shouted at the inoffensive instrument. "You need to grow up, fella, and learn to deal with the problem, instead of running from it."

She gulped at what had burst from her mouth and then sat down at the computer, ready to write him a blistering e-mail. But the tears blurred her eyes so badly she couldn't see the screen to know what she had typed. *If Martin really loves me, why won't he talk to his boss? Why won't he try to help me come up with a solution?*

Out of the blue, two answers surfaced in her mind. Maybe he didn't love her anymore, and maybe the reason he wouldn't cooperate with her was because he didn't really want her to move to San Francisco.

Hurriedly, Andy dried her tears and punched out a hot one-liner: <Martin, do you still love me?>

Surprisingly, his reply e-mail came back immediately. <What a stupid question. Of course I still love you.>

"Then prove it. Tell your boss my circumstances."

Looking in the mirror after a night of crying was not a good idea. Her hair looked as though she'd stuck her finger in a light socket—gray caught the light, bright silver against the dark mink strands. When had all those appeared? She moved closer to the mirror and looked at her bloodshot eyes. Martin always said she had laughing eyes. Well, not today. They were so swollen it would be impossible for anyone to discern that they were hazel. Green and red were great Christmas colors, but they did nothing for her eyes and skin. She turned to head back to bed but sat down at the vanity instead. Perhaps if she applied a mask and left it on for a week, it would tighten the drooping under her eyes and the corners of her mouth.

"You look terrible," her mother said when Andy walked into the workshop.

"Thank you. Good morning to you too, Mom."

"Something's very wrong, so you might as well tell me and get it over with." Alice turned from the bench where she'd been filling the lace sachets she'd sewn the night before.

"You're not going to like it."

"Let me be the judge of that. All I know is that you've been sighing, and you're walking around with the weight of something really terrible on your shoulders." Alice leaned back against the workbench and crossed her arms over her midriff.

Andy caught herself in another sigh. Might as well get it over with. "Martin has been offered a big promotion."

"I know, he told me."

"Did he also tell you that the job requires us to move to San Francisco?"

"No, but the way you've been acting, I was afraid he'd asked for a divorce or something irreparable."

Andy sighed again. "It might come to that."

"Not if you don't let it."

"Mom, he wants us to sell the house and the business." Andy watched her mother's face, saw the tightening of her eyes, the jaw line.

"I know what you're thinking, honey, that we—your dad and me—won't be able to get by without you, but the way things are going, we can probably hire a part-time employee to fill the gap."

"Maybe after the next big order, but not right now. And the problem is, we don't know when the next big order will come." Andy pulled out her latest business analysis and showed it to her mother. Then she launched into a full retelling of Martin's giving her his news, ignoring her concerns, and refusing to help her find a resolution.

"You're risking your marriage, honey. Your dad and I would never forgive ourselves if you and Martin split up because of us. We can work the business without you, and if it's too much for us and we still can't afford an employee, then we'll sell it, along with the farm. We should get a pretty penny out of the place, the way real estate prices have been soaring. Enough to last us the rest of our lives. Lots of people are looking to get into good home-based businesses these days." She took her only child's hand in hers. "We've been so fortunate to have all of you, Martin and the children, right here on the farm with us all these years. I thank God every day for—" Her voice broke.

"No, Mom, listen to me. I don't want to move to San Francisco." Andy told her mother all the personal reasons why, the same ones she had told Martin, only this time she added, "I wasn't cut out to be a corporate wife. I don't like charity balls and women's club lunches. I like it here, with you and Dad and the animals. And I like being a businesswoman again. I'm good at it, and I get a lot of personal satisfaction out of it. I gave all that up once for Martin, and I'm not going to do it again."

"Not even if it means losing him?"

Andy fought the tears, but when she reached out to hug her

mother, they collapsed in each other's arms. "He…he never even acted pleased about the Nordstrom order," she sobbed. "I…I have always cheered him on, but he shrugged off my good news like it didn't mean anything." She clung to her mother, a little girl again, a little girl whose kitten had just died.

That night, Andy brought herself back to stare at the face in the mirror. "God, what am I going to do?"

Are you going to trust Me?

"Yes, I trust You, but that isn't what I asked." *At least, I'm trying to trust You. But You have to help me out here, so I know what to do.*

Chapter Four

Kansas City

Julia Collins accepted the congratulations of her trial assistant with a smile. "Thanks, and thank you for finding that last witness. She was the clincher. I wouldn't have laid money on the outcome before you brought her into the picture."

"Something just kept niggling at me and wouldn't let go, so I went back through all the transcripts until I found her name." Adam Jefferson, fresh out of law school, was also Julia's latest hire, and she had no doubt he would be a keeper.

"Well, anytime you feel a niggling, you follow it." She turned to accept the grudging congratulations from the opposing lawyer, a good friend of hers outside the courtroom. "Thank you, Glen. I can't say I'm sorry you lost this one."

"Luck of the Irish, I tell you." The man shaking her hand shook his balding head at the same time. "I thought sure he was innocent."

Julia tucked a strand of deep brown hair with auburn highlights back behind her ear. "Pretty weak strain of luck, I'd say. Just good work on my assistant's part here. Adam, have you met Glen Heinsmith?" She kept a smile on her face in spite of the weariness that nearly knocked her knees out from under her. If only she could fit in a massage this afternoon to work the kinks out of her neck and shoulders. Although she was known in court as the picture of calm, that image frequently came with a price.

Dreams of her granddaughter, Cyndy, had awakened her three times last night from sleep that was already too short because she'd been fighting to bring this case to a satisfactory conclusion.

"May I take you to lunch?" Glen asked, a hopeful note in his voice.

She started to say no, then thought better of it. "I'd like that. Thank you. Just give me a second." She turned to her assistant and handed him her briefcase. "Please take this back to the office and ask Joanne to cancel my appointments for the afternoon. There's not much on the calendar anyway." At his nod she said, "Thanks." After handing over her briefcase, she turned to Glen and slung her black leather purse over her shoulder. "It's been too long since we've done this."

"You're telling me." He tucked her arm through his and led her toward the exit.

"We'd better not appear too friendly, or our media friends might get the wrong idea." She took back possession of her arm and smiled. For the first time ever, she had a feeling that if she made any move to deepen their relationship, Glen would take her up on it. Her next thought was, *What is wrong with that?* She filed the thought away to contemplate another time. Right now, she needed to gird up to face the wolves.

They rode the elevator to the street level in silence.

As soon as the elevator doors opened, Glen bent his six-foot-three, former-baseball-pitcher frame to whisper so the two other occupants of the elevator wouldn't be privy to his suggestion. "We could duck out the back, you know."

At five-three in sensible heels, Julia always wondered if some of their conversations didn't give him a crick in the neck. "Thanks, but no. I'd just as soon get this over with. That poor woman deserves this moment of triumph." Her client had suffered a stroke not two weeks before, a possible by-product of the head injury that her husband swore he didn't inflict. This case had been fought long and hard, because no one wanted to believe that a man with the public persona of Jerry Drysome would ever beat his wife. Reverends just didn't do that sort of thing.

Julia blinked at the bright sunlight that greeted her outside the building. At least five reporters were there, their cameras flashing one on top of another. Julia stepped forward and said, "I'm only going to say this once, so be ready." Her smile took the sting out of her words. As one of the leading family lawyers in the Kansas City area, she tried to be fair with the media, in the hopes that they would be fair with her, which they usually were. "We fought a hard battle, but like so many, it turned on the smallest piece of evidence. I'm grateful to the newest and youngest staffer in my firm, Adam Jefferson, for his impeccable research. This case garnered far more publicity than it was worth, but that's what happens when someone is already in the public eye. I can only hope that a lesson has been learned and that next time you guys let the lawyers try the case instead of you trying it in your newspapers."

Her comment caused a ripple of laughter, which she knew the press would turn around to their own advantage. But that's the way things worked with the media. She shook her head at the barrage of erupting questions and followed Glen, who'd also been asked questions but had ignored them, out to the parking lot.

"Woman, you've got more nerve than sense at times." His chuckle said he approved. "You want to ride with me or follow?"

"I'll take my car, thanks. Where are we going?"

He named a restaurant known not only for its good food but also for its privacy, and slid into his silver Lexus.

Julia walked two more parking spaces over and unlocked her plain blue Ford sedan. A blast of heat hit her when she opened the door, reminding her that she'd forgotten to crack the windows. Again. She'd arrived at the courthouse early that morning to meet with another client before the court was called into session.

Once they were seated in the coolness of a leather booth in the back of the main dining room, Julia set her purse down next to her and reached up to disengage an earring. "Ooh, I've needed to do that for hours." She massaged her ear, thought to reinsert the post, and instead shook her head, removing the other earring too, and tucked them both into her bag.

Glen had loosened his tie and folded his suit coat and laid it on the seat. "Now that we're comfortable…"

"Amen to that." She thought of removing her suit jacket too, but the air conditioning that felt good blowing down on her now would be chilly soon. "So how've you been, my friend?"

"Getting by." He nodded.

"It's been how long now, more than a year, right?"

His lips twitched. "Eighteen months, actually." He lined his utensils up so that all the ends made a straight line before looking across the table at her. "But I've learned that I'm ready to live again, and while Beverly will always be part of my life, I need to make a new life." A smile started, gently curving his lips and then wandering up to his eyes, eyes that had borne the weight of grief and now sparked with remembered joy. "She's in that perfect place."

Julia felt herself start to tear up and took a deep breath. "Yes, she is."

"I guess I forgot to tell you this—I've had a lot on my mind—but before she died she made me promise her something."

"What?" Julia couldn't help but smile. His fingers had rearranged the utensils again, she was sure without his realizing it.

"She made me promise that I would take you out to lunch first and then see."

"See what?"

"What happens."

Feeling a chuckle bubbling up, Julia leaned back against the leather seat and stared at him. "Do you mean to say…?" How odd that not fifteen minutes ago she'd wondered about deepening their relationship. And now…this.

"I'm not saying any more right now, but you know we've been friends for a long time. Good friends."

"Yes, we have," she agreed. Julia and Beverly had been friends for over twenty-five years, having met at church back when Julia had been struggling at being a single mother, going to law school, and trying to cope with a daughter like Donna, who'd been determined to follow in her mother's footsteps. The rebellious footsteps, not the "go to school and make something of yourself" footsteps.

Glen and Beverly had been her family when Donna got pregnant in her sophomore year. Like Julia, Donna had insisted on keeping her daughter instead of giving her up for adoption. Glen and Beverly had consoled her when Donna quit high school and decided to move to Minneapolis with a man she'd just met. While it didn't seem possible that matters could get any worse at that point, they did. Donna took baby Cyndy with her.

Darling little Cyndy, the light of her grandmother's life and a hope for a brighter future. Cyndy was six when Donna put her on a plane and sent her back to Julia to deal with. Though she was only in first grade, Cyndy showed signs of having some serious problems. Julia did everything she knew how to do: she hired therapists, moved Cyndy into a private school, provided her with tutors, and gave her unconditional love. Nine years later, the day of Cyndy's fifteenth birthday, the girl borrowed Julia's ATM card, took five hundred dollars from her checking account, and left the ATM card wrapped in a note saying that the house rules were too strict and that she was going home to her mother.

"Have you heard from Cyndy?" Glen's voice penetrated the bubble that had transported Julia into the past. "Where is she now?"

Julia's demeanor changed instantly; her smile turned into a frown. "Back in Minneapolis with Donna. I haven't talked to her in a couple of weeks." She mentally counted back. Maybe it had been longer than that. With her heavy caseload lately, the days had slipped away. "Perhaps that's why she's been on my mind and in my dreams lately." *Or else she's in trouble.* Julia changed the subject. "How are your kids?" She laughed. "Well, I know they're not kids anymore, but…"

"But when do we quit calling them that?" He shook his head. "I don't know. Both families are doing fine. I've become a well-behaved spectator grandpa." One eyebrow arched. "At Joe's insistence. He said I couldn't attend the ball games if I didn't lay off the umps."

"You'd think you would—"

"Know better?" he interrupted.

"Something like that."

"That's the problem. I know the game too well. Never could abide lousy calls." He took a bite of his salad. "Beverly always said I either had to coach or shut up."

"And you shut up?"

"Well…" He paused, made a bit of a face, and raised both eyebrows. "Sort of."

Julia chuckled. "Those were the days, right?" How she wished she'd been able to go to her daughter's games or dance recitals or plays. But Donna would have none of that.

The waiter returned with their entrées, and Julia smiled over the fact that she'd ordered fish. A creature of habit, that was for sure. She squeezed lemon juice over the grilled filet and looked up to see Glen watching her.

"What? Did I squirt you?"

He shook his head and dug into his pasta, a half smile playing at the side of his mouth.

They finished their meal with desultory conversation.

"Can I interest you folks in one of our fine house-specialty desserts?" the waiter asked as he cleared their plates.

Glen looked to Julia, but when she shook her head, he did too. "No thanks. Just our bill, please."

"So what are you doing the rest of the afternoon, if you're not going back to the office?"

"I'm getting a massage and buying groceries, and then I'm going to take a long very bubbly bath and be in bed by nine."

"I have tickets to a jazz concert for Sunday afternoon. Would you like to go?"

Julia paused, studied his face, and nodded. "Yes, I'd like that."

Back in her car a few minutes later, she thought back to their conversation, then burst out laughing. So Beverly had actually told him to come find her when he was ready to go on with his life. Teeth nibbling on her lower lip, she turned up the air conditioning and wheeled out of the parking lot to get her massage, which she had been looking forward to all day. Life just might be taking an interesting turn.

Once home and in a sublimely relaxed state of mind, she obeyed an inner prompting and dialed the last number she had for her daughter. Surprised when Donna answered the phone, she sat back, hoping for a reasonable chat. That was always her hope.

"What do you want?"

"Actually, I was hoping we could talk. It's been a long time."

"I got nothin' to say to you."

Julia tried to trap a sigh but failed. She wished just once Donna would try to have a civil conversation with her. Even if it was just a few short sentences, she would be happy. Instead, Donna acted as if she were the enemy. What had she done to warrant her daughter's hate? Julia remembered doing everything she could to make sure Donna never felt neglected while she was young. She remembered being too tired to think after a long day of classes but still taking time to play with her little girl, read to her, help her with her homework. When Donna turned twelve, she started to change, and by the time her daughter was in high school, Julia not only didn't recognize Donna, but she also didn't know her. *You haven't done anything. It's the drugs. The drugs took Donna away from you.*

"Donna, honey, please. I don't want to interfere in your life. I just want to know how you are." She heard someone whispering in the background and knew Donna wasn't alone.

"Like I said, I ain't got nothin' to say to you, so—"

"Would you tell Cyndy I called? Please?"

"She don't live here no more."

Julia sat up straight. "What? Since when?"

"Oh, month or two ago." Donna's voice faded in and out, as if she were just coming down from a high or just going up.

"Where did she go?" *Oh, Cyndy, honey, why didn't you call me? Why?*

The background whispers grew louder, urging Donna to hang up the phone, with foul language that made Julia cringe. "California," Donna said at length. "She said she wants to get into the movies. I told her it would never happen." The phone clicked.

Julia waited until the dial tone buzzed in her ear. Cyndy, on her own in Los Angeles. *No wonder I've been having bad dreams.*

Chapter Five

Julia

"You could file a missing person's report, but since she left on her own…"

Julia turned up the volume on the office speakerphone. "She's under eighteen—that makes her a runaway. Listen, Fred, there must be something more we can do."

She felt like throwing the phone against the wall. Fred Smith, a PI she'd hired from a firm she knew in Los Angeles, had come up with nothing. Like too many other Hollywood hopefuls, Cyndy had fallen into the maw of the city and had yet to be burped out again. She hadn't found employment anywhere, signed up with any talent agents, gotten any traffic tickets, or been charged with any violations. So far, she had no paper trail of any kind.

"You're not her guardian, Julia, and unless her mother signs papers, there's nothing the police can do." He paused a moment, then continued. "I showed her picture around, so someone might still get back to me. I'll let you know if I hear anything."

"You tried canvassing the studio cattle calls?" Julia didn't know much about Hollywood terminology, but she knew that when a movie needed to cast minor parts and extras, the studio people put out a general casting call, which ran in various daily industry publications.

"Yep. There's a big one next week for a new Brad Pitt film. If she's in town, I'd think that would be one she wouldn't miss."

"She's probably like every other young aspiring actress and thinks someone is going to see her walking down the street and say, 'Ah, you're the one I need.'"

"That does happen, Julia. It happens all the time, but not for Brad Pitt films or any other respectable film."

Julia gasped. She knew what he was referring to, but she couldn't bring herself to say it. She closed her eyes, sorting through her mind to come up with any other avenues to search, and she couldn't think of a thing. "Well, keep looking, please, and let me know if you come up with anything new. We'll do a retainer."

"Sorry I haven't been much help."

"Two weeks isn't a long time. Thanks for calling." She hung up and leaned back in her chair. Two weeks wasn't a long time, unless you were on the streets with no safe place to sleep and you hadn't eaten. *Dear God, watch out for her, please keep her safe, and let us find her somehow.*

Julia worked out at the local club, dealt with her clients, and had dinner with Glen—always with thoughts of Cyndy hovering at the back of her mind. Glen accompanied her to church on Sunday. During the sermon, she saw herself carrying her granddaughter to the altar and laying her down, but when she tried to leave the burden there, she couldn't. *I know You are watching out for her, Father, but I can't seem to leave her in Your hands.* She felt like a small child who wanted to share her favorite toy, but as soon as she turned away, something compelled her to grab it back.

She felt a presence beside her and turned a tear-streaked face to see Glen gazing at her, utter compassion glowing from dark eyes that were shaded by bushy eyebrows.

He has Jesus eyes. The thought made her want to throw herself in his arms and cry out her fears against his broad chest. Her hand sought his, and its warmth brought her comfort. She turned her gaze back to the rugged wooden cross that towered behind the marble altar, and she knew she was far from being alone in her search for Cyndy. When the choir began singing, Julia threw herself wholeheartedly into worshiping God, who promised to always be there—and to send help.

Later, during dinner, Glen rubbed a spot on his jaw line while he listened intently to her list of attempts to locate Cyndy. He made a couple of suggestions, only to be met with, "We've already done that."

"Then it looks to me like you're doing all you can. It's time to let God do His job."

"I keep telling myself that, but the telling is always easier than the doing."

"You have circles under your eyes." He stopped her restless hand with his.

"You're not supposed to see them. Lancôme promised me that their concealer would hide them." She made a good attempt at a smile that would pacify him.

"You're not sleeping, and it looks to me like you're not eating either." He nodded to her plate, where she had been moving bits of chicken around rather than eating it.

"You see too much."

"That's what friends are for. Finish your dinner, and let's go for a drive. I need to go look at a piece of property."

"Are you buying or selling?" She obediently took a bite and chewed. The chicken Marsala was delicious, and suddenly she was hungry. She finished the penne pasta and the crunchy roll, and drank her coffee, listening to him describe the lakefront property, asking the appropriate questions and enjoying the sound of his voice.

Two days later, Fred the private investigator called. "I have good news and bad news. Which do you want first?"

"The good. I could use some good news right about now." She'd spent the morning in court, watching as a well-prepared radiologist was awarded custody of his children and the family home in a decision that should have gone to the wife. Julia hated to lose any case, especially when the man had squirreled away assets in advance and had the soon-to-be-trophy wife waiting for him.

"I got a call from a young woman who had seen Cyndy's picture."

Julia's heart started to race. "Thank God."

"Well, yes, but…"

Her mind leaped ahead, and she began to shake. "Go ahead."

"She said Cyndy had been her roommate."

"Had been?" If this was the good news… "And the bad news?"

"Cyndy left LA and headed north to San Francisco. Someone promised her a screen test. That's all I know."

"When? When did she go to San Francisco?"

"Two weeks ago. My contact said she'd call again if she hears from Cyndy."

Feeling a little lightheaded, Julia sat back. "At least I know she's alive. Did the woman give any more information?"

"Only that Cyndy had been trying really hard to make it in the entertainment industry."

"Did she say what Cyndy was living on?"

"No, but I have a feeling my contact was the one providing the room and board."

"Did she ask you for money?"

"Not in so many words. I have her phone number, and she said she would be glad to talk with you."

"Wonderful." Julia took down the information and, after thanking Fred, hung up. Some news, not what she'd wanted, but anything was better than nothing. At least Cyndy was seen alive and well two weeks ago.

What now? she wondered. Hire another PI in San Francisco? Or go there herself? She studied her calendar. After this next court date, cases could be rearranged, reassigned.

Once that was taken care of, she could take a leave of absence and continue the search for her granddaughter on her own.

Chapter Six

Hope

San Francisco

Hope Benson, the director of a woman's shelter known as J House, stared at the faded brick edifice that once housed a thriving congregation, which had since moved to the suburbs.

"If only it could look as friendly on the outside as it feels on the inside," she said, shaking her head. On the upper walls, the bricks were hidden beneath a black frosting of neglect. Lower down, within reaching distance, layers of spray-painted graffiti had been scrubbed off until the terra cotta skeleton glowed orange in the morning light.

Hope and Adolph, her eighty-three-pound Lab-shepherd-something cohort, had just finished power-walking the sun up. Now it was time for coffee and a shower, or a shower and coffee, the order depending on how badly her husband Roger's back ached from the previous night's horizontal torture.

Roger had threatened to sleep on the futon, but that hard surface gave him a headache fit to lift his thinning hair right off his scalp. During his days as a police officer, he'd learned the hard way that spines and slugs didn't go well together, that is human spines and 9mm slugs. Though he complained very little, Hope knew he suffered a great deal. If only there was something that would give him relief, something *she* could do to help him.

Hope was forever *if only*ing. If only she could do more to help the women who came to the shelter. If only she had more time to spend with the children. If only she could find more resources to support the shelter. Hope sighed as she continued around the building to enter the private quarters by the side door. If only God had given them children of their own.

"*Buenos días,* Miss Hope." Celia, Hope's kitchen and front-desk assistant, greeted her. Celia was kneeling in front of the south-facing cold frame, where she was starting cabbages for the fall planting. Once a hard-core delinquent, the woman now took all her anger out on the compost pile.

"Good morning to you too. You're out early." Hope had discovered that for many—even the most desperate—gardening was an outlet that promoted healing.

"Bad dreams," Celia replied as she tenderly transplanted a seedling from the tray she had started under lights in the pantry. "Adolph, get away." Adolph loved Celia and licked her every chance he got. Celia wiped a sloppy kiss from her cheek, leaving bits of soil on her olive skin. "Ugh. I hate it when he does that."

Hope tugged on Adolph's leash. "You got enough there to plant an acre."

"I know. Who would've thought so many would make it this far? I'll take out every other one later and throw the greens into the soup pot."

Celia's gap-toothed smile reminded Hope that she needed to hassle Social Services to get dental help for several of her girls, but primarily for Celia.

"See you later." Hope bent to give the woman a pat on the shoulder. "Come on, Adolph."

"Oh, wait a minute," Celia called. "That sleaze-ball lawyer called." She rocked back on her heels and swept away a neon-blue lock of hair with the back of her hand.

Hope stopped with a groan. "Again?"

"Told 'im you call back when you come home from South America." Her twittering laugh followed Hope inside.

Hope leaned over to remove Adolph's leash. So what did the creepy lawyer want now? she wondered. She felt the urge to call him one of the names she'd used so freely before she became a warrior for her Lord, instead of a profitable lay for her warlord. She overrode the temptation, knowing full well that once she used that language again, she'd be using it on a regular basis.

The smell of fresh coffee told her Roger was up. She poured herself a cup and walked out of the kitchen and down the hall to the office-turned-exercise-room. "Hey, mon, thanks for the java." She lifted the cup in salute.

"Uhh." He carefully settled the bar onto its rack with a click. He lay there, broad chest sprinkled with gray swirls rising and falling while he caught his breath. "How was your walk?"

"Edie, mon. Be warmer in Jamaica." She often reverted to her native brogue just for the fun of it, but these last few days, the desire to revisit the islands of her birth had been nagging at her. Must be the travel article she'd read in Sunday's newspaper.

Roger laughed and sat up. "There's a new girl coming." He wiped his face with a towel, then draped it round his neck. "Ten o'clock. Some of the guys at the precinct thought we might be able to do something for her."

"Do you know anything about her?" Hope asked, her brogue giving way to her business voice.

He shook his head. "Not much. She's a prostitute who got caught up in last night's sweep."

Hope held her coffee close to her chest and savored the warmth. She dealt with girls and women coming to the shelter from all walks of life, but the prostitutes were the ones she had the most compassion for and related to the best. "How old?" Hope leaned against the doorframe.

"Sweet sixteen."

A sixteen-year-old prostitute had stopped being sweet a long time ago. "I'd better hurry up and take my shower."

With Adolph lying on the floor watching her every move, Hope braided her wet hair to counteract the curl. A few months ago, she had stripped the black out of her hair and dyed it a lighter color. The orangy result, while not exactly what she'd been striving for, was striking, and a near match for the freckles that dotted her broad nose and high cheekbones. Her café-au-lait skin tone came from the mix of African Jamaican via her father and Caucasian from her mother.

Roger came up behind her as she brushed her teeth, nuzzled a kiss on the back of her neck, and crooned, "Have I told you lately that I love you?"

She spat toothpaste froth into the sink. "How much is lately?"

"Always the wise guy." He slapped her gently on the rear and turned on the shower.

Glancing in the mirror, she flinched at the scar on his back. No matter how often she saw it, she could not keep from shuddering, at least inside. A perfect body, a perfect career, destroyed in seconds by a bullet.

"You want breakfast?" She raised her voice over the moaning water pipes.

"I already fried some bacon and onion. By the time you scramble up some eggs, I'll be ready." Roger was known for fast showers.

Hope dressed in khakis with a woven belt, tucked in a collared polo shirt, and, already on the move, slid her feet into well-worn huaraches. Once in the kitchen she let Adolph out into the walled garden with Celia, then went about fixing the rest of their breakfast. Humming the tune Roger had started in the bathroom, she took the grated cheese from the fridge and added it to the frying pan of scrambled eggs.

Adolph whined outside the back door to be let in.

"What, did Celia run you off again, or did you smell breakfast?" she asked as she held the door open for him.

Tail wagging, Adolph walked past her, sniffed at his dish, raised his head to check the air for flavors, and, tongue lolling, stopped in front of the stove.

"Yours is in your dish."

His tail thwacked across her knees, as if to say, "I don't want what's in my dish. I want what's on the stove."

Hope shook her head. "I don't care how much you wag. The vet said dog food only."

Adolph sat down and scratched his ear with a back foot, the foot thumping on the floor practically rattling the windows.

Just as Hope was putting the plates on the table, Roger entered the kitchen. "Perfect timing."

Hope nodded toward Adolph. "Tell your four-footed friend that table scraps are no longer his divine right."

"Sorry, Adolph, the boss has spoken," Roger said, his voice grave.

Just as Hope sat down, the phone rang.

"Let the machine pick it up." Roger bowed his head. "Father God, we thank Thee for food, for home, and a work that we pray always honors You. Amen."

Hope raised her gaze to look at the man across from her. Succinct and to the point, that was Roger. *Thank You, Father, for this man. Thank You for his love and for his strength.*

She'd taken two bites when Celia knocked on the back door and entered before they could invite her. "They're here early." Hope groaned, took another bite, and put her napkin on the table.

Roger put his hand over hers, staying her. "They're early. They can wait. You eat."

"Yes, dear." Hope smiled. His thoughtfulness always stirred a warm glow around her heart.

"Now, that's a first," Celia said beneath her breath, then poured herself a cup of coffee. "You want me to get started on the paperwork?"

Roger spread grape jam on his toast. "No, they said ten, and it's only eight thirty. They're going to have to learn that we have lives too. Have you had breakfast?"

Celia shook her head. "I ain't hungry."

Adolph plunked himself down beside her, his head just beneath her fingertips. When he didn't get the ear scratches he was hinting for, he lifted his head and whined.

"You surly mutt." Celia's fingers tapped the top of his head. "So what's on the list for today?"

Hope thought while she ate her eggs. "The duty roster needs to be updated to work this new girl in. Someone needs to go to Costco. And the checklist needs to be gone over for the market tomorrow." She paused, glanced at the clock, then at Roger. "We need to see if Starshine is back. I'd like to talk to her if she's in. Oh, and I have a meeting with Peter Kent at eleven thirty, and you"—she looked at Roger—"have one this afternoon at…"

"Two o'clock," he supplied. He glanced at his watch. "I'll do the Costco run first thing this morning."

Celia ignored Adolph's whines for more pats. The dog was never satisfied. "And I'll do the roster, call Starshine, and go over the market checklist."

Hope's thoughts were already elsewhere. Intake was always Hope's department. *Please, God, let this child be clean.* While she knew

the prayer was pretty hopeless, she nevertheless lived up to her name
—and hoped.

Casa de Jesús started as a dream in Hope's heart after she gave her
life to her Savior. It became a reality thanks to a grant from an unknown benefactor that covered purchasing the building. Money came
in from several sources: her church gave her a small budget for daily
expenses; the Saturday Market, held in what used to be the church's
parking lot, brought in money through space fees charged to the vendors and through the sale of deep-fried dough called elephant ears,
chai, and coffee to the shoppers. A good portion of their budget came
from Social Services.

Still, they struggled to keep the doors open. Every day brought a
new challenge that tested Hope's creativity and her resourcefulness.

After breakfast, Hope and Roger worked side by side to clean up;
then they were off to their individual duties. It was a little after nine
when Hope left the kitchen. She waved to the two girls cleaning the
common area as she headed toward her appointment.

"Good morning, Officer Langley." Hope reached out and shook
the young woman's hand. They had met before under similar circumstances and had found that they shared a common goal, helping
the girls and women get off the street and into a safe environment.

"Sorry to spring this on you," the officer said, "but you know
how things are…"

"Could you use a cup of coffee?" Hope asked.

"No thanks. Celia kept our cups full."

Hope smiled at the girl sitting beside the woman in uniform,
then extended her hand. "Hi there, I'm Hope."

No response from the emaciated teen dressed in black leather
short shorts and a black bustier that only emphasized a flat chest. She
wore four-inch spike heels and fishnet stockings that had seen better

days. Her bleached blond hair had been teased to near extinction, and her long jagged bangs fell like a curtain over her eyes.

As she did with all the young girls who came through the doors of J House, Hope wanted to tuck the hair behind this girl's ears, wash her face, and hug her close. It was the unfulfilled mothering instinct in her coming out. She longed for children of her own but had been told she would probably never conceive because her internal damage was too extensive.

"Come on in so we can talk." Hope led the way to her office, ignoring the reception area's stacks of file folders and papers, awaiting a magic fairy to put them into file cabinets that didn't exist. "Is she court-mandated to be here?" Hope asked, walking around her desk, a 1940s oak monstrosity that she'd found at a yard sale for twenty dollars. Her entire office was furnished with yard sale finds, and though nothing matched, the office had a warmth that Hope loved and that seemed to put other people at ease.

Officer Langley walked behind her young charge and indicated that she should sit in the chair closest to Hope's desk. "No. We just hoped you'd have room for her."

Hope poised her pen over a pre-printed admittance form. "What's your name?"

"Kiss."

She wrote the name down, then looked up and saw the girl cross her legs. "Is that your street name?" Kiss shrugged, her skinny shoulders reminding Hope of the way she'd looked at the end of her own street career. "Where are you from?" Something made Hope think the Midwest, though she wasn't sure why.

"Just around," Kiss said, deliberately evasive. She wiped her runny nose with the back of her hand.

Hope handed her a tissue.

A spark of anger widened Kiss's eyes, which were enlarged by a thick line of black pencil and layers of mascara. "I don't have to stay here, you know." Her voice rasped, as if she had a bad cold. She ignored the proffered tissue.

Hope didn't let the girl's obstinacy get to her. In her own special way, she understood how Kiss felt. She tossed the tissue in the trash. "No, you don't, and nobody will force you. But whether you decide to stay here or not, you might want to take advantage of a hot shower, a decent meal, and a soft bed—all to yourself. No strings attached."

"King will come for me." The tough-toned words belied the hands clenched over her bony knee.

"King—he's your pimp?"

Kiss turned her head and stared at the gold-framed print of the San Francisco Bay.

Hope glanced at Officer Langley, who nodded and mouthed, *He's bad.* Taking a deep breath, Hope scooted her chair back and stood up. "We've dealt with King before, Kiss. Tell you what. Let me show you around. You can talk with some of the girls who live here, then decide if you want to stay." *Please, Lord. Help us help this one.*

"I'll be on my way, then, Hope." Officer Langley stood and shook Hope's hand, then touched Kiss's shoulder. "These people can help you if you let them."

Kiss jerked her shoulder. "Fat chance."

Hope escorted Officer Langley to her office door. "Come on by the market tomorrow, and I'll treat you to an elephant ear."

"Oh, thanks for reminding me. My son wants to see the clown again. He kept that balloon hat he got last time, until it shriveled down to nothing."

"See you tomorrow, then."

"So what now?" Kiss asked, getting up.

Hope watched her and wondered what she would look like without all that makeup, and with her hair clean and soft around her face. "Well, that's up to you. Once we leave this office, you can either go out the front door and back to your life, or you can come with me and meet some of the other girls." With a confidence born of experience, Hope walked out into the reception area and headed toward the shelter's kitchen. She smiled when she heard Kiss's spike heels tapping after her.

The J House kitchen was the heart of the shelter. Here the guests worked together, talked, and shared their lives. The walls had been painted sunshine yellow, and the cupboards were the color of light cream.

"Hi, girls, this is Kiss." Hope motioned to the two young women chopping vegetables at the counters. Steam rose from a tall pot of some kind of soup, and the aroma of applesauce spiced with cinnamon emanated from another pot on the stove. She sniffed the air. "Whatever you're cooking smells wonderful."

"Thanks," one of the girls said with a smile. "Welcome, Kiss."

"Lunch is at noon, but if you need something now, we've got some of last night's dinner in the fridge." Hope snatched two pieces of carrot and handed one to Kiss, who shook her head and shrugged—a gesture that seemed to be her main mode of communication.

Hope kept up the one-way conversation as they climbed the stairs. "Everyone works here at J House. That's part of the agreement for those who stay. We have schoolrooms, and up here are the dormitories and a few private rooms, where the mothers with young children live." Hope explained each area as they passed it. "We have room for twenty guests, many of whom are out working right now, since we are sort of a halfway house for those who really want to change their lives." *Oh, my dear little one, I do hope you are one of those.*

While Kiss wasn't committing to anything by word or gesture, at least she was looking around. If she was feeling anything—anything at all—she was hiding it well. What had happened to her to cause her to be so withdrawn and sullen? Every girl had her own story, some worse than others. Some left before they had a chance to recuperate from their physical and mental wounds, some healed quickly and then left...and some never healed. And some like Celia never left.

They continued down the hall, Hope leading the way, Kiss following at a safe distance. "Here are the showers," Hope said, opening the door to a huge bathroom that had been transformed by a former guest into a garden of hand-painted sunflowers. "There's soap and shampoo, and the towels are over there." She pointed to a floor-to-ceiling set of shelves. "We ask that you use only one towel, and when you're finished with it, please dump it in the hamper. While you're showering, someone will bring you clean clothes."

Kiss stepped back. "You're not going to take these," she said, sticking her hands in the pockets of her leather short shorts. "These shorts cost me big time."

"No one will take them, but after you've eaten, you might want to throw them in the wash with the rest of your things. We have washers and dryers in the basement."

Kiss walked over to the shelf and grabbed a towel. "I'll take a shower, but I'm not staying here," she said, turning to Hope.

"I see." Hope glanced down at her watch. "Lunch is at noon if you decide you're hungry." She waited a moment, hoping for some response, but when none came, she smiled and left.

How many times over the last couple of years had she played this wait-and-see game? Dozens. If only there were something she could say or do that— She broke off, laughing at herself. She was doing it again—*if only*ing.

Chapter Seven

Hope

Too much coffee leads to indigestion.

Hope knew no other way around the pressure, or so it seemed lately. She rubbed her midriff and felt a belch rising. Not now. But then, why not now? She was alone in the mauve and gray waiting room, so nobody would hear her. Better now than later, when she was in the middle of a conversation, she thought, putting her hand in front of her mouth to muffle the sound.

Feeling somewhat better, she eyed the large silver sculpture that stood near the receptionist's desk. She knew nothing about contemporary art, but knowing Peter, it stood to reason that the sculpture had been created either by one of his clients or by a renowned artist.

Too bad it didn't have a brass nameplate, like some of the oils, so she could tell what it was. She cocked her head this way and that to study it from different angles, but she still had no clue as to what it might be. Finally, she gave up and took a recent copy of *Architectural Digest* off the small glass table next to her chair. The featured homes were like nothing she had ever seen, and some of them were like nothing she ever wanted to see. She quickly thumbed through the pages, hoping to find a house she could relate to, but they were all too formal or too exotic or just "too too."

She returned the magazine to its pile and picked up one of the three issues of *Smithsonian Magazine.* An article on Jamaica caught her eye, and the first line grabbed her and carried her into the story and back to her beginnings.

"Mr. Kent will see you now." The svelte personal assistant, or so her nameplate read, appeared as if by magic and nodded toward the double doors leading to Peter's office.

Hope debated taking the magazine with her, and begging Peter to give it to her, or leaving it behind. The day's busy schedule loomed in front of her, telling her there would be no time to finish the article. No surprise there. These days there was hardly time to breathe. She put the magazine down and followed Miss Swaying Hips into Peter's office. *How does she do that?*

"Ms. Hope Benson to see you, sir."

Hope rolled her eyes. As if Peter didn't know her name. He had been on the board of directors for J House for over two years. *I must be PMSing. She's new. She doesn't know me.* "Hello, Peter." Hope crossed to the huge free-form desk. No drawers, no files, just glass, the color of which reminded her of the clear blue waters of Montego Bay, the prettiest bay in all of Jamaica.

Peter Kent stood up behind his desk. "Good to see you, Hope."

He had aged since she'd seen him last. When was it? Three months ago? His dark hair was now silver-streaked, and a once healthy tan now appeared faded and splotchy. Dare she ask after his health? He was a very private man.

He came around the desk and indicated they should sit in two leather chairs, which bracketed a small table of the same blue glass as the desk. "Let's sit here, where we can be more comfortable."

Hope felt the now familiar heartburn start to creep up her esophagus. *Go away!*

"Coffee? Tea? I have iced tea."

How about a milk shake of antacid? "Iced tea would be fine," she said, glad for the offer. "And artificial sweetener, if you don't mind." She saw him nod toward his assistant. Miss S.H. nodded back. It wasn't difficult to spot the resentment in the young woman's eyes, even through all that mascara. She didn't appreciate playing maid.

"So what brings you here today?" As usual, Peter got right to the point.

In for a dollar, in for a dime. Her mother had loved old sayings. "Peter, are you all right?" she asked, concern overriding polite correctness. "You look…" She clamped her mouth shut when she saw him glance at Miss S.H., as if to say, *Wait till she leaves.* So he didn't want to say anything in front of her.

As soon as the door closed, Peter answered her question. "I'm happy to say I'm recovering."

"I didn't know you had been ill." She leaned forward. "What was wrong, if you don't mind my asking? You know how incredibly nosy I can be." There were times she wished she weren't so nosy; this was one of them.

"I had part of a lung removed. Malignancy."

The personal assistant returned a few minutes later and set a small lacquered tray down on the table. "Will there be anything else?"

"No thank you," Peter said, flashing her a quick smile. "That will be all for now."

Wordlessly, the young woman left the room.

Hope leaned forward, took a packet of Splenda off the tray, tore it open, and poured it into the tall, frosty glass of tea.

Peter simply picked up his coffee cup and took a sip.

"Six months ago, if you remember, I would be lighting up about now. But no more. I've learned my lesson about smoking."

"Oh, Peter, I wish you had let me know." No wonder she hadn't heard from him. *I should have called when I thought about him.*

"There's nothing you or anyone could have done."

"Sure there is. We could have prayed for you."

"Thank you, Hope. I appreciate the thought, but you know how I am. Anyway, I'm doing fine now. God was good to me and gave me a reprieve." He smiled, leaned against the chair back, and steepled his fingers. "Now, I know you didn't take time from your crazy schedule to come here and drink iced tea with me. What can I do for you?"

"How about getting us a million dollars?" she said with a half laugh.

He tilted his head slightly and raised one eyebrow. "No takers yet, huh?"

"Not yet." Hope failed at trapping a sigh. "I admit I'm a little worried."

"A *little* worried?"

"Okay, so I'm a lot worried," she amended. "I thought for sure that by now, what with all the letters we've put out, *someone* would have stepped forward to put Humpty Dumpty back together again."

"Retrofitting an old building like J House isn't cheap, my dear."

"But I thought big corporations were always on the hunt for a good tax write-off."

"There are a lot of worthy causes out there. You aren't the only ones seeking help."

Hope sighed. "No, I suppose not." She took a long cooling sip of her drink. "I keep reminding myself that our heavenly Dad owns all the cattle on a thousand hills. I need to ask Him for more help—a big corporate donation for J House and the wisdom for me to not panic."

"Wisdom is something I should have asked for a long time ago," he said, indicating the empty ashtray sitting on the table.

Hope sucked in a deep breath. "Believe it or not, money isn't the reason I'm here to…day." A belch snuck up on her and came out with the word, lowering her voice an octave. "Oh, excuse me. I have a little heartburn."

He smiled at her over the rim of his cup. "You're excused."

She pulled three letters from her briefcase and handed them to Peter. "They're all from the same company. The last one came a couple of days ago, and there's something about it… Read them in the order they were sent and tell me what you think."

He unfolded all three, then arranged them by date. "Blakely Associates," he said, reading the letterhead. "Never heard of them." He read the rest of the first letter in silence. "It's an offer on J House." He looked up at her. "That's nothing new. There aren't many lots the size of yours left on Telegraph Hill. You have a prime building location, especially for condos."

"Roger looked them up," Hope said. "They're a consortium out of Los Angeles."

"Hmm. They're offering a decent package. You could easily buy another place that didn't need major repairs."

"We've had this discussion before, Peter. Yes, we could sell out and move to the Tenderloin, but by being where we are, my girls get away from the street life, and they get a taste of the possibilities of a new life. A move would be disastrous. We'd lose Mai's restaurant, and you know how many of my girls she hires. And what about the Saturday Market? You've seen how that works. It brings the whole neighborhood together. We make a difference where we are, Peter. We make a difference in the lives of the women and girls we take in, and in the lives of our neighbors. A move is out of the question."

"You'd think after everything, I wouldn't forget all of that," Peter said, looking suitably ashamed of himself. Ever since Hope and her crew had helped his little sister get clean and sober, Peter Kent, attorney at law, had been a strong supporter of Casa de Jesús.

"Read the other two and tell me if you don't start to see a difference in tone."

Hope watched Peter's expression change as he read them.

"I see what you mean. The wording gets stronger in the second letter and almost sounds like a threat in the third." Holding the third letter, he read several lines aloud, " 'We dislike reminding you yet again that the time for negotiating a deal that will give you the means to move and relocate is running out. Be assured that we are aware that on January 1, if you have not begun the necessary repairs, the city of San Francisco will condemn the property and you will be forced to vacate. Rather than wait until that happens, we hope that you will accept this very generous offer.' " He rubbed his chin. "They certainly have all the information correct. This last part, about what they'll offer once J House is condemned, is sort of unsettling."

Hope felt like rubbing her midsection again but refrained. Instead of feeling better, she was feeling worse. "They remind me of vultures waiting for the kill." *Please Lord, I can't lose J House. Please. You know that's my dream and reason for being.*

"That's the way some companies do business." Peter pulled his PDA from his coat pocket and clicked out the stylus. "I think it's time for a board of directors' meeting. How about four o'clock Wednesday?"

Hope checked her pocket calendar. "Fine with me. Here or at J House?"

"Here. I'll have dinner brought in. In the meantime, I'll do a little digging and see if I can find out why Blakely Associates wants J House so much."

Hope thought about walking back to the shelter, but she caught the bus instead. She greeted the driver, found an empty seat, and nodded to the petite Japanese woman sitting next to her. *"Konnetchewa, obasan."* Hope said, using the traditional Japanese greeting.

"Hai." The woman sketched a slight bow, then in perfect English said, "Thank you for speaking my language."

Hope returned the bow. "You are most welcome."

An elderly man, who lived in Hope's neighborhood and sometimes attended Sunday services at J House, got on the bus at the next stop. "Hey, Hope. Good to see you." He smiled as he found a seat.

"And you," Hope returned, trying to remember his name.

"You have a good name," Hope's seatmate said, nodding.

"I thank my mother for that." Times like this, Hope was grateful she'd learned greetings in several of the many languages spoken in San Francisco.

"I get off next." The little lady stood and gathered her parcels. "Sayonara."

Hope smiled after the woman, then settled into her thoughts. *Thanks, Big Dad, for Peter and for all those You bring our way.* She blew out a breath at the fumes seeping in the window. *Kiss, what am I to do with her? Lord, please get her to stay long enough for us to help her.*

Knowing her stop was coming up, Hope stood and made her way to the front of the bus. "Thanks, Juan. You're the best driver in all of San Francisco."

"You take care now." The bus driver waved a good-bye. She stood on the sidewalk and waited for the signal to change. She only had a couple of blocks to walk, but they were uphill, and she wasn't feeling her best today.

The common room rang with the laughter of playing children, led by one of the younger women who was well on her way to a second month of clean and sober living and a fifth month of impending motherhood.

Hope loved the sound of the children's laughter. Too many of them had little to laugh about before coming with their mothers to the shelter. Several had been living on the streets; others had been on the run from an abusive relative.

Hope waved at their greetings and headed down the hall for her office. "Have you seen Kiss?" she asked the woman with the cornrows, who was mopping the hall.

"She the new girl at lunch?"

"Yes."

"She lyin' on her bed."

"Could you please tell her I'd like to talk with her?"

"Sure 'nough."

Hope set her briefcase down behind her desk and checked the list of messages. She had three calls to return, and Roger had left the day's mail stacked in the middle of the desk calendar.

She sat down and started going through the mail. Five credit card offers! The days were gone when she could just toss them in the trash. Now she had to shred them to protect herself from identity theft. What was the world coming to?

She swiveled her chair around toward the window and smiled at the blown-glass hummingbird suspended by a piece of fishing line from the top of the window frame. She leaned forward and tapped it with her finger. Refracted dots—every color of the rainbow—bounced against her walls and made her smile. Roger. Wise, wonderful Roger. He was constantly looking for things to make her smile. *What would I do without you?* She thought to go find him, but just then the office door was pushed open and Kiss came in.

"You wanted me?"

"Yes, please come sit over here so we can talk." Hope indicated the chair closest to her desk.

Kiss perched on the edge of the chair. She looked more than ever like a lost waif now, dressed in a denim skirt and scoop-neck T-shirt striped in various shades of red. Without all that makeup, she appeared to be the picture of innocence.

"Thanks for coming."

"Did I have a choice?"

"Here at J House, you always have a choice," Hope assured her.

"Yeah." Kiss looked away, her gaze taking in the colored dots hitting the walls and ceiling. One thumb worried the other on her clasped hands.

Hope tapped the hummingbird again. "Pretty, isn't it? My husband gave it to me to make me smile." She got a pencil and dug out from under the mail the admission form she'd started earlier. "I really do need to get some information from you."

"Why?"

"Government regs. We have to follow certain procedures."

Kiss shook her head, her soft hair swaying with the small action. "Why bother? I'm not staying."

"I'm sorry to hear that. Can you tell me why?" Hope kept her voice soft and gentle, as though she were taming a wild creature.

"Because if he finds me here—"

"Who? King? Are you afraid he might try to hurt you?"

Kiss rolled her eyes. "Well, duh."

"I understand," Hope said. Kiss's expression said she didn't believe her. "No. I do. Really." *Should I tell her why? No. She probably wouldn't believe me anyway.* "Let's forget about him for a moment and just talk. Where are you from?"

"You mean now or—?"

"Before you hit the streets."

"Kansas." Kiss stared at the moving dots. "Forever ago."

"Do your parents know where you are?"

She shook her head, again that soft curtain of swaying hair, innocence in motion.

"You can call them if you want." Hope put her hand on the phone. "Right now, or anytime you feel like it."

Kiss made a face and shook her head. "Nah, my mom, she's glad I'm gone."

Ah, little one, I have serious doubts about that. Try another tack. "Have you thought about what you want to do with the rest of your life?"

"Not really." Kiss's shrug carried the weight of dreams never born.

"We can fix that." Hope kept her voice soft and conversational, when inside she was screaming, *Let us help you. Please, Kiss, let us help.* If lost wore a face, Kiss could be a poster child.

"Have you ever been arrested?" It was all Hope could do not to get up, give the girl a hug, and promise her a new life.

A nod. "But they let me off."

Hope filled in a few of the form's blanks. "What was the charge?"

"Trickin'. What do you s'pose? The cops rounded up a bunch of us."

"The mayor's way of cleaning up the streets?"

"Yeah, picked up a couple of homeless women, too."

Hope nodded. "You know, Kiss, you're welcome to stay here, but we do have rules. You will need to stay clean and sober, take part in group, and do your share of chores."

"Like you think I'm a druggie?" She had a should-I-trust-you look written all over her face.

"Aren't you?"

Kiss shook her head. "No! I tried it once, but I didn't like it."

One of the lucky ones. Why does she stay with him if she's not hooked? "What about booze?"

"Some. You can stop with the questions. I'm not stayin'."

"Look, Kiss, I can understand why you're worried, but there's no reason for him to look for you here. According to the paperwork I have, you were picked up way out on the other side of town. And if for some reason he does come here, we won't let him have you."

"You won't?" Kiss's shoulders curved in, a cloak of protection.

"No, we won't."

"Why you bein' so nice to me?" She looked Hope right in the eyes.

"This is Casa de Jesús, Jesus House, and we want to be like Him."

Hope returned the look, all the love and concern she felt packed in tight.

"Figures." Kiss rolled her eyes and shook her head. "Jesus freaks, huh?"

It was Hope's turn to roll her eyes. She hated that term. Just because you loved Jesus, you were a freak? Please. "Yeah, and proud of it."

The office door opened, and Celia poked her head in. "You need to come out here. Got a real angry man lookin' fer his wife," she said, glancing over her shoulder, warning Hope of danger. "Mister Roger comin'."

Hope got up and started for the door. "Dinner is at six. Why don't you go help the other girls in the kitchen?"

"Yeah. Okay." Kiss got to her feet and followed Hope from the room.

A man's voice echoed from the common room at the front of the building.

Fear flashed across Kiss's face.

"It's not about you," Hope said in a rush, turning to Kiss and placing both hands on the girl's upper arms. She turned her around and pointed her toward the kitchen. "Go on. We'll see you at dinner."

Once Kiss was heading in the other direction, Hope sucked in a deep breath of courage and sent her prayers heavenward. Then she headed for the commons area, where a man was shouting loud enough to be heard two blocks away.

"I know she's here!"

Hope entered the room, assessing the situation at a glance. Roger was already there.

"Sit down so we can talk." Roger's voice was conversational as he nodded toward the chairs by the window.

Hope walked over to them. "Would you like some coffee?"

The man swore at her and took a step forward. "You got my wife and kids."

Roger stepped between the man and Hope. "Maybe. Maybe not. What are their names?"

Roger's rigid shoulders told Hope how much he hated these confrontations—and having to be polite when his instinct was to throw the man out bodily, after an "accidental" roughing up.

"Maria Saunders. She took my boy."

"What makes you think she's here?" Hope sat down first, in the hopes he would follow suit. He did.

"One of the neighbors told me she was coming here."

Hope shook her head. "I'm sorry, but we don't have anyone by that name here." *Whew, glad we didn't have to lie for this one.*

"Have you tried Social Services?" Roger asked. "Was there a reason she would want to leave home?"

A tale of lost jobs, evictions, and a downward spiral of their relationship flowed out of the man. "I didn't mean to hit her, but..." Head in his hands, he scrubbed rough fingers through dark hair.

"When she's been gone twenty-four hours, you can file a missing persons report at your local police station." Roger's clipped voice sounded official. "In the meantime, you might want to get cleaned up and go apply for unemployment..."

"That ran out long time ago."

"You can file for an extension, or perhaps for welfare."

"I don't want an extension or welfare. I want my wife and kid back!"

Roger sniffed the man's breath. "As a punching bag or..."

"I told you. It was an accident." The man came halfway off his chair.

"There's an AA meeting at six o'clock. I'll go with you," Roger volunteered.

"Don't need no meeting. Just need my wife and kid." This time he did leave his chair and, at the same time, swung his fist in an arc, catching the lamp on the back swing.

Roger was on his feet before the lamp shattered on the floor. "Enough! We tried to help you, but grace just ran out. Out!"

"But I didn't mean…"

Roger grabbed the man's arm and, with a smooth action, locked it behind his back. "I know, I know, you never *mean* to do anything. You're out of here, buddy."

Hope watched her husband escort the man to the door. Hopefully, he wouldn't be back.

Chapter Eight

Andy

Andy wasn't surprised when Martin didn't come home as scheduled the weekend after their standoff. Neither was she surprised that he didn't mention talking to the powers-that-be about her business and her not wanting to move to San Francisco. What did surprise her was that he could tell her he loved her and yet treat with so little regard her, her parents, and the business she'd built. From the moment he'd told her he wanted to move, it had been his way or no way.

Had he always been like this, and she just hadn't noticed? *Don't go there, Andy. Don't start analyzing your past. You've been happy until now. Whatever happens, you can't forget that.*

To keep from crying, Andy picked up the mail and immersed herself in the dozen or more envelopes. Three were credit-card offers, which she quickly shredded, five were bills, and the rest were orders and checks. She continued to busy herself with office chores, when the animated dog popped up on her computer monitor and barked, alerting her to a new e-mail. It was from a catalog company, an order totaling four thousand dollars in bath and body products. While the order wasn't nearly as big as the one from Nordstrom, it wasn't anything to sneeze at either. She felt a thrill just reading it on the screen.

Andy pushed her chair back and stared at the monitor. Was her prediction of more company orders like the Nordstrom order coming true already? This new order really would wipe out the inventory. But not for long. She'd shipped the bulk of the harvest off to the manufacturer ten days ago, so it would only be a couple of weeks before the new products arrived and her inventory was back up to what she'd started with, plus some. For the first time since she'd gone into commercial sales, she would be in the black, and there would be money left over to buy more equipment, expand the product line, or hire an employee.

She thought about her conversation with Martin. She'd told him she couldn't afford an employee. But that was then. Though only three weeks had passed, things had changed, and it wouldn't be fair if she failed to recognize the possibility.

But oh, the bother of hiring someone—an ad in the paper, interviews, training… If only she knew somebody who knew a little about gardening and bookkeeping, someone who could find her way around a computer. Somebody who was flexible, who wanted to work for the fun of it, not to support a family or to build a career.

Chai Lai, her faithful companion, sat curled up on the desk beside the keyboard, blinking blue eyes and twitching the tip of her seal-point tail. Andy marveled at the cat's calm. Nothing worried her. Andy sat staring at the cat, her mind doing a search of everyone she knew: her parents' retired friends, her friends, her neighbors.

A thought popped into Andy's head, and she looked at Chai Lai. "You know what I'm thinking, don't you?" Chai Lai's ears perked. When Andy leaned forward, the cat stretched out a paw to touch her face. Andy'd had cats all her life, but never one who did that. Andy liked to think of it as a loving gesture, similar to squeezing a person's hand or giving a quick hug. "What do you think Shari would say if I asked her to work for us? She's always volunteering to help out around here. I bet she'd be glad for the opportunity. It would take her mind off her empty nest."

Andy gave her idea a few minutes of serious consideration, and the longer she thought about it, the more she liked the idea. Shari would be the perfect choice. She was honest, organized, and had a good head on her shoulders, which could be turned into a good business head with a little training. Shari loved gardening and had even given Andy a few tips that had helped her be more productive. She didn't need a job; her husband made a good salary, so she would be working for the fun of it. And she could probably be flexible.

Andy spent the rest of the afternoon analyzing her books to see if hiring a part-time employee was really feasible. If Shari could work four consecutive days a month, Wednesday, Thursday, Friday, and Saturday, Andy would be able to visit Martin in San Francisco. She could leave early Wednesday and come home Sunday afternoon. Hopefully, Martin would see that she was making an effort—and maybe he would make one too.

Help me, Father. Help me make this work. Her gaze fell on the open Bible on the table. Often, during the day's work, she would take a moment to glance at the verses she was meditating on. "But above all, put on love," she read out loud.

I love Martin too much to give up on him, she decided, *or my marriage.* He had been a good husband in all the ways that were important. Other than wanting her to move, she couldn't remember the last time he'd asked something of her, which was probably why she'd thought he was happy with the way things were. As far as being inconsiderate of her feelings and not acknowledging her accomplishments, she could forgive him—this time—because he had been so excited about his promotion.

Andy put the computer to sleep, turned out the lights, and called Chai Lai. The cat was slow to get up, slower to stretch, and slower still to jump off the desk, cross the floor, and go out the door. Somewhere

Andy had heard that you don't own cats—they own you. Whoever came up with that must have met Chai Lai.

On her way to tell her parents her idea, Andy stopped and stared out at her burgeoning rows of lavender. A sheen of silvery purple above the mounds of gray foliage showed the late bloom. She sniffed the lavender-perfumed air and was instantly calmed. Everything would work out. God had a plan for her, and all she had to do was keep listening and she would learn what it was.

Andy reread Martin's e-mail three times; then she read between the lines. <I'm looking forward to our time together. Friday night we're scheduled to go to dinner with my bosses and their spouses. I haven't told them that you won't be moving here, and please don't you. I'm not convinced that you won't reconsider, especially now that you're hiring an employee. Saturday morning, I thought we could go out together to look at homes. I'm not suggesting we buy, only that we look. I've lined up a Realtor to take us around. Saturday night I have tickets for *Beach Blanket Babylon*.>

Friday night dinner with the bosses and their spouses was not what Andy had had in mind when she'd called Martin and told him she could come to San Francisco, not for five days this first time, but three, Friday through Sunday. Here again was a case where he should have consulted her before making plans. Why didn't he? What had happened to common courtesy? The thought of having to play the part of the good little corporate wife, of wearing the right clothes, of watching every word she said and smiling until her cheeks ached made her want to cancel her flight and tell Martin something had come up.

Andy opened her desk drawer and sorted through the files, tossing old papers. It wasn't a closet, but it did the job. So he wanted to keep the fact that she wasn't moving to San Francisco under wraps, did he? Fine. She would go along with that for now. Obviously,

Martin was worried what his bosses would say if they knew how things were between them.

But he was wasting his time if he thought he could convince her to move. Apparently, he still didn't get it, despite repeated explanations via e-mail about what the family home and Lavender Meadows meant to her.

She didn't mind going out with a Realtor. She had always enjoyed looking at model homes and open houses. Again, however, she wished he had consulted her first. She really would have to make herself clear on that. Making plans of any kind without consulting her first was just plain rude and inconsiderate.

Andy checked the clock. She had four hours to get ready. Good thing Medford wasn't one of those two-hours-in-advance airports. She filled hummingbird feeders, seed feeders, and the chickens' automatic feeder and waterer, then soaked the pots and hanging baskets on the deck and porch, pinched seed pods off the fuchsias, and deadheaded other flowers as she went.

When she had finished, she checked her house computer one last time for any e-mails. Martin's e-name popped up: mtaylor@aes.com. Andy clicked on the message. <Something's come up, and I'll be delayed, so I can't pick you up at the airport. Just follow the signs to BART and take it into the city. I've booked us a room at the Sheraton Palace. You get off at the Montgomery Street station and use the left exit up the escalator. Call me at the office when you check in. See you soon. M.>

"No, no, no. You are not going to do this to me, Martin Taylor!" She slammed her fists down on the desk, scaring Chai Lai. "After all I've done to make this trip happen, you tell me something's come up and you can't pick me up? And worse—you can't even pick up the phone and call to tell me?" She shook her head, refusing to accept that Martin would do this to her. He knew she hated traveling alone.

Crowds frustrated her, and SFO, the San Francisco airport, was always crowded. It had been a long time since she'd flown in or out of there, but she remembered hearing Martin say that an international terminal had been added and that it was far more complex. And as for using BART! Not in this lifetime. She would hire a cab to take her right up to the door of the hotel.

The anger she'd been trying to keep under control skipped over orange and red and flared white hot. "What is the matter with him?" The trip had started out as a goodwill gesture, but now it would be a confrontation. She was sick and tired of being treated like an entry-door rug, and she intended to tell him so.

She sucked in a deep breath and wiped off the streaming tears. Calling her husband names along the line of "ungrateful wretch" and "workaholic who thinks of no one but himself" helped to let off steam. If only she could quiet the little voice that kept reminding her that Martin had put his dreams on hold for all of them. But then, so had she. She had given up her dreams of business success to share their dreams of home and family. But thanks to her love of gardening, Lavender Meadows was now her dream.

"But above all, put on love." The verse wouldn't leave her alone.

I'm not feeling very loving at the moment, she thought, heading upstairs to pack. She wasn't sure what a corporate wife should wear, but she couldn't go wrong with her black slinky, a sparkly necklace, earrings, and bangle bracelets. Voilà. It would work. Slinky styles had become her equivalent of the little black dress all the fashion magazines said was de rigueur for cocktail parties and dinners with bosses. Her stomach took three flips and a swan dive. Was a hostess gift appropriate? It wouldn't hurt. People always liked gifts. But what kind of gift? A bottle of wine? A gift certificate to a restaurant? She shook her head. Hardly. Lavender wands? She only had three left, but they would have to do.

Back to packing. She added a black-and-silver shawl and a silver belt that would make the slinky outfit work for Saturday night at the theater, strappy sandals for both evenings, the remaining necessities, Bible, and journal, and left the suitcase open on the bed for anything she'd forgotten. After laying out khaki pants, rose cotton sweater, navy blazer, walking shoes, and gold jewelry, she stood back to study the mix. She added a blue oxford shirt in case it was warm, but the time she'd been in San Francisco before, she'd nearly frozen to death.

Before showering, she rushed back out to the workroom, wrapped the lavender wands in tissue paper, placed them carefully in a white box, then tied the box with a bit of lavender ribbon. She'd kept just enough room at the back of her suitcase for the gift. Snagging a handful of business cards, she locked the workroom and headed back to the house.

It seemed strange to leave her car in the parking lot. Usually, she was dropping off one of the children. *Perhaps this will be good for me, going alone, taking care of everything myself,* she thought as she checked in. *Maybe next summer I'll be flying off to France to visit lavender farms and practice my French. Ah, mon chéri. Mon petit chou. Combien? Quelle heure est-il?*

Pulling her bag, she made her way to the America West waiting area, found a seat, sat down, and stared out the window. Her thoughts went over everything Martin had said and everything he hadn't said. She had always envisioned them growing old together at Lavender Meadows, enjoying their grandchildren who would miraculously live nearby. Not in Seattle or Montana, but within a few miles in Medford. She'd thought Martin had the same vision. How could she not have known?

Her thoughts scattered when the agent called her section for boarding.

She felt like a wood chip on a raging stream when she deplaned at SFO. Crowds, speaking languages from every country in the world and dressed in clothing from around the globe, poured both ways on the concourse. And no one to meet her. She comforted herself with the knowledge that no one could come to the gates any longer without a ticket. As she dodged her way to the exit, she hoped Martin had had a change of heart and would meet her at the screening area. She followed the signs to the exit and passed through the crowd waiting to claim their relatives and friends. Several people waited toward the back, holding signs for the people they were supposed to meet; a family converged in a hugging match; and a young couple kissed as if they were alone in their bedroom.

But no Martin.

Swallowing her disappointment, she scolded herself for even thinking Martin would be here. He'd given her instructions and gone about his business, knowing that capable Andy would manage.

She kept a polite smile in place, all the while seething inside. She stopped short when she saw the BART signs. Yes, it would be easier to take a cab, but she'd come this far alone successfully, so why not go the distance? If she could do BART without Martin, she could do France with or without Martin.

The ride into the city passed without difficulty. Trying to ignore the homeless man sleeping against the wall in the station, she took the escalator up the steep incline to the street level. She should be right in front of the hotel. But she wasn't. The Sheraton Palace was across Market, a street as wide as her lavender nursery field and filled with cars, trucks, trolleys, buses, and the stink of gas and diesel. Street people lined the sidewalks, one of them a toothless woman rocking and singing to herself, eyes closed, a clawlike hand clutching the blanket tight around her shoulders.

"Miss, can you spare a dollar?" a black man with one eye importuned, his smile hopeful.

Martin always told her to never give anyone money.

But Martin wasn't here. She pulled two dollars from her purse, stuffed it in his can, and joined the throng at the stoplight. How could anyone function with all this—the noise, the smells, the hurry that rode the crowd like a jockey driving for the finish line? The light changed, and she walked with the rest of them, keeping one hand on her shoulder bag, the other clenched to the handle of her suitcase. If she'd read the instructions better, she would have saved herself this trek.

"I hate city life," she muttered. Now she was getting as bad as those people on the sidewalk who were talking to themselves. Poor things. Yet she'd read about the problems of the homeless. Most of them, not willing to stay in shelters or to be retrained for a productive life, chose street life. The problem in San Francisco was endemic. Not that she believed everything she read. She entered the hotel by the door on Market.

Perhaps Martin would be in the room. She trundled down the hall, past the dark-paneled Pied Piper Bar and Restaurant and the vaulted Garden Court to the check-in counter, where a smiling young woman greeted her.

"Ms. Taylor, there is a message for you. You'll find it waiting on the phone in your room."

"Thank you." She glanced toward the Garden Court. "Does one need reservations for the Sunday brunch?"

"Yes. This Sunday?"

"Please. For two."

"Would nine be too early? That's all I have."

"Fine, thank you." Andy smiled at the young Eurasian woman. The contrast between the feeling of elegance within this building and the chaos across the street almost made her close her eyes as she turned to find the elevators. *Lavender, think lavender.*

She took the elevator to the twelfth floor, following the signs to her room. With only one bag, she didn't bother with a bellman.

The fragrance of Martin's aftershave greeted her when she opened the door, but other than his toiletry kit in the bathroom and his clothes hanging in the closet—as usual, the original neatnik, she'd so often called him—the room bore no trace of her husband. She pushed the button on the phone to retrieve her message.

"I'm running late, so please be ready at six sharp."

She hung up. No "Glad you made it safely." No "Welcome to San Francisco." Don't waste words. Yes, that was Martin all right. Endeavoring to stay calm, she unpacked and shook out her slinky outfit. Ah, the bliss of "no ironing needed." Within half an hour, she was dressed with fresh makeup and the sparkly paste jewelry she loved. The only diamond she owned occupied the third finger of her left hand, in a set of rings she'd taken off only when the hospital insisted for the births of her children and for her hernia surgery.

She stared in the mirror. "Andy, m'dear, you clean up real good." She turned to study all sides. While she wasn't fat, her size-12 curves didn't match the current style of skinny and emaciated. She smiled at the face in the mirror. How long since Martin had seen her dressed like this?

With half an hour to go, she thought about leaving a note that would say "Meet me in the bar," but since she'd never done such a thing before, she figured now was not a good time to start. Instead, she picked up the *Guide to San Francisco* and flicked through it. A short while later, she heard the key card in the door.

Let the games begin.

Chapter Nine

Andy

"You look striking." Martin gave her an appreciative once-over.

Andy smiled up at him. "Thank you."

"I'm really glad you could come."

Andy saw the opportunity to play her first game piece. "I told you that as soon as the business could afford to hire an employee, I'd hire one. I just didn't think it would happen so quickly." She had decided not to tell him whom she'd hired, unless he asked, because she knew he wouldn't see Shari as a real employee. "Of course, it's just part-time, but if everything works out, I'll be able to come once a month."

"Really?" He sounded surprised. "The business is doing that well?"

There was something in his expression and his voice that made an alarm go off in her head. Could he be jealous, as Shari had suggested? Was he one of those men who was intimidated by his wife's success? She considered her answer carefully and decided to downplay the business, in case he was suffering from a case of green-eyed monster. "It's doing okay, growing some every day."

"That's great," he said, then gave her a bland smile.

For the first time in their marriage, Andy felt like she needed to tiptoe around Martin. She hoped that by the time Sunday came around and she was on her way home, she would know for certain what was going on with him.

Downstairs at the main entrance, he handed her into the cab the doorman had whistled up. "Masa's, please." He gave the driver a piece of paper on which the address had been neatly penned. That was Martin, always paying attention to the smallest detail. The cab roared away from the curb, hung a right, and hit warp speed in thirty feet.

"I'm looking forward to tomorrow," Andy said, in an effort to ease the strain that she couldn't help but feel.

"About tomorrow." Martin cleared his throat. "I thought I would be able to go with you, but—"

"Martin!" Andy interrupted, turning in her seat. "Don't you dare tell me you have to work."

He shrugged. "Well, I do."

She glared at him. "I came here to be with you, not with your bosses, not with your colleagues, and certainly not with some real estate agent." She turned back around and stared over the front seat, out the driver's window. Anger boiled just below the flash point. She should have known better than to think he wanted her there because he missed her. All he wanted her there for was to do his bidding, to be his nice corporate wife, to be his house-hunter, to be his... She was so mad she shuddered.

Biting down on her tongue was the only way Andy could keep from saying anything else. She held the box of lavender wands tightly in her lap and watched the city go by.

"There are some things you need to know before we arrive," Martin said, as if nothing were amiss. He briefed her on the guest list. There would be three other couples. She had met two of the couples at previous events. The new couple had been brought in from another company, and the wife was now the new senior vice president of something or other.

When he was through, she realized she had only heard half of what he'd said. Was it Jo or Joe with the last name Waters? The new senior vice president, should she be addressed as Mrs. or Ms.? Until she knew for sure, she would avoid addressing anyone.

Martin adjusted the knot in his tie. Again. He was nervous. Funny, she didn't recall him having any trouble in the past at functions such as this. Was he worried about the dinner in general, or was he worried she would mention the move that wasn't going to happen? She supposed she could reassure him, but right now she wasn't in a particularly charitable mood. On top of backing out of looking at houses, he hadn't even asked how her trip had been into the city, or if she'd had any trouble with BART.

At the restaurant, Martin paid the driver and handed her out. Acting the perfect, thoughtful husband, he put his arm around her and escorted her up the red carpet. If she weren't so mad, she would feel like a queen. At the door, he quickly moved in front of her and held it open. The smile he gave her reminded her so much of their early years that the tingle went clear to her toes. Now, though, every nice thing he said and did only aroused suspicion.

Lord, please get me through this occasion with my social face intact. Playing the game of corporate wife had often been a joke with her, one that Martin never found humorous. He had always been far too serious about his job. As they wended their way between the white-clothed tables, Andy told herself to make nice and remember to smile.

Then she saw them, six of them, seated at a rectangular table toward the back. Were they late? Martin was never late to anything. She used to tease him about being early to his own funeral, just to make sure everything was in order.

Andy squared her shoulders and lifted her chin. *Good little corporate wife.*

The three men rose from their chairs simultaneously. Black suits. Starched white shirts. They looked like a line of dominoes, standing up instead of falling down.

"Good evening, Andrea." Brad Grandolay, head of the company, greeted her. "I'm glad you could join us." He turned slightly, indicating the woman beside him. "I don't believe you've met my wife, Sophia."

Andy put on her brightest smile. "I'm so happy to meet you, Sophia." This was not the same wife Brad had been married to a few years ago. Andrea reached out to shake the woman's hand and was blinded by the diamond—as big as a bantam chicken egg—on her finger. Vaguely, Andy recalled Martin saying that Brad's first wife had left him to pursue a career in something or other. *Yeah, right.*

"Thank you. It's a pleasure to meet you, too," Sophia said with a distinct southern drawl.

The syrupy drawl, combined with the blond hair and the chicken-egg ring, told Andy that Sophia could find her way around Saks blindfolded and that it would be hard to strike up a good conversation with her.

Andy drew her hand back and went to the next introduction. "And this is our new senior vice president of R&D, Ms. Waters."

Andy nodded and smiled, but before she could say anything, the fashionably thin woman extended her hand. "Please call me Marcelene, and this is my husband, Joe." The way she said it made it clear that Marcy was not an alternative. Her husband might have a nickname, but she didn't.

Andy shook hands with her and then with Joe. "I'm glad to meet both of you. Martin said you came from Dallas. Welcome to the West Coast." She greeted the other couple, whom she'd known from company Christmas parties and summer picnics, and sat when Martin pulled out her chair. Laying her box on the table, she untied the bow and lifted out the lavender wands, wrapped so carefully in tissue paper with a lavender bow, and handed one to each of the women. "A token from Lavender Meadows."

"How lovely." Each woman held the wand to her nose and smiled in delight at the fragrance.

"Did you make these?" Marcelene turned the ribbon and lavender wand and admired the handiwork.

"Yes, they are one of our specialties. They last a long time, and when the fragrance fades, you can brush them gently to release new scent, or add a few drops of essential lavender oil."

When Martin cleared his throat, Andy glanced at him and detected a hint of annoyance in his expression. Why would just mentioning Lavender Meadows earn her that look? *Oh, Martin, what has happened to you?* She felt herself shrivel inside.

Forcing herself to smile, she tucked the box down at her feet with her evening bag.

At least the women seemed to appreciate her gift.

The waiter arrived with menus, explained the evening's entrées, took their drink orders, and left. It was Joe who started out the conversation, lightening the mood with a humorous account of their move to San Francisco.

Andy liked Joe. Not only did he have a good sense of humor, but he was also a good storyteller, which he came by naturally, she learned a few minutes later. He was a novelist. Somehow one comment from Brad turned the conversation, however, and before she knew it, they were talking about company business.

"So I understand you're going out with a Realtor tomorrow," Brad said, catching Andy off guard.

"Why, I—" She glanced at Martin and saw the look in his eyes. "Yes. First thing in the morning." *Sorry, Lord.* Now she would have to go. Lying wasn't something she took lightly, and spending the day with a Realtor in this city hovered somewhere between having a root canal and a mammogram.

Brad nodded. "We ask a lot of our executives and their spouses, but we'd like to think we make it worth their while."

I wouldn't know, since my husband hasn't told me how much of a salary increase you gave him, or how much the bonuses will be or—anything else. Andy's first thought was to tell Brad that some things couldn't be bought, things like family roots, dreams, and happiness. But she kept still.

"If there is anything AES and I can do to help you, feel free to ask."

Again Andy smiled. "Thank you. I will."

The conversation turned to expansions and acquisitions, which was frankly boring, as far as Andy was concerned. She glanced over at Joe and saw him watching his wife, his smiling eyes telling Andy that he was proud of her. Picking up her glass of iced tea, she looked over the rim at Sophia, who was watching the candlelight reflect off her diamond ring. The other woman, Denise, who sat at the opposite end of the table, nodded at everything her husband said. She reminded Andy of one of those plastic dashboard dogs.

Feeling guilty for being bored, Andy made a real effort to attend to the conversation. If only Martin had discussed his job from time to time, she might appreciate the expansion that they were talking about.

During a lull, Joe put in a word or two about sales techniques, based on his experience selling computer equipment back before he started writing. "I remember my boss telling me, 'The customer is always right, even when they are wrong.'"

A round of subdued laughter followed. They obviously thought the concept ridiculous. But Andy didn't. She followed the same credo. "Joe has made an interesting point," she said, putting a stop to their laughter. "It's not an easy thing to do, but it's highly effective, and it wins the customer's loyalty."

"You don't say," Marcelene said, looking at Andy with new interest. "Give me an example."

Andy felt Martin's foot land squarely on top of hers and knew he thought she'd spoken out of turn. She considered just shrugging it off, then thought better of it. She was an intelligent woman, and there was no reason why she couldn't add her two cents. She couldn't imagine Marcelene or any of them thinking less of her for it. It seemed to her that they would think better of Martin.

"Last week I had a customer who complained that the bath and body products we sent her were not what she ordered. But they were. She'd obviously not correctly read the instructions on our Web site and had selected the wrong boxes." Andy discreetly pulled her foot out from under Martin's.

"So what did you do?" Marcelene asked, leaning toward Andy.

"We told her to keep the merchandise we had sent her as a gift, and we would send out a new order right away, at no extra charge. Before she hung up, she ordered a case of lavender tea and our honey sticks." She chanced a sideways look at Martin and knew he was hard pressed to control his anger.

"Bath and body products? Teas? Honey sticks? Web site?" Marcelene shook her head. "Martin told us that Lavender Meadows was just a little hobby, but it sounds to me like you have a real business going there. Have you sold it or—"

"No," Andy cut in. "Lavender Meadows has been my family's home for three generations. We won't ever sell it, but the business belongs to my parents as well, and we've hired an employee to help out."

Smile, Andy. Smile if it kills you. She remained silent for the rest of the evening. By the time Brad Grandolay bade everyone good night, she had mentally planted the rest of the acreage, one plant at a time.

"Good luck on your search tomorrow, Andrea. What an exciting track you are on." He shook her hand, then Martin's. "Life will be so much easier for both of you, with less time on the road. I know you've been looking forward to this."

Andy and Martin rode back to the hotel in silence. Once inside their room, Andy put her hand on Martin's arm and stopped him from taking another step. "Sit down, Martin. We're going to talk."

Andy woke at six o'clock, sat up, and saw Martin across the room sitting on the couch working on his laptop.

"Don't you ever take a break?" She yawned and stretched, staring at the face in the mirror across from the bed.

"Of course." Already dressed for the day, he closed the lid on the computer and carried it back to the table.

Looking in the mirror across from the bed, Andy saw that her hair was spiked and that a sleep-crease slashed across her cheek. Definitely not a trophy wife. *Is that another part of his dream?* The thought stopped her. Never had he given any hint of straying, and never had she been given to suspicions.

What would happen to their marriage if she refused to move? What a silly question. Of course their marriage was sound and could weather any storm. Look how they'd handled the separations all these years. While sometimes she'd grumbled, she understood that a man did what he had to do to make a living, especially to maintain the style of living to which they'd all become accustomed. Not that they'd had money to throw around, but the bills were paid, retirement funded, and they'd put two of their children through college and were working on the third. They drove decent cars, paid their tithe at their church.

Are you going to trust Me?

That prompting again. *Lord, You know that I trust You.*

Do you?

She got up and went to the bathroom, turned on the shower, and washed her fears down the drain. Their "talk" last night had not accomplished what she'd hoped it would. She'd let Martin know in no uncertain terms that he was treating her like a doormat, and that from now on he was to consult her before making plans of any kind. He apologized, blamed it on being overwhelmed by the job change, and promised it wouldn't happen again.

He was so contrite, she decided to cut him some slack. She told him that she would go out with the real estate agent as planned but that it was just to kill time while he worked, because she had no intention of moving. She pointed out that between her five days a month with him in San Francisco and his one or possibly two weekends a month in Medford, their lives would continue as they always had.

By the time she'd finished with all of that, she didn't want to stir things up again by talking about his behavior at the restaurant. If indeed he was jealous, which seemed likely, she would need professional advice on how to deal with it. Meantime, she wouldn't mention it, and she would be extra careful in what she said to him about the business.

She stepped from the shower, wrapped a towel around herself, and grabbed another to dry her hair. As she opened the bathroom door, she heard another door click closed. A note lay on the table.

Decided to go in early. Enjoy your time with the Realtor. We have tickets for Beach Blanket Babylon *at 8:00. We'll catch a bite to eat first here at the hotel. M.*

Ten minutes before nine, after enjoying her room-service breakfast, she sipped the last of her coffee, laid down the paper, and did her final bathroom sweep. With fresh lipstick in place, she checked her bag to see if she had everything, including her room key, and as she left made sure the door clicked behind her. *Please, Ms. Real Estate Agent, do not be a cute young thing who thinks everyone in her right mind would*

*want to live in San Francisco. Wonder what would happen if I just blew
this off and went shopping for the day?* The thought made her roll her
eyes.

"Mrs. Taylor?" The soft voice with a slight southern accent made
Andy turn from studying the vaulted glass-paned ceiling of the restored
Garden Room, a historical feature the Palace was renowned for.

"Yes."

"I'm Suzanne Solby, Benchmark Realty." Thick white hair cut to
swing freely at midear framed dark expressive eyes and an oval face.
While her business suit said *professional,* her feet in walking shoes said
comfort.

By three o'clock that afternoon, Andy was certain she'd been run
over by an eighteen-wheeler named Suzanne. They'd traipsed through
lofts with two-story ceilings and windows to match, condos smaller
than her kitchen–family room at home, condos palatial but with a
two-million-dollar price tag; Andy could hardly breathe. Places with
views of the bay, others with views of the city. She now knew the difference between Telegraph Hill and Russian Hill, North Beach and
the Marina. Her feet screamed, and her head pounded.

And all for nothing. Well, maybe not for nothing. Today's house
tour reconfirmed that she would hate living in the city, and that even
if she did like it, she and Martin couldn't afford to buy anything
unless, of course, he was turning straw into gold. The prices were out-
rageous! She wondered if Martin had any idea what kind of money
they would have to spend to get a place.

"Martin and I have reservations tomorrow for breakfast in the
Garden Room at nine. Would you like to join us?" Andy hated to
admit it, but she was setting the woman up for a fall. Once Martin
saw the pictures and then saw the prices, there would be no more talk
about moving.

"How lovely. Thank you. I'll see you then at nine."

Chapter Ten

Hope

Hope loved the sounds of the Saturday Market, from the moment the vendors began setting up at seven a.m. until they all packed up and went home again after noon. Preparations had started at J House with mixing the whole-wheat yeast dough for the elephant ears at four thirty in the morning. Since she was usually awake by then anyway, she'd taken on that job. There was something about the yeasty fragrance of rising dough that met a need deep within her.

Maybe it even went back to biblical times and Proverbs 31, where the perfect godly woman provided for her household. Or perhaps she just loved yeast dough. It all depended on how spiritual she was feeling at the moment. She'd mixed the first batch, set it to rising, mixed a second, and filled the two thirty-cup coffeepots with water. Thank God for the ten-cup coffee maker, or she'd be in caffeine withdrawal.

Celia's cry meant the Saturday Market was officially open for business. "Elephant ears, get your hot elephant ears and coffee here."

"Hey, Starshine, how've you been?" Hope greeted the aging hippie who still insisted on wearing peasant blouses and long skirts with gathered rows. Multiple strings of beads adorned a neck going wattly, and a knitted shawl, in glorious shades of purple shot with silver, warmed the woman's shoulders.

Starshine's knitting needles clicked along as she visited. She sold her hand-knitted wares right off her back, along with those piled on the tables of her booth. In addition to selling her own product, she was in charge of collecting the vendor fees and crisis solving. The most volatile disagreement was usually over who got what booth space. They'd started out on a first-come-first-served basis, but after all these years, those with the longest attendance got their pick of locations.

"Doing better." Starshine tucked an errant strand of graying hair back in the loose bun she wore, a bun that always seemed to be on the verge of collapse.

"You had your coffee yet?"

"No, thanks, brought some herbal tea today. Swearing off caffeine." Starshine refolded shawls and scarves as she talked, stacking colors to set off each piece for best show.

"We really missed you." Hope leaned across the table to give her a hug and whispered, "Was it malignant?"

"Yes, but it's gone now. Snip, snip, and my youth is over. No more babies for old Starshine."

"Did you want more?" Somewhere Hope remembered hearing of Starshine's children, and it wasn't a pretty story.

"No." A lock of hair slipped down at the vigorous shake of her head. "But it's the thought of it, you know, the finality." Starshine smiled, revealing a missing canine tooth. She worked hard at her knitting; there was always a started project in her hands, needles flashing. But like so many other people, she couldn't make enough to buy medical insurance, let alone dental coverage. And yet she made too much money to qualify for welfare, where she could at least get medical care.

"If I can help you with some of the medical costs…"

"Hope, you cannot afford to write checks for my medical bills."

"No, I can't, but I have a discretionary fund for J House, and a friend or two with deep pockets." She ignored the sheen of tears in her friend's eyes. "When I think of all the people you've helped."

"I don't do…" Starshine started to protest.

Hope shook her head, eyebrows raised. "Sometimes one has to be on the receiving end of help."

"Hope!" A man's voice rose above the market's hum.

Hope waved to signal she heard, then turned to Starshine. "I have to go, but you think on what I said." Hope squeezed her friend's hand and threaded her way between the vendors, answering greetings as she made her way to the steps where Roger waited for her. "Hey, mon, what's up?"

"Bad news." Roger lifted his hands in defeat. "Kiss split."

Hope closed her eyes and took a deep breath. "When?"

"No one knows. She left this note." He held the folded paper out to her.

Thanks for the shower and food. Wish I could stay, but I can't.

"Can't?" She looked up at her husband. "Strange word, don't you think?" She read the note again.

"That got me, too. The others assured me they'd told her we could deal with an angry pimp, that there are safe houses and that we'd get her into one."

"Did he come for her?"

"Not that I know of."

"Guess we'll just pray she finds her way back to us. We're the best chance she has."

"Unless she goes home." He handed her half an elephant ear. "Have you had anything to eat this beautiful day?" He glanced up where the sun was already burning off the fog, leaving wisps around the granite towers of Grace Cathedral up on Nob Hill. North Beach and China Town still lay in the shadows.

"Nope. Just coffee." *Probably the reason for my indigestion.* "Maybe I'd better give up on the hard stuff." She rubbed her middle, all the while keeping eyes on the shifting kaleidoscope that was the Saturday Market.

"Cream in it might help. Maybe you ought to go have a checkup?"

"For an upset stomach? Hardly. I'll get a couple of antacids." She and Roger paused shoulder to shoulder for a moment, looking out over their neighbors gathered in one place and obviously enjoying it. She waved back at Pierre and Brian, the two men who had recently purchased Speedy's, the grocery at the corner of Union and Montgomery. They'd come from New York and discovered the store, which had been a neighborhood icon for fifty years or more but had been going downhill. With a new look, a good cook, and friendly servers, the deli section was quickly becoming a gathering place. The men bought a lot of fresh produce from the Saturday Market vendors.

"We need new dough," one of their girls sang out as she returned to the kitchen for the next batch.

"That's the second one already. And the coffeepot is half empty."

Hope watched as more customers strolled in from the street. One of these days they might have to rent a cop to direct traffic. The article in the *San Francisco Chronicle* about their market being a good Saturday destination, in spite of the main one down at the Ferry building, was bringing in plenty of newbies.

Thanks to the early morning chill, she recognized several of Starshine's shawls warming shoulders. You could count on San Francisco fog through the summer and much of September, as long as the inland valleys remained hot.

"Who's shopping for us today?" Hope asked.

Roger held up two string bags. "How about you and me?"

"I'm game." Hope waved at the two musicians who were just setting up. "Hey, guys, you're late."

"I know. The traffic is getting worse and worse." Rafe, the darker one, took his hammered dulcimer from the case and set it on the frame while his partner tuned his guitar. The worn guitar case lay open in front of them, waiting for donations. The two men—one with dreadlocks tied back, the other with head shaved and shiny—had been playing at the market for the last couple of years, even though they now had more real gigs than they could handle. They often boasted the Saturday Market had given them their start.

The notes of "Scarborough Fair" wended their way through the hum of conversations.

Roger and Hope had just purchased a crate of late peaches when Roger laid a hand on her arm. "We've got trouble." He nodded toward three men, all in black, strolling into the lot. A diamond ring caught the sun's rays when the man in the center raised his hand.

"You know him?" Hope slit her eyes against the sun's glare.

Roger nodded. "King D'Angelo. I'll bet he's Kiss's pimp. She said King, right?"

Hope nodded but didn't ask how he knew the man. His years in vice while on the San Francisco police force had put him in touch with much of the thriving lowlife of the city. She touched his arm. "Be careful."

Roger rolled his eyes at her, squeezed her hand, and melted into the crowd.

"I'll carry that in for you." The young fruit vendor took her box of peaches and headed for the side door to the shelter.

"Thanks." Hope busied herself searching for the best buys on tomatoes, salad fixings, and vegetables, all the while hoping she wouldn't hear angry shouts or gunshots. *Keep him safe, Lord. He's my mon, my life, my love.* "I'll take that full box of tomatoes. I know they're pretty ripe. We'll make sauce." She took a quick look around and didn't see anything out of the ordinary. *Don't worry. He's good at what he does.*

Hope moved on to a different stall. "Hi, Nita," she said, finger-
ing the mounds of cabbage and bok choy. "How much?" When the
older Filipino woman named a price, Hope shook her head. "No,
you're not charging enough. I know you would get more from someone else. I'll wait to see what's left."

"No, no, that for you." Nita leaned under the makeshift counter
and brought out a box. "I bring you this special." She handed Hope
long slender Japanese eggplants that glowed in the sunlight, a deep
purple with slashes of cream, as if lit from within.

Hope's face brightened. "I thought these were done for the season." Coveting eggplant was probably not against one of the com-
mandments, but oh, she loved it diced with garlic and onion and
stir-fried in sesame oil. Nita had given her the recipe several years earlier. Rarely did she find this kind in the grocery store. "You are so
good to me."

"Least I can do."

When Hope pulled her money from her pocket, Nita, black eyes
snapping, flapped her hand and shook her head. "No, no, gift for you."

"You'll never make a living giving the good stuff away."

"Look who's talking." Starshine stopped behind her.

"Oh, hush." The three woman laughed together. Shaking her
head, Hope continued on to the next stall.

The hot oil of the spring-roll booth joined the other smells, drawing Hope to the far corner, the spot for her friend and mentor, Mai.
A line had formed right after opening and hadn't let up. Mai made
two kinds of spring rolls, vegan and pork. While she'd expanded her
business from a handcart to her own restaurant down the street, she
still ran the cart herself on Saturday mornings. When Hope asked
why, she said it kept her in touch with the neighborhood and was the
cheapest form of advertising she could find.

A refugee from Vietnam, Mai always wore two black-lacquered

sticks to help hold her thick dark hair in a swirl on the top of her head. A number two pencil shoved over her ear had become her trademark. Petite and as active as a young girl, Mai made change while chatting with the customer.

"You not been to my restaurant? Ah." The look of horror would have done a cinema queen proud. She reached under the cash drawer. "Here, you bring this, one free dinner." She handed the couple a coupon and their spring rolls, laid in flat paper cartons with a container of sweet vinegar. "Use for dipping. Eat those, come back for more."

They left smiling, and Hope stepped up. "Two pork."

"On the house."

"Mai."

"No. No say nothing." Mai, her dark eyes laughing, dished up two. "Where that man of yours? Swear off spring roll?"

"No." Hope started to take a bite. "Ouch."

"Sign say hot spring roll. You never learn."

"We need to talk." Hope blew on her spring roll and dipped it in the sweet-and-sour sauce.

"I take one more girl for now." Mai handed out another order while her assistant kept the spring rolls frying in the deep-fat fryer.

"Thank you. I have a girl about ready." Hope glanced over at the sound of raised voices, then realized the voices were not in anger. Where was Roger? "But I mean we need one of our real talks."

"Been too long." Mai whipped out another coupon. "Only for special people like you. Come to the restaurant, ask for me. I make you something extra good." She waved her customers on and greeted the next one.

"We'll talk later." Hope raised her spring-roll container. "Thanks." She closed her eyes, the better to savor the mingled flavors. She had tried once to learn the minute chopping and mixing required for the filling but had quickly run out of patience. Somehow the ones here at the market tasted even better than those at the restaurant. Perhaps it was the sunshine and the view. Off to the east the Transamerica building added its unique spire to the city skyline of the financial district. White-painted Coit Tower topped Telegraph Hill. From this vantage point, its cylindrical shape was hidden by the surrounding two- and three-level flats, but it was always there, a sentinel that welcomed those coming from the sea, a reminder of bygone days.

Ah, but she loved San Francisco.

The local bus stopped and disgorged another group of customers for the market. The locals always came early to get the best produce, then went about their busy Saturday lives. Applause rippled on the air. Most likely the clown with long skinny balloons had come to entertain the children. Sometimes a mime showed up. Several artists had set up their jewelry and art booths, like those provided for the tourists along the sidewalk by Ghirardelli Square, Maritime Park, and Fisherman's Wharf.

Hope wound her way back to the side door and slipped inside. Good smells came from the kitchen as those with cooking duty prepared lunch. She put her bagged eggplant in the small refrigerator in her apartment. Tonight she'd make stir-fry for just her and Roger.

"Someone waitin' in your office," Celia said, looking up from chopping cabbage for the cole slaw.

"You should have come for me."

"Not me. You looked to be havin' a good time—about time."

"Who is it?"

Celia shrugged. "Dunno."

"Have you seen Roger?"

"Nope."

Concern wiggled its maggot way into worry. Should she call his pager? If he had it on vibrate, he wouldn't mind. But then she still wouldn't know where or how he was. Surely, she would have heard by now if there'd been any trouble.

"Please apologize for me and tell whoever is waiting that I had to run out for a second. I'll be right back."

"Whatever."

Chapter Eleven

Hope

The visitor had left by the time Hope and her husband returned.

"I forgot all about her," Hope said, then gave Roger a look of reproof. "You could at least have called me or told someone where you were going."

"Like I said, I just wanted to follow them a ways to see if they would double back." He showed her his cop face. "But they took off in a Lexus parked three blocks away." Roger had a healthy streak of wife-protectionism that sometimes drove her nuts. "Pedro was sitting on his corner. He said D'Angelo has a well-known stable of girls. It's funny how quickly he came into power."

Her anger lasted all of one second. "He wasn't around when you were on the force?"

"No, I never heard of him until Kiss mentioned him." Roger furrowed his brow, obviously flipping through back files to locate any mention of D'Angelo.

It had been four years since Roger had been shot, and what with his long recovery and then a bout of depression, he had lost touch with a lot of the street people. Once he'd officially retired, he renewed some of his contacts. Now both he and Hope were known as friends by many of the street people, who knew more about what was going on in the city than did most of the city officials.

Roger returned from his thinking place—as Br'er Rabbit would have said—and gave his wife a winning smile. "You weren't worried about me, were you?" Roger loved the Uncle Remus stories, which were no longer PC, but then he'd never been worried much about being politically correct anyway.

"Not a bit," Hope said, crossing her fingers to negate the lie.

Roger rolled his eyes.

Hope shrugged, then picked up a business card that had been placed in the middle of her desk calendar. "Hmm. Julia Collins, an attorney from Kansas. I wonder what she wanted." She turned the card over to find a local phone number, certainly a hotel, since there was a room number also. She looked up to see Roger watching her.

"Someone looking for someone?"

"I don't know, but if that's what she's doing, she sure came a long way, when a call might have answered any questions." Out of the corner of her eye she saw Roger knead his back and tilt his head from side to side.

"Need a rub?"

"Please. Carrying in that box of peaches, that's what did it."

She gave him a questioning look. "You didn't carry them in. The fruit vendor did." She knew he'd not slept well. After tossing and turning in bed for a while, he had gotten up and gone into the other room to read. She wasn't sure when he'd come back to bed, but he'd been deeply asleep when she got up this morning to start the dough for the elephant ears. "Sit." She pointed to a chair and went to work on his shoulders and neck. "You're due for a real massage."

"Not until payday." His voice already took on the gentle throb of relaxation. "You have such good hands, Hope, darlin'. More to the right."

While she dug and pressed to loosen muscles tightened by pain,

Hope found the movements soothing for herself. As she told him to relax, her body did the same. Except for the queasy slosh in her middle that called for more Tums.

He yawned, then said, "I think I'll go get a nap."

"Good idea." The moment he left the room, she dug in her desk drawer for the bottle of antacids and chewed two to powder.

"Miss Hope, you get the paperwork done for Jessie?" Celia stuck her head in the doorway.

Hope shut the desk drawer so Celia wouldn't see what she was doing. "I thought you went home." She didn't want Celia on her case. The woman was worse than a mother hen.

"You know, stuff to do."

Hope searched through the stacks of papers on the right side of her desk. It was inevitable that what she was looking for was in the last stack, on the bottom. "Here it is." She gave it a quick once-over. "Nope, I didn't finish it, but I can do it right now." She pulled out her chair and sat down. The amount of paperwork that came across her desk was ridiculous. There were forms for this, forms for that. She was always behind, but there was just never enough time. Time or no, it had to be done in order for Social Services to release the money needed to run J House.

Celia stood beside the desk, waiting. "Did you call that lady lawyer?"

"Not yet. Did she say what she wanted?"

Celia shook her head. "But she seemed real upset."

Hope handed Celia the signed and dated form, then picked up the phone and dialed. She was about to switch the handset to her other hand when she heard a hello. "Hi, this is Hope from Casa de Jesús returning your call. I'm sorry I couldn't see you before you had to leave. Saturdays are crazy around here. How can I help you?"

"I'm searching for my granddaughter," the woman said, getting right to the point. "The local police station suggested I check with you." The voice sounded professional, a bit clipped.

"What's your granddaughter's name?" Hope waved Celia off and started taking notes.

"Cyndy—with two *ys*—Jacobson. She's sixteen, almost seventeen, a natural blonde, slender, about one hundred thirty pounds, five foot five. She wants to be a movie star. I started my search for her in Los Angeles and made contact with a girl who claimed to be her roommate. She told me Cyndy had been offered a screen test in San Francisco."

A screen test in San Francisco didn't make a lot of sense, at least not for a street kid, but Hope had long since stopped trying to make sense out of the crazy things people did. Hope asked questions about Cyndy's past: what her home life was like, had she been abused, was she pregnant, on drugs or alcohol. The woman on the other end of the phone didn't have a lot of information, but she was forthcoming with what she did have.

"I don't know why Cyndy left home. I do know that she and my daughter don't get along. They never have. I don't get along with my daughter either. I regret to say we have something of a dysfunctional family. My daughter, Donna, became a mother at a very early age and never quite took to the job. On top of that, she has a drug problem and—other problems, too. I tried to talk Cyndy into coming back to live with me, but she said she'd tried living with me before, and I put too many restrictions on her. I suppose I did, but it was only because I thought she needed some boundaries. A teenager has to have boundaries or else…" Julia's voice faded out.

Hope's heart went out to the woman. "Julia, just so you know, we are not in the business of searching for runaways, but we run across a lot of them. As a matter of fact, we had a girl about that age and general description come here the day before yesterday, but she left, and…"

"Oh no, you should have stopped her!" Julia cut in. "It could have been my Cyndy."

Hope was used to people overreacting, so she'd learned to exercise patience and understanding. "We don't operate like that here," she explained, purposely keeping her voice soft and gentle. "We're a refuge, a safe place for girls like Cyndy to come, to get a shower, a good meal, and a place to sleep. It's up to them if they decide to stay. If they do, we try to help them in any way we can."

"I'm sorry, I—"

"I understand what you're going through," Hope said. "I don't know if this girl—she called herself Kiss—is your Cyndy or not. All we can do is pray she'll come back. Do you have a picture that you could give us? That would help immensely."

"Yes, I do. I'll go make some more copies and bring a few by later today, if that's convenient."

"I'm planning on being here, but something could come up. Even if I'm not here, put her name on the picture and leave it with whoever is here. It'll get to me." Hope had no sooner said good-bye and hung up the phone than she heard a crash, followed by a colorful expletive, coming from the other room. A moment later, a small child began wailing in the playroom, and an ambulance siren pulsed up Kearney Street a few blocks away. Adding to the noise level, doors slammed out in the parking lot as the vendors loaded up their vehicles. All the normal Saturday noises of J House.

Hope walked out of her office and saw myriad papers, file folders, and pamphlets scattered across the floor. It looked like a dust devil had just blown through.

"What happened?"

"Don't ask," Celia snapped as she knelt to gather the mess.

"I won't. But I'll help after I see what's going on in the playroom."

"Ophelia's found another bug."

"Oh." Today was turning into an eye-rolling type of day. Hope shook her head as she opened the door to the children's playroom, where a little black girl, her hair captured in many short braids with bright ribbons, stood screaming in the middle of the room. Her wails had made two other little girls begin to cry—a chain reaction.

"Okay, sweetie, what is it?" Hope knelt in front of the four-year-old and looked into her frightened eyes.

"A bug. A bug." Ophelia pointed at a big black beetle trying to escape into the corner.

"Did it bite you?" she asked, gathering the child into her arms. She smelled so clean and sweet, just like a little girl ought to smell. Night after night, Hope dreamed about holding a child of her own like this, but that's all it would ever be—a dream. She'd given up on having children a long time ago. She'd done a lot of stupid things during her rebellious years and, like most kids, never imagined how things might end up. For Hope, it had been a hospital bed, a long recovery, and the reality of never bearing children. Too much damage, the doctor said.

The little girl shook her head and sniffed. "No bugs, Hope. No bugs."

At least it's not a roach. "Okay, okay, let's put him outside."

"No-o-o. Kill it."

"But why? He didn't do you any harm. Bugs need to live too."

"No-o-o. Bad bugs." She scrubbed her eyes with little pink-palmed fists.

"Where's your mommy?"

"I dunno," she cried, then wrapped her arms around Hope's neck.

"Okay, okay." She carried Ophelia over to a chair. "You sit right here, and I'll take the bug outside." She waved the other two girls over. "You two sit right here, next to Ophelia."

Rub-a-dub-dub, three little girls in a tub—chair. All three curled up their legs and watched as Hope caught the shiny-backed beetle with one of the shirts from the dress-up corner. On her way to the door, she tried to remember who had playroom duty today. A little boy named Conner sat in the corner watching the goings-on, his thumb in his mouth, dark eyes cautious. He'd been there a week and had yet to say anything to anyone.

Hope planned on getting his hearing tested. Conner and his mother had come to the shelter because the father beat the child until his ears bled. When the police went to arrest the father, he'd disappeared, and thank God, he hadn't come looking for them.

Hope put the bug outside, the girls returned to their play, and Conner smiled at her. Feeling ten pounds lighter, she returned to the mess around the front desk.

"We need more office help." Celia held a stack of papers against her prodigious bosom and stared switchblades at the desk, counter, and credenza, all mismatched donations or yard-sale finds, and all buried in stacks of file folders and papers.

"Somehow, I think we've said that before." Hope squatted to gather more of the errant papers into another pile. "I think that anytime paper gets in a stack, it breeds more paper. Have you noticed that?"

Celia shook her head. "*¡Qué asco!* I can't keep up, and you can't keep up."

"I know. I know. Let's set these along the wall where no one can bump into them." Hope put her armful down and straightened it as best she could. When she raised up, a wave of dizziness sent her grabbing for the desktop, which sent another stack tumbling. "Oh, brother."

"Sister and mother, too. What's wrong?"

"I must have stood up too fast. I'm a little dizzy." Hope blinked and stood still until the dizziness passed.

"Dizzy, tired all the time, poppin' antacids like candy—it's time you got yourself to the doctor." Celia set the final stack against the wall and came over to feel Hope's head. "No fever. You had anything to eat today?"

"Spring rolls, an elephant ear, and a peach," Hope said. What she didn't say was coffee, coffee, and more coffee.

Celia rolled her eyes and pursed her bright, red-defined lips, foot tapping. "You get back to your office, and I'll get one of the girls to fix you somethin' that's good for you. Go on now, *¡ándale pronto!*"

"Okay, but you have to promise not to say anything to anybody, especially Roger. Promise?" Celia crossed her heart. "And check the duty roster to find out who's supposed to be supervising the play-room, and tell them…"

Celia took her by the shoulders, turned her around, and marched her toward the office.

Thank God for Celia. As maddening as she could be at times, the woman had a heart of 18-karat gold and a work ethic that made her the most valuable worker at J House.

Once back in her office, Hope sat down at her desk, leaned back, and closed her eyes.

Maybe this was God's way of trying to tell her she needed to sit down and do paperwork. If it wasn't… She thought back over the past couple of weeks—the tiredness, the heartburn, the upset stom-achs…and now dizziness. *Like I need a health problem right now. Big Dad, God of all healing, you know how I hate doctors. Whatever this is, just take care of it, please. I don't have time to be sick.*

Chapter Twelve

Clarice

Tampa, Florida

Was California much farther from Florida than Florida from New York?

Clarice Van Dam, once widowed, twice married, stared at all the moving boxes, most of which she had packed herself because she couldn't bear to let strangers handle her things. All her treasures were now wrapped and packed. She'd heard the packers talk about her interfering, but she didn't let it bother her. Some of her collections were extremely valuable, not only in dollars but in memories.

"A new life" this new husband of hers, younger by twenty years, had promised her. What was wrong with the old life? At sixty-seven, wasn't one supposed to settle in and enjoy the so-called golden years?

"Now, darling, you aren't worrying about all this, are you?" Gregor put his arms around her from behind and kissed her under the ear, where he knew it would give her the shivers. That she could still get the shivers at her age had been a surprise. *I wonder what Herbert thinks about that!* She talked to Herbert every day, just as she had when he was alive. Herbert, friend of her childhood, love of her life, and dead at fifty-nine of a heart attack. She had told him to slow down, and when he did, kaput, just like that, he was gone. She had to think he would be glad she had found happiness again.

She leaned against her husband's strong chest and reached up to pat his cheek. "No, dear, not worrying so much as just thinking."

"Ah, California, here we come." He hummed the tune in her ear, turned her around, and danced her around the room, threading their way between the boxes and twirling her under his arm at the arched doorway. "We are going to have a glorious life. Perhaps you could become a Hollywood star. I can see it now: 'Florida Woman Takes Hollywood by Storm.'"

Clarice laughed at his antics and batted his arm. "The way you go on. I'm an old woman, ready for bridge and bonbons."

"Not you, my love. You are far too alive to spend your time playing bridge with old biddies and gossiping your life away. Besides, you have me to do all your worrying." He hummed a few more bars, this time switching to "I Left My Heart in San Francisco." He pulled her more tightly to his swaying body, cheek against her ear. "Just think, we will have a hundred-and-eighty-degree view of the San Francisco Bay from our tenth-floor condominium on Russian Hill." His arm marked the pretended scope of their view. "Over here"—his arm pointed to a stack of shipping cartons—"is Fisherman's Wharf and the Golden Gate Bridge." He swung to the boxes on the right. "And here is Grace Cathedral, and there you can see the tops of the Bay Bridge between the skyscrapers of downtown. The world-renowned San Francisco trolley goes right in front of our building, The Frederick."

"It sounds wonderful." She leaned against his chest, picturing the places he described, imagining the two of them exploring the city together.

"You said you'd dreamed of living in California someday, and our someday is now." He checked his watch. "The movers should be here any minute, but first, I have a surprise for you."

"You are always full of surprises."

"For you, my dearest Clarice, as a reminder of our new adventure." He drew a small package from his jacket pocket and handed it to her.

She glanced from the box to his smiling eyes. "You are so good to me, but this is not necessary."

"Open it."

His excitement always set her heart to pounding. She slid the bow off the long, narrow box. Surely not more jewelry. But a charm bracelet lay nestled in a cotton bed. It held three charms. She turned them to study each one. The Statue of Liberty.

"For your New York life." He turned the palm tree over. "For Florida."

She giggled at the third. "A trolley car."

"We'll add more when we travel." He lifted it from the box and snapped it around her wrist, his hand under hers to hold it to the light. "Beautiful." He cupped her jaw with loving hands and kissed her lips, her cheeks, nose, and back to her mouth, lingering there as if reluctant to let her go.

Mother Mary and Joseph, this man has bewitched me. How can I be so fortunate?

"I'm sorry I won't be flying with you"—he kissed her again—"but I'll be thinking of you every moment, even when I'm finishing things up here. You go to New Jersey, have a good visit with your sister, and by the time you get to San Francisco, I'll already be there, and I'll meet you at the airport when you arrive. Do you have all your tickets now and everything you need?"

Clarice nodded. "I'm only taking a weekender. As you said, I need to learn to travel light." She reached up and kissed his chin. *My Greek god,* she thought again as she stroked the dark curly hair that just covered the tops of his ears. "How will I find you there? I hear it is a huge airport."

He handed her an envelope. "I'll meet you at the baggage claim area for your flight. But just in case something goes awry, everything you need to know is right here—directions to our new home, phone numbers, my cell number, just in case you have a problem. I do wish you would carry a cell phone." He gave her a slightly exasperated yet indulgent look. "Then I wouldn't have to worry that you might need something, and I'm not there to provide it."

Clarice rolled her eyes and shook her head, a tiny "tsk" escaping. "All right. I will take a cell phone." She gave a slight shudder. "My carry-on and purse are going to weigh two tons by the time I get there." She eyed her mink coat that he'd insisted she take along.

"That fog comes in over the city, and you'll be glad you listened to me. And besides, you know how you freeze on airplanes."

Even though she had argued, he'd been adamant, and as usual she gave in. Being cosseted took some getting used to, but she had learned to adapt.

"Now remember to turn your rings to the inside so no one is tempted to steal them."

"Yes, Mother."

"Are you sure you wouldn't rather have that one shipped?" He referred to the ring he had designed for her, using the stones and melted gold from her original wedding ring. She now wore that one on her right hand and her new ring set with its very large diamonds on her left. She never took either of them off. "No? I see that stubborn look in your eyes. *Cara mia,* I am going to miss you." He stared deep into her eyes.

A horn honked.

"The taxi is here." Gregor glanced out the bay window. "And the moving truck right behind." He picked up her coat and took the handle on her suitcase. "Come on. Say good-bye to the old life and hello to the new."

Clarice took one last look around, then dabbed her eyes and walked out the door.

Gregor handed her into the cab, leaned in to kiss her, closed the door, and waved her off. Clarice sat back in the car's seat. Gregor had kept her so occupied she had forgotten to talk to Herbert today. "I hope this new venture has your blessing, Herbert, dear. Be happy for me, please." She whispered low enough so the cabby wouldn't think she had lost her mind.

One week later, after a marvelous visit with her older sister, marred only by comments about "that gigolo," as Nadia insisted on calling Gregor, Clarice stood in the tiny rest room aboard the flight from Newark to SFO, as she was learning to call the San Francisco airport. She touched perfume to her neck, reapplied her lipstick, and made sure every strand in her highlighted, warm-blond hair fell perfectly. She'd spoken on the cell with Gregor just before her flight lifted off. He couldn't wait to see her. Their furniture would be arriving sometime this afternoon, but she wouldn't have to lift a finger.

After checking to make sure no lipstick had smeared on her front teeth, Clarice left the rest room, returned to her seat, and buckled up for the landing.

"California, here I come…" The tune had been on her mind all day. A thrill of excitement rippled from heel to head.

People deplaning lined the aisle, and when it came her turn, the nice man in the seat across the aisle motioned for her to go in front of him.

"Thank you."

"You are indeed welcome. Are you sure you're being met?"

"Oh yes. Thank you for your concern. I have most enjoyed our visit."

She followed the other passengers up the aisle. Gregor had said he would be waiting for her at the baggage claim, and all she had to do was follow the signs.

But he wasn't there. And when she called his cell phone, all she heard was voice mail. Disappointment burgeoned. But, she reassured herself, he'd most likely been caught in traffic. He'd warned her how bad California traffic could be. The same nice man lifted her suitcase off the baggage carousel when it came around, so she thanked him again, reassured him that she was all taken care of, and followed the signs to passenger pickup. She could hear Gregor as if he were standing right there.

"Now if something comes up and I can't make it, all your instructions and the key to our new home are right here in your envelope. I don't foresee any problems, but it is always better to be prepared." He'd shown her the contents and tucked the envelope into her handbag. *"Even I cannot control California traffic."*

A frisson of what?—concern, worry, fear?—snaked up her spine. *Holy Mary, Mother of God, protect me.* She sucked in a deep breath. Should she wait or should she go? If only he would answer his phone. She dialed the number again, only to hear his dear voice instructing her to leave a message, and he'd return the call as soon as he was able.

She waited for half an hour. No call. No appearance. So she flagged a taxi, something she knew well how to do after her years in New York City, and gave the driver the address.

After what seemed an interminable time, with the fare ratcheting up, the cab climbed one more hill, steep enough to slam her against the seat back, and stopped in front of a not fancy but friendly appearing building, smack on top of the hill. A brick edifice with cut gray stones around the entry beckoned her. *The Frederick* had been carved into a marble face over the entrance.

"Here you are. That'll be forty dollars," the cab driver said when he'd finished unloading her bag from the trunk.

She pulled the bills from her wallet and handed them to him. Her cash was dwindling rapidly. Thank heaven for credit cards. With her heavy purse propped on the handle of her suitcase, she tugged the pieces up the three steps and made sure they were stable before pulling out the envelope again and removing the key. The instructions said this key would open both the front door to the lobby and the door to their condominium. She peeked in through the glass wall. A lovely interior awaited her, a warm pool of lamplight around a chair created before her time. How she loved antiques. A stunning arrangement of flowers that looked to be fresh reflected in a mirror behind the carved library table.

She sighed with pleasure. *Ah, Gregor, how perfect. Now if you were only here to enjoy this first minute with me.* She inserted her key into the lock and turned it. Or rather tried to turn it. Nothing. She tried again, the other way this time. Nothing. The key refused to turn. The door refused to open. Now what? She searched for a buzzer that would call the building manager. None.

She tried the key again. Her hand shook slightly.

Panic tasted bitter.

Chapter Thirteen

Andy

Andy hummed a Celine Dion song as she put on her liquid founda-tion. They still had a half hour before they were to meet Suzanne in the dining room for brunch.

Last night, Andy had seen glimpses of the old Martin, the fun Martin, the interesting Martin, the attentive and charming Martin. Throughout dinner they talked about Morgan, her homesickness, and what they could say and do to get her through it so she could get the education she wanted. During the play, Martin seemed to genu-inely enjoy himself. He laughed and clapped and kept a smile on his face until the very end. Afterward, in the cab on the way back to the hotel, he put his arm around her shoulders and held her close. Once in their room, he reintroduced her to the romantic Martin, the man she'd fallen in love with over thirty years ago.

Andy closed her eyes. *Thank You, Father, for last night. Thank You for reminding me what a wonderful man Martin is and how lucky I am to have him.*

If every visit to San Francisco could be even half as wonderful as last night…

She laughed to herself. *Now that would be an unrealistic expecta-tion, old girl.* First of all, the circumstances would never be exactly the same, and second… Her smile turned into a frown. What if last night was just Martin trying to butter her up so she would reconsider sell-ing everything and moving? She banished the thought and told her-self he wasn't a schemer, nor would he ever resort to emotional bribery to get what he wanted.

Last night was just what it was—a wonderful night to be grateful for and remembered fondly.

Do you trust Me?

I want to. I really do. If only I could keep my faith in front of me like a shield and use it to protect myself from feelings of frustration and anger.

"About this new job of yours," she said now, hoping he would be as talkative as last night. "You haven't told me much about it. Will you have more responsibilities than you do now?"

"Not more, just different. I'll have people working under me, doing what I have been doing."

One question. One answer. So far, so good. "You mean the traveling?"

She saw him nod in her mirror, then check his watch. "Yes, we'd better hurry."

She began applying her eye makeup. She could hear Martin straightening things up behind her. "Are you saying that your travel-ing days are over?"

"Not entirely. I'll still be required to make an occasional trip, but not more than two or three times a year."

"Do you think you'll be happy working in an office, day in and day out?"

"I'm tired of living out of a suitcase and eating hotel food. I can't wait to have my own office with a desk and file cabinet where I can put things away at the end of the day. But even more than that, I can't wait to come home to my own house and my own bed."

In all the years he'd been traveling, he'd never complained or mentioned wanting something different than what he had.

"The grass is always greener on the other side, Martin. What if you don't like working in an office? Can you go back out on the road?"

Watching him in her mirror, she saw him stop what he was doing and stare at the wall.

"No," he said after what seemed like a very long time. "There's no going back."

"Why not?"

He shook his head. "It's just not an option."

Andy opened her mouth to tell him that wasn't any kind of an answer but thought better of it. He'd just raised a blank wall, which told her there was something he didn't want her to know.

If she wanted their conversation to continue, she would have to content herself with the answer he'd given her and move on.

"You were right," she said, throwing him a smile over her shoulder. "I had fun yesterday with Suzanne."

"Did you see anything you liked?" He sat on the bed.

"There was one possible condo, but I didn't like the area much. It had a price tag of over a million dollars. Have you researched the housing prices?"

"Some. I've been checking out those real estate magazines and looking online at realtor.com."

She heard the zipper of his toiletry kit open, and she caught a glimpse of him taking a pill out of a small brown container and putting it in his mouth.

"Do you have a headache?"

"Huh?" He twisted around to look at her. "No, I…" The phone rang and interrupted whatever he'd been going to say. "Hello? Good morning, Suzanne." Andy watched him in the mirror. "Oh, okay. Of course, I understand. No, my wife is leaving early this afternoon for home." Holding the phone between his ear and his shoulder, he zipped his toiletry kit and put it into his weekender. "Sure, she's right here."

Finished with her makeup, Andy stood up, slipped into her shoes, then walked across the room and took the phone. "Hi, Suzanne." She listened while the woman repeated what she'd told Martin. A family crisis, she explained. Nothing serious. "No problem, really. Besides, I didn't really see anything yesterday that was worth further discussion." She saw a look of disappointment cross her husband's face, but she knew that would change with her next words. "But I'd be happy to look at anything else you come up with. You can e-mail me the listing information, and if I see anything I like, I'll get right back to you." Martin's eyes widened. "Yes, thanks. Bye." She hung up and waited for Martin to say something.

"Does that mean that you've reconsidered?"

Andy sat down on the bed next to her husband. "That means that I'm open to discussion if you are." *Come on, Martin, work with me.* She saw his eyes narrow but was encouraged when he didn't get up. "Yesterday Suzanne showed me listings that ranged from a million to two million dollars. I'm sure she wouldn't waste her time showing me properties that weren't in the price range you gave her. I know what your salary is now, and while generous, it isn't enough to buy a million-dollar-plus home."

She could literally hear him changing gears. "I told you not to worry, that AES is giving me a big raise and bonuses."

"Yes, but you didn't tell me how much of a raise or the amount of the bonuses. Is there a reason you don't want me to know?" *If that isn't laying it on the line, I don't know what is.*

"Of course not." He looked down, his expression contrite. For a moment it seemed he would continue to keep his secret. Then he looked up and said, "The raise is eighty thousand a year with two fifty-thousand-dollar bonuses, besides moving expenses and housing assistance."

Andy smiled. "Wow. I'm impressed. They must have big plans for you."

He smiled back. "They really liked my proposals to boost sales."

Andy nodded as if she knew what he was talking about. Another secret? "Whatever it was, it must have really been something for them to give you such a big raise." She was careful to avoid sounding sarcastic. This walking on eggshells was for the birds, but it was working.

"I know I told you, Andy," he said, gazing at her as though she'd lost her mind, "that they offered a cash incentive."

Andy shook her head. "No. You never mentioned anything like that to me." She shrugged. "Sorry."

He exhaled, shook his head. "No, I'm the one who should be sorry. I meant to tell you—both things—but I guess it slipped my mind.

Right! She got up and busied herself with packing her suitcase. She needed a moment to remind herself to trust in God to help her and to not let Martin's inconsiderate behavior and lame excuses get the best of her. *Help me, Lord. Help me say and do the right things. I don't want to end this trip in an argument.*

"Let's go eat," she said.

All through brunch, it was as if Andy and Martin agreed to keep the conversation light. They talked about the artwork of food, the ice sculptures, the glory of the arched glass ceiling and crystal chandeliers. But even the harp music failed to calm the raging argument in her mind.

Back in their room, Andy zipped her suitcase, pulled up the handle, and turned around, ready to say what she needed to say and catch any arrows he might shoot at her. "I know how much this job means to you, and I can appreciate your wanting to comply with every request, but you should have consulted me before you agreed to move here. As husband and wife, we're supposed to be partners, and we're supposed to talk to each other and listen to each other." She paused and sat down in the chair across from his so she could see his face. "You didn't talk to me about your promotion, and you didn't listen to me when I told you what Lavender Meadows and my home mean to me."

He looked for all the world as though he was truly sorry. "I guess I just got carried away in the excitement."

She leaned forward, her hands capping her knees. "Whatever the reason, we now have a major problem, and unless you're willing to compromise, we'll have a bigger problem." She took it for granted that he could put his own name to the problem.

He looked up. "What kind of compromise?"

"Now that I know how much your raise is, I don't see any reason why we couldn't buy a small, low-maintenance home here in the city." His eyes rounded with surprise, and she realized she hadn't made herself completely clear. "We have enough in our money-market account to make a respectable down payment, and your raise will more than cover a second mortgage." When his mouth opened, she raised her hand and pointed her index finger. "Let me finish, please. If the new employee works out the way I think she will, I'll be able to fly down here once a month on a Wednesday and leave on Sunday. If you think about it, along with your weekend at home, a week a month is more time than we've had together in years," she said, adding emphasis where needed.

He looked her straight in the eye, then shook his head. "Two houses? Two mortgages?"

"Don't make it sound impossible, Martin. The last time I refinanced the house, I took out a fifteen-year mortgage, and it will be paid off in three years."

"It doesn't matter. We can't afford two mortgages."

"Yes, we can, but we have to be realistic about what we can buy."

"I don't want you to have to work," he said.

"I love what I do, Martin. Just like you love what you do. What with Morgan in college now, I wouldn't know what to do with myself if I didn't have the business."

"No," he said, shaking his head. He stood up and walked over to the window. "That isn't going to work for me."

She sat back in the chair. "Why not?" Frustration throbbed in her voice. *Help me out here, Lord.*

"Because…because I don't want a part-time wife."

Andy heard herself gasp. Of all the things he could have said, that was the one thing he should not have said. The arrow hit her straight between the eyes. "Martin Taylor, you listen to me," she said between gritted teeth. "Ever since you started traveling for AES, you've been a part-time husband and father. We were lucky to see you more than two full weekends a month. And even when you were home, you spent every waking minute reading company reports and going over paperwork." Anger oozed out of every pore. "In all those years, I never once complained, because I knew you loved what you were doing. I never dreamed of asking you to give it up."

"I was doing it for you and the kids," he flashed back. "So you could have the best of everything."

"All we wanted was you, Martin. Just you! But we couldn't have you, so we made do without." *Easy, Andy, calm down or you'll be saying things you'll be sorry for, things you can't take back.* Taking a deep breath, she continued, "Let me be very clear here. I am *not* going to leave our home, our church, my cat, my dog, and everything else I hold dear to move here so that I can be a *full*-time wife. You're a workaholic. You'd rather work than eat. You may not be on the road anymore, but I know you. You'll be gone by eight in the morning, and you won't be home until after nine. You'll grab breakfast at the coffee shop, eat warmed up-dinners, and be in bed by ten. And where will that leave me? Stuck here in a city I hate, in a house that isn't a home, without my animals, without my parents or my friends, and with nothing to occupy my time." She stood up, grabbed her purse in one hand, her suitcase handle in the other, and started for the door. "When you're ready to talk, Martin, you give me a call."

The phone woke her to sunlight pouring through the windows. Not the pale yellow of early dawn, but full-blown, close-the-blinds hot September sun. Sometime during one of the worst nights of her life, she had pulled the comforter over her, and now she felt hot and sticky. Her eyes burned from all the tears. She ignored the ringing phone and lay there, her gaze roving the familiar and loved room. All the school photos of the children, including graduations, covered two walls. Except for Morgan's. She had yet to get that one framed and hung. A two-way sheaf of lavender hung over the door, symbolizing peace and prosperity. Both of which she'd had until a few weeks ago.

The phone rang again. Surely it wasn't Martin, not during working hours. Unless of course he wanted to apologize. Fat chance.

She reached for the phone, then stopped herself. *Do I want to talk to anyone else? Not really.* She brought her hand back to her side. The answering machine downstairs would pick up.

You have work to do. Get up! All of the psychologists said self-talk is the most powerful motivator. Not this morning. She teared up at even the thought of yesterday morning's conversation.

Martin could just do his thing, and she could do hers. Maybe, after a while, he would miss her so much, he would be willing to compromise. She sniffed again. *Martin, we've never fought like this. I hate it.* If only she could say this to him.

She stumbled from the bed to answer nature's call. Chai Lai, tail straight in the air, marched into the bathroom and demanded her morning meal. Her name meant "beautiful girl," but right now she was acting like an imperial queen.

"I'm coming. Let me get a shower—oh, all right."

Downstairs she poured out the dry cat food and, in penitence, opened a can of fancy cat food and put it on a plate. Filling the coffee-pot, she glanced at the blinking light on the answering machine. She could listen to the message later. Like she could check e-mail later. Besides, if she heard Martin's voice or saw a message from him, she'd want to destroy the messenger.

All she wanted to do was crawl back under the covers.

"Andrea Taylor, you can't go back to bed. Look at all you have to do today." At the tone of her voice, Chai Lai flattened her ears. *Ask me if I care.* Fury turned her tears to steam. She stomped upstairs, turned on the shower, and washed her hair so hard her head ached. She'd just donned her undies when Comet's barking told her someone was approaching the house. She glanced out the window. Shari's car. Was she supposed to come this morning? Probably so, to give her a rundown on how things had gone over the weekend.

Andy finished dressing, slid her feet into her clogs, and moussed her hair before running a comb through it.

"Andy! Andy! Are you all right?" Shari's voice preceded her up the stairs.

"In the bathroom. The coffee is hot." Andy stared at her red, puffy eyes. No amount of makeup would help that, and besides… "Ask me if I care." Her mutter propelled her to hang up her towel and straighten the bathroom mat as usual. When she was the only one here, she could blame clutter on no one but herself. Somehow, she did care enough about that to put everything away.

"I thought you fell and hurt yourself or something. You always answer your phone." Shari met her at the arch to the kitchen with a steaming mug of coffee. "You look terrible."

"Thank you." Andy took the cup. "Just what I needed to hear."

"Are you sick?"

"Sick and tired…"

"Of?" Coffee cup in hand, Shari took a seat at the counter.

"My husband."

Shari sipped her coffee. "I was afraid that was coming. What happened?"

Andy went over the entire weekend in detail. "When he told me he didn't want a part-time wife, I came unglued, and the worms came crawling out of the can."

"So where does that leave things?"

"Well… " Andy thought a moment. "I don't know. The way I feel right now—I'm still so mad…" The word *divorce* popped into her head, but she couldn't bear saying it out loud. Surely it wouldn't come to that. Would it? If divorce was in her future, it wouldn't be because she wanted it. *That would be Martin's call, and I'd fight him all the way.*

"I've been praying for wisdom for you." Shari refilled her coffee cup and held up the pot.

Andy shook her head. "I already feel like I'm stretched tighter than a mandolin string."

She reached out and picked up the picture frame that sat next to the telephone. The picture had been taken a couple of months before she and Martin got married. They looked so young, so innocent in it. "You know, when we got married, I pictured myself as being the perfect little wife, who would take care of her husband and her children and make them a wonderful, loving home. The first couple of years after Martin started traveling, I called him whenever anything went wrong—a leaky faucet, a bounced check, a problem with the kids. No matter what the problem, he would always say the same thing, 'Do whatever you think is best, Andy.' So I did. After a while, I stopped calling him for the little things and eventually even for the big things."

"He should have been there for you and the kids more than he was, but we've talked about that before, and you told me you'd come to terms with the role he forced you to play."

"I did come to terms with it, but I'm just now realizing a few other things." She watched Shari pick up her cup and look at her over the rim. "I'm not the same Andy. There used to be a time when Martin would say, 'Jump,' and I'd say, 'How high?' When he first started traveling, I was weak and dependent. I didn't think I was capable of being the head of the house and making all the decisions."

"And now you know differently. You're like that song—'I Am Woman.' You're capable, strong, and independent. That is not a bad thing."

Andy stared at Shari. "Not for me, no. But I think Martin wants that woman I used to be—the little wife. I don't think he even realizes that I'm not her anymore." She looked out the window and saw a stiff breeze bending the tree branches.

"Oh, I'll bet he does."

"We went out to dinner with his boss and the new vice president of R&D—a woman. I hated every moment of it. I am not and never will be a corporate wife. I'm Andy Taylor, lavender grower and purveyor of fine lavender products."

"So I take it you're not planning on selling out and moving to San Francisco."

"I offered up a compromise. A small second home. I pointed out that my being there with him five days a month was as much time as we've had together for years." She frowned. "And that's when he said, 'That isn't going to work for me. I don't want a part-time wife.'" Tears started to fill her eyes. "I really didn't want us to end our weekend together in another argument, but we did." She plucked a tissue out of the box.

"Did Martin do or say anything to make you think he might be jealous?"

Andy nodded. "During the corporate dinner, he gave me a look—you know—really annoyed, and then later he put his foot down on top of mine to let me know that he wanted me to exit a conversation about dealing with difficult customers. Both times, what I was saying was in reference to Lavender Meadows."

"Well, then. At least you know what you're dealing with."

Andy used a dishtowel to swipe down a cobweb, a sign of an opportunistic spider. In the short time she'd been gone, the spider had moved in. "Yes, but how do you handle it?"

"Counseling?"

"Martin would never consider going to a counselor."

"I know that, but maybe if you went, you might be able to find out how to deal with the problem. Or maybe you could find the answer in a book. You know, one of those relationship books. Somebody must have dealt with this problem before."

Are you going to trust Me, Andy?

"I keep hearing God saying, 'Are you going to trust Me?' He must know something I don't, so I think the best thing to do is pray and dig into His Word."

Chapter Fourteen

Clarice

"Ah, ma'am…ma'am, can I help you?"

Clarice looked up to see a woman with a friendly smile. The warmth of the smile and voice made tears burn her eyes.

"I-I'm just moving here, and my key won't work in the door, and I didn't know how to call the manager, and I…" She stopped to catch a breath.

"Sometimes new keys are hard to work. Would you like me to try it?"

"Oh yes, if you would." Clarice handed her the brand-new key ring that Gregor had made especially for her. "My husband was to be here. I just don't know what happened to him."

"Traffic can be so terrible here. Where is he coming from?"

"Florida."

"Oh, my, quite a ways." The woman smiled over her shoulder as she inserted the key. Nothing happened. She tried again, with the same luck. "You were right. The key doesn't work. Come on in with me, and we'll call Frank, the manager. He'll take care of this."

Clarice got to her feet, knees creaking in the process. "Like some man said, getting old ain't for sissies, that's for sure." She clutched the handle of her suitcase and proceeded through the door the woman was holding open.

"Such a lovely place. My husband said I would love it here, and I'm sure I will."

"Why don't you sit in that chair, and I'll get Frank?"

"Of course." Clarice parked her suitcases by her side and sank into the wing chair, absently stroking the carved wood part of the arm. The room looked as warm and inviting from this view as from beyond. The flowers on the carved walnut library table were indeed fresh: lilies, gladiolas, and chrysanthemums in lovely rust and orange shades, along with greens and baby's-breath. Classy and friendly at the same time.

She knew she'd love it here; Gregor always had her best interests at heart. *I can't wait to tell him how thrilled I am.*

"I'm sorry, I didn't get your name." The woman had returned, man in tow.

"Mrs. Gregor Van Dam. Clarice."

Frank scratched his chin, hesitated, then asked, "You said you were supposed to be moving into this building today?"

"Yes, is there a problem?" Something uncoiled in her midsection.

"Well, ma'am, I hate to say this, but there is no one moving in here today, or even this month. We have no vacancies."

Clarice cleared her throat. "Why, right here I have all the instructions." She dug in her bag and pulled out the envelope. Opening the sheet of paper, she pointed to the paragraph that included the name of The Frederick and the address. "See."

"I believe there is some major misunderstanding here. As I said…"

"So you mean he is already moved in."

"Not unless he moved in six months ago. And I know those folks. They still live here. I don't know what to tell you."

There is some mistake, all right. Clarice could feel her heart thudding in her ears. "I need to get in touch with my husband. Surely, he…" But when she punched redial, the same voice message came on. She clicked it off without leaving a message as instructed.

"Clarice." The voice seemed to come from a distance. "Are you all right?"

She pulled herself back from the edge of what looked to be a precipice and blew out a breath. Voices of her sister, her friends in New York, others in Florida, shouted in her head. *"He's no good." "Too smooth." "You'll be sorry." "No fool like an old fool." "Don't come crying to me."*

Her hands shook so badly she could hardly put the envelope back inside her purse. She who had always been so strong. *Herbert, what have I done? Where is Gregor? You can see him. I know you can. Surely there is some mistake.*

But right now talking to her long-dead husband failed to bring her the usual comfort.

"Perhaps you would like to check into a hotel until you decide what to do?" The woman offered the suggestion gently.

"I could call you a cab." Frank leaned closer. "Unless there is someone local you could call."

"I don't know anyone local." She tried to put some starch in her voice, but that failed too. "Yes, please call a cab."

"Mrs. Van Dam, do you have a preference as to which hotel? We have all of them."

"One that's close, not too expensive, but safe. You wouldn't believe the stories I've heard about this city." *Get your gumption back, Gerty. You start to cry now, and you'll dissolve into some kind of puddle.*

When the taxi arrived, the two people helped her in, and Frank told the driver to take her to the Holiday Inn on Van Ness. "That's the closest to here," he told her. "I do hope everything will be all right."

"Thank you, you've been most kind."

Clarice collapsed against the seat back. Surely once she'd put her feet up for a bit, she would be fine. She'd talk with Gregor, and all this would be food for laughter someday—when she'd recovered. She clutched her fur coat closer around her. Fear always made her cold.

The cab driver came around and opened her door, then lifted out her bags. "You need help with these?"

"No, no, thank you." She handed him five dollar bills, one of which was a tip.

"Thanks."

She watched him drive off, then resolutely turned to the door. Good thing it was an automatic door, because right now she didn't have the strength to push it open.

Pulling her luggage, she approached the desk and joined two others in line. *Please, please, Mother Mary, have mercy on me. Let there be a room.*

The young man greeted her with a nice smile when her turn came.

"You have a room?"

"Yes, smoking or non?"

They went through the routine, with her growing more weary by the second. When he asked for her address, she gave the one at The Frederick, for she had no other.

When he asked for a card, she handed him her Visa and shifted from one foot to the other. Why had she insisted on wearing heels on a trip like this? Even though they were only two inches, right now they felt like four. Her legs ached, her shoulders felt like she'd been pulling that suitcase for a week, and some demon was stabbing pins in her feet. Hatpins.

"I'm sorry, ma'am, but your card was declined."

"Declined! Why, that cannot be. Run it through again." She pursed her lips. "Please."

He shook his head but did as she asked. When her third and last card was declined, she sagged against the counter.

"But I don't understand."

"Would you like to call your bank and see what's wrong?"

Was he being sarcastic? She looked back at him, but he seemed sincere.

"There are phones right over there."

"Th-thank you." The space across the lobby looked like a mile.

She carefully called each card. The answer was the same. "I'm sorry, but that card is over the limit and cannot be used."

She set the receiver in the cradle and leaned back against the wall. What could she do?

Blessed Virgin, if I ever needed help, I need it now. Where can I go? I can't sit here in the lobby. Another call to Gregor's phone yielded only the same answer.

Do not cry, you old fool! Something terrible has happened to him. Had there been a plane crash? That wouldn't be in the papers on the rack today. She needed to see a television. Watch the news? Could one call to see if a plane had crashed?

The war in her head and heart drained all her energy as she staggered to a chair and sat down. *What can I do? Where can I go?* Like a gerbil on an exercise wheel, her thoughts went nowhere. Her stomach knotted; heartburn gnawed at her esophagus. *Surely, I'm having a heart attack. If I have a heart attack, they'll call an ambulance. I'll have a place to sleep. You silly old fool. No, something has happened to him. Gregor loves me.*

"Ma'am…ma'am…ma'am." Someone was tapping her shoulder.

Gregor, no, he wouldn't call her…ma'am. She tried to open her eyes, but the weights holding them closed were so heavy.

"Ma'am…ma'am, are you all right?"

She nodded and won the battle with her eyelids. Straightening, she swallowed and looked around. The young man from behind the desk stood in front of her.

"Please, is there someone I can call for you? You cannot stay here. I'm so sorry." He glanced over his shoulder, as if afraid someone was coming for him.

"I— May I use the rest room?"

"Yes, of course. It's down that hall."

"Thank you." Clarice walked as though she were in a fog, unable to see more than one step at a time. Two steps too fast, and she might pitch over the cliff.

After using the facilities, she washed her hands and peered into the mirror.

Her eye makeup was smeared, her powder looking like a distressed finish on antique furniture. She applied lipstick, more by feel than sight, took two steps, and remembered how her feet hurt. Sitting on a padded bench, she removed her heels, stuck them in her suitcase, and pulled out a pair of walking shoes. If she had to walk all night, at least her feet would not hurt so terribly.

She trundled her cases out the door and into real fog, the San Francisco kind that seeped into the bones and broke the will. She fastened the closures on her coat and struck out for the street. With her shoulder bag banging against her side, she stopped again and unbuttoned her fur coat. Taking her arm out of one sleeve, she put the strap over her head, and with the bag under her arm, she shoved her arm back in the sleeve and closed the coat. With the collar turned up, she felt warmer than a moment ago. At least she was doing something.

Was everything in this blasted city on a hill? She paused in a doorway, out of the wind.

"Keep movin', lady, this here's mine." The voice came from down by her feet.

"What?" Something bumped her ankle. She started, stifled a

scream, and leaped out onto the sidewalk again. She dragged her suitcase, bumping over curbs, stepping around sleeping forms covered by papers, blankets, rags. A dog growled at her.

Hearing footsteps behind her, she tried to pick up her pace. Was she being followed? Were there no police?

"Hey, lady, ya' got a dollar, change, anything to help a…"

She staggered off without responding. *Keep going, keep going.* Going uphill set her to panting and puffing. Her shoulder ached from dragging the weight. *Let it go.* She clenched the handle with all her might. From streetlight to streetlight, she staggered as if drunk, finally to lean against a wall, unable to go any farther.

"Hey, get that old broad." The voice almost penetrated her inner fog that drifted like the silver mist around her.

"Git outta here. You git!" The voice roared out of nowhere, followed by the sound of hard objects striking something softer, screaming profanities, and shoe soles slapping against concrete.

Clarice huddled into her coat, making herself as small as possible.

"You all right, there?" The voice of a thousand cigarettes and an ocean of booze grated in her ears. When she failed to answer, the voice dropped to a sibilant whisper. "You keep movin', or they'll strip you nekkid."

"I-I cannot."

"You ain't from these streets. What brung you here?"

"He didn't come."

"Ah, a man. More trouble than they're worth." Her cackle made Clarice shiver.

"I-I don't know where to go." She forced the words past a throat clogged with the moisture she'd been sucking in.

"Where you from?"

"Florida, Miami."

"I alles wanted to see Florida."

God, if only I were there. So heavy. Eyes, head, if only to melt down into the cold cement that was now eating into her posterior, even through a fur coat.

"Ya heard of J House?"

"I've never heard of anything."

"Run by woman named Hope. You go there. She'll find a place for you."

"Why don't you go there?"

"Ah, ain't no hope for me. Can't abide by the rules."

"Rules?" A shudder racked her, clattering her teeth, knocking her knees.

"No drinking, gotta be sober. Life's hard enough drunk, let alone sober."

"I see." Clarice sniffed but hadn't enough energy to dig into her purse for a tissue.

"Na, you don't see. You get to Hope, you hear?"

"Who are you?"

"Name's AA, ain't that a—?"

"AA?"

"You go on to see Hope."

"Where?"

"Ask one of the coppers. One will come by soon. Be out on the curb. Wave. You don't look like one of the ladies."

"How do you know what I look like?"

"Don't, but I can guess."

Clarice leaned forward, looking both ways on the street. "There's a white car coming."

"Be ready." AA gave Clarice a push. "Get you on out there."

Clarice used the wall as a support to lever herself to her feet. Clutching the handle of her case, she staggered to the corner, right under the streetlight.

"Help, please help me!"

The car, with a light bar on top, pulled over to the curb. "What do you need, ma'am?"

"Please, sir, I'm from out of town and I'm lost and AA said I should go to see Hope at…at, oh, I don't remember. Some place."

One of the officers got out of the car and came to stand beside her. "Your name, ma'am?"

"Clarice—er Mrs. Van Dam. It's a long story and not a nice one."

"Where you from?"

"Miami."

"You want to go to J House?"

"I-I have no money for a hotel."

"Get in." He opened the rear door and handed her in, followed by her case. "How you got this far without being robbed is beyond me."

"Grace of God, sir. Grace of God. And an angel named AA."

"I'm sure…ah…Annie's not been called an angel in this life."

"She has now." *When I get help, I'll help her any way I can.*

Chapter Fifteen

Clarice

"What? What?"

"We're here, ma'am. Let's get you inside." The policeman shook her arm gently.

"Here? Where?" Clarice blinked again, and the last few frightening hours came sneaking back like the fog that dimmed the streetlamps. "I'm sorry, I must have fallen asleep." She thought she remembered answering their questions.

"That you did. And you'll have a bed here to do so again. You need a hand?"

"No, no, thank you. I can manage." But when she put any weight on her feet, they screamed as if they'd been sliced. She swallowed and wiggled her toes, bending her ankles, anything to get the circulation going again. She felt for her purse, still under her arm where it belonged, and scooted sideways, now ignoring the pain in her feet. Holding out a hand, she allowed the officer to assist her out and clung to his arm to get her balance. "You'd think I'd been drinking."

"Many do." He pointed her up some broad stairs. "This here is Casa de Jesús, better known as J House. Run by a husband-and-wife team, Hope and Roger Benson. It's a women's shelter. They'll get you some help."

"How can I begin to thank you?"

The other officer came around, and they each took an arm and helped her up the steps, then pushed a lighted button by the door. "This used to be a church."

"I see." *But really I don't. There's as much fog in my mind as is floating around out here.*

They waited a bit, the walkie-talkies on the officers' belts sounding more like static than any real messages, but at one point the man on her right spoke into the microphone on his shoulder.

The door finally opened, and a man who'd obviously just gotten out of bed ushered them into the entry hall.

"Sorry to wake you. Not your normal company, Benson. We got an older lady who's been locked out of her new house and all her accounts frozen. She needs a bed."

"Hi, I'm Roger Benson." He held out his hand.

"Clarice Van Dam." Somewhere she'd dropped the Mrs. "I'm sorry to bother you."

"We'll be on our way, then. Thanks, Roger." The policemen said good-bye to her, too, and headed back to their patrol car.

"You can tell me your story in the morning." Roger took the handle of her suitcase and slung her carry-on over his shoulder. "Can you walk all right?"

"Easier since I'm not carrying anything. Thank you."

"Nothing fancy here; the one bed we have is in the dorm. All our girls are far younger than you, and we reserve the private bedrooms for mothers with children. Breakfast will be from six thirty until eight, but if you sleep in, we'll find you something to eat. There are showers and bathrooms through that door." He paused at the top of the stairs for her to catch up. "Sorry, can't turn on the lights, but I'll keep the door open so you have light from the hall. Put your cases under the bed. Your eyes will adjust, and there's light from the windows too."

"This will be just fine. Sure beats sitting against the wall with AA."

"Ah, Annie sent you."

"You know her?"

"Of course. Long story that I'll tell you in the morning." He patted her shoulder. "Don't worry. You are safe here. Good night."

Never one for fussing, Clarice slid her cases under the bed, spread her coat across the bottom in the hopes that her feet might finally get warmed up again, and, laying her glasses on the small table beside the bed, tucked her purse under the pillow and crawled under the covers, too weary, too foggy to care about a nightgown or washing her makeup off. Surely, when she woke up, this would all prove to be a far too vivid nightmare.

Staggering through the fog, dodging hands that sought to drag her into lairs, rain, hills, dark, darker, streetlamps glowing amber in the dense mist, *keep going, keep going.* Fighting to catch her breath, Clarice battled her way out of the dream to find herself in a bed she'd never known, a room she'd never seen. *Gregor, where are you?* She flopped back on the flat pillow. *Jesus, Mary, and Joseph, what has become of me?*

"Shh, let her sleep."

Clarice heard the whisper and the tiptoeing feet going away, but opening her eyes took more effort than she could marshal at the moment. Besides, floating in the fog seemed far more appropriate for now. But when her bladder insisted on attention, she forced her eyes open and let her gaze wander. Water spots, tan surreal art on the ceiling, a mural painted on the far wall, a window high above her bed, long room, two beds, and an aisle wide. Too many beds to count, and where was the bathroom?

Somewhere children were reciting, a small someone was crying, a dog was barking, a car horn was honking, a bus was shushing to a stop, then roaring to start again, a phone was ringing. The sign above the arch read Bathroom. Following signs showed she was at least cognizant again. Last night she'd not been. Who was the young man who'd shown her to the room? No name came to mind. There'd been a ride in a police car, two officers…names, surely they'd had names.

A woman who'd befriended her on the streets, in the creep of the fog, AA, that's right, Angel Annie. Bits and pieces of the former day returned. The key not working, the manager saying no room, no room at the hotel, her credit cards being rejected. She made her way back to her bed and sank down on the edge. Her head felt too heavy for her hands, so she lay back down. What would become of her? Who could she turn to? How to find out what terrible thing had happened to her husband?

That brought her back upright. *Get showered and dressed and go find a phone. That is the first thing you will do.* Out of long years of habit, she made her bed and took her things to the bathroom to shower and dress. With her face in place some time later, she felt strong enough to follow the smell of coffee downstairs. The young man had said something about food available, although for the life of her, she couldn't remember where she was staying. Fear tiptoed in on feline feet and wound itself around her ankles.

Clarice shuffled down the stairs and followed her nose to the kitchen. Empty. Did she dare help herself? Yes, to the coffee at least—with a heavy dollop of half-and-half and sugar, so that hopefully her brain would begin to function. What if it never worked right again? What if she'd had a small stroke wandering the streets and hills like that last night? *Could the fog in her brain be from something like that?* Leaning against the counter, sipping coffee, she eyed the institutional-sized refrigerator. Surely a piece of cheese or…

"Hello." A front-heavy woman in stiletto heels blew in the door. "You must be Clarice."

"Yes." *Although at the moment, I'm glad I don't have to swear on a stack of Bibles as to the truth of that.*

"Have you eaten?"

"No. I just came down."

"I see." The woman handed out slices of bread. "There's the toaster over there." She popped out of the refrigerator to point the way, then leaned back into its maw. "Butter and jam." Pop out. "Would you rather have peanut butter? I love peanut butter."

"No, butter and jam are fine." Clarice crossed to the four-slice toaster and set the slices in the slots.

"There's bacon and eggs if you want."

"No, this is fine."

"Lunch will be in an hour or so. Where's Linn? It's her day to do lunch."

"Ah, Miss, Ms...."

"Just call me Celia. Sorry I forgot to introduce myself. Hope's always on my case about my manners."

"Hope?" The name rang a bell, only so faintly she could barely hear it.

"Hope Benson runs this place, along with her husband Roger. You met him last night."

"Thanks." *At least now I have a name to go with the shadow.* How truly embarrassing not to remember that.

"She said for you to come to her office soon as you can. But no rush." Celia emerged from the refrigerator with two stalks of celery and a plastic carton of white something. "I'm trying to cut back, but somehow celery just don't cut it. Salad dressing helps."

Clarice spread butter, then jam, on her toast and put her meal on a plate she found in the cupboard before ambling back to the coffee-pot for a refill. Already, she could tell her head was clearing, at least somewhat. Dare she confide in this rather unusual woman? She'd never had a conversation with someone wearing one slash of magenta and another of fluorescent blue in her hair.

"Ah, Celia, do you think my purse and things are safe on my bed?"

"Not if you got any money in there." She dipped her celery in the dressing and munched. "We like to hope things is safe, but I personally don't trust nobody. Other than Hope and Roger. Ask Hope when you meet with her. That some coat you got up there."

"Thank you. It was a wedding present from my husband."

"You're one lucky woman."

"How so?" At the moment, *lucky* was not a term she would ever think of using in regard to herself.

"That you still got it, wandering the streets like you were. Actually, that you got anything left, including your life." She nodded to the rings on Clarice's fingers. "People get killed for a lot less than what you're wearin'."

"I had them turned inside so they couldn't be seen." Clarice studied the rings. Gregor had put them there and kissed them in place. Such a romantic. She set the plate down with a clatter. "I'd better find a phone. I'm sure something terrible has happened to my husband."

"Plates go in the dishwasher." Celia pointed to that appliance. "Rinse first."

"Ah yes, of course. How careless of me." Clarice did as told, went upstairs for her purse, and then came back down, peering into rooms that had open doors until she came to one where a woman sat staring at a computer screen. "I'm looking for Hope?"

"Aren't we all?" Hope turned from the screen with a smile. "That's kind of a punch line around here." She stood and reached out a hand. "I'm Hope Benson. Welcome to J House."

Clarice shook her hand. "Th-thank you. What do I do to find a phone?"

"You're welcome to use the one at that desk in the corner, but I'd appreciate it if you would fill me in on a few things first."

"Oh, of course, it's just that—well, have you heard of any plane crashes?"

"No. And Celia keeps us up to date on any calamities, pretty much around the world. Why?"

"Well, my husband didn't show up at the condo he bought for us, and I just know something has happened to him." Tears threatened to choke her.

"If you'll give me his name, I'll get Roger to look into this. He's an ex-policeman, so he is very good at searching for someone. What airline was your husband flying?"

Clarice removed her envelope from her purse and unfolded the sheet of paper. She started to read, then stopped. "Would it help if I just gave him this paper? You see, some things are really strange. My key didn't work in the lock at The Frederick, and the manager says we do not own a place there. I tried to check into a hotel, but my credit cards were all maxed out."

"How long have you been married?"

"To Gregor? A little over a year. I never dreamed someone my age could be so happy again. I was married to my Herbert for forty years, and then one day, he just keeled right over. They said he was dead before he hit the floor. I was a widow for nine years, and then…" She stopped and looked at Hope. "Sorry, I'm rambling. And that's not like me either."

"Let me call Roger in, okay? He needs to hear all this."

Clarice watched her go. *Now, you must keep the faith,* she ordered herself. After all, Gregor could be in terrible straits. *Or Gregor could have skipped.* The nasty little voice crept in and curled up on her shoulder. *Remember what Nadia told you. "Gregor is a gigolo and on the make. He's going to take you for every dime you let him."* But she'd so hated taking orders from her older sister. All her life she'd been the youngest, with two bossy older sisters. Especially Nadia. For years after she and Herbert hit it big, they'd been jealous.

Her mind, which seemed on such a capricious bent today, floated back through the years. Three little girls playing dress-up in the backyard of their New Jersey home.

"You be the baby, Clarice, and I'm the mommy, and Bernice, you have to be the daddy."

"No, I don't. I'm the rich auntie."

"Then who's the daddy?"

"He's at work. That's what daddies do."

And that's what their daddy did, and that's what Herbert did. Of course, Nadia said she was making a mistake, marrying a nonentity like Herbert. But he never went out boozing with the boys, like Nadia's husband, Earl, or played the ponies like Bernice's husband, who finally ran off with the hostess at the track.

Boring Herbert, they called him. *Ah, Herbert, what am I going to do? You know how I prayed to Saint Jude that I was making the right decision. And you never said anything either. You know other times I had a feeling that you wanted me to go here or do that, but nothing about Gregor. I thought you just wanted me to be happy again.*

"Hi there, Mrs. Van Dam. You're sure looking more chipper than when I saw you last." Roger perched on the corner of his wife's desk while Hope sat back in her chair.

"Thank you again for taking me in."

"That's why they call J House a women's shelter. We take in women and girls who need a ready hand." Hope propped her chin on her hands. "Now, how about telling Roger all that you've told me, and we can go on from there?"

Clarice told the story again, feeling even more apprehensive. "I haven't even tried to call his cell phone today. Perhaps he's been trying to reach me." She reached down for her purse at her feet.

"Let me get a bit more information, and then I can get on this while you do that."

"Okay." She clutched her purse on her lap.

"Your husband's full name."

"Gregor Lucius Van Dam. That's capital V and capital D, two words."

"Do you know his Social Security number?"

She shook her head.

"Place and date of birth?"

"Nineteen fifty-seven in Atlanta. I met him after I moved to Miami. Herbert and I had always dreamed of retiring in Miami, so I went down there to live by my cousin. Bernice came down later, but Nadia stayed in Newark." *You're babbling again.*

"And you'd been married how long?"

"Just over a year. It's been about the happiest year of my life since Herbert passed."

Roger nodded. "Okay, that should do it for now. You try calling his cell phone, and I'll make some phone calls too. You might try calling the banks that issued your credit cards and ask to speak to a supervisor. Perhaps you'll get some information there."

"Yes, I will." Her hands shook as she drew her cell phone out of her purse. She pushed the key for his number, only to hear, "The number you have dialed is no longer in service. Please check the number and dial again." She did, dialing the complete number this time rather than depending on the number in her phone list. The same.

She stood to go back to the kitchen, but her knees were so weak, she sat down instead. It seemed like just yesterday he'd kissed her good-bye, not a peck-on-the-cheek kiss either, but one that seared her soles. Such wonderful plans, a new life in San Francisco, an adventure. She leaned her head against the wall and shut her eyes. If only she could go to sleep and wake up to this all gone.

"Mrs. Van Dam?"

Clarice opened her eyes. Hope knelt in front of her. "Call me Clarice."

"Are you all right?"

"No. His cell phone is no longer in service."

"I see. Let me get you something. Coffee, tea, iced tea?"

Clarice shook her head. "No thank you."

"Come on. Let's see what Roger found out."

"I'm not sure I can even walk down the hall." *That would do a lot of good. Fall down and break your neck, and with your luck, you'd end up quadriplegic.*

"I'll get Roger." Before Clarice could say no, Hope had disappeared through another door.

"I'm still working on this." Roger's calm voice lent strength to her soul. With his arm around her, they made it down the hall without a stumble. He pointed to the phone. "Go ahead. Call your banks like I said. Let's see if we can get to the bottom of this."

Half an hour later she had her answer. "I'm cleaned out. All but for these rings on my fingers and the fur coat on my bed."

Roger entered the room. "There is no Gregor Lucius Van Dam. It's one of several aliases for Lucien Gregson."

Chapter Sixteen

Hope

What a way to start the morning, puking your guts in the commode. Hope closed her eyes and wished she could plug her nose. She waited for her insides to stop roiling. They didn't. She rinsed her mouth out and stared at the black circles under her eyes and the gray look about her mouth. *I'm never sick. What's the matter with me?* Possibilities popped up like the gopher game at an amusement park. She mentally slammed each one with a bat. Ulcer. *Slam.* Gallbladder. *Slam.* Stress. *Slam. Slam.* Cancer. *Slam. Slam. Slam* again.

"God, please, You know what my calendar looks like for today. There is no time for this."

She turned on the shower, stepped into the stall, and let the water do its trick. *How can I help anyone if I'm sick? If You want me to do Your bidding, then You have to keep me healthy. With any luck, it'll just be something minor, and they'll give me a pill and send me on my way.*

Once out of the shower, Hope quickly french-braided her hair, dressed, and meandered into their private kitchenette. Even with the door to their private quarters closed, she could hear the sounds of the shelter, the day-care children playing, someone singing, the phone ringing. All normal.

Then a door banged. Not normal. It not only banged, but was

slammed against a wall with force. Was Celia at the front desk? What was going on?

A whisper came over the intercom. Hope strained to hear Celia's voice. "Call 911."

Dear God, keep her safe. Keep them all safe. Hope's prayers flew upward as her fingers hit the keys. The moment the dispatcher answered, Hope said, "This is Hope at J House, there's something going on in the main room and Celia just told me to call you."

"Anyone down?"

"Not that I'm aware. I'm in our apartment, so I can't see anything. Is this JuJu?"

"Yeah, honey, I'll get a car right out there. No sirens." JuJu and Hope had worked hotlines together a few years back.

"Thank you, bless you." As Hope pushed the End button, she heard a man yelling.

"I want her back, man! She owes me big time."

"I don't know who you're talking about. We don't have anyone by the name of Kiss here," Roger said, his voice calm and controlled, as he'd been taught in Crisis 101.

Hope heard a scuffle, then a thud. It was everything she could do to stay where she was, but she knew better than to interrupt when Roger was in the middle of a crisis situation. She turned toward the window and saw two black-and-whites pull up. Relief no sooner flooded through her than she heard a crash that kept on crashing, then police shouting orders.

And after it all, Roger laughing.

Perplexed, Hope opened the door and started toward what used to be the church sanctuary, now their common room. Celia was standing at the end of the hall, and scattered on the floor in front of her were files, dozens of files, with papers sliding out of them.

Just beyond her were the three men who'd come to the farmers' market the day before. Hands raised, they stood in a row facing an officer holding a gun while two other officers searched, then cuffed the men.

Roger came from behind the door, his face red with laughter. He gave Hope a slow wink with a slight nod of approbation toward Celia. "They'll handle things from here," he said, taking Hope and Celia each by an arm and escorting them back down the hall.

"What's going on?" Hope asked, when finally they were alone.

"Celia's the heroine of the hour," Roger said. "She's better with those files of hers than I ever was with a gun."

Celia started to giggle. "I didn't know what else to do. It looked to me like that one—the big one—was going to start a fight with ya', so I jes gave those files a shove, and up they flew and down they came…"

Roger laughed again. "I wish I'd had a camera. We could have won the big prize on *America's Funniest Home Videos*. D'Angelo was swatting at those file folders like they were bats."

Hope ate a piece of toast, tossed back some tea, and snagged her purse before heading out the door. Good thing the free clinic was only three blocks away. "Where's Adolph?"

"Out in his run. He missed all the fun." Celia wiggled her rear, hands fluttering in the air. "Hey, I'm a poet, didn't know it."

"Right."

"If you see Roger, tell him I had to go out for a little while." She felt a little guilty not telling anybody about seeing her doctor, but she didn't want to worry anyone, especially Roger. He had enough to worry about.

Since she'd missed her power walk that morning, striding down the hill felt good. She turned right on Kearney and kept up her down-hill pace, arms and hips swinging freely. *I feel great. Look at me. The picture of health.* She conveniently ignored her posture of supplication at the porcelain throne earlier that morning.

The clinic was open seven days a week, and no appointment was needed. Even if Hope had the money to go elsewhere, she wouldn't. She loved the women at the clinic.

"Hey, Hope, haven't seen you for, like forever." The Hispanic woman behind the counter reached out and shook Hope's hand.

"That's because you never come around. You know where I am."

"Yeah, and who to thank." Teresa Gonzales had spent several months at J House, gone back to school, and, thanks to Hope's recommendation, been hired as a receptionist at the clinic. "Did you know I'm taking classes to be a medical tech? I'd go for nursing school if I could, but with two little ones at home yet…"

"You know they could come to day care with us." *If only all of our girls were doing as well as Teresa.*

"Day care isn't the problem. It's night care I need. As soon as they go to school, I'll go to school." She pushed the clipboard across the counter. "You know the drill."

Indeed she did. She'd brought enough of her girls here and filled out the paperwork for them. She stood at the counter, read over the questionnaire, and put check marks in the appropriate boxes: nausea, fatigue, dizziness, severe heartburn, poor appetite. Under medications, she wrote Tums. She slid the clipboard back across the counter. "What's the wait time?"

"About five minutes."

Hope sat down and out of habit checked her watch. In less than five minutes, a woman called her name.

"Doctor will see you now." The woman smiled and stood back to allow Hope to pass. Hope headed for the scale, set down her purse, took off her shoes, and stepped on it. The woman reached in front of her and jiggled the weights. "One-twenty-two." She glanced down at the chart. "Have you been dieting?"

"No. I just haven't felt like eating a whole lot lately."

While Mindy—that was the name on her name tag—wrote down her weight, Hope headed toward the examination room.

Mindy followed her in and closed the door. "It looks like it's been over a year since you were here the last time."

Hope seemed genuinely surprised. "Has it been that long?"

"I'm sure Doctor will want to do an annual." She opened the drawer and pulled out a blue cloth gown. "Please take everything off and tie the gown in the back. We'll also need a urine sample. You'll find the cups and lids in the bathroom."

Ten minutes later Hope lay down on the examination table to await the doctor. Mindy had taken her temperature, gotten a blood-pressure reading, poked her finger, and drawn enough blood to do a transfusion. A yawn caught Hope by surprise, and the next thing she knew Dr. Cheong was shaking her shoulder.

"Wake up, Sleeping Beauty." A gentle voice, laced with laughter, brought Hope back to attention. Even in a white lab coat, Dr. Cheong wore elegance as if the coat were made of silk.

Hope yawned and blinked, blowing out a puff of air on her way to awake. "Sorry."

"So what are all these check marks on your chart?"

"I'm thinking I need to cut down on the amount of coffee I drink."

"Okay, let's have a look." Dr. Cheong palpitated Hope's abdomen and checked her breasts for any lumps. "Do you do self-exams regularly?"

"Um. How do you define regular?" Hope lifted her right arm over her head.

"Oh, once a month, every other month, that would be acceptable."

"Somewhere around in there." Hope flinched slightly.

"Tender?"

"A little."

"Localized?"

"No, general."

"So when did all this start?" Dr. Cheong went about the routine of a pelvic as they talked.

"Three or four weeks ago, I think. But this morning when I woke up and had to run to the bathroom to throw up, I figured it was time to find out what was going on."

Not a minute later, the doctor snapped off her gloves. "You can sit up now. I'll be right back."

Hope stared at the closed door but remained lying down. Now she was scared. Why had Dr. Cheong fled the room like that? What was wrong?

Dr. Cheong returned momentarily, smiling as if she'd just invented a cure for hair loss. "I don't know how to tell you this, but—"

Hope's heart flip-flopped inside her chest. Whatever it was, it was bad. Really bad.

"Don't look so scared." She held up a small stick. "See that? It's blue, my friend. Congratulations. You're going to be a mother."

Chapter Seventeen

Andy

<You want to know what's wrong? I'll tell you. Your father has decided to fulfill his lifelong dream—that he only just shared with me—to live in a city. San Francisco.> She wrote a detailed account of everything that had happened. <He is over the moon with joy. I, on the other hand, your loving mother, am...> Her fingers flew over the keyboard. When she was through, she went back and edited the lengthy e-mail, deleting the names she had called Martin, the sarcastic remarks about his sanity, and whatever else sounded unmotherly.

Andy read her message one last time, then pressed Send. Her children had all been bugging her to know what was happening. Now they would know.

The teakettle whistle brought her out of her reverie. She dunked a tea bag with her special blend of tea flavored with lavender and waited for it to steep. The English china teapot, her favorite, held several cups, so one bag in a full pot made the tea weak enough for nighttime imbibing. She poured a cup full and drizzled in honey that, due to the hives being set in her lavender fields, tasted slightly of lavender also. Chai Lai jumped up on the counter and rubbed her head under Andy's chin, her rumbling purr telling Andy she was in a loving mood.

The ringing phone nearly made her drop her teacup. She glanced at the clock—too late for Martin, too early for Morgan.

"Hello?"

"Mother, wow. That's the biggest news that's ever happened to our family. Why are you so against it? I think you and Daddy would have a wonderful life there. And I'd be able to visit a lot more often."

Andy set her cup and saucer on a round lamp table and sank into the chair. She looked at the computer screen and wondered if she had accidentally edited out the part where she'd said how Lavender Meadows was finally supporting Grandma and Grandpa, and that they'd gotten a big order from Nordstrom and smaller, but still very significant, orders from other chain department stores.

"Yes, it is the biggest news that's ever happened to our family. Unfortunately, I don't think it's good news, and I don't see how you can." She had to make Bria understand why she felt the way she did. She hated to think that Martin would use Bria's opinion against her, but she knew he would.

"But wouldn't it be great to get out from under all that work on the farm and…"

"All that *work* is work I love doing, or are you not aware of that? And have you forgotten that Lavender Meadows is supporting your grandparents, and that they would have to give up their home if we sold this place?" She had done her best to raise her children to think about things before they jumped in with both feet. Right now Bria was up to her waist in mental muck.

Bria's voice went from wildly enthusiastic to embarrassed. "Um, I guess I forgot about that."

"Did you also forget that this farm has been in our family for three generations and that you and your brother and sister stand to inherit it and the business?"

"Okay, you're right. I really wouldn't want to see you sell it," she admitted. "How does Daddy feel about all of this?"

"He wants me to sell out, move to San Francisco, and be a full-time wife that he can take to corporate parties."

"Gag me with a spoon."

"Exactly." Andy rubbed her forehead. "Bria, would you call your father a workaholic?"

A slight chuckle came through the wires. "That would be an understatement."

"Takes one to know one, right?"

"I take after him, but Mom, don't you have a few of those tendencies yourself?"

"I never let things keep me from the three of you. I was always there when you needed me, and your activities came first."

"That's true, but you weren't the breadwinner. Daddy did all he could with us when he was home."

Interesting how age had given her oldest daughter a different perspective on things. When Bria was ten and in the Christmas play, she cried her eyes out because Martin couldn't be there to see her put the star on top of the Christmas tree. And the day before she was to graduate from junior high, she called him in New York and told him he'd better be in that audience or she would go back to seventh grade. By the time she finished high school, she'd given up and had stopped asking him to come home for anything extra.

A sound clicked on the line. "Hold on, let me see who that is." Andy pushed a button. "Hello?"

Bria's voice answered. "It's still me, Mom. Whoever that is can call back." The slight impatience in Bria's voice spoke of an oft-repeated lesson on how to work Call Waiting. When was Mom going to come up to speed on the technologies that were supposed to make her life easier? "So what are you going to do?"

"Pray. Can you think of something better?"

"Nope. I'll pray too. Okay?"

"You'd better. Love you. Bye."

Andy spent the next few days harvesting the last of the lavender crop. By the end of the week, her drying racks as well as her bins were full. Now she and her mother would begin making the sachets and potpourri for the Internet sales.

Andy didn't tell her mother what had happened in San Francisco. She glossed over the house-hunting expedition and pretended that everything was fine between her and Martin. If her mother got wind of what was really happening, she would feel guilty and insist on selling the house, the farm, and the business.

Saturday morning Andy went over the quarterly sales report that her mother had generated on QuickBooks. The good news was that they were well into the black and had money to spend on new equipment. Lavender Meadows was growing at a rate that would require either more planting or buying from another grower. In the spring, she would start selling her field starts after transplanting them to gallon containers. She could also sell far more rooted plugs than she had.

So much to do.

She called up her database and entered the names and addresses of new people who had signed her Web-site guest book. A mailing list of nearly a thousand wasn't bad for three years' time.

When the phone rang, she picked it up without taking her eyes from the computer screen.

"Lavender Meadows."

"Hi, Andy, this is Suzanne, your Realtor from San Francisco."

"Oh, hi."

"I think I found you a place."

"Oh?" Andy fumbled for politeness. "Really?"

"I'm going to send you the pictures I have. I snapped them yesterday when I took the listing. I have to tell you this property won't last long. It's one of those once-in-a-lifetime chances, if you know what I mean."

"So tell me about it." Andy minimized her database and opened her e-mail.

"It's a house, not a condo or loft, and it borders a garden. Grace Marchant's Garden. Have you heard of it? It surrounds a series of stairs going down the north side of Telegraph Hill. I'll be up front. The house needs some work, but it has everything your husband said he wanted." She rattled off, "It's twenty-four hundred square feet, three stories, but the top floor is a loft, sixty years old, with the kitchen, dining room, and living room on the main floor. Three bedrooms and two bathrooms are downstairs on the same level as the main entry. The main floor is open, so it has a surprisingly big area for entertaining, which your husband stressed was really important."

Entertaining? *Oh, goody. I can't wait to make a tray of hors d'oeuvres and put out the cocktail napkins.* "How much?"

"Four hundred seventy-five thousand, with conditions."

"What kind of conditions?"

"First of all, it's 'as is.' The woman who owns the house is quite elderly and incapable of making any repairs."

"Okay, that's understandable."

"There's more. She wants to pick the new owners. And she wants the new owners to adopt her cat. She's moving to a retirement home and can't take it with her. She also wants the new owners to promise to feed the parrots."

"Parrots? I would have to adopt her parrots, too?"

"They are a wild flock of parrots that frequent the area."

Andy thought fast. The price was right, and the size sounded right. Maybe if she flew down and took a look, she could get Martin to come around to her way of thinking. She flipped through her datebook. Bible study tomorrow morning and then—nothing. Could she catch an afternoon flight? "Let me see if I can get a flight. If I can, I'll e-mail you my arrival time. If I can't, call me again when you have something else." She said good-bye and hung up, then went to Outlook Express to check expedia.com.

She typed in her dates and destination and within a few minutes had a flight to SFO for the next afternoon. Not particularly wanting to talk with her husband, she sent him an e-mail.

<I'll be arriving at SFO tomorrow afternoon. Are you in town or traveling? Suzanne has a house for me to look at. It sounds perfect for a second home. But we have to act quickly, or it will be gone. You can e-mail me or get me on my cell phone.>

She stared at the words she had typed and knew that he would know by the words *second home* that she was still wanting him to compromise. Was that throwing down the gauntlet or what? Adding <Love, A.> she hit Send.

Never had she taken such a stand, but then never had she been forced to.

Chai Lai jumped into her lap as soon as she pushed the chair back from the computer desk. "Well, I guess we'll just have to wait and see what happens." Chai Lai stood up, put her front paws on Andy's shoulders, and licked her face.

"Your tongue scratches." Stroking the cat always calmed both of them. Andy leaned back in her chair, eyes closed, and called herself several highly uncomplimentary names for letting Suzanne's call change her resolve to wait for Martin to miss her enough to give in to compromising.

Since coming home from San Francisco, she'd spent hours reading her Bible and praying.

Maybe Suzanne's call was God's answer to her prayers. Maybe He wanted her to swallow her pride and make the first move. And maybe the elderly woman selling the house had been praying too. Praying for an animal lover to buy her home and adopt her cat.

So many maybes.

Andy glanced at the computer screen. The little dog icon was telling her she had an e-mail. She clicked her mouse and found Martin's name on the screen. "Here we go."

<I'll see you tomorrow, then. I'm at the Residence Inn.> He gave her the address. <It'll be easier if you just take a cab from the airport. Love, M.>

Andy studied his reply. Why couldn't he have said something like, "I'm sorry, honey. I was a real jerk, but I promise I'll make it up to you"? Because Martin never said anything like that. He never admitted to being wrong. She clicked the New Mail icon and typed a message to Suzanne to give her flight details and when she would be available. She was about to turn off the computer when she remembered the pictures Suzanne said she'd sent. "Please, please, please make it be what we need."

She clicked on the little paperclip in the corner of the e-mail, caught her bottom lip between her teeth, and waited for the attachment to come up. The first picture showed the exterior. It reminded her of a stack of boxes. The second one was of the living room, which looked bleak but roomy. The others showed the bedrooms, baths, kitchen, and last but not least, the view. A truly magnificent view of the Golden Gate Bridge, across to Sausalito and even the Bay Bridge.

Andy turned off the computer and went outside, Chai Lai walking behind her. Fall was definitely in the air. She inhaled the sweet smell of lavender and wondered how she could survive the smell of smog and gas fumes. Then she reminded herself, *You will only be there five days out of a month.*

Chapter Eighteen

Hope

"Blue! You mean...?" Hope felt her jaw drop. She shook her head in utter disbelief. "No, it can't be. You said I couldn't..."

Dr. Cheong nodded. "I know what I said, but this is pretty conclusive." She handed Hope the stick. "The only explanation I have is that I think God wants you to have a child of your own." She shared a smile with Hope.

"You're sure?"

"I can run it again, but your body shows all the symptoms. When did you have your last period?"

"I don't know. You know how it's been. Sometimes I have them, sometimes they are terrible, and sometimes I don't."

"No problem. We'll go on fetal development. Another month or so, and we'll do a sonogram, especially since this is your first."

"Oh, my." Hope stared at the stick. "I-I'm going to have a baby." Softly, reverently, she repeated the words. "I'm going to have a baby." Still lying on the table, she smoothed a hand over her nearly concave belly, then looked up into her doctor's dark eyes. "There really is a baby growing in there?" A tear leaked out and rolled down her temple.

Dr. Cheong stood and retrieved her prescription pad from the counter. "You need to get on some good prenatal vitamins." She scribbled down a couple of brands, then ripped off the page and handed it to Hope as she was sitting up. "And cut out the caffeine."

"Wait a minute." *No caffeine. How will I function with no caffeine?*

"No smoking, no drinking, not that you do, but just so you know. You're going to need plenty of rest. Your power walking is fine, but no marathons, and tell Roger I want to see him."

"Why? Is something wrong?"

"No, but I'm sure you aren't going to tell him all this, so I will do it for you. Remember, you are up in years for a first baby. We'll need to be a bit more cautious."

"A baby," Hope whispered again, still in a state of shock, then stared at her doctor. "I sure wasn't prepared for this. I thought I had something wrong, gall bladder or acid reflux or—" She stroked her middle with a gentle hand. "You'll deliver him or her, won't you? I don't want to have to switch to an ob-gyn."

"There's no reason for you to switch unless you need a specialist. Get dressed now, and I suggest you and Roger make a list of all your questions after you have time to absorb this." She patted Hope's shoulder. "Make an appointment for next month on your way out. And make sure you keep it. Monthly exams are very important."

"Yes ma'am." Hope all but saluted.

Dr. Cheong picked up Hope's chart. "Remember, I know where you live, and I'll come looking for you if you don't show up." She handed Hope a packet of information and some sample vitamins.

"Doctor who makes house calls?" Hope raised an eyebrow, and the two shared a comfortable smile. Over the years, Dr. Cheong had often come to the shelter when Hope had called her, but never for herself, always for one of the shelter's women or children.

As soon as the door closed, Hope got off the examining table, stuffed the packet and vitamins into her purse, and started to get dressed. Her thoughts were so consumed with the news that she put her panties on backward and had to take them off and start over. *I'm going to have a baby. We're going to have a baby.* She left the building in a virtual daze.

Outside the clinic, she took a deep breath, closed her eyes, and lifted her face to the sun. She recalled one of her favorite lines by an early Catholic saint, Dame Julian of Norwich: "All will be well, all will be well, all manner of things will be well." For years after she and Roger were married, she'd asked God nightly to heal her so she could become pregnant. Eventually, she'd given up. She felt ashamed of herself now. She knew God's promises, at least most of them. She should have had more faith.

She started for home, her thoughts flitting as fast as hummingbird wings. A baby. A little baby to love and cherish. She would need a crib and bottles and diapers. They would have to clean out the storage room and turn it into a nursery. If it was a girl, she would want to name her after her mother, and if it was a boy, she would want to name him after Roger's father.

Roger!

Her thoughts came to a bone-jarring halt. What would Roger think? She grabbed the bench at the bus stop and tried to get control of her thoughts. In her excitement, she had momentarily forgotten about Roger. She smiled when she thought about how he would react to the news. Long before they even talked about getting married, she had told him she was incapable of having children. He'd been disappointed at first, but he accepted it and said that God had a reason for everything. When they'd begun their work with the shelter, both of them had known without question what the reason was.

She picked up her pace, eager to get home. How would she tell him? Should she find some knitting needles and yarn and start knitting baby booties, like in the old movies? Or maybe she should buy a book on baby names and leave it on his pillow. Or maybe she could play twenty questions and see if he could guess the answer.

Back at J House, Hope fought to keep her feelings under control. He would never guess.

"So what did she say? Do you need more tests?" Roger studied his wife's face, his expression telling her he was worried.

"No, not right now, but I have to go back next month and the month after that until…" She saw his brows furrow and felt guilty for prolonging his agony.

"Hope, for Pete's sake…" Roger took a step toward her. "You look like the cat who killed the cream and licked the bird, and yet it sounds like you're telling me something is really wrong."

Hope beckoned him with a head motion, then walked toward their apartment, begging off the calls for her attention from Celia and one of the other girls with a wave of her hand. She didn't care what they wanted; they could wait a few minutes while she told her husband their news.

Roger, darling, this will be the shock of your life.

Preceding Roger by seconds, she quickly dug the packet of information Dr. Cheong had given her out of her purse, scanned it, found a drawing of an embryo at two months, and clutched it to her chest.

"Okay, what is it?" Roger closed the door behind him.

"What is something we've wanted and couldn't have?" Hope tried to act calm, but she couldn't still the tremor in her voice.

"All the bills paid?" He rolled his eyes when she shook her head. "Hope, you know how I hate guessing games."

"This something takes nine months and…" Hand trembling, she handed him the booklet. "Right there, that's what's been making me feel sick."

Roger's eyes widened, and he stared from the cover of a booklet titled *So You Are Pregnant* to his wife, and back to the booklet in his hand. "Oh, my…" He choked and swallowed. With a whoop, he tossed the pamphlet over his shoulder and gathered Hope into his arms. "We're pregnant?"

She nodded. "We—you and me—we're going to be parents. A real mom and dad." She rubbed her belly. "And here I was afraid it was a malady of some kind." She leaned her forehead against his chest. "Can you believe it? I hardly can, and I've been the one with my head over the commode."

He stroked up and down her back and kissed the side of her face. "How is this possible? Dr. Cheong said you would never get pregnant."

"When I mentioned that to her, she said the only answer she could think of was that God wanted us to have a child of our own."

Roger rocked her back and forth in his arms. "I've never been this close to a pregnant woman before. I've never been around babies either. What if I—we—don't know what to do?"

"Well, I guess we're going to learn." She pulled back and offered her mouth to his.

"Phone for Hope," Celia called from beyond the closed door.

Hope sighed and stepped out of Roger's arms. "I'll take it in here," she said, opening the door a crack. She kissed her husband one more time and picked up the phone. "Hope speaking." How she loved to answer that way, corny or not. "Sure, just a minute." She covered the mouthpiece. "How about gathering the troops? Meeting in my office in fifteen minutes."

Roger nodded and left the room with a wink while she returned to her phone call. "Sorry. Now, how can I help you?" She grabbed a pen and pad. "With kids or without? When would she be coming?" She shook her head. "She has to come on her own and be willing to accept help, you know that, Charles. Court mandates don't count unless she is willing. There are no bars here." Yes, they had a high success rate, she knew that. But it was because she was careful about who could come. Even then, some of the young women had left, like Kiss the week before, or gone back to their old life when clean and sober and a regular job got too hard.

"Yes, I'll give her an interview tomorrow afternoon, say three. Okay?" Hope hung up the phone and doodled around *Serena,* the girl's name. Since one of the girls had left while she was at Dr. Cheong's, she had one bed available, and right now it was first-come, first-served. She ripped the sheet off the pad so she could write the appointment on her office calendar before meeting with the others.

Her stomach rumbled, so after a bathroom break, she helped herself to a piece of cheese from the fridge, then opened the door and walked across the hall to her office.

Trying to appear nonchalant when she was about to burst at the seams took supreme will. They all checked her face and then lined up on the couch and bench, silent. The last ones leaned against the walls or sat on the floor.

Finally Chelsea, who at fourteen was their youngest resident, except for the children, burst out. "You ain't gonna die, are you, Hope? Please don't die."

"No, Chelsea, don't be— Whatever made you think such a thing?" Hope could feel her bangs tickle her eyebrows. As soon as Roger closed the door behind him, she reached for his hand. "I just wanted you all together so I didn't have to say this a hundred times. As you know, I did go for my doctor's appointment this morning." She glanced at Celia. "In spite of files scattered all over the floor." Snickers danced around the room.

"Cops helped pick some of them up too." Celia nodded. "Now, what was it you have to say?"

"I'm… We're…" Hope took a deep breath and grabbed Roger's hand. "We're going to have a baby."

"Y-you're not dying." Chelsea leaped to her feet and rushed

around the desk to throw her arms around Hope in a monster hug. "A baby. You're going to have a baby."

"You sure that's safe, old as you are?" Celia hung back, eyes narrowed.

"God must think so because this is a miracle pregnancy, according to Dr. Cheong." Hope stared across her desk at the woman who had become closer than a sister in their years of working together, since even before Hope and Roger had struggled to get pregnant. Celia knew the whole story.

"Yes, and while I am getting close to forty, I am wonderfully healthy, and she sees no problem." Hope paused. "I'm supposed to be a bit more cautious and make sure I get extra rest."

"And no caffeine." Roger laid his hand on his wife's shoulder.

"Lord, preserve us." Celia looked toward heaven. "We're gonna need another miracle here!"

Hope had often and with some gusto delivered her opinion of decaf anything.

"That means no chocolate," Celia said firmly.

"No, it means no coffee." Hope stared at her friend. "There's caffeine in chocolate?" The despair in her voice brought on another case of snickers from those gathered. *How will I live without coffee and chocolate?* One to get her going and one to keep her going.

After answering a barrage of questions, many of which she had to respond to with "I don't know," the group filed out one or two at a time, chattering and giggling.

Hope could tell something was already afoot by the glances and giggles thrown her way. She started to say something to Roger when the phone rang.

"Hope here. Oh, hi, Julia. What's up?"

Chapter Nineteen

Andy

Andy collapsed in the wing-backed chair. The flight had been turbulent. They had landed at SFO after circling for what seemed like an hour, and BART had been delayed for some unknown reason. The headache had started with the bumpy flight.

"You look terrible. Are you all right?" Martin hung his suit coat in the closet and pulled a cotton crew-neck sweater over his shirt. The little alligator on the chest used to be a joke between them.

"Right now a headache is making my eyes hurt. I'm going to lie down for a few minutes and see if that helps." She stood carefully, as if balancing a tray upon her head.

"Did you take something for it?"

She didn't bother to answer. He should know better than to ask such a stupid question.

Of course she had taken something, both for her head and her stomach. She wasn't one of those people who would rather suffer than take a pill. She stretched out on the bed and breathed deeply to hasten relaxation. Two more deep breaths, hold and exhale, she counted them out, and the warmth started in her feet and worked upward. If only all things in life could be dealt with by taking three deep breaths.

Twenty minutes later she walked out of the bedroom, calm, lipstick renewed, hair fluffed, and best of all, pain free.

"You look much better."

"I feel better."

"Tell me about the house Suzanne is showing you."

"All I know is that it's on Telegraph Hill, it has a view, and it's within *our* price range." She stressed the *our*. "She said it would need some work, and we would have to adopt the owner's cat, because she's moving into a retirement home and can't keep it with her."

He groaned. "Well, that's an unusual condition. What time is your appointment?"

"Nine. Do you think you might be able to get away from the office and go with me?"

She knew the answer to the question even before he shook his head. "Okay, then, just so you know…if I like it, I'll put in an offer. If I don't, I'll tell Suzanne to keep looking."

She could see that he was uncomfortable with the idea of not being consulted, but if he couldn't make time to go with her, she wasn't going to worry about it.

"I'm hoping you'll still reconsider selling the house and Lavender Meadows. It would make everything easier, and we could save more money for retirement."

She didn't give him the benefit of a look but cleaned out her purse instead. "Selling isn't an option, Martin, so you might as well give it up." She sounded like a mom telling her kid for the tenth time, "No, you can't have that toy." She wadded up a couple of used tissues and tossed them into the trash. "You know, if I didn't know better, I'd think you were jealous of my success with Lavender Meadows." There were times when she surprised herself with the things that came out of her mouth.

Martin snorted. "Don't be ridiculous. What's to be jealous about?"

She walked right up to him and stood toe-to-toe, face-to-face. "That's what I'd like to know."

He started to walk away, but she stepped in front of him and clasped her hands around his upper arms. "Lavender Meadows is a home-based business that by the grace of God brings in enough money to support my parents and gives me something fun and interesting to do with my life." She saw him blink and thought maybe she'd gotten through to him.

"I can't believe you want to sabotage my career." His reply made her blink. Did he think of nothing else but Martin, Martin, Martin?

Help me, Lord. Give me patience and understanding. "How can you say something like that to me with a straight face? Your boss isn't going to care that your wife and in-laws own a small business and property in Oregon. He isn't going to care that I don't live in San Francisco 24/7. Lots of people have two homes. Call Lavender Meadows your summerhouse."

"But if we can't afford a decent place in the city, we will not be able to entertain, and…"

"Ah, are we playing keep up with the Joneses?"

"Don't be juvenile." His sniff added punctuation. "There are ways things are done in the corporate world."

"Oh, for heaven's sake, Martin—" Andy cut herself off. So he wanted to play corporate one-upmanship. "Watch it, bucko, you're fast becoming a corporate snob."

She could see him making an effort to control himself.

Calmly, too calmly, he said, "I really thought that with the children grown, we could start over, and this seemed like the ideal way. A whole new life in a new house, a new location. Not stuck forever in podunk Medford."

"I happen to love podunk Medford, and while I'm trying to figure a way we can both have our dreams, you go on as if what I want has no value at all. I love our house, I love my business, and I love the sense of home there. I'm willing to buy a second home here and to make monthly visits." She straightened her shoulders. "But that's it, Martin. Any more compromises are up to you."

She met Suzanne in the lobby at nine. After the greetings, they drove on out Columbus and turned right on Union.

"Thought I'd show you the area a bit, then we'll go to the house itself. Our appointment is for ten."

"Fine with me."

"Many of these are single family homes. You'll find lots of fun shops on Kearney. That old church is now a women's shelter called J House, for Casa de Jesús, and there's a farmers' market every Saturday in that parking lot. I think you'll really enjoy that, and maybe you could sell some of your lavender things there." She pointed up the hill. "That little store on the corner is becoming quite the gathering place. I stop there when I am in the area to take home some of their soup. It is really good."

They turned left on Montgomery. Suzanne pointed up the hill to the right. "There are steps down to where Montgomery picks up again and heads down into the financial district. A bus turns around here in this intersection, so public transportation is really convenient."

Where the road split, they took the lower right-hand lane, the divider filled with pine trees, juniper, and some shrubs. A huge pyracantha shrub with red berries covered a brick wall on the driver's side.

"You'll often see the wild parrots feeding here."

"You're not serious?"

"Of course I am. Perhaps we'll see them when we go down to the house." They parked in a turnaround in front of a worn brick wall. "That's Castle Julius there, one of the longstanding restaurants in the city and a wonderful place to bring visitors to watch the sunset from that upper balcony."

"How's the food?"

"Not the best, but not bad." Suzanne waved to the greenbelt park. "These are the Greenwich Steps that run from Coit Tower down to the upper part of the Levi Center. The steps are bordered by houses on both sides, and the people who live here maintain the garden area around their own houses."

Suzanne sat forward and pointed. "The house I want to show you is down this way. There was no parking place on the street when we came by. Aren't the brick wall and stairs lovely?"

"But you can drive to the house too?"

"No, the only parking is that area just off the street, in this turn-around here or on the street." She led the way back up Montgomery to another set of stairs, opposite the bush with the berries. As they started down, she motioned to a weathered brass signpost.

"Grace Marchant's Garden?" Andy stopped to read it.

"Yes, Grace was a Realtor who moved here in 1949 and started pitching the debris over the cliff as she cleaned up so she could begin planting trees, shrubs, and all kinds of flowers. When the ground was ready, she started planting the open space. Eventually, her garden was known across the country. When arthritis slowed her down, friends pitched in to help. Now residents have continued her work, and there are building restrictions and requirements."

"Like the Greenwich Steps?"

"Yes." Going down the steps, Suzanne pointed out plants and other houses, then turned right to what looked like a series of boxes with vertical siding stained a rusty brown. Square thigh-high cedar planter boxes held sweet-smelling jasmine climbing on a tower and a Japanese lace leaf maple, underplanted with variegated hostas and alyssum.

"The entrance is on the lower level, and the main living area is upstairs, where the view is. Why don't we look at that first." She motioned up the stairs. A circular stained-glass window scattered shards of jewels over the landing, making Andy catch her breath.

"How beautiful."

"Isn't it? I do love stained glass." She walked ahead of Andy. "I always like to see the main living space first, and here, the view is worth the mortgage." Suzanne stopped in front of the bank of windows that comprised the north face of the house.

Andy caught her breath. From the towers of the Golden Gate Bridge at the far left to the Bay Bridge, San Francisco Bay lay spread out before her. "I see what you mean." *Oh, Martin will love this. Fiddle on Martin, I could love this.* She turned to look at the living space, which was basically one long and comparatively narrow room. A fireplace on the back wall blended into the dining area, and a bar for lower cabinets set off the kitchen.

"Mrs. Getz planned to update the kitchen someday, but you know how *someday* things don't always get done. Then, after her husband died, she retreated into her painting."

Andy nodded. It really wouldn't take a lot to remodel the kitchen. The cabinets were dark, but they looked to be in good shape. The flooring needed replacing. A small table and two chairs in front of the window would be a marvelous place for morning coffee. She glanced back to the living room. "Does the fireplace work?"

"Yes, and there's a full bath on this floor, behind the kitchen."

Andy looked in and nodded. That needed updating also, but like the kitchen, it wouldn't need gutting, just cosmetic work. "How hard is it to get good help, laying floor and things like that?"

"I can recommend some contractors. Would you like to see the loft or the bedroom area next?"

"The loft, please."

Andy caught her breath at the full wall of windows again. "What did you tell me is the asking price?"

"Eight hundred seventy-five thousand."

Andy gulped. "I thought you said four hundred seventy-five."

"No, you must have misunderstood," Suzanne said, turning out the light.

Andy was positive she had not misunderstood. Suzanne had deliberately given her a wrong price just to get her here to see this house.

"As I told you, Mrs. Getz wants to meet and approve the buyers herself. She is very attached to this house and isn't pleased to have to give it up." Once outside, Suzanne checked her watch.

"So what do you think?"

"It's four hundred thousand more than what you told me. That's what I think."

"But it's wonderful, isn't it?"

"Yes, it is."

Are you going to trust Me?

Andy sighed. *This is not the time to ask me that unless You have an extra four hundred thousand dollars that I can have.* "Do you think she'll negotiate?"

"No. She's a smart cookie, and she knows that once the house goes up on the multiple there will be a bidding war."

"Okay, write it up, then."

"Well, it just so happens that I was so confident you'd love it, I already have the offer written up. I'll give it to her as soon as I drop you off, and if she takes it, and I think she probably will—because I wrote in there that you love cats—we can call on her tomorrow."

Chapter Twenty

Hope

"Here's another letter from Blakely Associates." Celia rolled her eyes.

Hope groaned. Had Peter not responded to them and told them to go bark up someone else's tree? "Here, let me read it and see what's going on." She used her letter opener to make a clean slit in the envelope, which was what she'd like to do to the Blakely group. While reading the letter, she shook her head repeatedly.

"So what they say?" Celia wanted to know.

"They have thoughtfully provided me with an estimate of how much it will cost to retrofit J House to meet the state's new earthquake standards." She stared at the figures, which were considerably more than the estimate she had received. But of course they were probably inflated by a few hundred thousand just to make it look grimmer than it already was. After the 1989 Loma Prieta earthquake, property owners had been put on notice to make seismic repairs. Hope had made several attempts at finding benefactors to fund the repairs, but there were no takers so far. *No one to help…not enough money… If God doesn't work a miracle soon, we are going to lose J House.* The thought made her want to put her head down and bawl. Instead she tossed the letter onto the one small patch of visible wood on her desk. Her goal for this morning was to eliminate the stacks of files and to clear the desk. She'd been doing better at tossing away stuff that she didn't need, but she had a long way to go before she could call herself caught up or organized.

Celia laid her hand down on the new pile of mail. "I already shredded all the junk mail and credit card offers, so everything here is stuff you gotta deal with. You gonna stay in here till this desk is bare as a baby's bottom. I'm gonna screen all your phone calls and take messages."

Hope stared at Celia's long purple fingernails and wondered how she managed some of the more personal tasks. "Slave driver."

"You'll thank me for it."

"You are so kind." Hope sat back in her chair and tapped the letter. "How about faxing this over to Peter? Let him deal with it. These guys don't understand the word *no*." She picked up her cup of decaf coffee, sipped, and shuddered.

Clarice poked her head in. "Got a minute?"

"Yes, but just a minute. Come and sit." Clarice walked around Celia and took a chair. "What's up?"

"Well, since I've turned this mess I got myself in over to the fraud squad, I have some time on my hands until I meet with the jeweler at one. I wondered if you have something I can do?"

Celia half covered her mouth and spoke sotto voce. "Last night while everybody was sleeping, this crazy woman cleaned and reorganized three kitchen cupboards and under the sink."

Clarice chuckled. "Well, you see, I'm on Eastern Time yet, and if I stay in bed, I start worrying. Then I make noises and wake some of the others, and they need their rest. So I came down to the kitchen and thought I'd fix myself a snack. When I looked in the cupboards and… Oh, dear, I hope I didn't offend anyone."

Hope looked up at Celia, who shrugged. "No. I don't think so."

"Oh, good."

"So you're an organizer?" Hope held her breath.

"Yes, you could say that. I used to be my husband's—my first husband's—office manager. I did everything: answered the phones, did the payroll, filed, did accounts payable and receivable." She laughed. "Why, I even took shorthand and typed up letters. I used to be able to type one hundred and ten words per minute, but I don't think I can do that anymore. I haven't done that kind of typing in years."

"Do you know your way around a computer?" Hope's brain was bursting with ideas.

"I made myself learn the computer so I wouldn't fall behind. I know Word, QuickBooks, and Excel, and I'm pretty good at Internet searches. Oh, and eBay. I'm really good on eBay, though I hate to admit it."

"Lord God, heavenly Father, we thank You, we praise Your name." Hope knew her grin was going to crack her face. "Where would you like to start?"

"What do you need done the most?"

Hope nodded to Celia, who had yet to close her mouth. "Celia is our office manager. I'll let her get you started."

"B-but, Miss Hope," Celia stammered, "I don't have time to show her."

Clarice stood up. "Let me start with filing. Just give me a stack of files that need to be put away, and show me where the filing cabinet is, or whatever it is you use. I won't be any bother. I promise."

Celia looked from Clarice to Hope. "Okay, but you better not be pestered me with a bunch of questions that I ain't got time to be answerin'."

The moment they left the room, Hope pumped one fist in the air. "Thank You, Father. Once again You have answered my prayers." She paused. "Now, about the retrofitting."

A half hour later, a discreet knock, and Celia poked her head in. "Your ten o'clock is here."

"Julia?" At Celia's nod, Hope said, "Send her in. Did you get that letter faxed to Peter?"

"Sorry, the machine is down again."

Hope groaned. "Did you tell Roger?"

"No. He's on the phone."

"Slip him a note."

"Okay."

Hope signed one more paper as Julia entered the room. "Have a seat and tell me what I can do to help."

"I just wanted to fill you in. I've distributed a thousand fliers to people on the street, and so far no one has come forward to say they've seen her."

"That's pretty typical."

"Your husband suggests that I might have better luck if I let some friends of his continue the search. He said they fit in better." She glanced down at her finely creased slacks and slubbed silk blazer. "I could go buy some clothes at the Goodwill, but he thinks I'd be better off to sit tight and let his friends do the looking. I can't just sit in a hotel room day in and day out, and I've already seen every movie worth seeing, so I thought maybe if I could keep busy... I've worked with young women before, coaching them in interview skills, preparing them for new jobs, self-image, that kind of thing. Is there anything I can do here to help out while I wait?" She leaned forward. "I can't go back home until I learn something about Cyndy."

Hope felt lightheaded. Two offers of help in a half hour. This was almost as good as Dr. Cheong telling her the stick was blue. "Thank You, Lord, I cannot believe this."

"What?"

"I'm sorry. I'm just so delighted to have you offer. And yes. Yes! I would love to have you working with the girls. If you could give me a couple of your ideas and an outline, we could set up an impromptu class this evening. What would you need in the way of supplies?"

"Pencils. Paper. Clipboards, maybe."

"You got it. I can think of three girls who will benefit immediately. Others are working now, but they need better jobs." Hope stood up. "Julia, you are a godsend. Tell Celia what you need, and you can work anywhere you can find chair and table. You'll be able to meet some of the girls at lunch."

With an effort Hope went back to work and, just before lunch, signed off the last of the overdue reports. If only she could spend more time and resources working with the girls rather than tangling with paperwork. But to get government assistance, especially grants, the reports were necessary. And to cover themselves in case of a lawsuit.

The intercom buzzed, Celia's way of sending a distress call. "Uh-oh." Hope pushed her chair back and stood up. She had learned that presenting a cool front won lots of battles, so before opening the door, she breathed her protection prayer. *Oh, Lord, with Thy strong right hand, deliver us.*

Celia was talking to a young woman with a blackening egg-sized eye, a split lip, and a ripped blouse. On her hip she toted a toddler, and she clutched the hand of a little girl who looked like she needed the other hip.

The mother glanced over her shoulder, fear widening her eyes.

Hope walked forward, surrounded by a gauzy cloud of serenity. "Hey there, looks like you've come to the right place."

"He might be after us."

"Okay, follow me, and he'll never know you're here. How did you get here?"

"I took a cab."

That was different. Hope showed her into her office. "Come in, and I'll have someone get you an ice pack for your eye." She nodded toward Celia, who nodded back in understanding.

"Do you have any diapers? He's wet."

"Sure." Over her shoulder Hope said, "A diaper, too, Celia."

"I'm so sorry to be such a bother," the young woman said, walking in front of Hope. She hadn't been seated for more than a moment when Clarice came in bearing a tray with a diaper, a wet cloth, a blue ice pack from the freezer, two juice cartons from the fridge, and a cup of coffee for the mother.

The aroma of the coffee made Hope salivate. *Dear Big Dad, what I wouldn't give for a cup of coffee.*

"I wanted to pack up some stuff, but I didn't have a chance," the mother said, putting the toddler down on the chair opposite her.

"It doesn't matter. We have everything you need here." Hope sat down and let Clarice distribute her offerings. Smiling warmly, she set down the tray and handed the little girl the carton of juice.

The little girl, eyes wide like the sad-eyed children in paintings, stared at the juice carton.

"Do you want me to open that for you?" Clarice asked, her voice soft, grandmotherly.

The child's nod came slowly, as if fearful of reprisal.

Clarice pinched the opening, pulled it wide, and stabbed the straw into it. "It's okay, honey," she said, "you're safe now."

Clarice smiled and left the room.

Hope was impressed. More than impressed.

With the toddler and the little girl sucking on the straws, Hope turned her attention back to the distraught mother. Would this one be willing to go after the brute and press charges?

Hope pulled the necessary paperwork out of her organizer. "What's your name?"

"Heather, and this is John Mark and Mary Ellen."

The children's names told Hope that their father was possibly a southerner. A master at keeping her thoughts to herself, she smiled, giving her face an extra dose of confidence and compassion, an easy deed, since her heart broke for this little trio.

"Don't forget the ice pack," Hope said as she wrote down their names.

"Oh, right." Heather angled the pack to cover both eye and lip, flinching as the cold penetrated the swollen tissue.

"Do you need to be checked at the clinic?"

Heather shook her head. "Pretty superficial this time."

"Meaning there have been other times?"

"Yes. He's beaten me before, but never the kids."

"Will you file charges?"

"I don't know. He might try to kill me then."

"He can't if we keep you hidden."

"You don't know my husband."

"We deal with your type of situation all the time." She smiled at the woman, hoping to reassure her. "I need to know more about you. Your clothes are better quality than I usually see here."

"You're very observant."

"In this business I have to be. You want to tell me your story? Right now Celia is on the phone to the various women's shelters to see who has a room for you. We will transfer you as soon as we can find a space."

Heather nodded and arrived at that expression that told Hope she trusted her. "This is the third time. I believed him the first time, when he said he'd never hit me again, that it was an accident. The second time he stayed with a friend for a week, then begged to come home. I insisted he get counseling, and he said he would. He said he would do everything he could to make sure this never happened again."

"Did you report him either time?"

"The second time, but I didn't press charges."

"So there is a record?"

"Yes."

"How long has he been verbally abusive?"

"How did you…?" Heather sighed, evidently reminding herself that Hope had seen and heard it all before. "You can't understand how I hate to be part of a syndrome. I believed him when he'd say everything was my fault. Before I met John, I was an independent and successful woman."

"What kind of work did you do?"

"I managed a small hotel, but we hadn't been married long when John convinced me I should stay at home to raise our children. I'd always dreamed of being a stay-at-home mom." Heather shook her head slowly, as if that took more energy than she owned.

Hope heard the click of Celia's spike heels before she knocked on the door.

"We found a shelter, and Roger can take her right away."

"Good." Celia closed the door, and Hope returned to her paperwork. "You didn't give me your last name."

"It's Gerritson. Mrs. John Gerritson."

Something clicked in Hope's brain. "You don't mean Councilman Gerritson?"

"Yes."

"I see." She wrote down the information. "All we need you to do now is to file charges."

"It might ruin his career. I'd rather file for divorce, but…" Heather closed her eyes and shook her head. "What would you do?"

Hope put her pen down and sat back. "I can't answer that question. All I know is that you have an obligation to your children to keep them safe, and to yourself to keep you safe."

"I'll do anything," she said.

"Does he know you're gone?"

"Not yet. He was sleeping when I left."

"Do you have joint checking and savings?"

"Yes, oh—" Understanding dawned.

Hope didn't usually make such ambiguous suggestions, but in this instance...

"When he finds out I drained the accounts, he'll go into a rage."

"So? You won't be around to witness it. I'll have my husband take you by your bank. Do they have a drive-through?" Heather nodded. "Good, then you won't even have to go in." She got up. "Call me if there is anything else I can do for you." Hope patted Heather's hand. "We'll put our heads together here too and see if we can find some answers."

A few minutes later, she watched Roger escort his charges out the back door and into a van with shaded windows.

Celia stood beside her. "Did she tell you her name?"

Hope nodded. "You don't want to know."

"Okay, then it's back to business. The toilet in the front bathroom is stopped up. I think one of the kiddies put something down it. Julia says she's got her outline finished, and Clarice has gone to her appointment. Lunch will be ready in a few, and DeeDee and Chelsea aren't speaking. Which is better than a catfight."

Hope flinched and stretched her upper torso around.

"What is it?"

"Pulled muscle or something." She rubbed her midsection. "I thought they said this was *morning* sickness." She headed for the bathroom, remembered the clogged plumbing, and veered off toward the apartment. *Please, Lord, let me make it.*

Chapter Twenty-One

Clarice

She should be out enjoying the lovely weather and the Saturday Market that everyone raved about, but Clarice felt like that fog that so often drifted in at night had taken up residence in her brain. And was not drifting on. She stared at the computer screen without seeing it.

How had he gotten away with everything? How could she have been such a fool? She'd asked herself these questions every day in the week she'd been at J House. "Herbert, you must be so disappointed in me. Losing all that you worked so hard to earn, all because of a charming smile and enough compliments to paint a two-story building. Why didn't I listen to Nadia?"

If someone came upon her talking to herself, her explanation that she was talking to her dead husband wouldn't do much to defend her case. *Sometimes I think I am going round the bend. Mary, Holy Mother, I know you haven't deserted me. Please, I need some saintly help right about now.* Clarice stared at her rings, rings that she thought had been her saving grace. But when she took them in to be appraised, so she'd know she had some kind of money to start over with, she'd learned the final depth of Gregor's perfidy. The diamonds were cubic zirconium. He must have had the excellent copies made of her rings when he so kindly took them in to be cleaned and their mountings checked. All three rings had a total value of about a thousand dollars, not the thirty to forty thousand they'd been worth several years ago. Her beloved fur coat was worth about three. She sniffed and dabbed at the tears that persisted, in spite of the good people who had taken her in. She'd sure proved out the adage that there is no fool like an old fool. No matter how much Roger tried to convince her that Gregor had been a master con artist and had fleeced other lambs as well, she beat herself blue and purple with blame—and shame.

"All right, old fool, forget your maudlin weeping and get the job done that you can do."

"Talking to yourself again, eh?" Roger propped a hip on the clean and bare credenza behind her. Gone too were the stacks on the desk.

"I just can't…"

Roger raised a hand, traffic cop style. "I thought we agreed that I would worry on Gregor and you would be kinder to Clarice."

"That's easier said than done," she mumbled to her now tapping fingers.

"I'll ignore that. Has Mr. Kent sent any response to that last letter we received from Blakely Associates?"

"Not via e-mail. And Celia has been answering the phones. She'd have left a message on Hope's desk." Clarice turned so she could see him better. Roger looked rumpled, as though he'd just gotten out of bed. "Back's bad again?"

"Must be a change comin' in the weather. Hard to believe I'm saying things like that. Always thought Peter's complaint about his trick knee was all made up."

"You tried a chiropractor?"

"Uh-huh. He helps keep me vertical. Some days are just bad."

"Couldn't have anything to do with the hours you spent on the roof yesterday, could it?" Clarice pasted an innocent look on her face, or at least she hoped it was innocent.

"Shouldn't leak any longer, and when the winter rains hit, we'll be

real glad of that. Whole building is held together with bubble gum
and duct tape." He flinched as he pushed away from the wall. "If Julia
comes by, tell her I'm in the laundry room."

"Washing?"

"No, fixing the dryer. Need it to last another week at least."

Clarice already knew he meant six months to a year. A new dryer
was one of the items on the donations list. Or else scheduled to be
replaced after the next fund-raiser.

*Lord, I'd buy them a dryer if we could get back some of my money. A
brand-new one, no hand-me-down that'd need fixing in a month or two.*
That thought alone was enough to clear the way for the doldrums to
attack again. Hard work had been her antidote up to now, and must
be again. The more physical the better.

A child burst through the front door. "I got to go."

Clarice pointed him in the direction of the bathroom. "And don't
forget to flush."

*Shame we never had children, Herbert. I would have made a good
grandma. But then perhaps that's one of the reasons I am here. I can
grandma some of these little ones.*

The door flew open again. Young Alphi, who had been living in
the shelter with his mother for a month or more, raced to a skidding
stop at her desk. "Where's Hope?"

From the look on his face, Clarice thought perhaps Roger might
be of more use to him. "She's out on the grounds somewhere, but
Roger is in the laundry room. Go get him." She pulled the walkie-
talkie from the drawer. Now if only she could remember how to use
it. Was it push to talk or push to listen? She pushed the button and
spoke. "Hope, you're needed in here."

Some static blasted her ear, then Hope's voice. "Emergency?"

"Alphi came racing in. I sent him for Roger."

"Be right there."

Roger and the boy rushed by her desk. "Call 911 and tell them we need a uniform or two."

Clarice had learned already that meant "No one hurt yet, but we need help." She dialed 911 and at the answer said, "This is Clarice at J House, and we need a uniform or two. I take it no sirens."

"What's happening?"

"I don't know. The Market is still in full swing, and one of our children came rushing in, and he and Roger raced out. That's all I know."

"Tell Roger or Hope the cars are on their way."

"Thanks." Clarice hung up the phone. *Lord, protect the innocent. Send peace to quell the violence.*

"What's happening?" Hope had come in through the side door and now stood at the desk.

"I don't know, but Roger asked for backup, so I called 911."

"Good. Who…?"

"Alphi. That's all I know."

"Hmm. I'll call you if we need more help." She touched the walkie-talkie clipped to her belt. Dressed in khaki shorts and a scoop-neck red T-shirt, she looked about as fierce as a Lhasa apso, but even sweet dogs have teeth.

Curiosity ate on her like a yellow jacket starving for protein, but Clarice forced herself to get back to work. The quarterly reports were already a month overdue, and if the grant application wasn't turned in soon, Hope would not get all the funds she was entitled to.

Running a nonprofit wasn't a whole lot different from running a hopefully for-profit business. Both had paperwork that could sink the Bay Bridge.

While she typed, Clarice kept one ear tuned to whatever was going on outside. No sirens, no gunshots, no screaming.

When Alphi and Roger finally strolled through the door giving each other high-fives, she blew out a sigh of relief with a breath she didn't know she'd been holding.

"What was it?"

"Pickpockets, and I saw them." Alphi pumped the air, then glanced up at Roger, who gave the needed approbation.

"He did at that. We shadowed them, and the cops caught them. Two young punks working as a team. They failed to explain in a satisfactory manner how they happened to have four watches, two pocket computers, three wallets—two with rather substantial amounts of money—a diamond tennis bracelet, and a diamond crusted lipstick case. Definitely not the normal paraphernalia of teen hoods."

"Don't forget the credit cards."

"Right. That would have been the long-term scam." Roger thumped Alphi on the shoulder. "Nothing better to catch a pickpocket than a reformed pickpocket."

"I was good."

Clarice kept her mouth closed, but only by a whisker. *This child had been a pickpocket? This sweet child with the choirboy's voice?*

"Not been for my friend Roger here, I'd a been stuck in juvie." He shook his head. "Who knows how long."

Clarice caught the look of love Roger showered on the boy. *Folks say Hope runs this place, but I'm thinking Roger is the backbone.*

"Wish a certain pickpocket I knew could be caught as easily."

"I'm working on it, Clarice. Now don't you go giving up. Remember, God says He is the vindicator of widows and orphans. It's not smart to invoke the wrath of the almighty God."

Clarice glanced up at the clock. One p.m. She planned on attending four o'clock mass at Saints Peter and Paul, on the other side of Washington Square. Today's weather was perfect for the walk.

If only she had money to stop by the Italian bakery and bring back macaroons for everyone. Perhaps selling her coat was the only option. Although Roger kept telling her to be patient.

After mass, she thanked the priest for his homily and headed back toward the shelter. Dusk softened the outlines of buildings, and dampness not quite dense enough to be fog hazed the streetlights. She buttoned her coat, as much for safety's sake as the chill. Interesting that her fur coat, Gucci bag, and matching shoes would brand her as wealthy, yet she had only five dollars left to her name.

Herbert, what would you suggest? You always had a good head on your shoulders. What kind of work can I do that would make enough money for me to live on? You know I don't ask for a lot, all that at the end, that wasn't me. You just wanted to give me all the things you thought I wanted. And I didn't want to hurt your feelings. But now everything is gone, and I need to depend on my wits again. Yes, I know, take stock. You were always taking stock, counting what you had and looking ahead.

She stopped to look in the windows of a store. She could work retail, a nice dress shop, perhaps. Not a big store like Saks, but a small, intimate shop where one could know the customers and call them when something special came in they would like. She waited for the light to change. Of course, she could work in a bakery or even a restaurant, but could her feet take that kind of punishment? An office, like she was doing now, would be the best, but who would hire a sixty-seven-year-old woman?

She started up Union to Casa de Jesús. Yes, indeed, the house of Jesus, and His arms encircled everyone who came there. With the new programs Julia was starting, a good office worker was needed all the more. Especially one who could organize things as she could. That brought up another thought. *How to do what I do best without stepping on Celia's toes? Her pointed remarks lately were about as subtle as her pointed shoes. I know—take time to build a friendship and get us work-*

ing together as a team. It's just that I get so involved and barrel ahead. I know, Herbert, I'll do better, really I will.

Back to living arrangements. Was living in the shelter a bad thing? No, other than it took a bed from someone who needed it worse. And they'd had to turn away a young woman who needed a bed.

Herbert, if you tell me to eat crow and go back to stay with Nadia, I will, but if I can do more good here, then just let me know. But I don't want to cost someone else something for me to stay. Got that? And you know something else? I really need a haircut. Jesus, Mary, and Joseph, the things I took for granted.

Andy

The view was even more incredible than she remembered.

"Andy, where are you?"

"Up here," she called down. She stood leaning against one of several stacks of still-full moving boxes, looking out the bank of living room windows at a freighter passing under the Golden Gate Bridge. She was enthralled by the way the fog licked the tops of the towers and then devoured the remainder of the span.

"Are you all right?" Martin stopped behind her and slid cool hands around her waist.

"Yes. Of course. Why?"

"You never stand still like this."

She could feel his warm breath on her neck. "I just can't get over this view. It's nothing short of spectacular." She leaned her head back against his shoulder. "Who would have dreamed…?"

"That we would be standing in our own house enjoying a view like this?"

That wasn't what she'd been going to say, but it didn't matter. She was happy that he was happy, that they weren't arguing, and that things were working out. Martin had his new house, a house he could be proud of when he entertained, and she had her house and Lavender Meadows.

It wasn't a perfect situation, but it was workable, at least for now.

Andy looked up at the clock. "It's only five thirty. What are you doing here so early?"

"Since I work in the main office, I leave when the others do."

Andy saw his briefcase and knew that even though he'd come home, he wasn't through working. "I didn't have time to get out to the grocery store," she said. "Suzanne left us some takeout menus. What do you say we order in?"

"Fine with me."

Andy turned and kissed Martin lightly on the cheek. "I'll get the menus." She headed for the kitchen. Her hurrying and scurrying the last few days had equaled higher winds than a class-four hurricane. From the signing of the contract with Mrs. Getz until now, it had been twelve days. In that time, Andy had flown home, hired a moving company, emptied the house of all the extra furniture and accessories, gone through every cupboard, drawer, and closet, and boxed up all the extra towels, sheets, and kitchen items.

The process had opened her eyes to her buying habits and her saving habits. She had bought items she already had and didn't need, and had saved items she should have donated to some worthy charity. The result was that she now had more than enough of everything to stock and furnish their San Francisco home.

Sunday she would return to Medford, make up a schedule for Shari, and teach her how to update the Lavender Meadows Web site. Andy was pleased with Shari's progress. She was proving to be just the kind of employee Andy had thought she would be, conscientious and hard-working.

Now that the lavender beds and fields had been put to rest for the winter, the outdoor agenda would slow down, but the office work, the order taking, and the making of lavender sachets and other hand-worked items would continue as before.

Once she got the San Francisco house in order, she would set up an office in the loft, buy a laptop computer, and have it networked to the Lavender Meadows computers so she could do her bookkeeping and monitor her catalog and Internet business when she was in San Francisco.

Dinner arrived forty-five minutes later. Coq au vin, marinated eggplant salad, fresh rolls, and apple crisp for dessert.

"This sure beats eating in a hotel," Martin said.

Andy saw through his innuendo. "It's still restaurant food."

"True, but I didn't have to go out to a restaurant or eat alone."

"No, you didn't," she conceded. "When we're through, do you think you could help me in the kitchen for a few minutes? I want to take off the cabinet doors so that when I'm here the next time, I can sand them down and paint them."

"The next time? When's that?"

Andy stared at him. "Next month."

"But I thought—" His expression grew hard and resentful.

"You thought what?" she challenged. "That I'd changed my mind and decided to stay here and be a *full-time* wife?" She saw him take a deep breath and knew he wouldn't answer the question. "Never mind. I'll take the cabinet doors off myself." *And here I thought he was happy and that things were working out. Call me a fool.*

Andy was up before sunrise. She wanted to get an early start on organizing the kitchen so she could spend the rest of the day stocking the cupboards with food and the bathrooms with their favorite personal grooming products. By seven o'clock, she was finished and had started breakfast.

Martin came to the table with a sour expression that told her he was still brooding. It pained her to see him this way, but until he could get over being jealous and accept the compromise, she would pretend to ignore him.

"I want to grocery shop today," she said, smiling at him from across the small drop-leaf table that had been stored for more years than she could count in the attic in Medford. "Do you have any idea where I can find a grocery and a drugstore?"

He took his electronic organizer out of his coat pocket and set it down on the table. "I saw some posters for a Saturday Market, which I assume is an outdoor produce market. But other than that…" He shrugged, then turned on the organizer.

With no small effort, Andy ignored his rudeness. "Did you happen to notice where the Saturday Market was located?" she persisted.

He looked up and met her gaze. "Next door to Casa de Jesús—that building on Union that looks like an old church."

"Okay. I think I know where that is. Suzanne told me about it, but I'd forgotten." He nodded, then took a bite of his eggs. "Would you like to go with me? It might be fun exploring the area together."

Shame on you, Andy. You're baiting him, and you know it. All that togetherness stuff he'd spouted was just lip service to lure you into moving here.

"No thanks. I'm going to spend the day getting myself organized. I thought I'd set up an office upstairs in the loft." He must have heard her quick intake of breath, because he looked at her strangely. "What?"

"Nothing," she said, lifting her shoulders and pasting on a bright smile. "That's a perfect place for an office."

He finished his breakfast and pushed his plate back. "Isn't someone supposed to bring Mrs. Getz's cat today?"

"Yes, around four, I think." She gathered up the dirty dishes. "I should be back by then, but if I'm not, don't let them go without making sure we have all his stuff." She took a pad of paper off the counter. "Here, I've written down everything Mrs. Getz told me came with him." Andy put away the butter and jam and tidied up the kitchen.

She still had time before her first shopping expedition to wipe down the cabinet framework. She filled the sink with Simple Green, scrubbed down the framework, then rinsed the soapy residue away with vinegar and water.

She didn't hear Martin get up from the table, but she did hear him upstairs moving furniture around, the furniture she had intended to use to make up her office. Oh, well, if it made Martin happy, she could deal with it. One of the spare bedrooms downstairs would do for her office just fine, even though it didn't have a view of the bay. The courtyard area would be lovely with some work. After all, she wouldn't be here most of the time anyway.

It was noon before she was ready to go shopping. Grabbing her purse, she yelled a quick good-bye to Martin from the door and ventured out. She climbed the stairs through the Grace Marchant's Garden, noting her neighbors' houses and even some of her neighbors. One day soon she would make the effort to meet them.

The walk up Montgomery gave her a chance to admire an ancient pink and purple fuchsia, watch for the parrots, and wonder about a brown shingled building whose signage proclaimed it a restaurant. It appeared to be abandoned. Houses needed to be occupied, or they fell too soon into disrepair.

She stopped to watch a photographer and his assistant shooting wedding photos with the Transamerica spire in the background. The bride's veil fluttered in the breeze. The groom, dressed in a traditional black tux, laughed at something she said. Love glowed from the two of them. They would have wonderful pictures, Andy thought. She just hoped the happiness would last as long as the photos. She crossed the street and glanced into Speedy's. Savory flavors of onion, garlic, and beef floated on the air. On the way home, maybe she'd buy a quart of the soup for dinner.

Cars lined the street, forcing a bus to drive right up the middle. She could hear music ahead and saw shoppers loaded down with their purchases walking toward their cars. Obviously, she was nearing the outdoor market Martin and Suzanne had told her about. Leafy lettuce, long ears of corn, and carrot tops smiled at her as they peeked out of brown paper bags. She picked up her pace, eager to start shopping.

Many vendors used the backs of trucks to display their produce. Others had set up tables. The vendors who had no shade brought their own: market umbrellas or tied-down canvas or plastic shelters. There was a variety of produce to choose from: tomatoes of every size and color from purple, striped green, and cherry to huge beefsteak; onions, green, purple, brown, and white; and leeks. On top of the produce were flowers: sunflowers, zinnias, and mums, both cut and potted. The array dazzled and intrigued. She followed her nose to the elephant ears cart and bought one, spread with melted butter and dusted with cinnamon and sugar.

"I ain't seen you here before. You new?" asked the woman behind the stand.

"Yes," Andy said, laughing. "Do you know everyone who comes?"

"No, but most. My name's Celia. Want some coffee?"

"Yes, please." Andy dusted sugar off her hand and reached for the steaming foam cup. She set both down and dug in her purse for her money. "We just moved into a house that borders Mrs. Marchant's Garden."

"Great. See the parrots yet?" Celia counted out change.

"No. Not yet, but hopefully soon." Pocketing her money, Andy nodded toward the rest of the market. "Is it always this crowded?"

"Nope, sometimes it's worse." Celia turned to wait on another customer. "Thanks." She turned back to Andy. "Most of our vendors are pretty regular, depending on what they have in season."

"I see. Who would I talk to about the possibility of having a table with lavender products?"

"You grow your own?"

"Yep. Up in Oregon."

Celia pointed a long, shimmering, gold-flecked fingernail. "See that tall woman over there with the knitting? That's Starshine, and she's in charge of vendors."

"Thanks." Andy raised her half-eaten treat. "And for this."

"See you 'round."

Andy ambled over to the knitting tables and drooled over the hats, scarves, vests, and accessories. She chose a matching beret and long scarf of fluffy turquoise with a thread of silver metallic running through it for Bria. Winters in Seattle could be bitter with the dampness. Then she found a brick-colored set for Morgan. Pacific Lutheran wasn't that far from Seattle.

"Welcome to the market. You must be new." Starshine shook out a bag for Andy's purchase.

"I'm still trying to get moved in. This is beautiful work. Do you knit all these yourself?"

"Got to have something to fill the long evenings. Did you see the mittens to match these?"

"No, I didn't." She "oohed" and "aahed" when Starshine showed her the cable-knit mittens.

"I'll take those, too." She patted other pieces while they chatted. The gorgeous yarns and patterns pleaded for her attention. "Celia said you're in charge of the vendors."

"Sure am. What do you have?"

"I raise lavender on our farm in Medford, Oregon, and I whole-sale and retail a line of lavender products, including my own brand of lavender tea. I'd like to try selling them here, if you think there might be a market for them."

"Lavender? Oh, sure."

"Is the market open every Saturday?"

"Up until Christmas, but you don't need to show up all the time.

Some come every other week, some just in the spring, others in the summer. The only rule is that whatever you're selling has to be raised, grown, made, and/or produced by the seller."

"Is this typical weather for October?"

Starshine nodded, setting her intricately beaded earrings to swinging. "October is our best month. Summer day fog is gone, winter rain not started. Good winds to blow away any smog, not that we get a lot of that."

Another customer held out a piece to be bagged, so Andy nodded her thanks and wandered on. She wished she'd brought a string bag like so many of the patrons had. Sooner or later the plastic bag handles would cut into her palms.

Two small children chased each other through the crowd, their laughter blending in with the music of a string group on the front steps of the old church and a wood flute from out by the street.

When she wandered by the elephant ears cart again, Celia called to her. "You met Hope yet?"

"Hope? No. I found Starshine." Andy motioned with her bag of purchases.

"Hope just went that way." Celia nodded toward the church. "She's the one who puts this thing together. You need to talk to her, too."

Andy smiled and shrugged. How would she recognize Hope in all this crowd?

As if reading her mind, Celia said, "Light brown skin with freckles, orangy hair in braids. 'Bout five two, dynamo. You can't miss her."

Andy nodded her thanks and continued shopping. After a while she realized a string bag wouldn't be adequate either. She needed one of those two-wheeled wire carts like some of the other shoppers were pulling around. She would have to start thinking differently if she was going to walk to and from shopping. Of course, she could take her booty home and return for more, but she hated to leave for fear she would miss something.

Noticing a poster on the church's door, she made her way between people sitting on the steps, visiting and enjoying the day, and started to read.

"We have services at ten, Sunday school at 8:45, including an adult class." The voice came from right behind her.

Andy turned around. The orangy hair gave the woman away. "You must be Hope." Celia had not mentioned the warm smile and laughing eyes.

"Sure enough. Celia sent you on to me?"

"I'm Andy Taylor, newly moved to Mrs. Marchant's Garden." She held out her hand.

"Hope Benson. I run the women's shelter here, Casa de Jesús, more commonly known as J House." Her smile widened. "I'm also the pastor."

"Wow, you must keep busier than busy."

"Yes, and I love it." She gestured to the crowd. "And we have a party every Saturday." She cocked her head. "You buy that brown shingled house with the view that never quits?" At Andy's nod, she continued. "Mrs. Getz came here to sell her paintings, up until a couple years ago when her health began to fail."

"I saw some of her paintings when I visited her. They're lovely." Andy set her bags down on the ground and rubbed her palms. "I was telling Starshine that I grow lavender in Oregon. I have a line of lavender products that I wholesale and retail. I was thinking that I might like to set up a table here at your market. What do you think?"

"I think that's great. Get the paperwork from Starshine, fill it out, and send it to me."

"Hope!"

Hope glanced around at the caller, then turned back to Andy. "When do you want to start?"

"Next month, about this time. It would take me that long to get my stuff together."

"Sounds good. Like I said, get the paperwork and send it in. I'd better go now and see what they need." She started to turn and walk away. "Maybe I'll see you tomorrow morning in church?"

"If not tomorrow, another Sunday," Andy answered, waving her away. "I don't live here full-time." Something told her Martin wouldn't think this congregation quite proper enough for his new corporate lifestyle.

Andy finished her shopping and trudged home. By the time she reached her entry, her hands were bloodless.

Martin greeted her at the door and took the bags from her hands. "Maybe you should have taken the car."

"Yeah, maybe, but there was no room to park." She gladly relinquished her bags, stumbled up the stairs, and plopped herself on the sofa. No sooner had she caught her breath than she heard a loud meow. She turned her head to the right and gasped at the huge tabby cat staring back at her.

"His name is Fluffy," Martin said, a look of disgust etching his features.

"But he isn't…fluffy," Andy observed. "He's a short-hair."

"Yeah, I know."

"Did they bring his stuff?"

"Oh yeah," Martin said, gesturing toward the pile in the corner of the room. "If we put all his stuff out, we won't have any place for our stuff." Martin walked over to the pile. "He has a bed for every room," he said, lifting them one at a time. There was a leopard chaise, a red velvet Victorian settee, and a black leather Harley Davidson chair. "He has an electronic, self-cleaning cat box that requires clump-ing cat litter. I repeat, clumping cat litter." Andy couldn't resist a chuckle, although Martin's face bore no trace of levity. He picked up the bag and pointed to the word *clumping*. "He has two scratching posts slash cat trees with holes that he can play hide-and-seek in. And he has a variety of toys." Martin picked up a large plastic bag, opened it, and spilled them out on the floor. "Remote control mice, cat-nip scented bubbles with a wand that we are supposed to wave to make the bubbles, and talking toys that have Mrs. Getz's recorded voice say-ing, 'Kitty kitty num-num' and 'Mommy loves Fluffy.'"

Andy's laughter escalated to the point where she couldn't speak. She had never in all her life seen Martin look or talk like this. With his straight face and his humorless tone, he could have won the best comedian of the year award.

At long last she found her voice. "Does he seem to be a nice cat?" She turned just in time to see Fluffy get up from a furry blue sofa bed and pad over to Martin.

"He hasn't bitten me or clawed me so far."

Fluffy stopped midway across the room, arched and stretched every muscle and ligament, then proceeded over to Martin, meowed, and twined around his ankles. Martin picked him up and held him against his chest, stroking his orange fur. The cat scraped his evening shadow of beard with his coarse tongue, the sound rasping in the stillness.

Andy could hardly believe what she was seeing. Martin had never picked Chai Lai up and held her like that. But then Chai Lai had never meowed at Martin and twined around his ankles. A thought came to her, but she quickly put it aside. Meowing and twining were not her style. She would have to find another way to get Martin to accept her compromise and put his jealousy aside.

Andy stood up and went over to pet Fluffy. "How much do you think he weighs?"

"They told me he weighs eighteen pounds, but that he's not fat, he's big-boned."

Andy burst out laughing. This was getting funnier by the second. "Did they give you his medical history?"

Martin pointed to a small plastic file box. "His vet is just a few blocks away." Still holding the cat, Martin walked over to the small portable television set Andy had confiscated from her sewing room at home. "These are his videos," he said, taking up the remote and pushing a button.

"Videos? What would a cat do with a video?"

The moment the picture came on the screen, Andy howled with laughter.

Saltwater fish of every color swam back and forth across the screen. Martin turned Fluffy's head, and the second the cat saw them, he meowed and scrambled to get down.

"They told me the fish are his favorite, but that we should rotate them so he won't get bored. Personally, I would think he'd like the mouse video over the fish. But what do I know?"

"Oh, Martin," Andy said, her laughter interrupting her voice. "I love you, honey." She walked over to him, twined her arms around his neck, and kissed him.

Chapter Twenty-Three

Hope

"Good morning!"

"Good morning," the congregation answered rather weakly, but Hope smiled at them with all the love she always shared so freely.

"Welcome to worship at Casa de Jesús this Sunday morning. Our opening song is 'Our God Is an Awesome God.' You'll find the words in your bulletin." She nodded to Roger, who held his guitar at the ready. He played the opening chords, and between the two of them, they led the singing.

"Our God is an awesome God…" Both the words and music always gave her a thrill. Much as "Holy, Holy, Holy" did those first years of her new life. Every Sunday, to open the service, they sang two praise songs and one hymn so that people would not forget the great hymns. Today her congregation broke into harmony on "Beautiful Savior," and she had all she could do to keep from crying.

When Roger sat down, Hope stood and tucked her bulletin inside her Bible. "I know that when you sing like that, we are all experiencing a little bit of what the music will be like in heaven. Let us pray."

As the rustling settled, she used a deep breath to calm herself, to prepare for the message. "Heavenly Father, we thank You for the privilege of worshiping You in freedom, all of us together; that we have a place to meet, to draw closer as members of Your family. We rejoice that You are our Father, the same yesterday, today, and tomorrow, that with You there is no shadow of change. We ask You to bless our worship today, that we may grow closer to You minute by minute. In Jesus's precious name, amen."

The "amen" returned, and Roger stood to lead the simple liturgy. He sang a line, and they all repeated it.

"Holy Father." They sang it back.

"Jesus, Son of God." His voice rose, lifting those who followed.

"Holy Spirit, Teacher of us all."

Hope watched her people singing, some so serious, others smiling. Some with lifted hands. A little girl swaying in time to the music.

"We worship You, we praise You, we sing Your names forever. Amen, amen, amen." Roger had written the words and set them to simple music so that all could take part.

"Celia will read our lesson, and then together we'll read the psalm."

Celia left her folding chair in the front row, took a couple steps forward, and turned to face the gathering. "Our lesson today is from Paul's letter to the Ephesian people, and I am reading from *The Message* so we can all understand it better. Got that?"

Hope had to smile at Celia's small addition. Many of their people didn't read well, and the more contemporary words made more sense to them.

Roger led them in the first verse of "Spirit of the Living God" before the gospel.

Hope had been preaching a series on the miracles Jesus performed, so she read the story of the man who could walk again. She prayed for guidance and wisdom, and that all would have ears to hear, and then she let the silence stretch. When she opened her eyes, she saw one of her girls wiping her eyes with the tail of her blouse. Always God amazed and delighted her when He spoke through the silence.

"Ah, my dear family, let's talk together about what Jesus did then and what He does today." She retold the story, then asked the question: "What would you have done if you couldn't walk and Jesus told you to get up?"

Alphi shrugged. "I'd get up and walk. Don't want to dis de man."

Titters danced like dry rustling leaves over the gathering.

"Good thinking, Alphi. Anyone else?"

"Had he been crippled for a long time?" came a voice from the back.

"We assume so from the story."

"He be afraid and wonderin', what if nothin' happen?"

"I'd think so. So why did he do it?"

"Jesus, He look you in de eye 'n' take all de fear away." A female voice this time.

Hope waited, letting the words sink in. "So how about us, today? Doesn't Jesus say to us, 'Take up your bed and walk'?"

"A whole bed?" One of the little girls squeaked.

More soft laughter.

"But I ain't crippled." A little boy stood up and spun in a circle.

Hope nodded. "We are all crippled in one way or another. From fear, from someone beating on us, from us beating on ourselves. We are crippled inside from hate and disappointments, from not enough love and too much violence from those around us. So we need to keep our eyes on Jesus, listen for His soft command, to rise up and walk, and keep on walking so that we can learn to love and to dance and to sing. Because de man"—she grinned and winked at Alphi—"said we can, and we must. Amen."

She nodded to Roger, who stood and strummed the chords for "Silver and Gold Have I None."

Everyone sang, "He went walking and leaping and praising God."

After the offering and Communion, where everyone took part of the small loaf of bread and a sip of the wine, they closed the service singing the "The Lord's Prayer," followed by the benediction.

Giving the blessing was one of Hope's favorite parts of the service. She raised her hands. "The Lord bless you and keep you. The Lord make His face to shine on you and give you His peace. In the name of the Father and the Son and the Holy Spirit, amen." She made the sign of the cross and added, "Go in peace and serve the Lord."

"Thanks be to God." Little Hallie broke from her mother and ran to throw her arms around Hope's leg, right around the simple robe she wore. "Jesus love me, huh, Miss Hope?"

Hope bent over and swung the little one up to her hip. "He sure does, and so do I." Kissing the soft little cheek, she reached out to grasp the mother's hand. "So how's life going? Sure glad to see you here."

"Ah, Hope, I just can't believe it." The young black mother had graduated from high school in June and from J House in August. They were living in a halfway house, one of the arms of J House that Hope would love to add on to. "I still have my job in the preschool, and I go to school at night." Her eyes brightened with tears. "I wouldn't have gotten this far if you hadn't kept on me. Sorry I wasn't brave enough to stand up and tell everyone, but most of them know."

"That's okay." Hope hugged the young woman and handed Hallie over, then hugged them both. "What about Jimmy?"

"He's in rehab, but I ain't makin' no promises. Clean and sober and a job. That's what I told him. He's workin' on walkin' with Jesus too."

"Well, we miss you here, but honey, we sure don't want you to come back, except for church, that is, and to any classes you want." Hope turned, stretched out her hand, and pointed. "That woman right over there, her name's Julia, you go talk to her. She's got some good stuff for you."

"Will do."

Hope glanced up to see Andy with a good-looking man beside her. While he was almost smiling now, he'd been frowning through much of the service. Shaking hands and patting shoulders, she made her way over to the couple. "Hi Andy."

"You remembered my name."

"That's not hard. You were here only yesterday. Glad you could come. I know moving in takes up lots of time." She turned to the man. "Hi, I'm Hope Benson. I really enjoyed my short visit with your wife yesterday. Hope to see you again."

"Thank you. I'm sure you serve quite a polyglot parish here."

And you want no part of it. Such a shame. Your wife would love it here. "Yes, we have an unusual ministry." Hope glanced around at the people talking in small groups, someone handing out cookies and coffee, children playing in and among the adults. She savored the bright laughter and was delighted to see several of the street people from the neighborhood, as well as some of the residents. Polyglot. A good word. "I do hope you'll come again."

"Thanks." Andy squeezed her hand.

"Hey, I just thought of something. There's a few of us meeting for coffee on Tuesday at ten." *Please, Lord, let my schedule be clear.* "You might want to come."

"I can't. My flight leaves this afternoon, and I won't be back for a few weeks."

"Next time, then. Maybe you can bring us some of that lavender tea Starshine said you have." She saw Hope's husband frown. He didn't like lavender tea? Or he didn't like discussions about lavender tea?

Andy smiled. "Well then, I'll make a point of bringing some back with me."

"Good. I'll see you soon." Hope smiled at the husband, but he was too intent in getting his wife out of there to look back. She watched them leave and thought she detected a look of disappointment on Andy's face, but she couldn't be sure.

A few minutes later she heard car doors slam outside. Four men entered, three uniforms and a suit. Their faces were blank.

"You're late for church, gentlemen." She gave them her brightest smile. "How can we help you?" Roger appeared from out of nowhere and stood beside her.

"We have a search warrant. No one is to leave this room. "

Roger looked incredulous. "Come on, Carlos. What's with the official face?"

Hope knew Roger was upset; he'd known Carlos for ten years or more.

"Just let me do my job, okay?" Carlos raised his voice. "Don't anybody leave this room," he said in a stentorian voice that bounced off the walls. He turned to the uniforms and gave a hand signal. "Make it thorough but make it neat." Then he turned back to Roger. "We'll make this as quick as possible."

"What are you looking for?" Hope demanded.

Roger took her arm. "It's gotta be drugs. You got a tip, right?"

Officer Carlos nodded.

Please, Lord God, let there be none here. While all the residents vowed they had nothing, to some of them a little marijuana meant nothing.

"You don't go messing up my undies drawer, you hear?" Celia shouted at their backs. She clamped hands on her hips and stomped across to face off with Carlos. "You know better than this. And on a Sunday mornin' even." She wagged a finger at him. "What's San Francisco's finest coming to?"

"I can help you search the kitchen if you like," Roger offered, stepping between Carlos and Celia.

"You know I can't do that. Come on, give a guy a break."

Hope raised an eyebrow. *I'd like to give you a break. How about an arm or a leg? Hope, you know better. What happened to "Love your enemies"?* Some of the people moved to the back of the commons area. Others shifted and re-formed into new groups. Some simply stood and eyed the man in charge with distrust. Why should they trust him?

Too many of them had been on the other side of the law and knew firsthand that there was a difference between the way the police handled the rich and the poor. Maybe because she'd been on the other side, the poor side, Hope had more resentment. Her feelings were intensified by how hard she and Roger had worked to guarantee a clean house, using a plan that the police had devised. The girls all knew that even one infraction meant they were out.

So who could have called in a tip? Someone they'd helped but had to let go? A relative who bore a grudge against one of the girls? Angry husbands were always a prime suspect. She leaned into Roger, the question in her eyes.

He shook his head. "I don't know. Somebody with a grudge."

"Any chance they'll find anything?"

"Nope, Adolph and I did a sniff test just the other day. We're clean." Roger had trained Adolph to sniff out drugs and firearms. Without anyone realizing it, the dog was always in the room when they admitted a new girl. He'd saved their reputation more than once. "We should have had him in here when they came in." He tapped Carlos's shoulder. "I need to let the dog in, okay?"

"Sure, Rog. Just be quick about it."

Within seconds Roger and Adolph padded back into the room, the dog's tail thwacking chair legs and peoples' legs as he walked by. Pink tongue lolling, he sat down beside Hope and gave each child that came up a quick face-washing.

Carlos's eyes narrowed as he looked down at the dog. "He's mighty big for a Lab, isn't he?"

"Yeah, might have a bit of Great Dane in him or mastiff, but the soul of a Lab. Couldn't find a better friend if you tried." Roger tightened the leash as Adolph sidled on over to the cop. He sniffed the man's pants, nosed up his leg, and planted his nose on the holster on his belt.

"What's he doing?"

"He doesn't like guns," Roger said in a voice that told Hope that he was proud of Adolph.

"Roger, for crying out loud, call off your dog."

"Adolph." Roger made a down motion with his hand. The dog looked at him, gazed with slightly slit eyes at Carlos, and backed off, never taking his gaze from the holster.

"He helps us on intake."

"I can just bet. I didn't know you were a dog trainer."

"Just one of those things to help pass the time when I was laid up. Some drink, some gamble or do drugs; I trained a dog."

The three uniforms clunked down the stairs and made their way back into the room. "Clean."

Carlos sighed in relief. "That's all, then." He turned to leave.

"You might want to apologize to all these good people for taking up their time." Roger spoke in an offhand manner, but one eye twitched.

"Listen, Rog, you know the drill…"

Adolph stood with his nose pointing to the men, his tail perfectly still.

Carlos raised his hands and let them fall to his sides. He turned to face the crowd. "Sorry, folks, for the inconvenience. You've been patient, and I appreciate that." He turned back to Roger and raised an eyebrow.

Adolph sat and yawned, mouth wide, showing the black spot on his tongue. Then after a gargantuan belch that made the kids laugh, he lay down with a sigh.

"Next time phone ahead, and we'll save you the trouble." Hope knew she should keep her mouth shut, but this burned her. As soon as Carlos walked away, she added, "They could have waited another half an hour. This was out-and-out harassment."

Roger gave her a thoughtful look. "Yeah, I wonder why."

Hope grinned at her husband. Once he put his snoop skills to work, all manner of interesting things happened. She locked her arm with his and raised her voice. "Lunch in ten minutes! There's plenty of food for everyone."

Before they all left, Hope acted on her idea. She invited Julia and Clarice to join her for coffee Tuesday morning. She was sorry Andy wouldn't be able to make it, because she sensed the woman could use a friend to talk to.

Tuesday morning, Hope fled to the john before even kissing her husband. Clutching the cold porcelain stool from a kneeling position reminded her to appreciate the days when this didn't happen.

Roger handed her a wet washcloth. "I thought you would be done with this by now."

"Me too." She staggered to her feet. "I never even had time to put the Sea-Bands on."

"Wear them to bed." Roger had thought the elastic bands with a knobby button on the inside were like snake oil, but he'd changed his mind when Hope wore them and had felt better.

"You want to go back to bed?"

"Only for a bit." Hope stumbled back to bed and sat down before digging in the nightstand for the package. "Not here?" She held up the empty plastic container. "You know where they are?"

"Nope, but I'll look."

"That should be helpful." Hope lay back down. Her husband might be one of the best snoops in the city, but he couldn't find his socks in the dryer. Arm over her eyes, she added, "I have a meeting at ten."

"I'll make breakfast."

She groaned and tried to think what she could throw at him without causing any head movement.

"You feeling all right?" Clarice asked when Hope entered the office some time later.

"Morning sickness. I'll be all right after I get some fresh air."

"I set up a coffee tray in the kitchen. Roger said he'd bring rolls from the bakery."

"Ms. Van Dam, how did we get along before you showed up?" Hope cocked her head. "Edie, mon."

"That's good. Right?" At Hope's nod, she continued, "I've been thinking…"

"Huh-uh, save it for the meeting. Adolph and I are going to walk around the block—or at least up to the corner and back—or perhaps around the garden."

"Did you try crackers?"

"Not much help. Have you seen my Sea-Bands?"

"Those gray things?" Clarice pulled open the shallow middle drawer of the wooden teacher's desk. She held up the bands. "Right here."

"I knew Roger wouldn't find them." Hope slipped the bands onto the proper places on her wrists and headed out the side door. Celia, earphones in place and rear wiggling to the beat of the music only she could hear, was kneeling on the flagstone walk, trowel in hand and a basket beside her.

"Where's Adolph?" Hope had glanced in his empty run. She tapped Celia's shoulder.

"Huh, no need to scare me white-headed! Couldn't you just yell or something?"

"I did the something. Where's Adolph?"

"Gone with Roger. You think I should put the tulips or the daffodils here?"

"Why not mix them together?"

Celia shrugged and put her earphones back in place.

Hope sucked in a deep breath and blew it out, rising up on the balls of her feet to loosen the ankles. She sure hoped she'd feel better at the end of the week than she did now.

Chapter Twenty-Four

Andy

Hope strode to the end of the block, crossed, and continued up the hill. Glancing up toward Coit Tower, she saw a familiar figure turn the corner on Montgomery and start down. "Andy." Hope called and waved.

"I know I'm early, but…"

Hope sucked in a deep breath. She hadn't taken the hill fast, so why was she dizzy? She staggered over and leaned against the light post.

"Hope, are you all right?"

"I'm not sure. I feel really dizzy."

"You're whiter than a sheet." Andy took her arm and guided her toward the curb. "Sit down and put your head between your knees." When Hope started to say something, Andy silenced her. "Don't talk, just relax."

"Yes, Mother."

"Sorry, sometimes I can be a bit bossy."

"Andy, I'm teasing." Hope eased upright, sucked in a deep breath, and let it out slowly.

"I sure thought I was through with this part of it—you know—the queasy stomach, the lightheadedness."

"Oh, I see. You're pregnant. Congratulations. I didn't know."

"Thanks." Hope took the hand Andy offered and let herself be pulled to her feet.

"Are you ready to amble back down to J House?"

"Yes, ambling would be good." Hope laughed, then waved at a woman climbing the block below J House. "That's Julia Collins, an attorney from Kansas City. She's looking for her runaway grand-daughter."

"Oh." Andy glanced sideways at Hope. "You collect all kinds of strays, don't you?"

"I collect interesting people, and I have a feeling we four women—" She stopped and looked at Andy. "Hey, I thought you said you had a flight."

"I did, but I decided to stay in town a little while longer, to get things in order. I spent all day yesterday buying stuff to stock the refrigerator and the cupboards so Martin would have everything he needed."

They stopped at the wide steps up to the front door. "There's Roger coming with the pastries. Just in time."

"I brought some lavender tea, by the way." Andy held up a zippered plastic bag.

"But how—?"

"I had my mom overnight it to me."

Andy kept an eye on Hope as unobtrusively as possible as the four women came together in one corner of the common room. Two wing chairs, one with fraying arms, and a well-loved sofa were pulled into a circle around a low table, inviting them to enjoy the coffee and now a steaming pot of lavender tea.

Roger set the box of pastries in the middle and took two out. "Come on, Adolph, let the ladies get to their meeting."

Adolph ignored Roger's command and stood staring up at Andy with eager eyes. She patted him and scratched him behind his ear.

"You better go now," she said, gently shooing him away, when she would have loved for him to stay. She'd only been gone from home a few days, and already she missed Comet and Chai Lai. Fluffy was a great diversion, but they hadn't bonded yet.

Hope sat forward. "Okay, ladies, we have lots of history to share. "I thought we'd start with my reason for inviting you all." She looked from one to the other. "I know I made it sound like we were going to meet for coffee and friendship, and that's really what I intended until God impressed on me that we need each other. Now, all I have to do is find out what He had in mind."

Andy's brow furrowed. What was she talking about? She liked Hope, but she didn't need her, and she certainly didn't need either of the other woman. She didn't even know them.

Do you trust Me?

The voice was so loud, Andy wondered if anybody else had heard it. She looked at each of the women. Their eyes were riveted on Hope, who was sipping her tea. Andy crossed her arms, physically and mentally closing down.

"The three of you are new to San Francisco, so you have a common thread. So how about each of us take a few minutes to give a bird's-eye view of our lives and how we came to be here?" She didn't wait for an answer. "I'll start," she offered, obviously eager to begin. "I was born in Jamaica and born contrary. Dr. Dobson calls children like me strong-willed. I have no idea where my father is, and my mother died of a drug overdose when I was fifteen. I did well as a hooker, but thanks to our heavenly Father, I never got hooked on the hard drugs. Booze and marijuana were bad enough. A young cop got through to me after I'd been badly beaten, and I took his advice in two ways." She held up two fingers. "I accepted Christ as my Savior, and I got off the streets. Thanks to a wonderful couple who had pity on one of God's least ones and put up with her mouth, I got my

GED, finished college, and Big Dad called me into the ministry. When I came back to the Bay area, I had a new name—Hope—and I married that no-longer-young, badly bent cop. Not too much later, God gave us J House. I was told we'd never have children because of my former lifestyle, but now here I am, pregnant." A slight shrug raised her shoulders and eyebrows. "Hey, mon, my story, all by the grace of the Man upstairs, Big Dad to me."

"So that's where your accent comes from." Andy made sure her mouth was still smiling. She'd never dreamed by looking at her that Hope had been through so much. What a story. Her admiration for Hope tripled.

Julia popped the last of her cannelloni into her mouth and dusted the powdered sugar off her hands. "I'm next." She pointed to her mouth. "As soon…" She wiped her mouth with her napkin. "I came here on a mission—to find my granddaughter, who, it seems, is now on the streets. I, too, was a rebellious teen, pregnant at seventeen, but God saved me from marrying the loser. I kept the baby girl, finished high school, hated menial jobs, and went to college. I am eternally thankful for government assistance and college and law school grants. My daughter was making all the same mistakes I did, so she and I battled. When she started doing drugs, my granddaughter came to live with me part of the time, but as she got older and I insisted on rules, she went back to Minnesota to stay with her mother. When that got to be too much, she split for California. I'm an attorney, currently on leave, who specializes in adoptions and family issues." She heaved a sigh of relief and sat back.

Andy shrank back in her chair, wishing she could be invisible. This kind of sharing was not her cup of tea. She was a private person, and she didn't particularly care to know this much about people she had only just met.

"I might as well go next." Clarice set her coffee cup on the table.

"I grew up in Newark, New Jersey, the protected daughter of blue-collar parents, and married my Herbert right out of high school. Herbert was a dreamer, but he also learned how to put feet to his dreams. A hard worker was my Herbert. In spite of all our prayers and novenas, we were never blessed with children, so when Herbert's tailoring business grew to needing help, I was there. He moved his shop to a bigger place, then went into making shirts, then silk shirts. He hired some women to sew, and pretty soon he was selling shirts in the finest stores: Bloomingdale's and Saks. Then, just as I had convinced him to retire, without any warning he up and died. I wasn't at all prepared. I sold everything, banked the money, and moved to Florida to be near my sister. And that's where I made the biggest mistake any fool woman can do. A good-looking younger man, name of Gregor, convinced me that he loved me." She grabbed the sides of her hair. "Oh, to think I was so stupid, so gullible," she said between her teeth. She sniffed and dabbed at her eyes. "He took all of Herbert's hard-earned money, even made copies of my rings." She held out her hands. "Good copies, but…" She sniffed again. "He promised me a new life and said we were moving to San Francisco. He said he had us a place to live, helped me pack, and bought my plane ticket. He was going to wind up his business and meet me at the airport." She shook her head, as if she could hardly believe her own stupidity. "I got off the plane, and no Gregor. I took a cab to our supposed new home, and no Gregor. Funniest thing, the key he gave me didn't work. So there I was all alone and in shock. I had less than fifty dollars in my purse, I learned my credit cards were maxed out, and I had no place to go. That's when I met Angel Annie, who made me flag down a cop, and he brought me here."

Andy was dumbfounded. How could a man do that to a woman? How could Clarice not have recognized what kind of man she was dealing with? She seemed to be an intelligent woman.

"I'm sure there's something we can do legally." Julia's voice snapped, matching her eyes. "We can't let him get away with this."

"Roger is investigating." Hope handed Clarice a tissue.

Hope nodded to Andy. "Your turn. You can't hide in that chair any longer."

"But I have a boring story."

"Thank God one of us does." Hope reached for a cannelloni. "Go for it." She stretched, rolling her shoulders forward and twisting at her waist.

"What's wrong?" Andy asked.

"I'm just feeling a little tight. I'm probably not getting enough exercise." Hope turned to Andy and gave her the nod.

Andy wished the chair would swallow her up. She really didn't want to do this, but if she didn't, she would look foolish. Maybe even snobbish. If only she had known that this wasn't going to be just a gab session. "I grew up in Medford, Oregon," she began. "All through school I was known as one of the 'good' girls. I met Martin in college. We both attended Pacific Lutheran. We married shortly after graduation, had our first child within a year, and then had two more. Martin provided everything, allowing me to be a stay-at-home mom. When my mother gave me a lavender sachet, I was so taken by the fragrance that I bought a couple of lavender plants so I could make my own sachets. One thing led to another, and when the children went to college, I started selling some of the sachets. At first it was just to fill my time, and then when I realized that with a little more effort the business's profits could help support my parents, I worked at making it grow. Everything was going great. Business was booming. Is booming. And then Martin came home and said he wanted me to sell out and move here. He didn't seem to—" With a start, she realized she was giving away far more information than she'd intended. She threw up her hands in a gesture that said she'd gotten carried away. "That's really all there is. I hope I didn't bore you."

"Your own business—in lavender, how wonderful." Clarice inhaled from the cup of tea she'd refilled. "It smells so good. Who would have thought of putting lavender into tea?"

"And scones and salads and… Lavender has many uses," Andy elaborated.

Julia sat up straight. "Well, if our goal is to help each other, I know where I can get right on it." She turned to Clarice. "You have to write down all you know about this Gregor jerk."

"We can find out from Roger what he's learned, if anything." Hope ran her tongue over her bottom lip. "I wonder if he fleeced any other women."

Julia wrapped her hands around one knee. "Sad thing is, too many women are so ashamed that they never tell the police. But let me check with some of my colleagues. We'll see."

"What about your granddaughter?" Clarice asked. "What's her name?"

"Cyndy. Roger has his contacts out looking for her. If something doesn't break in the next few weeks…"

Hope reached over and touched her arm. "It will. Have faith." She switched her gaze to Andy. "What about you, Andy?" Hope shifted in the sofa corner, her hand going to her middle. "What can we do to help you?"

Andy shrugged. "I don't know that I need any help, unless you want to help me paint my kitchen cabinet doors." Even as she laughed, she wished she had the nerve to ask them advice on how to handle a jealous and selfish husband. Out of the corner of her eye she saw Hope shift in her chair. She looked very uncomfortable. "Are you all right?"

"I need to get up and move, that's all." She stood behind her chair and stretched. "I have plenty I need help with. We need supplies for Julia's training classes and clothes for the girls who are going out on job interviews. The only way I know how to get the things we need is to solicit small businesses and corporate sponsors."

"Can one person do it, or do you need a committee?" Clarice asked, leaning forward.

Andy hung back. She'd solicited businesses before, when the kids were in school, so she knew how to go about it, but she didn't want to commit herself. She had all she could handle with getting her new house in order, not to mention Lavender Meadows. She just didn't have time to volunteer.

"I can help with that," Clarice volunteered.

"Great." Hope looked pleased. "Okay, now the big problem. J House needs retrofitting. We're looking at several hundred thousand dollars. We need to find a person or a corporation who needs a big tax write-off. Any ideas?" Blank looks all around. "That's what I was afraid of. Let's close with prayer now." Hope sank back in her chair, frown lines deepening in her forehead. "Father, You know our needs. We thank You for bringing us together with all our different gifts and lives. We are sisters in Your kingdom. Now help us to become sisters under the skin too." She twisted and groaned. "Amen."

"What is it?" Andy asked immediately.

"Cramps. Like premenstrual."

"Let's get you to bed and your feet up on pillows. What's the number of your doctor?" Andy took charge without a thought. *Lord, please don't let her lose this baby.*

Chapter Twenty-Five

Hope

Lord God, please don't let me lose this baby. Please. Jesus, Rapha, Healer, You said, "By My stripes you are healed." I claim that right now for this tiny baby in me. All the while Hope's mind pounded out the prayer, she watched the women care for her. Celia's fingers shook as she dialed the doctor, and Andy talked to her, Andy because she'd almost lost a baby once. Julia propped Hope's feet up while Clarice laid a cool cloth on her head and stroked her belly, all the while humming a novena. Hope knew it was a prayer, and she needed all she could get.

"Dr. Cheong says stay down and see if this goes away on its own. She called in a prescription, so Roger can go get it. She wants to know if there has been any spotting." Andy's voice radiated peace.

"Not that I know of."

"Easy, dear heart, relax, and let the worry go." Clarice's singsong soothed them all. "This baby is so precious."

"Ask her if a heating pad would help."

"Whatever you can do to relax those muscles." Andy relayed the messages.

"Ask Celia. She'll know where one is."

"Scoot down on the bed, and let me take the pillows away." Clarice motioned as she spoke.

"Why?" Julia stared at her like she might be crazy. "I think we should call an ambulance."

"I learned how to make my Herbert's back relax." When Hope had wiggled down, Clarice climbed up on the bed, kneeling at Hope's head. Digging, pushing, stroking, she hummed along, eyes closed.

"Better, Hope?" Andy had hung up the phone.

"Yes. This woman has healing in her hands, for sure."

"My Herbert called it love. Andy, you could massage her hands and Julia her feet, or vice versa. Use lotion, it will feel better."

"How'd you learn all this?" Andy sat down on the bed and, picking up one hand, stroked the back.

"Have you ever had a massage?"

"No, but who doesn't love a back rub?"

"This is more than that. It helps the circulation too. My Herbert would sleep like a baby after I worked all the kinks and knots loose."

"Herbert was one lucky man, is all I can say." Hope sounded half asleep.

"Are you better?"

"Uh-huh, more like a dull throb now. Never did like cramps and have had them most of my life."

"Here, Andy, let me show you how to really do that." Clarice settled Hope's head back on a pillow. "Sorry, but my legs were cramping so bad, I was about to scream." Clarice winced and groaned as she put her weight on her feet. "Now, like this." Using her thumb she rubbed along the bones in the back of the hand, dug in around the thumb, and used her thumb and first two fingers to stroke out each finger. She drew circles in the palm of the hand with her knuckles and then, cupping Hope's hand between her own two, just held it upright, the elbow on the sheet.

"Ah, I feel that through my whole body. What did you do?" Hope struggled to stay with them but let herself float instead.

"Just held your hand. Works with feet too."

"Clarice, don't you dare think of going anywhere else, at least until after this baby is born." Hope sighed, a long sigh that released every muscle and tendon. "God bless you all, dear sisters. I had no idea I'd be the one needing help—immediately."

"You want us to leave so you can sleep?" Andy asked. She patted Clarice's shoulder. "You ought to go into business."

"I don't think I have ever felt so loved and cared for in my entire life. I need to learn this so I can help Roger."

"Help Roger do what?" He stood in the door, staring from one woman to another. "What happened?"

"She cramped. The doctor called in a prescription, just in case. Right now she seems to have relaxed, but you might want to get the medication anyway." Andy continued with Hope's other hand.

Roger knelt beside the bed and stroked Hope's hair back from her forehead. "Are you telling me the truth?"

"I'm not quite all right, but much better."

"I'll have my cell phone on. Call me if you need me." He kissed her and stood. "If I'm ever in trouble, I'm calling the Girl Squad."

"Old girl, but…" Clarice glanced across the bed at Julia.

"But not too old to be…" She glanced to Andy.

"Ah, useful, effective…I'm stymied."

"I know, pure gold." Hope smiled while the others chuckled.

Celia appeared in the door. "Phone call from Peter Kent, the lawyer dude."

"Switch it in here," Hope whispered.

"No such thing. Mr. Roger, you take it," Celia said, her face stern.

"Right." He followed her out. "The Girl Squad, not too old to be pure gold. I think we got something there."

"I know we've all been praying in our heads, but Jesus said when two or three agree, He'd be right there in the middle. You think we can do that?" Andy looked to each of them. "I mean, not everyone has to pray aloud, if they don't want to."

"Sounds good. You lead it." Hope's murmur sounded as though she was tilting on the cliff of sleep.

"Okay." Andy took a deep breath. "Heavenly Father, I can't tell You how much this frightened all of us, but You know we want Hope and Roger to have this baby, and we know You do too. You promised to answer when we pray; You promised to be right here. Please send comfort and peace to Hope. Thank you for Clarice with her special gift that she shared with us. Thank you for bringing us together." She stopped to let someone else pray. The quiet in the room hung whisper soft.

Julia opened up. "I pray for Cyndy, dear Lord. Please protect her along with this baby."

Hope's voice was low when it was her turn. "Thank you for giving me these women right when I needed them. Big Dad, You do provide for our needs, we see that day by day, minute by minute. Thank You."

"Amen," the women said in unison, then kept silent.

After a bit, Clarice opened her eyes and glanced down at Hope. "Thank You, Lord." Her whisper caught the others' attention.

Hope lay sleeping, a tiny smile curving the sides of her mouth.

They filed out. The smell of tomato sauce floated down the hall.

"Spaghetti for lunch," Clarice said. "I started the sauce early this morning." She shook her head. "I'm not used to cooking for more than one or two, so who knows how it will turn out?"

In the kitchen, Julia switched to her attorney mode. "Clarice, I've been wanting to ask you some more questions. Would you mind?"

"No, not at all. I hope I know the answers."

"Do you need to help serve?"

"No, someone is assigned to that. Celia takes care of all the scheduling. We mostly have day-school children, a couple street people, the girls who don't have regular jobs or school, not a big bunch. You could all stay if you like."

"I need to get home, but I want to make sure Hope is all right." Andy paused and sniffed. "That sure smells good."

"Come on, let's sit in here for a minute." Clarice opened the door to the common room, where their snack things were still set up. "Okay, ask away, Ms. Lawyer."

"Do you know what Roger found out about your husband?"

"If you mean Gregor, I don't consider him my husband."

"But he is, if you had a bona fide wedding, with a minister or judge."

"He was a judge. Gregor said he'd been divorced once, so our priest wouldn't marry us. I have the certificate, er, I had it, in my safe-deposit box. When I emptied it, I put the papers in the locked drawer of my desk, and who knows where that is."

"No problem, we can get a copy from the county. Now, what did Roger find out?"

"That Gregor is not his real name." Clarice stared at the fake rings on her fingers.

"How many names did he find?"

A small shrug. "Two or three." Clarice wished she could disappear into the seat or under the rug. *How could I have been so gullible?*

"I'll talk with him and see if we can find more." Julia patted Clarice's hand. "I used to locate deadbeat dads. This guy hasn't got a chance. What about your mail?"

My mail. Of course. I-yi-yi, how dumb can I be? "I filled out a card to forward it to The Frederick. But since I don't live there…" Her shrug this time involved her whole body. "How could I have been so stupid?"

"Okay, no more of that!" Julia leaned close enough that Clarice could feel her breath. "You made some mistakes…"

"Yeah, threw away all Herbert's hard work. Oh, my poor Herbert, he must be so disappointed in me." She put her hands over her face and rocked back and forth. "I have nothing."

Julia gently pulled Clarice's hands away. "From all the things I know, I'm almost positive there is money for you somewhere. We'll find it, and we'll find that scumbag, too."

"Maybe you can keep him from doing this again." Perhaps there was hope after all.

"First let's see if we can find your mail. Let's call the manager of The Frederick and see if any mail has come for you. If not, then you give me more information, and I'll start a paper trail. Amazing the things one can find out from paper trails."

Clarice looked to Andy. "She's one smart customer, that one."

Andy nodded. "Glad I'm not some deadbeat dad. Or Gregor. I think he's going to get his comeuppance this time. He messed with the Girl Squad."

Clarice giggled. "I know I could have called my sister in Jersey, but she'd just say, 'I told you so.' She did, too many times, but I wouldn't listen." She put her hands over her ears. "I hate I-told-you-sos, and I could never lie to her." Her shoulders sagged along with her face, aging her ten years.

"What about your sister—your friends in Miami?"

"What can they do? What's gone is gone." She scowled. "I hate to say that I doubt they'd help me. Most of them were so jealous of my handsome young husband that they'd probably see this as my just deserts."

"Any other family?"

"All dead but a few nieces and nephews. They have their own lives. They don't want no old woman in their spare room." Clarice leaned forward. "Here I feel needed. More needed than since Herbert died. I want to help here as long as I can. If I can get the money for a little house or an apartment, that would be all I need. So I don't take a bed here that could be used for someone who really needs the help."

"From what I hear, you've been a mighty big help." Julia paused, and her eyes brightened. "How old did you say you are?"

"Sixty-seven."

"Are you getting Social Security?"

Clarice nodded. "I was. Gregor had it sent it straight to our savings account."

"Good. A place to start. We'll find out where it's going." She pushed paper and pen across the table. "Write down your Social Security number."

Celia stopped in the doorway. "Lunch is served. Come and get it while it's hot."

"I should get home," Andy said.

"Why? Painting cabinet doors can always wait. We've got to work on getting the money to retrofit this place." Clarice leaned close to Andy so she could whisper. "So much good they do, and so little money. They really need our help. What if they close this place?"

Chapter Twenty-Six

Andy

Four cabinet doors wasn't bad. Andy held her paintbrush back as she admired her handiwork. Like Shari said: I am woman.

The ringing phone jerked her attention from the cabinets to the window. It was dusk. Martin would be home soon.

She picked up the receiver. "Hello."

"Hi honey. Have you started dinner?"

"No. I got involved in painting and forgot all about it. Any preference for order in?"

"That's why I'm calling. I'm going to be stuck here for a while longer, and if I can't get this snag worked out, I'm going to have to fly to St. Louis in the morning."

She sighed heavily. "How long will you be gone?" Fluffy sat watching her from his Harley chair.

"Two or three days."

She started to clean up her mess, her mind running ahead of itself. "I thought you weren't going to travel anymore." *Here we go again. The honeymoon is over.*

A hint of steel entered Martin's voice. "I told you how things would be. I'll do my best to work things out, but if I can't, I can't." There was a short pause. "Andy, could you iron up a few shirts for me? I forgot to send them out."

"You don't like the way I do your shirts, remember? Besides, I've got to find a place to board Fluffy, since I'll be flying out about the same time you are." At his silence, she said, "I've already overstayed my time here this month. I need to get back and help get some orders out." *Andy Taylor, you're just playing get-even here. I'm surprised at you.*

In fact, her mom and Shari had both encouraged her to stay over a few extra days and get the new house in order. Everything was fine there, and while the orders were steadily coming in, they were also steadily being fulfilled and shipped out. All she could do was say okay, which was what she'd really wanted to say, especially with things going so well between her and Martin. And now there was the matter of Hope. She hated to leave, just in case Hope needed her for anything.

Funny how some people become friends faster than others.

"Why don't you pack them dirty and have the hotel where you're staying send them out?"

"Andy, just please do this for me. I'm up to my eyeballs here, and I can't think about the incidentals."

"Sorry, I just don't have time."

She listened for the click that said he hung up and realized he already had when the woman's voice said, "If you would like to—" Andy hung up the phone and glared at it.

What was it he'd said when they'd talked about his new job? That others would be doing what he used to do? So where were the others? Why couldn't he have sent one of them? Because Mr. Perfection believed no one could do the job as well as he could.

Andy gathered her painting gear together, all the while fighting guilt. *What kind of wife are you, who won't do up a couple of shirts for her husband when he's in a pinch? A wife who has been taken advantage of too long and whose husband is jealous of her business. That's who.*

She looked around the kitchen. She hated to leave her project half done, but she wanted to put Martin on notice that she wasn't going to stick around if he wasn't. Too bad Fluffy had to suffer in the bargain, but she was sure she would be able to find a boarding facility that would take him.

A half hour later the only evidence of her day's painting was the smell and the missing cabinet doors. She went downstairs to the spare room that she'd halfheartedly set up as her office. One thing about San Francisco that she did like was that she could pick up the phone and order anything. She could even have it delivered. Yesterday morning she'd called a computer store, asked a few questions, given them her credit card number, and a few hours later, a computer tech was at her door with a new laptop and a portable-size printer. Within a couple of hours, everything she needed was installed, and she was ready to go.

She sat down at her makeshift desk, an old vanity table that had been in Morgan's room, and booked a midmorning flight. Then she did a search for boarding facilities and found one just a few blocks away called the Pampered Pet. Pick up and delivery, the ad said.

Next, she accessed her e-mail. Her in-box was suffering overload. "Sheesh, I only skipped one week." She glanced at the dates on the messages. Fluffy hopped up on the desk, and after sniffing her chin, he curled up next to the keyboard in the pool of light from the gooseneck lamp. He liked the heat from the lamp, just like Chai Lai.

Andy clicked on the latest from Bria, <MOM, WHERE ARE YOU?> titled in caps, the equivalent of shouting online.

<I'm heading out of town on business, and I haven't heard from you in two days. Neither has Morgan or my dear brother, who says you are busy and not to worry. Now, who does that sound like? Like father, like son? However, if I don't hear from you tonight, I'll be on the phone, and you can guess it will be early, as I have a 6:00 a.m. flight.>

<Talk about like father, like daughter. Who's the parent here after all?>

Fluffy opened his eyes and made a gargling sound.

<Sorry,> she typed, <I've been painting kitchen cabinets and...>
She glanced at Fluffy and thought Bria would enjoy hearing all about
him. She hoped she could do justice to Martin's reaction to Fluffy. If
only she were a writer! She ended the lengthy e-mail by giving her a
blow-by-blow of J House, the tea/coffee she'd attended, and Hope's
baby. <I'm considering doing a little volunteer work at J House when
I'm in town,> she wrote, then stared at what she'd written in shock.
Where had that come from? She started to delete the line, but something told her not to. What would it hurt to give a few hours of her
time when she was in town and Martin was at work? They could use
her. Maybe she could be instrumental in finding a corporate sponsor
to retrofit J House. She could pick Martin's brain for ideas, that is,
when they were talking again.

<Blessings on your trip,> she typed. <I'm praying for you. Love,
Mom.>

Andy clicked Save Draft, Send, and then opened the message
again, made changes so that it would be personal to Camden, and
then repeated the process one more time for Morgan. If she'd blind-
copied the other two, they would have been offended. Ah, the games
a mother must play, on e-mail, no less.

She sent business messages into the files designated for them and
ignored the rest of the messages, promising herself more time online
when she got home. She clicked off before any of her children could
respond. She had a lot to do to get ready and didn't want to answer a
bunch of family questions.

Martin still hadn't come home by bedtime, and her eyes were no
longer focusing on the book she was reading. She closed the book
with a snap, set it on the table next to the bed, and turned out the
light. "Good night, Fluffy." She heard the cat purring from his bed on
the floor.

Martin arrived home sometime after midnight, packed, and climbed into bed. He was up at five, and while she might have enjoyed another hour's sleep, she decided to give him a wifely send-off by fixing him a nice breakfast.

He looked tired, but who wouldn't be with only four hours' sleep? She couldn't imagine that he really enjoyed traveling from city to city. He'd told her in the past that he never saw anything besides the airport, the hotel, the coffee shop, and the office. He read his reports in the cab on the way to wherever he was going, and it was dark by the time he got back to the hotel.

Years ago Andy had struggled with the fear that her husband might be unfaithful and that was the reason for all his traveling, but there had never been any hint or sign of impropriety on his part. His mistress was his work, and how could she ever fight against that?

Andy stared out at the Bay when she'd finished the dishes. The rising sun kissed the spires of the Golden Gate Bridge, tinting them gold. Another beautiful day on the Bay. She was sorry to miss it. It was raining in Medford, according to her weather check.

She looked up at the clock, and at the same time a horn beeped. "There's your cab," she said.

Martin took a last sip of coffee, got up, and bussed her lightly on the lips. "I'm sorry. I really am. I love you, Andy."

She smiled and kissed him back. "I love you too. Have a safe trip." She followed him to the door. "Fluffy is going to the Pampered Pet. I'll leave you the number to call when you get back. They'll deliver him." The phone rang behind her. She waved him off and went back to the kitchen.

"Hi Andy, this is Clarice."

"Hi, how are you? You sound stuffed up."

"Roger just took Hope to the hospital in an ambulance." Clarice sniffed again.

"Oh, dear God, help. Do you think she'll be all right? What can I do?"

"Other than pray, nothing at the moment." Clarice blew her nose. "Pardon me." Her voice wore the sheen of tears. "She was bleeding pretty heavy."

"Are you going to the hospital?"

"No, I'm needed here."

"I'll be there in an hour. Maybe I can do something to help you." Andy hung up, closed her eyes, and prayed harder than she had ever prayed in her life. Then she called and cancelled Fluffy's pickup and her flight. *Lord, save that baby, please, please.*

Chapter Twenty-Seven

Hope

"Hang in there, honey." Roger gripped her hand. The paramedics had tried to keep him from riding in the ambulance, but he'd forced his way in.

"The baby—I don't want to lose the baby."

"I know." His eyes told her he was scared too.

Hope felt his tears wet her hand. An IV drip had been started, and a blood pressure cuff squeezed her arm.

"You're going to be all right." The young female EMT smiled at her with reassuring calm.

"It's the baby I'm worried about," Hope said back to her.

"How far along are you?"

"The sonogram showed about three months."

"And that was when?"

"Just last week."

"Are you in any pain?"

"No. The cramping has stopped." She clung to her husband's hand. "Does that mean the baby is gone?"

"No, not necessarily."

Hope covered her abdomen with her free hand. "Please, baby, want to live." The siren bleeped as they pulled to a stop. Hope could see the emergency signs out the window.

"Okay now, we're going to take you in," the EMT said. "Mr. Benson, you can carry the IV bag. Keep it a couple feet or so above her."

The doors swung open, and away they went. Hope saw doorways, walls, and the ceiling whiz by; the wheels of the gurney clattered; and Roger kept reminding her to hang in there.

It's not me I'm worried about. Please, God, please.

They stopped. "I'm sorry, but you can't go any farther." The woman's sharp voice penetrated the fog Hope floated in.

Roger didn't argue. Hope looked up to see him hand over the IV bag, and then he bent over her.

"I love you, Hope Benson. You are more important to me than anyone or anything on this earth." He kissed her quickly, and then the gurney whipped through the open doors.

She must have answered questions, but later she didn't remember what they'd been. The next time she came fully awake, she was in a regular hospital room, and Roger was sitting in a chair beside the bed, holding her hand.

"Hey there," he said softly as if they were in church.

"The baby?" she asked, her anxiousness making her sound almost breathless.

He beamed at her, his laugh lines deepening to furrows. "He or she is doing just fine. It must be a tough little kid to cling so hard to life. I think the doctors were surprised too."

Hope let out a long sigh, and tears welled in her eyes. She had never been so scared in all her life. "Thank You, Jesus," she said, looking up at the ceiling. "Thank You for answering my prayer." She moved her gaze to the right and saw both an IV and a bag of plasma hanging on the pole. "I lost a lot of blood?"

"Not as much as you'd think, but they didn't want to take any chances."

"So when can I go home?"

"When they say so," he said, his expression telling her that this time she wasn't the one in charge. "For now, you're going to stay flat on your back."

Only then did she realize she didn't have a pillow. She'd heard of this kind of situation before, when a woman in jeopardy of losing a baby spent weeks, sometimes months in bed, flat on her back. "How long?" she asked, thinking about all the things she had to do, things that wouldn't get done if she didn't do them.

"I don't know, and neither do they. I guess it all depends on what your body does and what that little one needs."

"Worst case?"

"Until the baby is term. Every day in utero after six months is a gift to that child."

"I see." Hope took a breath, then let it out slowly. After the third time, she still felt like she couldn't get enough air. *Deep breaths, don't hyperventilate. Oh, Lord, this will not be easy.* She who rarely sat still. "How will we manage?"

Roger smiled at her. "God knows what's going on. He's not going to leave us to wander this alone. Where's your faith, Pastor Benson?"

"I guess it slipped a notch, but it's back in place now." She smiled back at him. "Maybe we could call on the Girl Squad?" For some reason, she already felt closer to those three women than to other women she'd known for years.

"If it is the worse case, maybe we can move a couch or daybed or something into your office. That way you won't worry yourself into a frazzle wondering what's going on out in the main rooms. We can get you a bell, and you can ring it whenever you need something." He started to laugh.

"Funny. Very funny." But in truth, she was glad for his humor.

A knock on the door caught their attention, and Roger called, "Come in."

Clarice peeked around the door. "The nurse said you could have visitors."

Roger waved her in. "How'd you get here?" He stood to let her have his chair.

"I brought her." Andy came in right behind. "And let me tell you, we had us quite a little adventure. I need to learn the streets of this city. We accidentally turned on a one-way street and almost got clobbered by a streetcar." She stopped at the foot of the bed and swapped a look with Clarice.

"The baby is fine," Hope said, knowing they were trying not to act worried. "Thanks be to God."

"Yes, thank You, God." Andy moved to the side of the bed and stroked Hope's tube-cluttered arm. "I was getting ready to fly back to Medford this morning, but when Clarice called… Anyway, I rushed over to J House and saw that Celia had everything under control, so we came here. Celia sends her love, by the way. She said to tell you"— she glanced at Roger—"that you don't have your cell phone on, or you forgot it."

He grabbed the phone off his belt. "The battery is dead."

Hope shook her head. "Not that you could have had it on in here anyway. But…"

"Well, no one reminded me to plug it in. A guy can't remember everything."

Hope rolled her eyes.

A nurse strolled into the room. "Okay, everybody. Vamoose! I gotta check this woman."

"But I'm her husband."

The nurse waved them all away like a flock of chickens. "I don't care if you're Antonio Banderas. Out! I won't be long, and then you can all come back."

Hope mimicked the nurse's gesture with her free hand, her grin reminding him to just do as he was told. Not that he'd ever been very good at that.

As soon as they left, the nurse asked, "*¿Cómo se siente?* I'm Maria, by the way. I'm going to be watching over you while you're visiting us."

Hope was intrigued by the nurse's personality. This was a woman who was comfortable in her own skin. "A little weak, but okay."

"You gave everyone a scare, huh?"

"Not on purpose." She waited while the nurse checked her over. "I'm kind of woozy."

"The medication is causing some of that. The more you relax, the easier on the baby."

"What caused— I mean, what did I do to cause…?"

Maria shrugged. "Probably nothing. Sometimes things like this just happen. It may sound harsh, but God knows what He's doing. If He wants you to have a baby, He'll make sure you'll have that baby. If He doesn't…" She shrugged, then wrote something down on the chart.

"My husband and I—we've been praying for a miracle for eight years. I was told I would never have a baby."

"So God answered you. Now you have to do all you can to keep the baby. And it looks like bed rest, at least for a couple of weeks."

"And then?"

"And then we see. You're that woman pastor over at J House, aren't you?"

"Yes. Why?"

"Oh, you made a big difference in the life of a friend of mine. Remember a girl named Juanita Alvarez?"

"Of course. How is she?"

"Second year of nursing school."

"Oh, wow. I knew she had it in her."

"You saved her life."

Hope remembered they'd gotten Juanita clean and sober and helped her dream again. When she was ready, they sent her to stay with some friends of theirs, who frequently took in girls needing a safe place, away from their usual environment. Juanita had struggled with school, but with their encouragement, she'd stuck to it.

"Thank you. I needed to be reminded of that right now."

The nurse took her hand. "Listen, hon, I won't pull any punches. This isn't going to be easy, with you being such an active person and all. But six months isn't forever, so keep your eye on your goal: a healthy baby. Meanwhile, you can catch up on your reading and play on the computer. You can even continue your counseling, as long as you do it from your bed and you don't get stressed."

Hope stared up at the ceiling. Flat on her back was coming to mean a whole new reality.

Roger returned seconds after the nurse left.

"What did she say?" He held a single peach rose and some baby's-breath in a bud vase with a sunset ribbon tied in a bow. He set it on her tray. "This is to remind you that life is beautiful, no matter what." He leaned over the bed rail and kissed her. "And that I always love you."

Tears brimmed again. "Oh, Roger, you shouldn't have."

"Too bad. I had to do something."

Clarice and Andy hesitated at the door. "If you two want to be alone…," Andy said.

"No, come in." Hope waved them in with her free hand. "Pull up some chairs, and let's do some thinking." *Relax.* She held a breath and breathed out slowly, concentrating on relaxing, her shoulders especially. Only when she did that did she realize she wore her shoulders hunched up to her ears much of the time.

"Okay." Clarice had taken a notepad and pen out of her purse. "I'm ready."

Hope rattled off the things that needed immediate attention. "And tell Celia"—she shook her head—"no, Roger, you tell Celia to please cooperate with Clarice, okay? That I need her now more than ever, and that as far as I'm concerned she is and always will be my executive assistant." She turned back to Clarice. "I know you know what the problem is. Celia is jealous of you and how capable you are. All her life people have told her she would never amount to anything, and so she had incredibly low self-esteem. And she's insecure."

"Boy, after what I've been through lately, I can relate," Clarice said.

"Then please, do whatever you have to do to work with her. Be careful what you say, and respect her space. Just remember that she feels threatened by you."

"I have been working on it, but I'll work even harder. I like Celia, and she's good at what she does."

"Yes, she is."

Maria knocked and entered. "Okay, boys and girls, time to go home. Our patient needs some sleep, and it's hard enough to get it here."

Clarice stuffed her paper and pen back in her purse.

Andy stood. "Ever obedient. Later today, if you can call me and tell me what you need, I'll get it together. Here's my phone number." She laid a card on the table. "I'll call Julia as soon as I get back." She patted Hope's hand. "I'll be praying."

When she stepped back, Clarice did the same. She waggled her fingers. "Tomorrow, if Nurse Ratched"—she whispered the name—"will let me, I'll massage your shoulders."

Hope grinned at the reference to Nurse Ratched. "I'll look forward to it. You are an angel unawares."

They all waved as they went out the door. Hope sniffed and wiped under her eyes with her fingertips. To think, three weeks ago she didn't know those women. Another one of those prayers God answers before you think to ask. *How would I have known to even ask for such friends? I thought my life was pretty full.*

I will never leave you nor forsake you. The promise came clear, as if someone had spoken from the head of her bed. Peace like the softest of airy blankets kissed her face and warmed her heart.

Hope woke to the sound of nurse's shoes squeaking down the hall. She'd been vaguely aware of blood pressure checks during the night but never fully roused. *Thank You, thank You, Father for sleep and safety.* She laid her right hand over her belly. *Bless you, little one, so strong and brave. Tenacious you are.* She let her mind float, thinking of a name good enough for this little life. *Boy or girl, we need a name for each. Esther? Joshua? Ruth? David?* She played through names she knew. Had Roger given any thought to a name yet?

A nurse stopped in the doorway. "You're awake."

"Yes. Am I allowed up for the bathroom?"

"No, sorry. I know the bedpan is uncomfortable, but…"

"Don't worry. I'll do whatever I have to do."

Once she'd washed her face and brushed her teeth, she felt better, and with the head of the bed cranked up a little, she saw the rose Roger had brought her. *Oh, Lord, how blessed I am with that man.* Seven thirty, time to call him. She dialed their private number and counted the rings. Three, four… *Come on, please don't be in the shower.* Five… The answering machine came on. She hung up, disappointment pulling at her mouth.

The door opened.

"Hey, beautiful, how's my favorite woman?"

"Better be your only woman," she said sternly. She reached for him. "I called, and you didn't answer."

"How could I? I wasn't there." He leaned over the railing and gave her the kind of kiss that she hoped never quit curling her toes.

"I missed you."

"No, you didn't, you slept all night."

"How do you know?"

"Nurse Maria said so, at eleven and three and six. We've gotten to be good friends."

"Oh, you." She stopped. "You didn't really call all those times?"

"Of course I did."

"Did you ever sleep?" She checked his eyes to see if they were bloodshot or had dark circles. "You look pretty good."

"You look wonderful. There's some color back in your cheeks."

"Roger, there's always color in my cheeks."

"Not last night, there wasn't." He set the bag he'd brought on her bed. "Here're some things I thought you'd need, and a few of Celia's 'must haves.' "

"Uh-oh. Dare I look?"

"Breakfast." The aide stopped at the foot of the bed. "Hi there, Miss Hope, remember me?" She set the tray on the bed table.

Hope eyed the young woman. "You sure look familiar. Refresh my memory."

"That's 'cause I look a lot like my sister, my older sister, Shelby. Shelby Clark?"

Hope tapped into her mental computer. "Runaway. Long time ago. How's she doing?"

"It's been rough, but once she got rid of that good-for-nothing husband of hers, she got back on track and married a real good guy. They have the cutest little boy. He's my man." She adjusted the bed table and pushed it into position. "I promised myself I was never going to mess up like she did." She turned to Roger. "After you told her that no man ever had a right to beat on a woman, she filed for divorce."

Hope eyed her breakfast tray. "Would that all our girls turned out like Shelby." She was starved. The cup of decaf coffee looked more like tea, but at least it smelled right. She handed it to Roger. "Here, you drink this. Next baby, you get to be pregnant, and I get to drink the coffee."

The aide left the room laughing.

"Celia is coming by to do your hair, and Clarice will man—or woman—the desk. Julia's first class is tonight, and she'll be by some-time this afternoon. Has the doctor been here yet?"

"Nope." Hope downed her orange juice. "Did Peter call?"

Roger nodded. "He said he called Blakely Associates and told them we weren't interested and to stop soliciting us."

"Something tells me they won't give up, that they'll do whatever they have to do to push us into a corner." She wondered if she should tell Roger what she'd been thinking. She didn't want to alarm him. He had enough on his plate right now. Still… "I know this probably could sound like I'm overreacting, but did you wonder if that drug tip last Sunday might have come from them?"

"It crossed my mind," he said, grimacing as he sipped the coffee. "Whoa! That's gotta be the worst coffee I ever tasted." He shook him-self all over like a wet dog. "I don't want you worrying about them. I've got some of my buddies checking them out."

"Anything new for Clarice?"

"Negative. Are you going to eat that toast and egg?"

Hope shook her head. "I'm good with the juice and the bacon." How come this morning bacon sounded good, and others it had sent her to the bathroom? She nibbled the crisp strip carefully. Nope, no problem.

Roger cleaned her plate and spread jam on the second piece of toast. "Sure you don't want this?"

"Mister Roger, why you eatin' all her breakfast?" Celia strode through the doorway, beauty case in hand.

"Because I'm hungry, and my mother told me to never waste food, to think of all the starving children in the world."

"Hey, Celia. Who's minding the store?" Hope smiled. She loved Celia like the sister she had never had. No one had a bigger heart than Celia.

"I got Clarice fillin' in. By the time I get back, she'll probably have scrubbed all the walls and sewed new curtains." She kept a straight face. "I woulda been here sooner, but..." She held up a square box.

Hope inhaled the heavenly fragrance of fresh doughnuts. *Thank You, God. Now, make them Krispy Kreme.*

"There better be enough in there for me, or it's contraband." Dr. Cheong eyed the box as she came through the door.

"I got a dozen just in case I had to bribe the guard." Celia set the box down and opened the lid. "Got napkins, too."

Hope all but groaned as the smell of sugarcoated raised doughnuts found its way to her nose. "Me first," she said, reaching out her hand.

"Who said you could have doughnuts, missy?" Dr. Cheong asked.

Hope's hand stopped midway to her mouth. "Tell me you're kidding."

Dr. Cheong started to reach for the doughnut, then stopped. "Okay, I'm kidding."

Chapter Twenty-Eight

Andy

Andy checked the messages on her cell phone. When she saw one from Martin, she pushed the button and listened. "I'll be back in San Francisco Monday morning. I'm really sorry I had to leave, but I don't have anyone trained yet. I'll hang the cabinet doors when I get home. Have a good weekend. Love you, Martin."

Ordinarily, she would have been tempted to throw the phone across the room, but not this Friday morning. She had been doing a lot of praying lately, for Hope, Hope's baby, J House, the Girl Squad, and for herself and Martin. One of the many things she realized was that if she wanted to save her marriage, she would need to try harder to understand what was going on with Martin.

Something had sparked when Hope told Clarice to tread carefully with Celia. Like Celia, Martin had a serious case of low self-esteem. Early in their marriage, he'd told her that his parents were losers, and that he'd struggled to make something of himself so he wouldn't end up like them. On the Internet, she'd read that low self-esteem often translated into insecurity, and that insecurity could result in jealousy. Even of his wife's business? The thought still made Andy shake her head, and yet…

On the other hand, it was hard to think of Martin as feeling inse-cure. He always exuded such confidence in everything he did. In fact, it was Martin's confidence and perseverance that had inspired her to take Lavender Meadows to the next level—from retail to wholesale.

Her Google search pulled up a lot of different possibilities for Martin's jealousy, but it was how to deal with it that remained the mystery. Obviously, more research would be necessary, more prayer, and back to her Bible. *If you believe that answers to all life's problems are in there, then you better go searching,* she reminded herself.

Long time ago she'd learned to pray first and read second, especially when she wasn't sure where to look. "Father, You know I am searching how to help Martin the most. Where should I look? Please speak to me through Your word; You promised You would." She caught herself in a sigh. Sometimes the unknown could sure seem insurmountable. "I'll give You all the praise and glory, amen."

First she reviewed the concordance for the word *jealousy,* but all the Old Testament strictures didn't seem to apply in this case. After all, neither of them had been unfaithful. Flipping through the New Testament, red words caught her attention: *"that you love one another."* Jesus had said that more than once. *But I do love him. That's not the issue here.* Another line floated through her mind: *"the greatest of these is love."*

"Okay, I know You're trying to tell me something here, but this is not new stuff. I'm looking for a solution to Martin's jealousy of my business here." She closed her eyes and let her mind float. *Symptoms.* She wrote the word on the pad in front of her and opened her eyes to stare at it. She boxed it in with pencil lines. Was jealousy a symptom? And if so, of what? Of his insecurity, of course. And that could be helped by... She waited again. *Love.* Of course.

But I've always loved him. Doesn't he know that? She huffed out a breath and dragged frustrated fingers through her hair.

This would be easier to figure out if I were home. I could ask our pastor, or my mother. She's wise. But she couldn't call them, not after ten at night. Sane people went to sleep instead of driving themselves nuts with hard questions. *If you want to know about love, go to the love chapter.* She turned to 1 Corinthians 13 and read it through once to herself, then aloud. "Love suffers long and is kind; love does not envy; love does not parade itself, is not puffed up; does not behave rudely, does not seek its own, is not provoked, thinks no evil;…bears all things, believes all things, hopes all things, endures all things." Tears burned her throat, making reading aloud impossible. *I haven't done this, have I, Lord?* She knew this was not a question but a confession.

"Please show me how to love this man in a way he can understand." She remembered something she once heard a speaker say. *You cannot change another; you can only change yourself. You must let God change the other person.*

She stayed up until the wee hours to finish painting the second coat on all the cabinet doors, trying in ways to show Martin how much she loved him. After all, there was no sense trying to sleep when her mind was going two hundred miles an hour. Saturday, she needed to be at the market by 7:00 a.m., not to sell her products as she'd originally intended, but to help out. She'd promised Hope.

Fluffy looked up from his Harley chair, evidently his favorite, since he spent most of his time in it. His low meow sounded more like a question than an answer. "What?" she asked as if the cat could really tell her. "I know you're not hungry, and I know—" The cat looked at her and blinked. "You miss Mrs. Getz, don't you?" For the first time since Fluffy had been delivered, she realized that he might be missing the love and affection the older woman had lavished on him. "I'm sorry, Fluffy," she said, walking over to him, then bending to pick him up. "I never even gave a thought to what you might be feeling. Poor kitty." Fluffy lifted his paw and touched her face—just the way Chai Lai did. "Oh, aren't you sweet?" She cradled the eighteen-pounder in her arms like a baby.

Fluffy was just one of several surprises that had come her way in recent weeks. She would never forget coming back to San Francisco and listening to Martin giving her a rundown on Fluffy's stuff—and then picking the cat up and holding him, like she was holding him now. That was definitely a side of Martin she had never seen, but a side she looked forward to seeing again. This house and its spectacular view had been a surprise, a very pleasant surprise that kept her in a constant state of appreciation for sunny days that set the bay to sparkling, fog in all its facets, and sunsets that burnished both hills and steel buildings. But the best surprise of all was the Girl Squad, led by one very special girl: Hope Benson.

"Oh my gosh, I haven't called Hope yet." She scrambled to find her purse and the phone number, but when she looked at the clock, she realized it was only nine thirty, not noon as it felt to her. She dialed J House. When Clarice answered, she paused. "Hi, I was ready to talk to Celia, and here you are on the phone."

"Celia went over to the hospital. What do you need?"

"Nothing. I was just wondering how Hope is."

"Stronger today than yesterday. The doctor said she would need to stay at least three more days so they can run some tests. If everything looks good, she can go home as long as she promises to keep to her bed for another week or so."

"Oh boy. How's she going to handle that?"

"That's where we all come in. I'm spelling Celia on the front desk so she can take over some other things, especially getting ready for the market tomorrow. Roger is lining up substitute pastors and meeting with the lawyer about some offer that they received on J House. And the dishwasher is on the fritz."

Andy groaned. "Why is it mechanical things always break when there is another crisis going on?"

"Murphy's Law."

"How did Julia's class go last night?"

"Great. Let me put you on hold for a minute—another call."

Andy waited after the click and thought about how hard bed rest would be for Hope. She tucked the phone between ear and shoulder, picked up the dry cabinet doors one by one, and leaned them back against the dining room wall.

"Sorry." Clarice came back on the line. "I had to find one of the girls."

"Is there some way I can help there today?"

"Not that I know of. Celia is a wonder when it comes to dealing with the girls and the children. The truth is, she's much better at that than with filing and writing reports, the kind of thing I have no trouble with."

"So I take it you two are getting along better?"

"Much better. It was really just a matter of asking her to tell me what she wanted me to do and what she didn't want me to do. But we still have our moments."

"Call me if there is anything I can do. Otherwise, I'll get some chores done around here this morning and go to the hospital this afternoon."

"When will your husband be back?"

"He said Monday, but that could change. Martin is a workaholic. If his company has something they want him to do, he makes sure he's available to do it."

"Uh-oh. I detect a bit of anger there. Resentment, perhaps?"

Andy was momentarily taken aback by Clarice's observation. She hadn't meant to air her resentment, especially to someone she barely knew. It was too late to take her words back, but she still might be able to do a little damage control. "Let's just say I've cleaned a lot of closets over the years."

"I used to do that when I was angry too."

"From everything you've said, I thought you never got mad at Herbert."

"Of course I did. I still get mad at him, and he's dead. Men can be so pigheaded, selfish, self-absorbed, and impatient. Did I say pigheaded?"

Andy laughed. "Yes, yes, you did."

"Andy, I'm probably speaking out of school, but after what I've been through, all I can say is, be thankful you have Martin, even if sometimes you want to kill him."

Andy swallowed hard and bit back tears. "Thank you, Clarice. I am thankful for him, but lately I haven't done much to show it. I'll see you tomorrow morning, bright and early."

Andy hung up and, curling into the corner of the sofa, started her list for the morrow. *Get change for the cashbox* topped the list. Fluffy leaped up beside her and stepped into her lap. After bumping his head under Andy's chin, he turned around several times and made himself comfortable in a circle, purring loud enough to shake the seat.

"You don't make it easy for me, you know. I mean to write. You mean for me to pet you."

Andy had just finished her lists when the phone rang.

"Andy, this is Julia, and I'm calling to ask a favor."

"What can I do?"

"You know that class I'm teaching, to help prepare these young women for real jobs instead of just menial jobs?"

"Sure. I heard the first session went great."

"It was great, but what they need now are suitable clothes. I'm going to find out when some of the church women's groups meet at other congregations besides J House and see if I can get them to help us out. We need shoes, purses, everything. Clarice said she would call the corporate offices of some of the retail chain clothing stores and ask for donations of leftover sale items and returns. Some of those things might need a bit of repair."

"Is there a sewing machine at J House?"

"I'm not sure."

"I have one. It's in Medford. I could pack it up the next time I go home, which should be in a few days."

"That would be good, but hang on until after Clarice makes her calls. Meanwhile, I'm going to try to get some corporate sponsorship for the program. The more girls we can get off the dole and working, the better off we will all be. Do you know anyone who teaches ESL?"

"ESL?"

"English as a second language. That's another ministry that could flow through J House. That and literacy."

Andy could hardly keep up with all of Julia's ideas. "Are you planning on moving here so you can see all these programs through to the end?"

"I… Well, no. But I can at least get a few of them started."

"Anything new on your granddaughter?"

"No. Roger is beginning to think she's gone somewhere else, back to LA or maybe Las Vegas, since she took dance lessons for a few years."

"I'll keep praying."

"I appreciate that. If you can get to any thrift stores and you find some things, make sure you keep the receipt, in case there's money to reimburse you."

"Will do." Andy said good-bye and set the receiver in the cradle. One more thing to add to the list. In her e-mail tonight, she'd ask Bria if she had any castoffs she could send. The next time she was home, she'd go through the boxes she'd stuffed in the attic. Surely there were some usable things there.

Hope wasn't in her room when Andy reached the hospital, so she checked the nurses' station.

"She's down for a sonogram. You can wait in her room if you like. She shouldn't be long."

"Thanks." Andy settled into a chair, took out the card she'd tucked into her purse, and wrote a note.

"Hey there." Hope waved when they pushed the gurney in and transferred her back to the bed. "Thanks."

The nurse rehung the IV, checked to make sure the drips were functioning correctly, and sniffed. "Sure smells good in here. What is it?"

Andy handed Hope her card. "Lavender. I tucked a sachet into the envelope."

Hope sniffed the card and smiled. "Andy has a lavender farm in Oregon," she told the nurse. She opened the card and sniffed the sachet.

"Well, you two have a nice chat." The nurse smiled and left the room.

"So tell me everything I've missed out on."

"I doubt you've missed a thing." Andy sat back and crossed her legs. "Julia called me earlier, and we talked about getting suitable clothes for the girls in her class to wear out on job interviews. As soon as I leave here, I'm heading for a thrift shop I saw the other day."

"I want to thank you in advance for helping out tomorrow at the Saturday Market."

"My pleasure. I plan on helping out Sunday, too. But Monday I'm staying home. Martin is due back Monday morning, and we have some things to iron out."

"Workaholics aren't easy to live with. Ask Roger."

"How…how did you know?" Was the woman a mind reader?

"Just things you've said. Besides, it takes one to recognize one." She laughed.

"Actually, I'm a recovering workaholic. If Roger hadn't sat me down and talked to me, we wouldn't be together right now."

"What did he say?" Andy leaned forward.

"Well, first of all he asked if I remembered why we had gotten married. Then he asked me what I wanted out of the marriage. He told me that we had lost sight of our early goals of intimacy and shared time. He said that to him, spending time with me was more important than anything else. Now, tell me, what can you say when the man you love tells you he'd rather be with you than eat?"

Andy sat back and let her mind drift. *What would Martin say if she put those same questions to him?*

"You have to be willing to accept the consequences, Andy," Hope said, again as if reading her mind. "There are things you might have to give up, things you love. The question is, do you love those things more than Martin? I'd be willing to bet he believes that his hard work is his way of showing you his love." Hope reached for Andy's hand and squeezed it. "I'll pray for you."

Driving up the hill past J House, Andy turned into the parking lot that would house the market in the morning. She wasn't sure what had possessed her; she had plenty to do at home. She parked the car and entered the shelter through the side door, almost wishing she hadn't, when she heard the laughter and screams of the children. Whoever had built this church must be turning over in his grave at the thought of children running and shouting in what had been the sanctuary. She heard Roger cheering them on. Church on Sunday, gymnasium on the weekdays, multipurpose all the time. She waited while Celia spoke with one of the younger girls.

"But if Hope ain't here, who's gonna help me with my English?"

"Don't be lookin' at me." Celia shook her head. "Maybe Mr. Roger..." She turned her head and saw Andy instead. "What do you know about English?" Celia's hair stood out as though she'd been tearing at it.

Andy handed Celia the blazer she'd found at a secondhand clothing store. "Writing or reading?"

"Both," Celia said, looking the jacket over admiringly.

"Well, it's been a while since I've been in school, but my youngest daughter just went away to college. I helped her some."

"Good. Would you help Tasha here?"

"When?"

"Now."

"Ah, well...sure." She shrugged. Talk about being at the wrong place at the wrong time. She hadn't planned on staying. On the other hand, she had asked what she could do to help.

"Natasha Woods, meet Ms. Andy Taylor. Tasha's gotten back in school since she came to us and is hoping to graduate."

"I go by Tasha."

"I go by Andy. What do you need?"

"I wrote out this paper, but I don't do good with grammar, punctuation, that kind of stuff."

Andy turned to Celia. "Where can we work? I can't hear myself think in here."

"Hope and me usually go in her 'partment," Tasha said.

"So go." Celia made shooing motions.

"Where's Clarice?"

"Helping in the kitchen. Teaching tonight's cooks how to make meat loaf. That woman is one fine cook."

Andy was glad to hear Celia say something nice about Clarice. She turned back to her pupil. "Do you have your paper here?"

"I'll get them. Meet you there." Tasha started away and stopped. "Hope usually brings sodas and cookies or chips."

Andy nodded, then slowly turned her head toward Celia, eyes narrowed. "How did I get into this?"

"You walked through that door. This is life here at J House. You never know what's going to happen next."

"I should have kept on driving up the hill. I need to finish getting ready for tomorrow." Andy made a face and sighed. "Okay, I guess I can do an hour."

"An hour is about all that child can handle." Celia winked. "You got a big heart, Andy. You just trying to hide it."

"Well, I'd better take my big heart in there and find the sodas and chips." She swung her purse over her shoulder. "Give that blazer to Julia," she called back. "It's for her girls."

Chapter Twenty-Nine

Andy

As soon as Andy started down Union, she could see the trucks lined up to get into the parking lot. Starshine was handing out numbers on cards, designating parking places.

"I thought I was early." Andy paused to greet the smiling hippie.

"You are, and so are they." Starshine indicated the line of cars and trucks with a nod.

"You know where Roger is?"

"Most likely setting up the coffee and elephant ear stands." Starshine handed out another numbered card and pointed toward the parking space.

"Thanks." Andy hurried across the fast-filling parking lot to find Roger.

"Hey there, glad you made it," Roger greeted her as he adjusted the shade umbrella for the elephant ear cart. "Have you got the change?"

"Yes." She showed him a bank bag stuffed with coin rolls.

"Good. Do you think you can work this booth with Celia?"

"Sure. How's Hope this morning?"

"Climbing the walls. She wants out."

"I can believe that."

"Who's going to sample the first elephant ear this morning?" Celia asked, holding one up with the tongs she used to turn the fried dough.

"You don't have to ask me twice." Andy dug in her purse for money. "But you better put lots of cinnamon and sugar on it." She glanced around the grounds. "When do you let the customers in?"

"Eight," Roger said. "You're ready to go now. Good luck. Make a million."

Andy walked around behind the cart. "How come you're already frying?"

"So I know I'm ready. I always have to get a few ahead, or I'm behind all day."

"Story of my life, it seems. What do you want me to do?" Andy asked, then remembered that those were the same words, or at least half of them, that Clarice had said to Celia.

"You can wait on the customers. I'll do the frying."

Julia came over, sniffing the air. "That smells so-o-o good, but don't offer me one. Deep-fried foods do a number on my stomach."

"So what's your job today?" Andy asked.

"I'm going to sell coffee." She glanced around, a smile warming her whole face. "I never thought I'd be doing anything like this. Somehow this doesn't fit the image of a successful family-law attorney." She laughed, obviously enjoying her own humor.

Andy had to admit she did look a little like a fish out of water. But then others were probably thinking the same thing about her. "Are you feeling anxious to get home and back to work?"

She shook her head. "No. Not at all. And the scary part is, if I weren't so worried about Cyndy, I think I might actually like it here. But I am worried." Her smile turned to a frown.

"I've walked most of the streets of San Francisco and utterly failed in finding Cyndy. Why is it I can help solve other people's problems, and yet my own life is in total disarray? I just don't get it."

"Join the club," Andy said, chuckling beneath her breath.

"Your life is in disarray? I don't think so. You have a great life, a loving husband, three kids on the track to success, a booming business. Where is the failure in all that?"

Having learned her lesson with Clarice, Andy thought about what she was going to say before she said it. "You're right. I guess I've just been away from home too long. I'm not big on traveling. And I really don't like cities all that well."

"As I see it, we're all sort of traveling right now. You, me, and Clarice."

The morning passed swiftly, slowing down after the first crush and then picking up again as late risers came by.

"You sell lavender tea?" An Asian woman stopped in front of Andy.

"I— Well, yes, but how did you know? You have the spring roll cart, right?"

"Yes, I am Mai. Hope is my friend. She tell me about you. I would like to buy some of your tea for my restaurant. You come to my restaurant? I make you good meal."

"I'd love to."

"Best in North Beach, maybe whole city." Mai gave a slight shrug. "You send tea, yes?" She handed Andy her business card, then shuffled off. Andy looked at the card and was glad to see an e-mail address. Once she got back to the house, she would send Mai the link to her Web site so she could order what she wanted.

Andy leaned against the cart. "My feet are killing me." She looked at Celia, who, as always, was wearing tall, spike heels. "How can you wear those things all day long?"

"I dunno. Been wearin' them since I was a kid."

Andy couldn't bear looking at Celia's shoes, so she turned around and indulged in a little people-watching. She had never seen such a diversity of nationalities, incomes, ages, languages, clothing, and hair styles. She dropped her gaze as two teens with spiked hair in fluorescent stripes of green, pink, and blue walked by.

"You're staring," a voice whispered into her ear.

Andy jumped. "Julia, you scared me half to death. Are you finished selling coffee?"

"Yep. Clarice came by and said she'd finish up. Nobody wants coffee much now anyway. It's too late in the day." Another group of teens walked by. Their faces were painted black-and-white. "Sometimes I wonder if I'd recognize Cyndy if I saw her. She has the thickest, most glorious blond hair. I always thought she could be a hair model, but she blew that off. Wanted the big screen." Her voice dropped. "Like so many others. When I think of her being on the streets, I…I…" Julia huddled into herself. "I get angry one minute and want to cry my eyes out another." She stared straight ahead. "How could she do this?"

"I don't know." Andy collected the money from another sale. A woman walked by holding a pumpkin. "Celia, have you ever carved pumpkins here at J House?"

"No. Whatcha thinkin'?"

"Well, what do you do for Halloween?"

"We have a party, don't do no trick or treating like I did as a kid." Celia handed out two more orders.

"We need to have a pumpkin carving party here."

"Now?" Celia counted out change.

"No, but sometime the week before Halloween."

"That's next week."

"Oh, you're right. Well, how about if I buy the pumpkins and the candles, and we'll have at it. How many?"

Celia wrinkled her forehead. "Ah, maybe seven kids."

"What about some of the girls? Will they want to carve?"

"I don't know. We ain't never done such a party." Celia handed off two more ears.

"You'll help, won't you?" Andy turned to Julia.

"I'll bring the apple cider and doughnuts. No Halloween party is the same without those."

"We could fry our own doughnuts." Celia pointed at the fry wagon. "Got to be outside, but…"

"Why not?"

"We better ask Roger."

"Right."

"Okay, you guys, man this, and I'll go pumpkin shopping." Andy grabbed her purse.

"Check with Alvarez. He had a whole pickup full."

"Where?"

"Over by the back fence."

A bit later Andy returned to her stand with two bags of fruit and veggies, then off she went, only to reappear with a pumpkin under each arm. "He's leaving fifteen by the back door, and Roger gave a thumbs-up."

Roger came from out of nowhere and tapped Julia on the shoulder. "Come with me for a minute. There's a possibility that Cyndy… I mean, just come and see."

Julia's face paled.

Andy grabbed her arm to steady her. "Go on, it's all right," she assured her, giving her a gentle push toward Roger. "Please, Lord, let it be Cyndy," she whispered as Julia walked away, then disappeared into the crowd. "Wouldn't it be something if it was Cyndy?" she said, talking more to herself than to Celia.

Minutes later, Julia came back. The look on her face announced the outcome. "It wasn't her, although she did look a lot like her. I have to give Roger credit for trying." She sank down in the chair next to the cart. "Why doesn't God answer our prayers? Bringing her back to me would be such a simple thing." She stared at the cracked asphalt beneath her feet. A dandelion raised a lone yellow face to the sun.

Chapter Thirty

How long had it been since she'd carved pumpkins? Once, years before, she'd gone to her sister's house and made Jack-o'-lanterns with her nieces and nephews. Surely, that had been a much quieter event than this. And far less messy.

"I want a jagged smile. You ever cut one of those?" Cassandra, one of the girls who also attended Julia's classes, gave Clarice a hopeful smile.

"I think the one I did had two teeth. Why don't you draw it on and see how you like it."

"Like, yeah, cool idea. Or should I start with the eyes?" Cassandra studied her pear-shaped pumpkin. "I never knew the insides of a pumpkin could be so gross."

"It's just stringy pulp that holds the seeds together."

"I know, but still…" Cassandra headed to the supply table and got a pencil.

"You know, I saw some pumpkins that had been hollowed out, and then only the skin was carved. Seems easier and looks wonderful."

"Like, what do you mean?"

"Well, see how Alphi has the eyes cut out on his?"

"Yeah, in triangles."

"Well, this is more like etching." The girl looked at her with one eyebrow raised, clearly not getting it. "Why don't you just draw a face on very lightly, until you get what you like? I'm getting me a pumpkin."

"Awesome, Mrs. C."

While Clarice checked out each of the remaining pumpkins, she thought about the name the girls had given her: Mrs. C. When she shuddered at Ms., they opted for Mrs. and C for Clarice, a mark of honor. It surprised her that she and the girls got along so well. Was it because she'd ended up at the shelter and didn't go home to someplace else every night? The night before, one of the girls had come and sat on her bed, just needing to talk. They'd gone down to the kitchen so as not to disturb the others, and Clarice mostly listened until one o'clock in the morning. *I can't believe this,* she'd told Herbert. *You know, honey, I'm even beginning to talk like them.* Their own life had been far simpler, and hard work never hurt anyone. Gave them less time for mischief, too. She glanced around the bustling room. With Hope in the hospital and Julia with a speaking engagement, she'd figured Andy would help out, since this was her idea. But Martin had finally come home, so Andy had called and asked if could she beg off. So far, she and Celia were doing fine. Everyone seemed to be having a grand time.

Clarice chose a pumpkin about the size of a flattened soccer ball and brought it back to the table by Cassandra.

"What you think?" The girl, whose black hair was showing brown at the roots, nodded to her drawing on the pumpkin.

"Cool. Fun face."

Cassandra stood with her knife, chewing on her bottom lip.

"What's the matter?"

"What if I make a mistake?"

"Hey, it's only a pumpkin. You could always turn it around and start over. Or work the mistake into the face like you meant it."

"Right."

"Just stab it somewhere. The hardest part of carving a pumpkin or anything else is always the first stab." As if she were a master at pumpkin carving.

Cassandra made a face herself and rolled the pumpkin on its back to have a better angle for cutting. She started with an eye and inserted the knife, sawing as she moved it deeper.

"That's the way." Clarice cut the top off of hers and took an ice-cream scoop to the insides, dumping the innards on a paper. Roger had decreed that all pumpkin seeds be saved and washed, to be roasted for the Halloween party. Clarice wasn't too sure about eating pumpkin seeds, but then there were a lot of other things she'd tried in California, some good, like guacamole, and others not so good. Menudo and sushi were not high on her list of edible foods.

"You makin' one too, Mrs. C?" Alphi stopped to watch her.

"Guess you can't keep an old horse out of the ring."

"Huh? You ain't no horse." He gave her one of those grownups-are-weird looks.

"Just a saying." Clarice picked up the pencil Cassandra had used. "Are you done with yours?"

"Uh-huh. You need some help?"

"Not really. I'm going to try something different." She drew eyes curved over fat cheeks, eyebrows, and smile lines at the sides of the mouth, then erased some lines and finished with earrings dangling from ears.

Alphi shook his head. "That no Jack-o'-lantern."

"Wait and see." Clarice transferred her drawing to the pumpkin, then stood there studying it.

"The first stab is always the hardest." Cassandra's grin drove right into Clarice's heart and took up residence. *So what if this girl looks like something out of a horror movie, with her black makeup and fingernails and hair? There's someone real inside.*

Clarice let out a breath and picked up the knife. After a few cuts, she realized she would have to make a groove along her lines if she was to get the effect she wanted. As an eye took on shape, both Alphi and Cassandra sighed.

"Cool."

By the time she finished, several others had gathered to watch.

"You're an artist." Celia crossed her arms and flicked one fingernail against her teeth.

"No, just patient." Clarice finally made the final cut and laid the knife down, dropping her shoulders at the same time. She stretched her neck, angling her head from side to side.

Celia stepped behind her, pinching and rubbing her neck and shoulders. "You too tight, woman, you relax."

Warmth flowed into Clarice's neck and shoulders, up over her head, loosening her scalp. She sighed. "Ah, Celia, I didn't know you had magic in your fingers."

"No magic. Hope say I got holy hands. Hard to believe there can be anything holy in this sister, but if it makes someone feel better, Lord, let these fingers work."

"You need a candle in your punkin so's we can light dem all." Ophelia pulled at Clarice's sleeve.

"I got one." Alphi set a votive candle by Clarice's hand. "Want me to put it in?"

"Of course."

"Everyone has a candle?" Cassandra went around checking them all. "Yup, they do."

"Okay, light the long candles and use them to light the pumpkin ones. Then, Alphi, you turn out the lights."

Several of the girls lit white tapers and walked around, lighting each pumpkin. The tops were set loosely back in place so the candles could burn.

Children and adults alike "oohed" as the faces came alive, but when Alphi threw the switch, a universal breath of delight circled the room. Lit by the pumpkin faces, eyes gleamed, and one little girl clapped her hands over her mouth.

"So pitty."

"Pretty."

"I say dat. Pitty."

Clarice chuckled with the others and stared in delight at her carving. Pitty was right. The light orange lines glowed against the uncarved skin in a face alive with laughter.

"That is indeed beautiful." Roger stopped beside her.

"Thank you. When did you get back?"

"In time for the lights to go out. Almost went to check the fuse box."

"How's Hope?"

"She can come home tomorrow."

"So she'll be here for the Halloween party."

"As long as she stays down. Any running around and…"

"She knows what can happen."

"You know that, and I know that, but some kind of emergency happens here, and she'll forget all about herself and jump right in."

"Then the rest of us have to get so good at dealing with emergencies that she won't have to do that."

"Right, and then she'll feel like we don't really need her. You can't win." Roger ran a hand through thinning hair. "I must be growing taller."

"Huh? I mean, what?"

"Well, see, my head is coming up through my hair."

Clarice blinked. Roger, trying to be funny? She chuckled—finally.

"That went over like a lead balloon."

"Uh, yeah."

The lights came on again, and they blew out the candles. Mothers guided small children up to bed, and the others joined in for cleanup, most of them coming up to Roger to ask about Hope.

Several gathered around to talk about the Halloween party and what they could do to help.

"I could do face painting, if we had some paints."

"Anyone have any games we could play?"

"Pin the tail on the donkey, if anyone can draw a donkey."

"We used to have costumes. I was Snow White one year."

We should have started this a lot sooner, Clarice thought. "We used to bob for apples."

"What's that?"

"You have a tub of water with apples floating, and with your hands tied behind you, you have to try to pick one up with your teeth."

"But you'll get wet."

"That's part of the fun." Clarice glanced around the group. Since Roger had gone to answer a phone call, no one seemed to take charge. They could sit here talking all night, but nothing would get done.

"Okay, Celia, would you please get us some paper to write on, pens, too? Each of you, think of one thing you could do to make this a fun party for kids of all ages."

By the time Roger returned, everyone had their assignment, and they were all heading for bed.

"What happened?" he asked.

"Got the work done. See you in the morning." Clarice had her master list in hand. "Why don't you look at this and tell me if we are missing anything."

"Now?"

"Before morning."

He glanced down the list. "I have one question."

"Yes?"

"Who's going to pay for all this? As usual, we have more month than money. The budget is busted.

"Oh, I know a couple good angels who want to see everyone have a good time."

"They couldn't go by the names of Andy and Julia, by any chance?"

"Could be. There's a letter came today."

"Not again."

" 'Fraid so. I put it on the desk."

"Did you open it?"

"No. Celia said we should just rip it up and pretend we never heard from those skunks."

"I wish to heaven it was that easy." Roger tapped her arm. "Thanks."

"You're welcome." Clarice watched the last of the girls head for bed, then turned out the lights. *Whoever would have thought that I'd be here at a women's shelter on the opposite side of the country and having more fun than I have since the days we were building our business? Herbert, honey, did you have a hand in all this?*

She did face and teeth and all the nighttime rituals, said her rosary, and slipped into bed. Thinking back on the evening, she had to smile. She did a pumpkin so differently, all because of a picture she saw in a magazine. And it turned out fine. She wiggled her fingers, fingers that were good on a computer keyboard and a deck of bridge cards but had never been used to draw or carve. Never been used to comfort a child, or at least not in a long, long time. She rubbed the tips of thumb and forefinger together. Her hand had cramped from holding the knife steady for so long. *God, am I to believe that You had a hand in all this?* She rolled over on her side, the narrow bed creaking in protest.

Someone coughed. Another whimpered. These girls. Never would she have dreamed she'd be not only rubbing elbows with druggies and prostitutes, but working in the kitchen with them, laughing at their jokes, and even carving pumpkins.

A scream woke her in the middle of the night. "No! No!" The scream rose and fell, making the darkness pulsate with evil.

Clarice threw back her covers, the hair standing on her arms and the back of her neck. Who? What?

"It's okay, easy. Hold on to me." The soft murmur came from the same part of the room.

Other girls sat up, questions, grumbles. Someone turned on a lamp.

"Turn it out," someone else hissed.

Clarice made her way in the dark, lit only by the slight glow of streetlights through the high windows.

"It's Tasha, flashbacks, she'll be all right." Cassandra sat with her back propped against the wall, holding the sobbing girl, stroking her dark hair and leaning her cheek on the twitching girl's head.

"How can I help?"

"Not the first, prob'ly not the last."

Clarice started to turn back to her bed, then sat down on the one that was still shaking from the girl's shudders.

What do I do now?

Pray.

As if whispered over her shoulder, the voice spoke again. *Pray.* She knew no one else could hear it, but what was she to pray about? How much easier it would be if she were in the chapel, lighting candles for her petitions, using her rosary. *Jesus, You know this child. I don't. I know You love her. Help. Oh, God, help.*

She laid her hand on the girl's leg and felt the twitching. *Lord, she is Your child, such a messed-up child, and she is wanting to live a better life now. Please take away this nightmare, this flashback. You can wipe clean her mind, and I ask that You do so. Heal her body, heal her mind, help her to know that we love her, that You love her just the way she is.*

A jerk, a convulsion that seemed to last for minutes, but had been only seconds. She started to rise. "I'll call 911."

"No. She's over it now. Doctors can't do nothin'."

The girl whimpered again, then she coughed and gagged.

Clarice stood and headed for the bathroom. A cup of water and a cold cloth might help. She had to do something.

She brought them back and laid the folded cloth over the girl's head. Setting the cup of water on the bedstand, she put her hand on the girl who was comforting the other.

"She's about asleep." Cassandra stroked wet hair back from the girl's forehead.

"Will she remember this in the morning? Will she be able to go to school?"

"Sometimes. She'll likely be tired. It takes a lot out of you. Been a long time since the last one."

"What causes it?" *Please, Lord, she's been clean and sober, at least since I got here. She's one of the real possibility ones.*

"Who knows. Some people have flashbacks for the rest of their lives." Cassandra slid out from under her friend's shoulders and laid her back on her pillow. "Most times we get Hope, and she get us through."

"But you did it this time." They kept their voices to a whisper so the others could sleep.

"I guess."

"I'm right proud of you, honey." Clarice caught a yawn behind her hand. "Get to bed, or you won't be able to wake up in the morning either."

Back in her own bed, she tried to settle, but after flipping from one side to the other and turning her pillow twice, she lay on her back and stared at the ceiling.

How different her life had been, BG, Before Gregor. But before Florida, back in New Jersey. *Herbert, why did you have to go and leave me like you did? Sometimes I get so mad at you that if you weren't dead, I'd have to kill you. And you better not be in purgatory either, because I need you to go directly to the Head Man to get all this straightened out. Looks to be beyond anyone's power but Him. He could send a few angels, had He a mind to.*

She sighed and turned her pillow again. Perhaps she should just get up. She could work in the office without bothering anyone.

I need to write to Nadia. A postcard, that would do it. And get another change-of-address card. How could Gregor do this to me? How could I have been such a dupe?

Chapter Thirty-One

Hope

Doctor Cheong stared at her over the clipboard in her arms.

"I know, I know. I have to stay down at least one more week." Hope felt like she was six years old again, with a case of the chicken-pox, and her cajoling wasn't working.

"What is your idea of staying down?"

"The sofa? I thought Roger could put a sofa in my office, and I could…" She saw Dr. Cheong's eyes narrow. "Please don't say I have to stay in bed. I don't know that I can take being cooped up in the apartment. I'll stay down any way you want me to, as long as it's not in the apartment." Hope sucked her lower lip between her teeth, then huffed a sigh. She knew by Dr. Cheong's raised eyebrows that she was considering not releasing her from the hospital.

"I don't know…"

"You know you can trust me," Hope said, using their longstand-ing relationship as a ploy. "This baby is the most important person in my life right now. I'll get rest, rest, and more rest. But can't I walk out to the common room and watch the kids carve their pumpkins?"

Dr. Cheong sucked in her right cheek, appearing to give the re-quest some thought. "Only if you promise to stay on the couch once you're there." She raised her hand and shook her finger. "I mean it, Hope. Pumpkins and bathroom breaks are the only reason to have your feet on the floor." She jotted a note and glared over her half glasses. "And keep those to a minimum. Otherwise, there will be a potty chair by your bed."

"Yes, ma'am."

Roger leaned against the doorframe and scowled at Hope. "Are you giving her a problem?"

"Not me," Hope answered. "I wouldn't do that." She stuck out her lower lip in a pout. She knew she was acting like a scolded teenager, but when she thought about all she had to do, it made her want to tear her hair out, one braid at a time.

"All right." Dr. Cheong turned to Roger. "You may take your cranky wife home, and may God have mercy on you and everybody else at J House."

Hope gasped in mock surprise. "That's no way for a doctor to talk."

Dr. Cheong leaned over, grabbed Hope's right ankle, and squeezed it. "When said doctor has been your friend as long as I have, I have full liberty to say what I want. I'll get your chart turned in, and as soon as the nurse comes back with your discharge papers, you can leave—by wheelchair."

"Yes, ma'am." Hope saluted.

Dr. Cheong shook her head, then threw Hope a departing smile and patted Roger on the shoulder.

Roger crossed the room to sit on the edge of the bed. "Anything new I need to know?" He kissed his wife, lingering over her lips, before kissing the tip of her nose.

"Oh, I'm sure the warden will leave detailed instructions."

"Feeling a bit prickly, are we?"

"No, *we* aren't the one lying in bed. I feel fine. I feel like an idiot. I have tons to do."

"Not as much as you think. The Girl Squad pitched in and whittled your paperwork down to one small stack."

"But how—?"

"Those are some very intelligent, hard-working women. What they didn't know how to do, they left, and that amounted to one small stack."

Hope couldn't fathom a clean desk with only one small stack of paperwork. She would have to see it for herself to believe it. She felt like a heavy weight had been lifted from her shoulders. Those stacks of forms, rules, regulations, and documentation meant that she could put hours and hours back into her life. Not for a minute did she think she wouldn't be able to locate the papers if she needed them. Clarice had developed a filing system that even Celia had been impressed with—and willing to learn.

"I do have one piece of interesting news. Blakely Associates upped their offer by a hundred thousand dollars."

Hope stared into her husband's eyes. "Good thing we own title. If the church still had title, we'd be looking for a new home tomorrow."

"To tell you the truth, I'm wondering if looking for a new home might just be a good idea. We haven't had one offer of help."

"I thought we made a firm decision on this."

"We did, but time is running out, and we're running out of options." He took her hand in his and stroked her fingers with his other hand. "I just want you to think about it, that's all."

Her eyes caught and held his. "Those people are sharks. They…"

Roger lifted a finger to silence her. "I'm not talking about them. Believe me, they aren't the only ones interested in buying J House."

They talked awhile longer, and an hour later, Roger looked at his watch. "I think I'll go check on those discharge papers."

When he finally held open the door to their apartment, exhaustion rolled over Hope like a tidal wave. She could hear children playing in the common room, but she had no desire to see them. She dropped to the edge of the bed and slid her feet out of her sandals before lying back on the pillow. She could hear Adolph bark as Roger let him out of the run, then she heard his toenails clicking on the hall floor. He whined as he approached the bed.

"I hear you, big dog. How are you?" She laid her hand palm up on the bed, and he laid his muzzle on it. She could hear his tail swishing the floor. After a moment, he wiggled closer, put his paws up on the spread, and stretched his neck out to kiss her cheek.

"Good dog, Adolph. I'm all right." She patted his broad head and accepted his snuffles. "I know, I smell like hospital."

Roger came in, carrying her bag. "Do you want something to eat?"

Hope kept her eyes closed. "Not now, thanks. I'll sleep for a bit, and then I want to talk with Celia." She turned over on her side and smiled at the scent of lavender that permeated her pillow from the sachet she'd placed underneath it. It was so much more comforting than the disinfectant smell of the hospital sheets and pillows.

"Come on, boy." Roger snapped his fingers.

Hope could hear the dog's tail thumping the floor. "You know he's not going to leave me."

Roger muttered something about how even the dog didn't listen to him, then carefully closed the door behind him.

She woke to the sound of small children giggling—close by—and Adolph's snores. He was stretched out on the bed beside her.

"All right, you monkeys, what's going on?" Hope kept her eyes closed. Adolph thumped his tail. Another giggle, and the door clicked shut.

Hope tossed back the throw someone had put over her and headed to the bathroom. While she felt fine, still she dreaded finding evidence that she was bleeding again.

No spots. She heaved a sigh of relief. *Lord God, thank You for protecting this baby.* She glanced in the mirror and made a face. Talk about bed head. Braids or not, she had hair sticking out every direction. Would Dr. Cheong consider a shower too much, after all she'd done today already? "God's love surrounds you, little one, little one." The beginning of a new song floated through her head, complete with tune. Once back in bed, she lifted her Bible from the nightstand, propped pillows behind her, and flipped to Psalms. Surely since God could see David hiding in a cave, He would keep this little life hidden and safe in the womb until the time came for birth.

She read Psalm 22 again, then turned to 139. *"For You formed my inward parts; You covered me in my mother's womb."* She closed her eyes and laid her clasped hands on the open Bible. *I praise You. In Your time, oh Lord. In Your time. Forgive my restlessness. You, who know all things, for some reason You think this is necessary. Right now, I commit these months to You and to this child. I rest in Thee.*

A feeling of being totally loved welled up so fiercely in Hope that tears overwhelmed her sniffs and rolled down her cheeks. No matter how many times she blinked and sniffed and wiped them away, the deluge continued. No sobs, no sorrow. Just liquid proof of pure joy.

Roger peeked around the door. "What's wrong?" Seeing her tear-streaked face, he rushed to the bed, concern warring with terror in his eyes.

"Nothing. I'm just so full of joy, it's brimming over, and I"—she sniffed again—"c-can't stop it."

"Ahh, joy?"

She reached for his hand and laid her cheek against the back of it. "Remind me of this when I get all grumbly and frustrated."

He sat down beside her and wiped the tears away with his thumbs. "Thank God. You scared me out of ten years' growth."

"Can she come out now?" Alphi's voice was a loud whisper.

"Yes, she can come out now," Roger said, his tone mocking the little boy's excitement.

Hope smoothed her hair back and walked slowly to the door. "Are you sure I can come out?"

More giggles.

Hope opened the door to the hallway and gave Alphi a hug, which made him blush and sputter. "Lead the way, mon," she said. He took her hand as if afraid she might break.

"You gonna be okay?" he asked, looking up at her, his little face full of concern.

"I'm going to be just fine." She ruffled his hair. "Something sure smells good."

"Mrs. C been cookin'. Now close your eyes."

Mrs. C? Clarice? Hope did as told, letting Alphi guide her.

"Okay!" he said a moment later, then tugged on her arm as though it was a pull string to make her eyes open.

All the shelter folk, her three new best girlfriends, Starshine, and several of their street people regulars clustered to the side. The dining room tables had been moved into the main room, all now decorated with carved pumpkins, cut-out paper leaves, and twining ivy. Every person wore a face painting of some kind, the children from lovely fairies to black cat whiskers and paper ears.

Hope stood still at the entrance to the room, looking from one smiling face to the other. This was what love is all about. Determined not to get overly emotional, she pasted a smile on her face and said, "Hey!"

A chorus of "hey's" came back to her.

The children ran up to her, grabbed her around the waist, and hugged her. "When it gets dark, we gets to light the punkins." Ophelia stood in front of her, her eyes dancing as if lit by candles already.

A dozen or more pumpkins sat on the tables. Some had been carved with ghoulish faces, some with happy faces, some with goofy faces. "Who carved all these pumpkins?"

"We did." The announcement was universal.

"That's where you sit." Alphi tugged on her hand and led her to a sofa with pillows and a throw. "So you can be part of our party." He seated her with a flourish.

Dinner passed with giggles and only two spilled drinks. Everyone inhaled the pans of fried chicken, mashed potatoes, green beans, and Jell-O Jigglers—Jell-O shapes of green and orange.

"Dessert is after the party, so everyone pitch in for cleanup." Mrs. C's voice could be heard easily above the chatter.

Hope glanced from Roger to Andy and Julia. "Who put her in charge?"

"Didn't you hear? Clarice and Celia worked out some sort of a truce." Roger finished off the last drumstick.

"Thank You, Lord." Hope glanced heavenward.

Roger leaned closer to her. "Clarice is a pretty amazing woman," he said. "One night Tasha had a flashback, and she and Cassandra handled it by themselves."

Hope was impressed. "Are you sure that's the same terrified woman we took off the streets, what, just a little more than three weeks ago?"

"Closer to four, but yes."

Julia wiped her mouth with her napkin. "Wait until you see your office. We all worked to go through all that paperwork, but it was Clarice who organized the effort. I don't think she sleeps."

"Perhaps no sleep is better than being homesick." Andy picked up Hope's plate. "Would you like anything else?"

"No thanks. But I have a feeling two other angel friends dug deep in their pockets so we could have all of this." She waved her hand to encompass the food and decorations on the table.

Julia shrugged. "Better'n buying a new skirt or something. I haven't had this much fun shopping in a long time."

An hour later, the party was in full swing, with some laughing at the apple bobbers. The smaller children lined up to pin the tail on a grinning black cat, and Adolph, looking mortified in orange tabby ears tied around his head, sat in the corner watching. To Hope's surprise, he didn't try to shake them off, but he did shoot her an under-the-eyebrow pleading look every once in a while.

"Police! Don't anyone move." Three officers pushed open the front door.

"Welcome to the party." Roger hoisted his apple cider. "We've room for all."

"No joke, Benson, this is official business."

"Not another raid," Hope said, suddenly feeling peevish. Why didn't they pick on someone else? And what right did they have to just come barging in without a warrant?

Ophelia started to cry, and Hope heard mutterings. One of the street people made to escape through a side door but was told to halt.

Somehow Roger managed to keep smiling. "Aren't you getting a little tired of all this foolishness, Korchesky?" When he didn't receive an answer, he said, "Tell you what, you search all you want and let us go on with the party. We promise no one will leave the room." He glanced around to make sure everyone understood.

Adolph shook off his tabby ears and crossed the room to stand by Roger.

"By the way, Korchesky, who's the new man?"

"Watson." Korchesky turned to the man on his left. "Officer Watson, meet Roger Benson, retired detective from SFPD."

Adolph left Roger's side and sniffed the man's shoes, tail wagging slowly.

Hope watched Adolph.

"He's trained to sniff out firearms," Roger said, explaining Adolph's actions. "Come here, boy. Sure they're packing. That's their job."

Adolph's tail stopped wagging. He stuck his nose on the man's pocket and kept it there.

Watson took a step back. Adolph followed. "Call him off."

Adolph lifted his upper lip and growled, a deep-throated rumbling that meant business.

Roger took a step toward Watson. "You know what this means?" He nodded at Korchesky. "Adolph never makes mistakes."

Watson kicked out at Adolph. "Call off that dog before I..."

"Freeze, Watson." Korchesky gave the order.

"What in the...?"

"Careful now," Roger interrupted, keeping his voice conversational. "We don't use foul language here. This is God's house. Now, show us what's in your pocket."

"You said he's a gun sniffin' dog. That's what he smells, my gun."

"Your pockets. Just do as the man says." Korchesky stepped closer.

"Are you going to let a civilian give the orders here? What kind of a department do you run?"

Korchesky put his hand in his own pocket. "An honest one. Your pockets."

Hope saw Roger block the doorway. *Please, Lord, no violence.*

"We already know what's there, Watson," Roger said. "Just show us how much."

Hope glanced around the room to see everyone wide-eyed and not moving. This was better than a movie.

Watson glanced down at Adolph, whose growl got suddenly louder as his teeth became more visible.

"He usually doesn't attack without command, but he hates dope, doesn't suffer fools easily either."

Watson, visibly shaken by Adolph's ferocious growl, dug in his front pockets, extracted two small plastic bags, and placed them in Korchesky's outstretched hand.

Korchesky nodded to the other officer. "Cuff him and take him to the car."

"Okay, everyone, show's over—let's party!" Celia clapped and danced around in a circle, grabbing Alphi and Cassandra as she went.

As the noise volume rose, Hope smiled and chatted, but inside she steamed. That man had been going to plant drugs in J House. If he'd gotten away with it, they'd have been closed down. Someone here would have been framed for possession. Who would want to do such a thing, and why?

The next morning Peter called on Roger and Hope. "I don't want to spoil everyone's fun, but we're going to have to make some decisions soon."

"I don't have to make decisions. I'm pregnant." Hope delivered her line straight-faced.

Peter grinned at her. "Congratulations. I hear you had a bit of excitement last night—dirty cop and all."

"You heard?"

"Everybody's heard," Peter replied. "Good old Adolph. Now to find out who's behind it. But our main problem—retrofitting this building—isn't going to go away. I brought all the letters of intent. I also have the letter from the historical society, reminding us that the exterior of the building has to be restored to its original condition. I've communicated that to all who expressed interest in purchasing J House, but that stipulation took several out of the running. But I still have three reputable companies, not to mention Blakely Associates, who would like to talk with you."

"I don't want to sell J House," Hope said, her voice firm.

"Just because you sell the building doesn't mean you can't continue with the shelter," Peter reminded her. "Now, one of these groups has presented an unusual plan." He handed Hope and Roger copies of the letter. "They have an apartment building on the edge of the Tenderloin they would offer you as part of the deal." He raised a hand to cut off Hope's sputtering. "I know you don't want to be in the Tenderloin, but I've inspected this building, and it could be easily made to suit your needs."

"What about the Saturday Market?"

Roger laid a hand on her arm. "Hope, honey, we can't expect to have everything we want."

"Why not? We're doing God's work here." Hope unfolded her arms. She had promised herself not to get upset, and she wouldn't. "We won't be the same without the market. What will happen to Starshine and some of the others? And the Tenderloin is really depressing. Here we're in a real neighborhood."

"The Tenderloin is better than out in the burbs," Peter pointed out.

"Depends on your point of view," Hope countered.

"I'll file for another extension, saying that offers are being considered, and let you know if we get it. I don't want the city closing the doors on you, any more than you do."

"I know, Peter." Hope dashed at the tear that managed to leak out in spite of her best efforts. "Forgive me and blame it on the pregnancy again. I seem to cry easily. Roger accuses me of killing the messengers. I don't want you to feel that way."

"I'm stronger than that." He gathered up his papers and laid them neatly back in his briefcase. "I'm assuming you want this kept quiet?"

"Yes, please."

Chapter Thirty-Two

Hope

Roger plunked down on the sofa beside his wife after moving a stack of papers. "You're supposed to be taking it easy."

"You think reading and making notes for Clarice to type up is hard work?"

"It's not what I think, but what Dr. Cheong thinks."

"I can't just lie here and do nothing."

"No, I don't suppose you can." He looked down at the paper she had been reading. "What's that?"

"An e-mail from Andy. She got her church in Medford to sponsor our job-training program. They're sending books on conducting yourself in an interview, on job qualifications, on talking to your boss, as well as clothing, shoes, purses, grooming supplies, even makeup."

"Wow! That's great. When's she coming back?"

"In a couple of days. She says that she's filled all her Christmas orders and that things will slow down now to a snail's pace. She wants to stay in San Francisco a couple of weeks and work on her house so she can have a Christmas party for some of Martin's fellow workers."

She finished the rest of the e-mail and laughed. "She says she's going to learn to be a good corporate wife if it kills her." She looked up at Roger. "Don't ever ask me to be a corporate wife, okay?"

He shook his head and started to laugh. "Don't worry, I won't."

He reached up and tugged one of her orangy braids. "I don't really see you as a corporate wife."

She broke into giggles. "Me neither. O-o-oh." Her whole body shivered, as if hit by a blast of cold air.

"Is Celia over her mood?"

Hope looked out the window. "I imagine there's not a weed left out there. Clarice does rather outshine her in the area of office skills and organization, and..."

"But Celia knows street smarts. And she always knows what our girls need before they ask," Roger said. "She saw the signs and kept Chelsea from splitting."

"I'm proud of Celia," Hope said. "She's made a huge effort to work with Clarice, and vice versa. If we could just get past this retrofitting stuff, the turf wars are in the bag." She kissed him lightly on the lips.

"Alphi's bringing over the checkerboard as soon as he finishes his homework."

"I'd better hide my ego. He's beaten me more times than I can count." She put Andy's e-mail in the trash pile, having promised herself she wouldn't save anything that didn't need saving. Clarice kept her honest and went through the save piles, pruning even more. "Have you told Julia about your lead on Cyndy?"

"Not yet. I don't want to raise her hopes. I should know more in a day or two. You know how these things work."

"Well, I've been praying that it's her and that she'll at least come to see her grandmother."

"Me too."

Hope knew she should head back into the bedroom and take a nap, but she loved her new position as mother confessor for the little ones. Earlier, Ophelia had brought over a doll and asked for help dressing her. Once that was done, Ophelia went to work setting up a tea party and inviting Hope to be her guest.

Would she and Roger have a little girl who liked to play with dolls and have tea parties, or would they have a little boy who wanted to play cops and robbers? She closed her eyes and pictured herself holding a baby, feeding it, nuzzling it. Shock jerked her eyes wide. She'd better find a baby or two and do some practicing. Roger, too.

Her thoughts turned back to the last baby who had come to J House—a three-month-old girl. The mother, a young woman in her early twenties, had come in the middle of the night, claiming that her husband didn't believe the baby was his and had threatened to kill her. Hope had granted the mother and child sanctuary, but the next day the woman left, saying that she couldn't live without her husband.

Later that evening, on the six o'clock news, Hope listened to the newscaster say that the mother had been brutally slain and that the child had been given over to Social Services.

For months afterward, she and Roger had petitioned the courts to let them adopt that baby, but the answer was no. J House, with its recovering addicts, its prostitutes, gang girls, and street people, was no place to raise a child. They'd finally decided they were to remain childless but for the children who came through their doors. Like Alphi.

"I'm ready." Alphi stood beside her, checkerboard and checkers in hand.

"Okay, hotshot, but remember it's my turn to win."

The look behind his smile dared her.

"I swear, Alphi, you are a mastermind at checkers." She flopped back on the sofa after being soundly beaten. "So if you're so smart, and I know you are, why the struggle in math?"

"You think I'm smart?" He stared down at the checkerboard. "You don't think I'm dumb?"

"I know you're not." She wanted to gather him into her arms and hug him close. "If I can find someone to tutor you, would you let them help?"

He shrugged, the one-shoulder kind that told her how he hated to ask for help. "You be my tutor?"

"We'll see. But if I find someone, you don't go givin' them no lip, you hear me?"

He ducked his head and grinned at her from under impossibly lush eye lashes.

You're going to be a heartbreaker one day, little boy. Lord, please keep him on the straight and narrow. "Go get your homework, and let's see how we do." They'd only worked a couple of minutes when Hope realized he had no grasp of the basics of math. She sent him to Clarice to get some school supplies. When he came back, she made a set of flashcards and wondered why she hadn't made some a long time ago. She might not be able to preach lying down, but she could teach.

Julia, looking like she needed someone to talk to, came in. She pulled up a chair and sat down. Hope explained what they were doing.

"Flashcards, eh? I haven't seen flashcards for so many years…"

"Mebbe a hunnert?" Alphi glanced up from under his lashes.

Julia pulled a face. "Oh, thanks, kid."

"I know I shouldn't tell you this," Hope said while she made another flashcard, "but Roger thinks he has a lead on Cyndy." She put up her hand. "It's just a lead, and it might be a couple of days before he knows any more."

"Anything is better than nothing." Julia chewed on the inside of her cheek, then teethed her lower lip.

"Trust me, he'll let you know as soon as he knows something. The only reason he didn't tell you is because he didn't want you to get your hopes up for nothing. I shouldn't have told you, but you looked so down. Is anything wrong?"

Julia shook her head. "No. I'm just homesick. Spent the last couple of hours on the phone with my assistant putting out brush fires." She flicked her hand as if clearing away debris. "Have any clothes come in for the girls?" She abruptly changed the subject.

"Funny you should ask." She told Julia about Andy's e-mail, and then she stacked the flashcards together according to the number sequence. They'd finished with addition up through the fives.

"I want to play another game of checkers," Alphi said, already bored with the flashcards.

"Julia, how about you take him on for one game?"

"Sure, I can do that."

"And then back to the flashcards." Hope looked at Alphi. "Okay?"

"Okay." His groan smacked of universal kid.

Celia strolled through the door, drying her hands on a towel, the knees on her jeans mute testimony to the war she'd raged outside.

"Feeling better?" Hope asked. The indelible frown lines on Celia's forehead had eased, she had a smear of dirt on one cheek, and a lock of hair hung over one eye. Thank God for the restorative values of gardening. The fact that Celia wasn't swearing a blue streak was proof that she was learning to deal with her frustrations, Clarice being the biggest one right now.

Julia made her first move, and Alphi quickly followed.

Five minutes later, Alphi jumped three of Julia's checkers. "Gotcha!" he shouted at the top of his lungs, then leaped up and danced around the room.

Julia looked at Hope, her face frozen in shock. "Why, that little stinker. He beat me."

"Yes, counselor, he did."

Both Hope and Celia burst out laughing.

So many—Lord, You said You'll fight our battles for us, but when?
Cyndy, the retrofitting, jobs for all my girls, this baby. When, Lord, when?

Chapter Thirty-Three

Clarice

They're out there having fun, and I'm in here slaving.

The thought shocked Clarice. Better to be hiding out than engaging in another skirmish with Celia. Who would have thought that the woman wouldn't want her pencils sharpened? She'd just been trying to be helpful. Well, that would be the last time she'd…

"I knew better," she said to the picture of Hope and Roger on the opposite wall. "I can't lie. I thought about asking her before I did it, and I didn't. But good grief!"

Herbert, what do I do here? You always gave me such good advice. You must be so ashamed of me, the mess my life is in, when you tried so hard to make things easy for me.

Celia stuck her head around the door. "You want somethin' to drink? I've got iced tea and coffee."

Clarice felt instant blazing heat flash upward. She'd been caught talking to herself. And by Celia, no less.

"What's the matter? You look funny."

Clarice thought quickly. "Hot flash. I'm having a hot flash."

"Aren't you a little old for hot flashes?" Celia asked, her expression telling Clarice that she wasn't buying it.

"Coffee, please." Clarice ignored the question. "No, better make that iced tea." She picked up a piece of paper and fanned her face.

"You got it." Celia disappeared.

Coffee sounded so much better, but the caffeine levels of coffee might be one of the things contributing to her insomnia. No more coffee after three. Or switch to decaf. She finished the typing Hope had given her, printed out the pages, and stacked them neatly, ready for signatures and mailing. Now, to start on another drawer. She'd set herself a goal of one drawer a day, to get the office and the reception areas organized enough to lighten the work load. She'd talked to Celia ahead of time and gotten her to agree to change the filing system so that the files were more specific to the contents, thereby making it easier to find things. Surprisingly, Celia had agreed wholeheartedly. Well, maybe not so surprisingly, since Celia didn't really have a filing system. She had a "stack" system.

It was good to feel useful. She'd loved the old days when she ran the offices for Herbert.

She liked to think that her organizational skills contributed to the company's growth, from one room to a whole floor, then to an entire building.

"J House," she said, answering the phone on the first ring. Incoming calls always gave her a tiny thrill of excitement. She never knew what problem or person would be next on the agenda. "I'm sorry, Roger isn't available right now. May I help you?" She picked up a pen and scooted a message pad around to use. "Yes, Hope is here, but she isn't taking calls for another week due to medical restrictions. Perhaps I can help you." The woman on the other end of the line told Clarice why she was calling. "If I may put you on hold, I'll ask."

Clarice pushed the Hold button, grabbed her pen and pad, and walked out to the common room, where Hope was congratulating Alphi for correctly answering a math question.

"I have Inez on the line from Social Services. She has a young girl who needs a halfway house. She's been in juvie for a month."

"Oh, boy." Hope closed her eyes for a moment. "We're full, but…" When Celia came out with a tray of beverages, she told her the problem. "What do you think? Can we make room?"

"I dunno. It's pretty tight right now."

"Clarice, tell Inez that we don't really have room right now, but we'll do everything we can to squeeze her in. Say you'll call back in a half hour and let her know. Then come out and join us so we can discuss what to do."

Clarice nodded, smiled at the others, and returned to the office, leaving the door open this time. So much for the next drawer. She relayed the message, promised to get right back to Inez, and then rejoined the others.

Celia had gone back to the kitchen and was returning with a plate of ginger cookies that Clarice had baked that morning. There was nothing in her demeanor to indicate the frustration that had made her want to dig holes in the earth.

"How you gonna find room for one more?" Celia asked as she passed around the cookies.

"I could set up a cot somewhere, if we have one, and she could have my bed," Clarice volunteered.

Hope shook her head. "The only place left is the office. Right now you spend most of your waking time in there, but do you want to sleep in there too?"

"At least then I wouldn't wake anyone when I can't sleep." Clarice sent a smile Celia's way. "When you get older, you just don't need as much sleep anymore."

Evidently, the idea didn't sit well with Hope, because she shook her head. "Isn't DeeDee about to leave?" She turned to Celia for the answer. "Would you please pull her file?" Residents were supposed to stay only long enough to get on their feet, but with the new programs Julia had started, none of the girls wanted to leave without the extra training and support.

Celia rolled her eyes. "I don't know where it is."

"I'll get it," Clarice offered. With all this running back and forth to the office, she was bound to lose a few ounces.

Minutes later Hope found what she was looking for in DeeDee's file. "We need to help her find a job and get her out of here. She's ready. Celia, call Mai and ask if she has any more openings at the restaurant, and then, Clarice, you call Inez back and tell her to send her girl over." She looked back at Clarice. "There's a cot in the storage room." Her eyebrows arched. "But only for temporary use."

Clarice hid a smile. When Hope got on a roll, things happened. The only bad thing about moving out of the dormitory was missing the late-night or middle-of-the-night comfort sessions. But if the girls needed her, someone would point them in the right direction.

Hope yawned, then rubbed her eyes. "Thanks, everyone. I think I'll go lie down before Celia's glares melt me into a puddle."

Celia put a hand to her chest, eyes widened to appear innocent. "Me?"

"Yeah, you." Hope swung her feet to the floor. "Is it all right if I stop by the john on the way, Madam Warden?"

"We could always get you a wheelchair."

"Just try it."

Clarice returned to her office and called Inez. She eyed the corner where she could set up a cot. Perhaps she could find a box, too, to hold a lamp. After Inez had thanked her profusely, Clarice hung up and sucked in an invigorating breath. Feeling useful was a better tonic than molasses in spring. *If only they could catch Gregor the jerk and get me back some money.* Was that an impossible dream?

Chapter Thirty-Four

Andy

Andy flagged down a cab. She would have taken BART, but she had two duffel bags full of clothes for the girls that she had taken from her own closet, a large suitcase full of Lavender Meadows bath and body products for gifts and for testing at the Saturday Market, her portable sewing machine, and her own weekender carry-on.

She hadn't seen Martin since he'd gone on his business trip. When he called to say he wouldn't be back on Monday as planned, she bristled and started to say the same things she always said. Then she remembered the promise she'd made to herself, to treat him with kindness and love, and she changed her tone. "I understand," she said. "I'm disappointed, but if that's the way it is, then that's the way it is." She was equally careful when she told him she would have to go home for a while, that she had things to catch up on, but that she'd be back as soon as possible. He seemed flabbergasted. Obviously, he'd expected a fight. "I love you," she ended.

She was glad she'd gone home. Her mother and Shari had deliberately not told her about the orders that had come in, probably because they wanted her to enjoy herself. There was another big order from Nordstrom and one from a small chain store called The Country Woman. At the rate Lavender Meadows was growing, she would have to build a warehouse to hold her inventory. But that was down the line. Way down the line.

In the cab, Andy wondered how Julia had fared with Fluffy. Julia had jumped at the chance to housesit until Martin got home. She said she was sick of staying in a hotel, despite the fact that she didn't have to cook or clean for herself.

Martin had gotten home Wednesday night, and they'd been in touch constantly by phone and e-mail. He seemed a changed man, perhaps because she'd committed to some changes herself. *You should have looked to your Bible a long time ago,* she reminded herself. No matter what the problem, the Bible always had the answers. If one looked for them. *Why do I always need reminders? Shouldn't this be habit by now?*

The cabby removed her luggage from the trunk and set it on the sidewalk. She handed him his money, which included a generous tip, and eyed the steps. *Good, Martin's home.* His car was in the slot. *He can come help me.*

Oh, bother, she thought. She grabbed the handle of her suitcase and the handle of the portable sewing machine and started down the steps.

By the time she'd reached their house, she wished she'd thought to pay the cabby to help her. She wasn't a slouch by any means, but she was no muscleman either.

She opened the door. "Martin?" Still no answer. He must be sleeping or something.

She set her suitcase inside the door, then went back out for the duffel bags. Huffing and puffing, she tossed her stuff inside and walked in to check the bedroom. No Martin. He must be up in the loft, so deep into his work he didn't hear her. *Typically Martin. Not here when I need him. Cancel that thought.* That was the old Andy. As she climbed the stairs to the main level, she noticed that the television was on. Had Martin fallen asleep in front of the TV? That wasn't like him. The view of the bay caught her attention when she reached the top of the stairs, as it always did.

"Martin?"

She turned toward the living room. "Oh, dear God, Martin!"

Her husband lay spread-eagled, flat out on the floor, the cell phone just beyond the tips of his extended fingers.

"Martin!" Andy leaned over him and put her face close to his to see if she could hear him breathing. *Martin, please be alive. Please!* She laid shaky fingers on the side of his neck to feel for a pulse. Weak, but there. "Oh, thank You, God. He's alive." She saw the phone and grabbed it. No dial tone. She pressed the button, held it, then pressed it again. The dial tone sounded. She punched 911.

"You have an emergency?"

"My husband is unconscious. His pulse is really weak. Send an ambulance." She held Martin's hand while she gave the address, including cross streets. She wanted to scream for the woman to hurry. "We're the second house on the right down the Filbert Steps."

"The ambulance is on the way. Does he have a history of heart problems?"

"No. None."

"Is he on any medications?"

"No." A picture of Martin swallowing a pill in their hotel room clicked in her mind. "Wait, I don't know. I'm not sure."

All the while she answered questions, prayers flew heavenward. *Dear God, help him. Please help him.* "Should I be doing something for him?"

"If you have a blanket close by, put that over him."

Andy dropped the phone and flew across the room. Out of the corner of her eye she saw Fluffy sitting by Martin's reading glasses, which had fallen on the floor. She grabbed the throw from the sofa and hurried back. As she was covering him, she saw him move his lips and tried to comfort him. "I'm here, honey. I'm right here. The ambulance is on the way."

His lips moved again, but no sound came out.

"I can hear the ambulance. They're almost here." *Please, Martin, please don't die on me.* She snatched up the phone again. "Sorry, I forgot you. I can hear the ambulance."

"Go open the door for them, and turn your outside light on."

"Okay." She picked herself up and raced downstairs. Where would they park? Oh, why don't they hurry? She flicked the switch several times to signal them, then bit her lip to keep from crying out when the flashing red light was reflected in the windows of the houses across the garden. The moment she heard them park and open their doors, she ran back up to Martin.

"They're here, honey. They're going to fix you up." While it seemed like forever, she could hear the men entering.

"Up here. We're up here," she called out.

Two men came up the stairs, laden with equipment. "Okay, ma'am. What can you tell us?"

"I-I came home and found him like this, then called 911."

"Any history of heart problems?" While they asked her questions, one knelt by Martin with a stethoscope and the other took out a face mask and slipped the elastic over her husband's head, attaching a line to an oxygen tank.

"Is he taking any medications?"

"I'm not sure. Is it important to know?"

"Yes. Can you find out?"

"I'll go look through his things," she said. She hated to leave him, even for a second, but if it would help… She hurried downstairs to their bedroom and made a quick check of the medicine cabinet, then Martin's bathroom drawers. In the bottom drawer, she found a bottle of 81 milligram aspirin, then behind that a small brown prescription container. She grabbed them both, finished looking through the drawer, then ran back upstairs.

One of the EMTs spoke into a microphone pinned to his collar, repeating what he knew. She handed him the prescription container and the aspirin. "Looks like he's taking 81 milligram aspirin and 10 milligrams Inderal twice a day. We're starting an IV." He looked at her. "What's your husband's name?"

"Martin, Martin Taylor."

"Age?"

"Fifty-two."

"We'll be taking him to St. Mary's if you want to follow us. Be sure to bring his insurance card."

She nodded. The only thing that kept her from screaming for them to hurry was the knowledge that they didn't need a hysterical woman on their hands.

Two firemen brought up a collapsible gurney and transferred Martin onto it with the ease of long practice.

"Okay, ma'am, you drive safely. We're going to be in a hurry, okay?"

Andy bit her lip, fighting tears. "Oh, I don't know where it... How do I get there?"

He gave her a card with the address printed on it. "Is there anyone who can drive you?"

"I don't know. Maybe." She followed them downstairs, out the door, and up the steps, as all four men carried the gurney like a stretcher. Tears cascaded when she saw them slide the gurney into the rear door of the waiting ambulance. *Dear God, please, please let him live.*

She stood there, frozen, her knuckles against her mouth. "Please don't let him die," she whispered.

The doors slammed, and the orange-and-white vehicle rolled down the street.

Back in the house, one of the firemen gathered up all the debris and stopped beside her. "You'll call someone?"

"Yes, right now. Thank you."

"He's in good hands."

She watched him go downstairs and stared out the window, the ambulance wail an echo of the cry of her heart. Sucking in a deep breath, she dialed J House.

"J House. Clarice speaking."

Andy gritted her teeth and took another breath.

"Hello, are you there?"

"Clarice, this is Andy."

"What's wrong?"

"They— The ambulance just took Martin to the hospital. I— They think he had a heart attack."

"Let me get Roger. Hang on."

Andy leaned her forehead against the coolness of the floor-to-ceiling window. What did she need to take along? Martin's wallet. She glanced over, and sure enough, he'd left keys and wallet on the counter as usual. Martin was nothing if not a man of habit and neatness.

"Andy, are you at home?" Roger's voice came through the phone, warm and strong.

"Y-yes. I need to go to the hospital, but I don't know where it is. They gave me a card, but…"

"I'll pick you up. Be outside. I'll be there in five minutes."

"Thank you." She hung up the phone and stared at her hand, as if checking to see that her fingers were indeed at the ends of her palm where they belonged. Shaking herself, she grabbed Martin's wallet and her purse and started down the stairs. "Oh no. Fluffy." The door had been open for who knew how long. "God, please, where is he?"

The meow came from her left. "Fluffy!" He was sitting in the same exact spot he'd been in earlier. She walked over, picked up Martin's glasses and Fluffy, snuggling him under her chin. "He'll be all right. We have to have faith. Be a good boy and take care of things while I'm gone." She set him down and hurried for the stairs.

Everything seemed to be moving in ultraslow motion. As she waited on the curb for Roger, she realized she didn't know what kind of car he had. And then a car was stopping and the door was opening, and the man inside was telling her to get in and buckle her seat belt. She handed him the card with the hospital's name and address, and then put her hands over her face and burst into tears. Roger drove slower than a Sunday driver, or that's the way it seemed anyway. "Hurry, hurry," she said, her right foot pressing on the floor board. "No, light, stay green." She clenched her hands so hard her nails bit into the palms. "Get out of the way, you fools."

Her mind raced with myriad questions. Had she paid their insurance premium? How much life insurance was Martin carrying? When should she call the children, now, or later after she knew more about what was happening?

Roger pulled the car into the emergency parking lot, flung his door open, and ran around the front of the vehicle to open her door before she could undo her seat belt. "Let me help you," he said, taking her arm and steadying her.

"I'm so scared," she said, clinging to him. "I don't know what I'd do without him."

"Don't think like that. Think positive. You have to think positive."

Andy nodded. He was right. She couldn't let herself think negative thoughts. Not now. Not ever.

"Julia should be here any second," Roger said, guiding her through the emergency room doors. "We'll get through this; you're not alone."

"If only I hadn't gone back to Medford. If only I'd been there for him…"

"No, don't play the 'if only' game. God is in control, and things happen the way they are supposed to."

Andy shook her head. "He can't die. Martin is the healthiest man I know. This is just crazy." She clenched her fists. "He's too young to die."

He guided her to the desk, where a woman smiled up at them.

"Hey there, Roger, what's up?" the woman said.

"They brought Martin Taylor in by ambulance. This is his wife, Andy. Can she go see him?"

"Let me check." She punched a number on the phone and smiled at Andy. "Hang in there, hon." After a minute of questions and pauses, she shook her head. "Sorry, the doctors are working with him now. You would only be in the way."

"Can you give us any information?" Roger put an arm around Andy's shoulders. "Anything would help."

The woman paused. "Let me go see." She reached over and patted Andy's hand on the counter. "Be right back."

"You want to sit down?"

Andy shook her head, as if standing would help Martin. She felt as though she was having one of those out-of-body experiences and looking down on all this. Another ambulance wailed and came to a stop just outside the automatic doors. Someone coughed from the rows of chairs in the waiting area. A white-jacketed doctor breezed past her, his eyes intent on the chart he was holding. On the fringe of the long hall leading to the examination rooms, another group of people waited—a teenage boy sat holding an ice pack on his face. From where Andy stood, it looked like it was the other side that needed it. His face looked as though it had been sprinkled with meat tenderizer and beaten with a wooden mallet. A young mother rocked back and forth. In her arms a baby coughed to the point of gagging. A gurney whizzed by, and the medical team pushing it looked on edge.

The receptionist returned. "The nurse says Mr. Taylor is responding to treatment, but he's still not stable. If you'll have a seat—I know how hard it is to wait, but right now there is nothing anyone else can do for him."

"Sure we can," a familiar voice said from behind. "We can pray for him."

Andy whipped around and flew into Julia's arms.

While Julia consoled Andy, Roger took a pen and a clipboard from the receptionist. "Let's sit down over there," he said, looking pointedly at Julia. "She needs to fill this out."

With Julia's help, Andy filled out the papers and put Martin's insurance card under the clip. She knew the drill, because she'd volunteered at their local hospital in Medford. But this time it was different. She was on the other side of the counter, and it was Martin.

While Roger took the clipboard and pen back up to the counter, Julia asked what had happened.

"I had a cab bring me to the house from the airport—" Andy cut herself off, realizing she didn't have to go through every step. "He...he was on the floor when I got home."

"Heart?"

"They think so."

"Martin looked like the last one who'd suffer from a heart attack."

"Type A personality all the way."

Julia nodded. "I thought so, but still..."

"He's so young."

"Which is in his favor," Roger said.

"This wouldn't have happened if..."

"No 'if's,' remember?" Roger asked. "There was nothing you could have done to prevent this. No matter how strong and capable you are, some things are beyond your control."

"Yeah, like Martin." Andy rolled her eyes.

Roger chuckled. "Spoken like a true wife."

A wailing baby came through the door, its parent trying to shush the noise.

The sound grated on Andy's nerves like the drip of a faucet. *Shut that baby up. What's the matter with me? Lord, I'm going loony.*

She watched the clock hands stutter around its face. She tried to pay attention to the conversation between Roger and Julia, but they might as well have been talking Swahili. She'd shredded every tissue Julia pressed into her hands, her cheeks feeling chapped and raw from the constant dabbing. Who'd have ever thought she had this many tears in her? They kept leaking out in spite of her stern orders to stop.

Most of the room had been cleared out, immediately replaced by new sufferers. Suddenly the woman who had been behind the desk was standing in front of them. "Mrs. Taylor, Doctor says you can see your husband, but you have to be quick because they're taking him up to surgery."

"Surgery?" Fear clamped off her air. She coughed. And coughed again. *Brace up, Andrea. Answer the woman.* "For what?"

The woman glanced at her clipboard. "Bypass. That's all we know for now. Come with me. Roger, you can come too."

"I'll wait here." Julia squeezed Andy's hand.

Andy stood, and Roger took her elbow. Comfort and strength flowed into her through that bit of contact. *Bless the man.* They followed the woman through a pair of doors and down a hall—a hall that seemed to stretch three city blocks.

Green-garbed staff were wheeling a gurney out into the hall.

"Here's his wife." The woman motioned her forward.

They paused, obviously impatient to be on their way.

Andy stepped up to the side, reached over the bars, and took Martin's free hand. She stroked his face. "I love you, Martin. You're safe in God's hands." A slight squeeze let her know he heard her. She stepped back, fighting the tears that refused to be fought. Standing in the hall, she watched them wheel him through another pair of doors, these reading No Admittance.

Bye, Martin. I love you. God be with you. If it hadn't been for Roger and the wall she stumbled to, she'd have collapsed right there in the hall. *Please, God, let him live.*

Chapter Thirty-Five

Hope

"So I hear you want off the couch." Dr. Cheong put her stethoscope back in her pocket and helped her patient sit up.

"Yes. How's the linebacker in here?" Hope laid a hand on her middle.

"Doing fine. Next month we'll do another sonogram. There's been no more spotting?"

Hope shook her head.

"Cramping?"

"Nope."

Dr. Cheong checked Hope's ankles. "No edema?"

"No, I run—er, walk—to the bathroom enough to get in a mile a day." She raised a hand. "I know… I've been staying down, but you make me drink gallons, even eliciting cooperation from my staff. Everyone's been against me, and I can't live in the bathroom."

"We could get you a potty chair."

Hope stared toward the ceiling. "Please, Lord, no."

Dr. Cheong half snorted, half chuckled. "If you can restrain yourself, I'd say you can be up and more mobile. But taking it easy is still the order of the day. Getting too tired, catching something, on your feet too long, all could lead to trouble."

"How do I know what is too much?"

"If you are tired, lie down, take a nap. Listen to your body. Don't push yourself to make commitments. In fact, don't make commitments, other than what is best for this baby. We all want you to carry this baby to term."

"I know. Me too." Hope thought a moment. "I have a question."

"All right."

"Are really oppressive nightmares typical for pregnant women?"

"No. You're having a bad time?"

"Yes."

"You might want to talk with someone about them."

"I'll see." Hope blew out a breath. "Can I walk outside?"

"Not power walk."

"Stroll?"

"Up to the corner and back. That is all—for now. You will find your stamina is greatly reduced."

"But other than tired at times, I feel really good again." Hope stared at her doctor, who was slowly shaking her head. "All right. And I see you again when?"

"Three weeks, unless there is a problem, and that I want to know immediately."

"Thank you. I'm sure you've already given the news to Roger."

"Not yet, but he is a persuasive man."

"That's one word for him. He could have just as well come in here."

When she finished dressing and met Roger in the waiting room, the smile that showered her with love also said he knew the good news. "I'll take it easy."

"I know."

They said their good-byes to the receptionist and headed out the door.

"I could even go out for lunch."

"I have meetings this afternoon—sorry."

"I know, but I could go out for lunch. And tomorrow I get to walk up to the corner and back. Outside. I will never take being outside for granted again."

"We have to have a meeting of all of us," Hope told Clarice.

Clarice shrugged. "How, when Andy is at the hospital all day, every day?"

"Her daughter's with her. Maybe she can stay with her father so that Andy can meet with us. Time is running out. I cannot believe how fast."

"Have you told Julia yet?"

"No. Do you have Andy's cell phone number? I want to leave a message. I'm thinking tomorrow afternoon might work. Let's see…" Hope studied the calendar pad on the desk. "The surgery was last Tuesday, he's been out of the ICU since Thursday, and this is Monday. He should be going home tomorrow, I think she said." Hope took the paper with the phone number that Clarice handed her and dialed. After leaving the message, she sat down in her office chair. "Okay, let's get on with whatever you have for me to do. I can guess the pile is three feet high."

"Not anymore, but the front of this file drawer has to be gone through, and only you can do it. The most important things are in the front. When you get to the middle, stop and take a nap."

"Who made you my keeper?"

"The man."

"Roger? Celia calls him the same thing. You're all against me."

The next afternoon, the four women met at one o'clock in the back corner of the hospital cafeteria. Andy had set the time, saying that

Martin usually slept right after lunch, and Bria could stay with him by herself for an hour or so.

"Okay, so what is going on that I don't know about?" Andy pushed her plate away, her salad only half eaten.

"First things first," Hope said. "How are you holding up?"

"Better with Bria. She's been a big help and a good listening post."

"And what's the latest on Martin's condition?"

"The doctor says he's right where he needs to be after the surgery, so that's a relief. He's scheduled to go home on Tuesday. Good thing he is going down the stairs to get to the house and not up."

"Roger will help," Hope said, knowing that indeed he would.

"I can't begin to thank you all for the visits and the prayers. You have truly become my family. Hope, are you sure you should be going to the hospital yet? You haven't been out of bed that long."

"Two days, and I'm being careful. Doc said I could walk every day, and my walk today is here at the hospital."

"The Girl Squad in action." Julia reached across the table and patted Andy's hand. "How are your kids doing?"

"Bria is doing fine. Of the three, she's the strong one. Morgan was upset that I sent her back to school, but I told her that there wasn't anything she could do and that she couldn't afford to be away from school too long or her grades would suffer. As for Camden, he was okay with going back to Montana once he knew his dad was going to be all right. He's working as a TA as part of his master's program."

Hope glanced at her watch. "We better get to business. Last week I met with Peter Kent, our attorney, and he reminded me that we only have until the end of the year to come up with the money for retrofitting, less than two months away. So unless God sends a miracle, J House will have to be sold." Her voice broke on the last words, and she cleared her throat.

"Well, then," Andy said, "let's ask Him for one—a miracle, I mean.

After all, He has done them before." Andy laughed, and it felt so good, she laughed harder.

Hope laughed at Andy's laugh, and then they were all laughing. "Okay, okay." Hope put up her hand. "That's basically what I was going to say. We need to get together and pray for Martin, for J House, for all of our needs, every week, and each of us needs to commit to praying every day. We have a prayer chain that I will put out the request on too."

"That's a great idea," Julia said, her expression eager. "I don't know why nobody thought of this before."

Hope blew out a sigh. "I'll be real honest with you. I'm at the end of my spiritual rope. Good thing I know Big Dad is hanging on to the other end, or I'd freak."

"You mean pray right here, out loud?" Clarice glanced around the room. The diners had thinned out, and no one was sitting near them.

Hope understood her discomfort. "No one will hear us. They're all busy doing their own thing." She smiled at Clarice. "Jesus said, 'Where two or three are gathered together in My name, I am there in the midst of them. And whatever they agree on, I will answer.' So let's just hold hands and close our eyes, and anyone can pray as the Spirit leads. Okay?" She glanced around at the others and saw them nod. She took Clarice's hand and squeezed gently to stop the shaking. "It'll be all right. Relax."

"Easy for you to say. The only prayer I ever said out loud was 'Now I lay me down to sleep, I pray the Lord…'" She yawned. "I do that every time, right in the same place. Isn't that funny? Oh, and the Lord's Prayer—and grace."

They all released the breaths they'd been holding and grew silent.

Hope could hear the kitchen workers and two people talking a few tables over. *Please, Lord, quiet my mind. Let someone begin.*

"Father, we're here because we need You. We've hit walls that we cannot knock down." Andy paused and sighed. "We ask that You take care of J House and all those who live there, that You provide housing and food, that You pay the bills. Lord, You said You have a plan for us, for good and not for evil, and we ask that we can see that plan in action."

"Thank You, Jesus." Hope waited again.

This time it was Julia who spoke. "Jesus, You said You are here, and You must be, because otherwise I would not be doing this." Julia sniffed. "Please bring healing to Martin's heart and the incisions. Make him well in all ways. Let him know that You are in control and that all he needs to do is let You do the work. And please bring Cyndy back to me."

Hope felt Clarice nodding clear through to her hands. *Oh, Lord, You are so gracious to bring us all together. Thank You.* She waited longer. The noises around them faded away, and it felt as though they were even breathing all together, in the same rhythm. "Big Dad, I know that You are listening and that You never go back on Your word. I am so scared for J House, or at least I was when we started. Thank you for reminding me that You will do what You will do." She dropped Clarice's hand so she could dig out a tissue and mop her nose. "We ask also that You take care of Clarice and her problem. Give her money back to live on, and You say that You are to do the revenge. Go for it, please." She paused again. The silence felt comfortable now, and Clarice's hands had quit shaking. Someone else was sniffing too. They should have brought a box of tissue. "Amen," she said, and everyone else echoed.

The others joined her, all of them blowing out sighs like wind. They mopped and sniffed and blinked a few times.

"You just talked like He was right there." Clarice looked around at each of the others. "No fancy words like *Thee* and *Thou*. That's all right? I mean—God doesn't mind?"

Hope patted the older woman's hand. "The best prayer of all is *Help!*"

"No, there's one better." Andy grinned. "*Thank You*. The words I never say enough."

"I could always talk better with the saints, because I could use regular language, not *Thee* and *Thou* or in Latin. This was so easy." Clarice dabbed at her eyes again. "So now what?"

"Well, I don't know about all of you, but I'm going back up to Martin."

"And we go back to J House."

"And we all expect a miracle." Hope did a thumbs-up. "Or four."

Chapter Thirty-Six

Julia

"Yahoo! I got him!" Julia came stomping into the office, sporting a Cheshire cat grin.

"Got who?"

"That…" Julia reined in her language. "The gigolo of all gigolos." She smiled down at Clarice. "Gregor, or whatever he's calling him-self—this time."

Clarice leaned back in the chair and stared at Julia. "How— What— Will I get my money back?"

"If he hasn't spent it all, yes. But if he has, you might have to be content with knowing that he'll never defraud anyone else. So far, it looks like you are wealthy widow number four. But now, thanks to certain friends in high places, his duping days are over! They picked him up and charged him last night for fraud and bigamy—no, it has to be polygamy. Seems he neglected to divorce the women he mar-ried, then divested of their money. Of course, he couldn't divorce any of them, or they would have come after him." Julia paused midrant. "He did tell you he'd been divorced, right?"

"He said once, when he was younger."

"I wonder what name he was going by then?" Julia's grin broad-ened. "Since he's likely a flight risk, the judge didn't set bail."

Clarice stared at the excellent fakes glinting on her fingers. "I'd like my real wedding ring back most of all." She stared at Julia. "This is so hard to comprehend. He seemed to have plenty of money."

"Sure he did. He used the money from the former wife…" She paused to think a moment. "I wonder if all the marriages were legal. Hmm, I'll follow up on that." She wrote herself a note. "Back to your question. He used the money from wife three to court you—soon-to-be wife four. I'm thinking he hasn't had time yet to find wife five. One of the women is from Texas, another California, then Oregon, and you lived in Florida. He moved around, so you'd never find out about each other. What a crafty…"

Julia sat down on the sofa across from the desk and ran her fingers through her hair, setting the caramel wavy strands to flying every which way before dropping back into place. "I'd like to have a crack at him personally before I sic the IRS on his tail. You can bet he didn't pay any taxes on all that he's stolen."

"He had me sign an IRS form, married couple, so we both signed it."

Julia stared over her glasses. "Are you sure he filed?"

"He must have. I never heard from the IRS…" Clarice paused, her eyebrows knitting in thought. At length she said, "But then I didn't pick up the mail. I let him get it. He seemed to take such pleasure in it." She sighed and shook her head. "There's no fool like an old fool."

Julia wagged a finger at Clarice. "Well, since you are neither, I guess that doesn't apply to you."

"Thanks, but—"

"No buts. He was very good at what he did, and like I said, I know of at least three other women that he pulled this on."

"So I'm either in good company or foolish company," Clarice said, not bothering to hide her resentment.

Julia pointed to the computer Clarice was working on. "The Internet is a wonderful invention. I think I'll start a blog for women who've been fleeced. I bet I'd get all kinds of interesting stories. And who knows? Maybe it'll be the launch of a whole new career for me."

"What about your practice in Kansas City?"

Julia put a finger to her cheek. "I don't know. Other than a glitch once in a while, they seem to be doing just fine without me. And to tell you the truth, I'm not sure I can work up any enthusiasm for family law again. I don't even know if I really want to go back to Kansas City."

"Has the City by the Bay stolen your heart?"

"Could be."

Clarice smiled. "It's certainly stolen mine. If I could get some of my money back, I'd rent or buy a little place near here. I don't need much." A slow smile curved her lips. "In Florida I had money and a handsome husband, but here—here, I have a purpose. Here, I'm needed."

"You'd stay here then—here at J House?"

"It's better than going back to New Jersey and listening to my big sister say 'I told you so.'"

"One thing to keep in mind, you'll have to go back to Florida at some time."

"Why?"

"To testify at this jerk's trial."

Clarice grinned and waggled her eyebrows. "With bells on."

Julia checked her PDA. "I promised to be up at Andy's in a half hour to open the door for the men delivering the hospital bed, so I'd better run."

"Martin's going home today—right?"

"Later this afternoon. Andy told me to have them put the bed in the living room so it would be easier on her. She's certain Martin will pitch a fit, but she says he'll forgive her once he's enjoying the view."

"I-yi-yi." Clarice threw up her hands. "Men can be so stubborn."

"Who you calling stubborn?" Roger leaned against the doorframe of the office.

"Men in general."

"Myself excluded, of course."

Julia tucked her PDA into her purse. "Do we want your opinion, since it could be slightly skewed, or Hope's?"

"Male bashing is not polite."

"It's not bashing if it's true." Julia sat forward, her eyes full of excitement. "Do you want to hear our good news?" At his nod, she told him everything she'd learned about Gregor.

"Good work, Julia. Maybe you should have been a detective."

Julia laughed. "I actually considered it at one time, but you know how that goes." She stood up, feeling better about herself now than she had in a long time. She refused to diminish her pleasure by wondering why, if she could find a man thousands of miles away, she couldn't find a sixteen-year-old girl a few miles away. Some things just didn't make sense. She waved on her way out the door. "See you."

Roger checked his watch. "If anyone calls, tell them I'll be back in a couple of hours. I'm going to the store, then over to the hospital to bust Martin out." He started to leave, then stuck his head back in the doorway. "Hope is sleeping, and while she asked me to wake her, I'm opting for her to sleep as long as she needs."

Clarice raised her hand. "I second the motion."

Julia stopped by Speedy's on her way back to J House and bought some chai. She had a taste for something warm and fuzzy, and spiced chai fit the bill. Clarice was still in the office, and Hope was in the common room helping Alphi with his math.

"Don't you ever quit?"

"Celia asked me that a little while ago. Herbert used to call me his little bulldog because I wouldn't quit until the job was done. Of course, that's also why he was so successful. The woman behind the man, you know."

Julia leaned forward and whispered, "How are you and Celia getting along? I haven't seen her out in the garden playing gopher in a few days."

"We're getting along just fine. As a matter of fact, she actually asked me to teach her how to use Word Perfect. She said she wanted to write a book about her life. I told her I would be happy to teach her. Now, all I have to do is get her to let me edit it!" She chuckled at her own joke.

"Do you have time to help with the girls tonight?"

"Of course. Thanks for asking. Helping with their training makes me feel useful. They've come a long way in the few weeks you've been doing this." She glanced at the calendar. "What, four weeks now?"

Julia nodded. "We need to find places for them to intern, to use their newfound skills in a real office setting."

"Oh, I forgot to tell you," Clarice said quickly. "I asked Peter Kent about that, and he said he could take one or two of them, and that he'd ask some of his friends if they'd be willing to do the same."

Julia leaned down and gave Clarice a hug. "You are amazing."

Clarice blushed. "Thank you. I was afraid you would think I overstepped my bounds. That's why I didn't ask first." The phone rang. Clarice answered, then held up a finger to catch Julia's attention. "It's for you."

"Who is it?" Julia whispered.

Clarice shrugged. "One moment, please." She handed the receiver to Julia.

"Hello? This is Julia. Hello? Hello?" She stared at the receiver, then at Clarice. "They hung up."

"It was a she. A young voice... She sounded like she was crying or plugged up with a cold."

"Cyndy?" Julia sank down on the sofa.

"I don't know but"—Clarice huffed a disgusted sigh—"I should have asked for more information. I know better than that."

"It's not your fault," Julia said, her voice dragging with defeat. "It must have been her. She probably heard I was here looking for her... God above, I'd give anything to see her again, to hug her. Why would she rather be on the streets than with me? I love her. I want to give her a wonderful life. I don't understand." She shook her head, tears sparkling at the corners of her eyes.

"If that was her, maybe she hung up because she was afraid someone might hear her. Maybe she's with someone who doesn't want her getting in touch with you."

"You mean like that *pimp?*" Julia spat out the word.

"Remember that girl who came over from juvie? She was on the run from a pimp."

Julia covered her face with her hands. "I can't bear the thought of Cyndy working as a prostitute. I know too well how bad it is." She took a deep breath and worked on composing herself. "If it was her, maybe she'll call back. Do you have my cell phone number?" She reached forward and grabbed a pencil and a scratch pad. "If I'm not here, give it to her. Tell her I want to talk with her, that I won't pressure her, that I love her and just want to help her." She handed the note to Clarice.

Clarice put her computer to sleep, got up, and signaled Julia to follow. "Come on, both of us have had a big day. Let's get a soda or something."

"I've got chai." Julia pulled two little packages out of her purse.

"You mean t'ai chi?"

"No, chai. It's a tea. All we need is hot water."

That night back in her hotel room, Julia stared at her most recent photo of Cyndy. "Lord, You said You keep track even of all the sparrows, and I know You think Cyndy of more value than a little bird. Please watch over her and protect her—in spite of herself. And bring her back to me." She sank to the floor and brought her knees to her chest, soaking her slacks with her tears.

Chapter Thirty-Seven

Hope

"Huh? What did you say?"

Roger crawled into bed beside her and put his face on the pillow next to hers. "Blakely Associates was behind our drug raids."

Hope tried to make sense out of what he was saying, but her brain refused to cooperate. "Roger, what are you talking about?" She glanced at the clock and groaned. "It's three a.m., Benson. You are losing your mind and taking mine with you." She closed her eyes and tried to ignore him, but his breath tickled her face. "Would you mind taking your head off of my pillow?"

"Not until you hear what I have to say."

She stretched her arms out to the sides and rolled her shoulders. "This better be good, or you're going to be on my list."

"It is good. Blakely Associates—you know, the consortium that sent us all those letters? They were behind both drug raids and our crooked cop."

She could tell by his voice that he was trying to be cute. "Really? How do you know?" She pushed her pillows against the headboard and propped herself up with a groan.

"Korchesky called a couple of hours ago and told me to come down to the station so I could hear Watson's confession on tape."

She was wide awake now.

"He confessed to taking ten grand from Blakely's CEO to plant drugs on the property."

"Wow! They must have really wanted J House to do something like that."

"J House sits on some prime property, honey. You know that. A savvy developer could make a fortune." Taking her hands in his, he smiled into her no-longer-sleepy eyes. "Blakely Associates is in serious trouble. Korchesky has a warrant and will be bringing all the company's officers in for questioning this morning. He also has a warrant to search their headquarters and their personal homes."

"What about Watson?"

"He's behind bars, and I imagine that's where he'll be staying for quite some time."

Hope stared at him a moment, her thoughts whirling. "So my instincts were right," she said, recalling the letter she had taken to Peter.

Roger raised up and kissed her nose. "I should have paid closer attention to your instincts and been more watchful. You can go back to sleep now. I'm sorry I woke you up, but I wanted to tell you so you wouldn't be afraid anymore."

"Ah, if that were the only thing I've been afraid of."

"Other than a forced closing of J House, what else?"

"Isn't the forced closing of J House enough?"

He got out of bed and tucked the covers around her. "Sleep tight."

"You betcha."

Hope woke to fog-shrouded windows and the penetrating chill of a cold wind tossing the tree branches and seeping in like a bad odor. The clock said nine. How had she slept through the bedlam of breakfast and people getting off to school and work? Roger must have threatened a slow and painful death to whoever woke her up. It wasn't like she hadn't been up and down half the night anyway, with a baby lying right on her bladder, or at least giving it a good kick now and then. And she still had three months to go.

She threw back the covers and headed for the bathroom and a shower. With the hot water pounding down on her, she thought back to Roger's news. *Thank God for Adolph. If not for him, we might have been facing more than the closing of J House. A lot more.*

Dried and dressed, she sat down on the bed to rub dry and braid her hair. "This is the day, this is the day, that the Lord has made, that the Lord has made, I will rejoice, I will rejoice, and be glad in it." She sang the song softly, when she'd rather be shouting it aloud. But if she made any loud noises, everybody would think something was wrong and come running.

She needed to sing the song in church on Sunday. Funny how you could forget one of your favorites for a while, and then the Holy Spirit would bring it back. Singing Bible verses always made her feel better.

Hope left her apartment and went to the kitchen, where she poured herself a cup of decaf coffee. Sipping her coffee, she walked down the hall to find Celia hard at work. "Good morning." Celia mumbled something that might have been a reply without taking her eyes off what she was reading. "Do you know where Roger is?"

"Nope."

Hope set her coffee on the desk and tried to see what it was that Celia was working so hard on. "What are you doing?" she asked, her curiosity getting the best of her.

"Studying."

"Studying what?"

"Word processing."

Hope recalled that Celia had asked Clarice to teach her word processing so she could write a book. *Thank You, Father. You did it again.*

Admittedly, for a while she'd begun to think that peace and harmony between Celia and Clarice was an impossibility. "You can always use word processing, just like you can always use typing," she said, being careful not to make too much of it, or else it would embarrass her. "Now, is there anything that I need to know this morning?"

"We got another call for Julia, but the caller wouldn't give her name. And the Dragon Lady, she didn't press her."

"Celia!" Hope shook finger at her. "Does Clarice know you call her that?"

"Of course. Why would I do something behind her back? She thinks it's funny."

What could she say to that? *Let it go, Hope. They're working it out their way.* "How did Julia's classes go last night?"

"That Julia get more out of those girls than I ever thought possible. They sayin' 'yes ma'am' and 'no ma'am' and wearin' longer skirts and buttoning up blouses." She indicated her own rather obvious cleavage. "I like the part where they answer the interview questions she fires at them."

Hope sighed. "I just wish we could accommodate everybody who wants to take her class, but we just don't have the resources. Someday, maybe." She looked at the phone messages Celia had taken and put them in the order of who needed to be called first. "I just had a thought. Tell Julia I want to see her when she comes in. What do you think about having graduation exercises for the girls who complete Julia's training?"

"Sounds good to me, but she's already here. She's been here since real early this morning."

"Oh, good. I can't wait to tell her my idea." She started to leave, then turned back and asked, "How are Thanksgiving preparations coming?"

"We have pies made and in the freezer. Tonight we're baking cookies. That Fawna, she's turning into a real good cook. I showed her a thing or two about spices, and the Dragon Lady gave her some baking tips. Now, she's got it in her head that instead of goin' to school to learn nail art, she wants to learn how to be a chef."

Hope laughed, then shook her head. Every day there was something new, something exciting, and most times, something wonderful happening at J House. Again, she started to leave, only to have Celia call her back.

"I almost forgot," she said. "Peter Kent called. I didn't put it on a message. He said not to call him, that he was gonna come by about lunchtime. Said he would like it if you could get everybody together. I told him I couldn't guarantee that, but we'll try."

Lunch was clam chowder and a salad of fresh greens from Celia's garden topped with pine nuts and sliced apple and covered with raspberry vinaigrette. The crowning glory, however, was freshly baked focaccia bread.

Peter Kent offered to say grace, after which he asked, "Since when do you have a chef here?"

"One of our girls, Fawna, wants to be a chef. We let her work in the kitchen, and Celia and Clarice have been training her." Hope smoothed the white tablecloth.

"Has she ever worked in a restaurant before?"

Clarice answered. "She did some fast-food cooking, but she isn't interested in getting back into that. What we need is to find her a restaurant—a good restaurant—where she can work and train at the same time. Then she can see if she really likes cooking enough to make a career of it. Ideally, the restaurant needs to be someplace close by so she can continue to take part Julia's class and her GED classes."

Peter appeared to ponder the situation. "Let me talk with the chef in our building. Maybe he would be willing to take her on." He drank the remaining coffee in his cup. "Okay, if everybody's ready, we need to get down to business. I have another meeting this afternoon."

Roger scooted his chair back. "I knew better than to think this was just a pleasant call with an old friend. Before we begin, though, I want to tell you our news about Blakely Associates."

"Sure." Peter reached down to his briefcase and pulled out a file folder. He started to look through the folder, but as Roger's story unfolded, he put the folder down on the table and gave Roger his full attention. "That's incredible. If it hadn't have been for Adolph…who knows what might have happened?"

Clarice piped up, obviously eager to add to the excitement. "And Julia here has found that jerk who fleeced me! I can't wait to go back and testify against him. I hope they put him someplace where the sun doesn't shine!"

"Congratulations, Julia," Peter said. "I wish we had someone like you working in our firm. If you ever decide to practice law in California, let me know."

"I hear the California bar is a bear to pass."

"You're a smart woman. You could do it."

"You're right. I could. Thanks for the offer. Just don't be surprised if I take you up on it."

"Well, now," Peter said, "in regard to the retrofitting, it looks like you're out of options. You're going to have to sell J House."

Chapter Thirty-Eight

Andy

Andy stared out the windows to the lights on the Bay Bridge. Even at this time of the night, she saw car lights blink as they crossed the final span from Treasure Island to the city. *I don't care how lovely the scenery is, I want to go home.* Just today she'd read the saying "Home is where the heart is," and she'd been thinking about it ever since. San Francisco wasn't where her heart was, and she was doubtful it ever would be.

If only Bria had been able to stay longer, but I know she had to get back to her job. That's one thing this family does, always gets back to the job. She turned away from the window and chastised herself for acting like such a baby.

Okay, so she was trapped here for the time being, but it wouldn't be forever. Only until Martin recuperated. Then she could resume her life.

She got the milk out of the fridge, poured a mug full, and stuck it into the microwave to warm. She saw Fluffy coming up the stairs from the bedroom. Fluffy hadn't left Martin's side except to eat and use his cat box since Martin had come home. She'd heard of dogs acting this way, but never cats. Cats were said to be too independent. Obviously, Fluffy was an exception.

She sat down at the kitchen table and gave in to her frustration by slamming her fist on the table. The doctor had warned both her and Martin that some depression was frequently a side effect of open-heart surgery. But Martin didn't seem to be making any effort to pull himself out of it. And why did he have to drag her down too? While she was grateful, grateful beyond measure, that Martin was still alive, he didn't seem to care one way or another. If she'd heard it one time, she'd heard it a dozen: "You'd be better off without me. An invalid. Struck down in my prime." The doctor had given him a regimen of exercise, which Martin had promised to do, but whenever she reminded him of it, he said he was too tired or in too much pain.

Maybe she was expecting too much. She couldn't imagine herself acting that way, but then she wasn't the one who'd nearly died.

Tomorrow he had a doctor's appointment, and maybe the doctor would have some encouraging words. She glanced over at the hospital bed that she'd rolled into the corner. She needed to have it picked up. Martin had walked from the parking space, down the stairs, and into their house, then to their bedroom, where he collapsed and said that was where he would stay.

She'd been up and down the stairs a million times since then, getting him this or getting him that. Sometimes she wished she'd never thought of the baby monitor she'd hooked up so she could hear him if he called out. He didn't seem to care one whit that he was making her life ten times harder. Was lack of common courtesy also part of depression?

The microwave beeped. She retrieved the mug from the microwave and her bottle of Tylenol PM from the counter, then she headed for the couch. If Martin needed her, he would call. He didn't have any trouble calling for her on the monitor, no matter where she was or what she was doing. As far as she could tell, only his mouth was getting any exercise.

Her last thought before drifting off to sleep was that Thanksgiving was only two days away, and she'd not even bought the turkey.

❦

"Your incisions look fine. How are you doing with the exercises and walking?" The doctor paused in his examination when Martin didn't answer.

It was all Andy could do to keep her mouth shut. *He's not doing anything. He's not even making an effort.* When the doctor glanced her way, she shook her head.

"Having a bit of a problem with pain?"

Martin nodded, a scant nod that would have been easily missed but for the doctor's focused attention. "I have a hard time getting enough oxygen when I move around a lot."

"Your heart sounds fine." The doctor took out his stethoscope and checked again. He pressed gently on Martin's calves and ankles. "You've got to get moving. I'm going to send a therapist over, say two or three times a week. I know I told you not to go running any marathons, but walking is really important."

"When can I go back to work?"

"That all depends."

"On what?" Martin asked.

"On whether or not you obey your doctor's orders."

Andy rolled her lips together to stifle a grin. *Way to go, Doc. That's putting it on the line.* Now, the question was, would the promise of working again get him up off his duff and exercising?

"All right, I'll exercise."

"Good, but that's not all you're going to have to do. You need to make some lifestyle changes. Your wife told me that you've been on the road four to five days a week, every week, for a number of years. That kind of life takes a toll. My guess is that you work long hours, eat lots of fatty fast food, and don't get any exercise at all."

"Yes, but that's changed. I have an office job now."

"Nine to five?"

When Martin didn't answer, the doctor turned to the counter to write out a prescription, then ripped it off and handed it to Andy. "Here's for the physical therapist. I've written the name of the group associated with us. Insurance will cover it."

"Thank you." Andy sucked on her bottom lip.

"I gave that prescription to your wife, because I understand she didn't know about your heart condition. You were fortunate that she found your medication. She probably saved your life."

Andy hadn't dreamed that the EMTs would pass that information along. Now that the proverbial cat was out of the bag, she wanted to know why he hadn't told her. On second thought, she knew the answer. He believed he could take care of everything on his own, that it wasn't important enough to mention.

"Is it okay for him to be left alone now?" Andy asked.

"You have a job to get back to?"

Yes, but it looks like it will be a long time before I can. "No, I mean for grocery shopping, that kind of thing. Our kids are coming for Thanksgiving and…"

"For short periods, yes." The doctor extended his hand to shake Martin's first, then Andy's. "I hope you folks have an extra special Thanksgiving this year. I'll see you in two weeks, Martin. I'd better not hear that you aren't doing your exercises or that you're keeping any more secrets from your wife. I want to hear that you're planning to change your work habits."

After the doctor had left the examining room, Andy helped Martin with his shirt, then stuck the *Sunset* magazine back in the rack. By the time they got home, Martin was gray with fatigue.

"I never realized a doctor's appointment could be so tiring." Once in the house, he sat down on the edge of the bed, closer to collapsing than sitting.

"Can I get you something to drink—orange juice, hot tea, iced tea, coffee, Diet Coke, water?"

"Is the water bottled?"

"Yes, of course." She hated to drink the city water and knew that he did too. Ah, for the sweet well water of home. "You want ice with it?"

"No thanks, just the bottle will be fine." When she brought it, he asked, "Would you please turn on the TV?"

"You're staying down here?"

"I'm too weak to go up the stairs right now."

Andy put the back of her hand against his forehead and cheek. No temp, but gray still bracketed his mouth and eyes. She stacked extra pillows against the headboard. "There you go." It would be so easy to remind him that if he'd been doing his exercises, he wouldn't be in the state he was in now.

How could I know how he feels? I've never had major surgery of any kind. She trapped a sigh and went back upstairs to the kitchen to set the teapot on. Hot tea sounded not only good but necessary, especially her own blend. Right now she needed the comfort of lavender.

If only she could spend another hour or so with the Girl Squad. Their prayers at the hospital meant more than she could find words for. Why couldn't she? She picked up the phone and dialed J House. Clarice answered. "I know this is asking a lot," she said, trying to hold herself together. "But will all of you come here this afternoon for the weekly prayer session? The doctor said I could leave Martin for short periods of time now, but he's in such a depressed state that..."

"Let me check with everyone," Clarice said. "I don't think it will be a problem. I'll call you back in a few minutes." Good to her word, Clarice called right back and told her they'd be there at four.

Andy was beside herself with excitement. She bustled around the kitchen making scones and lavender tea. Just before four, she checked on Martin to see if he needed anything.

"The Girl Squad is coming over," she said. "They won't be here long."

He held out the remote and turned down the volume on the TV. "What are they coming for?"

"For a prayer session," she said, cleaning up the mess on the nightstand. "We all get together and pray for J House, for each other, and for ourselves."

"Why do you need to pray for J House?"

"The city has ordered that the building be retrofitted by the end of the year, and there's no money to pay for it. We pray that some big corporation will come forward and donate the money." A thought came to her. "What about AES? Could they use a big tax write-off?"

Martin rolled his eyes and snorted. "Why don't they just sell? That's prime real estate there. They could get a bundle for it, proba-bly enough to buy a bigger place in a lower rent district that doesn't need retrofitting."

"Roger and Hope—they don't want to sell. They love J House. It's their home, and it's been the home to many a girl in need. They've saved lives there, built dreams there."

"It's just a building, Andy."

All she could do was stare at him. "It's not just a building. It's a dream. You don't understand what it means to them, just like you don't understand what Lavender Meadows means to me."

"Don't look at me like I'm some freak from outer space. I'm sorry I don't understand why people get so attached to houses or land. They don't mean anything to me, never did and never will."

Andy's anger died an instant death. An overwhelming feeling of sadness assailed her. He had no frame of reference. He'd grown up moving from place to place. He'd grown up without a place to call home. She had accused him of not being able to understand, but it was she who had not understood.

Chapter Thirty-Nine

The Girl Squad arrived promptly at four. They spent a good fifteen minutes sipping tea and eating scones. Hope mentioned that several boxes had arrived from the church in Medford. They planned to open them after Julia's next class.

Clarice briefed Andy on recent events: Blakely Associates' demise, Gregor's being found, and phone calls from a girl they thought to be Cyndy.

When they gathered in a circle to pray, a sense of peace floated among them. They fell silent, exhaling any sense of hurry. After thanking Big Dad for the prayers He had already answered, Hope prayed first for J House and then for her unborn child. No longer hesitant, Clarice thanked God and praised Him for Julia and her successful efforts in finding Gregor.

"And please, Lord, give that man his just deserts, which You can do so much better than we can." That gave them all the giggles as they let their imaginations speculate on just what that would be. Julia prayed to be reunited with Cyndy. For the first time, she added a second prayer, for her daughter, Donna.

I don't want to burden them all, Lord, Andy prayed silently. Such a long and convoluted tale. But once she began, it was like God opened the floodgates and her story poured forth. "Amen's" and "Please, Lord's" punctuated her silences when the tears became too much.

"I blamed Martin for everything, and Father, You showed me that I needed to practice love, real love, the kind You talk about in Your Word." She took the tissue someone handed her. "I resented him for wanting to move, for being so unsympathetic to my business, my parents' needs, for all the times he went ahead and made decisions without considering me or the kids." Between sobs she added anything else she could think of. "Lord, I don't ever want to have to go through this again. I'm a mess." She blew her nose and cleared her throat. "But God, You are so good; You really let me see that love works." She blew out a sigh. "Thank You, Father, for these women. I know that if I hadn't come here in spite of myself, I'd never have met them." She gave them each a wavering smile.

"Amen to that." Julia echoed. "I'd never make it without all of you."

"Amen," they all said together.

Later that evening, after dinner, Andy sat down at the table to write a grocery list. She'd go shopping after picking up Morgan from the airport tomorrow.

The phone rang. Andy answered it on the first ring and heard Bria's perky voice.

"How did Dad's appointment go?"

"Very well. Doctor said his heart sounds great, and the incisions are looking good." She recalled her last trip downstairs, seeing that Martin had rolled onto his side and seemed to be sleeping peacefully. She'd gotten used to seeing the furrows on his forehead that indicated discomfort.

"I'll either rent a car or come into the city via BART, so don't worry about me, okay?"

"When are you arriving?"

"I'm taking the early flight, so I should be ahead of the masses on Wednesday morning. What time is Camden coming in?"

"If the flights are all on time, he and Morgan are within an hour of each other, about four tomorrow."

"Okay. Here's what we'll do. I'll come straight to your house. We can go grocery shopping, and then I'll head out and pick up the others. I'll e-mail them where to meet me, and they can call me if there is a problem."

"Thanks, honey."

"Are you all right, Mom?"

"As good as can be expected, I guess. Just please remind them both that this will not be a normal Thanksgiving."

"All that counts is that we'll all be together. Oh, I forgot to ask, are Grandma and Grandpa coming?

"They're driving, in spite of Dad dreading the trip."

"Wonderful. I've been thinking, we could order one of those cooked turkey dinners from a restaurant or grocery store."

"I think you have to do that before the last minute."

"Hey, we're two days out, what's this last-minute garbage? Give Daddy a hug from me, and I'll talk with him later. I love you, Mom."

"And I, you." Andy blinked back the tears that hovered so close to the surface.

She finished her grocery list, including a reminder to buy pies. She'd never bought pies for Thanksgiving in her whole life. They always had pumpkin pie, made from their own pumpkins left from Halloween, apple pie, and lemon cheese pie, her specialty. Homemade rolls, perhaps she could still make them.

"Andy, could you help me please? I'd like to come upstairs." Martin's voice came through the baby monitor.

"I'll be right down." Had she heard him right?

Coming up, he took the steps slowly, with her one step behind him. If he would only try harder. But then, she didn't always do what was best for herself either, she reminded herself. It had only been two weeks since the surgery. *A little patience wouldn't hurt, Andy.*

She almost snorted at that. Since when had patience ever been one of her stronger attributes?

Martin settled on the sofa and used his TV remote to turn on a music station. "Soft rock okay?" he asked.

"Sure." She sat down beside him and leaned her head on his shoulder.

He reached up and cupped her cheek. "Thank you for being such a good nurse."

"You scared me half to death."

"I scared myself."

They sat just so until he shifted and flinched.

"I'd better get dinner going," she said, giving him a quick kiss before getting up.

Fifteen minutes later she had a chicken casserole in the oven and a salad chilling in the fridge.

She looked over at Martin and saw him staring out the windows.

Was the stress of his new job the cause of Martin's heart attack? Or had he been leading up to this for years? The doctor had told him point-blank he would have to make some lifestyle changes. What would Martin do to comply? Would he ignore that suggestion the way he'd ignored the doctor's order to exercise?

The problem was that this house was surrounded by steps, which would make taking a walk difficult. If only they were home in Medford. He could walk forever among the lavender plants and never encounter a single stair.

Fluffy jumped up on the table in front of the living room window and meowed.

"Hey, boy, what do you want?" Martin asked, moving his head this way and that, trying to see what Fluffy was seeing.

Fluffy sank down on his belly, the tip of his tail twitching back and forth.

Martin got up and went to the window. "Are there birds out there?"

"Maybe it's the parrots," Andy said. "I've heard them several times, but I haven't actually seen them." They were a pair, man and cat, looking out the window.

"I guess it was a false alarm." Martin returned to the sofa and changed the station to one that played worship songs and hymns. The familiar music lifted Andy's heart. Maybe that was why the Bible said to sing songs of praise, no matter what. The thought made her smile. Maybe so.

The ringing phone snagged her attention, and she could feel the smile clear to her toes when she recognized Camden's "Hello."

"Hey, Son, see you soon."

"I hope so. I thought I'd better warn you, though, that we have a Northerner coming in, high winds and heavy snow predicted."

"Oh no. We'll all be so terribly disappointed if you can't make it."

"I'll call you tomorrow when I know what's happening."

Fog blanketed the entire West Coast for forty-eight hours, stopped all incoming and outgoing flights, and closed Interstate 5 in both directions. After the last phone call from SeaTac, Bria had taken Morgan home to her apartment so at least two members of the Taylor family were together. Camden had given up on Wednesday morning and went to stay with a friend.

Andy locked her arms around her middle, hands clutching her elbows. The only reason she and Martin were having any kind of Thanksgiving dinner today was because she had walked up to Speedy's and bought the last frozen turkey breast they had, along with stuffing mix. Never before had she made Stove Top Stuffing Mix.

To think that she'd left what she thought of as the fog capital of the world only to get socked in in San Francisco. Delayed flights in and out of Medford, however, did not make a difference in worldwide traffic—like SFO. She thought back to the conversation with her daughter.

"We can drive all night, taking turns sleeping and driving," Bria had offered.

"The news says it is all up and down the coast. I'd rather know you are safe and alive than think of you driving in fog for twenty hours or more."

Morgan took over the phone. "But, Mom, I want to. I need to see you and Daddy. He needs us."

"Thanks, sweetheart, but we need you safe even more." They'd never know what it had cost her to say those words.

"God, right now I am having a real hard time being grateful." She heard the toilet flush and knew Martin was up. Time to make the coffee and see what he wanted for breakfast. He was moving about a bit more, had even taken Fluffy outside to look for the parrots, but his appetite was still poor. She'd cooked all manner of things to try to entice him, only to have him take a couple of bites and push his plate away. She felt like a short-order cook, a waitress, and a busboy all in one. *Andrea Marie Taylor, you have to do something with all this anger you're carrying.* She waved away the Bible verse that floated through her mind. So what if Paul had been in jail in Rome when he wrote, *"I have learned in whatever state I am, to be content."*

The coffee fragrance followed her downstairs to find Martin sound asleep again. She glanced at the clock. Nine. "Martin, I'm starting breakfast. What would you like?"

"Huh?" He blinked and glanced over at the clock. "What did you say?"

"Breakfast. You have to eat so you can take your meds."

"Oh. I—all right."

"You want help with a sponge bath?"

"I'd give my left arm for a shower."

"Better keep that arm, you might need it. After you eat, I'll wash your back and give you a rub if you want." Keeping the incisions dry was still necessary.

Back upstairs, Andy set water boiling and coffee dripping, fed the cat, and stepped outside to cut lavender stems off the potted plant she'd bought at the grocery store. She cut several and held them to her nose. The scent reminded her of home so much that tears threatened to swamp her.

By now she would have had the twenty-pound turkey on the Weber kettle outside on the patio. The pies would be all baked and the green bean casserole ready for the oven. Her mother would bring candied yams and a salad and some new recipes that she always tried out on them. Some had become classics, like the cranberry salad; others, like the oyster stuffing, had been discreetly set aside after being sampled. Oyster stuffing had turned into a family joke.

This house felt resoundingly jokeless. She wished she could have invited Mrs. Getz to dinner or taken Hope up on her invitation to join them at J House. But the doctor had made it clear that Martin wasn't to be with other people other than the children. In his present weakened condition, there was too big a risk of his catching something or picking up an infection.

She cracked the eggs one at a time into a saucer and slid them into the softly bubbling water. Plunking the toast down, she set the tray with a fall napkin for decoration, next to the bud vase. It would sure be easier if Martin came upstairs like two nights ago.

With the eggs cooked just the way he liked them, she made her way carefully down the stairs. All she needed to do was fall and break something. *All right, woman, this is the time to think some positive thoughts, or you'll be as depressed as Martin.*

He pushed his pillows up behind him and smoothed the comforter to make way for the tray she set across his knees. "Thanks."

She slid her plate out from under his and transferred one of the eggs and a piece of toast to her plate. "You need anything else?"

"No, this is fine." He rubbed his chest.

"Hurt?"

"No, itches."

She watched as he ate a couple of bites and then moved the rest of the eggs around on the plate. "You have to eat."

"If you knew how I feel…" He focused on his buttered toast and drank from the cup. The orange juice sat untouched.

"Taking those stupid pain pills makes me constipated." He rubbed his abdomen.

The phone rang, and he looked toward her to answer it.

"Martin, it is right by your hand." At his look of beaten supplication, she set her plate and silver on the end of the bed and huffed her way to the phone. This was getting ridiculous. "You don't have a broken arm. Hello?"

"Happy Thanksgiving." Both Bria and Morgan spoke together.

"Happy Thanksgiving to you, too. Did you have a good dinner?"

"Bria sure knows how to order in."

"Don't give away my secrets."

Andy laughed at their antics. They sounded like her children of a few years ago.

"Mom, are you all right?" Bria's voice clicked into concern.

"Of course." Andy forced herself to sound cheerful. "How's Seattle? It's clear here."

"No flights yet, although it isn't as bad as yesterday. So did you get groceries to make dinner?"

"Frozen turkey breast and Stove Top Stuffing."

"Mom, you didn't." Morgan burst into laughter.

"It was better than frozen TV dinners." Andy laughed again with her girls.

"Is Daddy near the phone?"

"He's right here. I'll talk with you later. I love you, and have a fun weekend together." She handed the phone to Martin, then picked up his tray, added her things to it, and headed up the stairs.

How do I keep from comparing this Thanksgiving to the years before? Pretty soon I'll feel as depressed as Martin does. Lord, this isn't fair, You know that?

Chapter Forty

Hope

"Roger, I have a favor to ask." Clarice was placing turkey-shaped cookies on the serving tray.

"Sure, what's up?" He turned to smile at her, continuing to peel potatoes, as he and Alphi had been doing since early morning.

"I would like to go find Angel Annie and invite her here for dinner. Would you drive me? Julia would, but she has no idea where AA hangs out."

"She's usually over on Market. Sure, but don't be too disappointed if she refuses. She's not known for her sociability."

"You keep saying that, but she saved my life. She didn't have to take care of me like that."

"True. You know that Angel isn't her first name?"

"To me she is. And if she won't come, then I'll take dinner back to her."

"The irresistible object has met the immovable force. We'll see who wins. When do you want to go?"

"Well, I thought we could offer her a shower and maybe clean clothes, if she'll let us."

"We can offer. Let me get these potatoes soaking, and then we'll go."

"Roger Benson, you get my vote for sainthood." Clarice leaned over and kissed the top of his head.

"You messed his hair." Alphi slapped his knees and nearly fell off his stool laughing.

Roger smoothed a hand across his spreading dome. "Knock it off, kid, or you peel by yourself." He pointed to the forty-pound bag still to be opened. Several of the women working at the counters around the room joined Alphi's giggles.

"Not much to mess with, is there?" Celia didn't even try to stem her taunting laughter.

"There's too much jollity going on in here." Hope paused in the doorway. "And Roger, it sounds like they are picking on you."

He nodded, trying to look pathetic, which set Alphi off again.

"Roger, the can opener is stuck again," Tasha called from across the room.

"You got to admit, you one popular dude." Celia nudged him on her way back to the stove.

Roger heaved himself to his feet, giving the stool a slight kick so that it banged against Alphi.

"Hey, Dude." He strung the short word into three syllables.

Clarice rapped Alphi on top of his head. "What's seven times nine."

"Not math on Thanksgiving. Dis a holiday."

"Come on."

"Sixty-three."

"Yes, you, boy, are the winner." Clarice handed him the tail part of a turkey-shaped ginger cookie.

"How come I don't get one?" one of the girls wailed.

"This was broken, so it needed to be eaten before it dried out."

"Gee, and since it was broken, all the calories ran out."

"You like him better 'n me, that's all."

"My kind of cookie." The banter kept up, bouncing around the room like a wayward SuperBall.

Clarice checked the yeast dough she'd set to raise at five thirty this morning. "Someone want to form the rolls?"

Two hands went up, so she beckoned the two girls over. "You ever made rolls before?"

Both girls shook their heads.

"Okay, I'll show you a quick way." Clarice sprinkled flour on the steel table surface, cut off two pieces of dough, set them on the flour, cupped her hands over them and rolled each bit of dough on the counter into a ball, then plopped them in the pan.

"Hey, cool." One girl tried it, but her dough didn't look anything like the smooth balls Clarice had made.

She showed them again and began cutting pieces of dough, while they practiced until they were both laughing at their success.

"You teach me that?" Fawna, their chef-in-training, came over to admire the smooth balls of dough lining the pans.

"Watch them." Clarice nodded to the girls, who were racing to see who filled a pan first.

"Homemade rolls for Thanksgiving at J House. This gets out, and we'll have to lock the doors on the hordes of guests." Hope snitched a bit of the dough and headed back out the door laughing. "We're near to setup out here." She led the team that set and decorated all the tables.

"Okay, Clarice, let's go. I found another sucker to finish the potatoes." Roger announced a few minutes later.

She nodded to her two helpers. "You can finish?"

"Go on, he waitin'."

She stopped at Fawna's side. "The rolls need to rise double in size, then bake for fifteen to twenty minutes at 350 degrees. I used to take a cube of cold butter and use it like a crayon to butter the tops of the baked rolls while still hot."

"Okay, and they need to cool on racks like cookies?" the chef-in-training smiled.

"That's right. And you might threaten anyone who snatches one with no dinner." She leaned closer to whisper. "There are two more bags of rolls in the closet in the office. I baked them the other day. "

Fawna snorted. "I wondered where they went."

Roger and Clarice found Annie right in her normal spot, her trash bags of belongings surrounding her.

Clarice, wearing her fur coat against the cold wind, got out of the car and crossed the sidewalk. "Annie?"

"Yeah, who's askin'?"

"You probably don't remember me, but one night you told me to flag down a cop…"

"Yeah, I remember. You so dumb you wearing that same coat?"

"Only one I have."

"Someone gonna knife you for that coat."

"No, they won't. I live and work at J House. I'm not living on the streets, thanks to you."

"Ah."

"We are serving Thanksgiving dinner, and I want to invite you to come with Roger"—she motioned to the car with the door open—"and me to have dinner at J House. I can offer you a shower and clean clothes too, if you'd like."

"I leave and someone steal my spot."

"Come on, Annie, no one would dare to steal your spot," Roger called from the car.

"No, no." She shook her head and shrank back into her heap of ragged blankets and canvas. "You can't make me."

"I'm not trying to force you. I just want to repay you for saving my life."

"No, no, go 'way." Her voice rose as if someone were beating her.

"Easy." Clarice stepped back and shot Roger a pleading look.

He shrugged. He had warned her.

Clarice nodded. "All right, then I'll be back later with food for you and perhaps some of your friends."

The man on the next spot of sidewalk guffawed. "A-Annie don't got no friends."

Clarice drew herself up a good three inches. "Her name is Angel Annie, and she does have friends." She pointed to the car. "Roger and me and lots of others. I'll be back."

"Bring a bottle with you, honey." The man pulled a piece of plastic tarp closer around him.

Clarice sighed. At least she'd tried. But this wasn't the end of it. If there was a way to get through to Annie, she'd find it.

And if not, she'd done her best. Maybe Annie didn't realize she was an angel. She'd been called by that other obscenity for so long, she probably believed it.

When Roger and Clarice got back, the aromas of roasting turkey and baking rolls, all overlaid with laughter and the hum of busy people, floated out from J House like a welcome beacon. A line had already begun to form outside the front door.

"Let me check and see if you can wait inside," Roger told the gathering.

The crowd had tripled or more by the time the serving lines were set up, those serving the food wearing hair nets and clear plastic gloves, per the health department regulations.

"Okay, everyone. Can I have your attention?" Roger raised his voice and said it all again, waving his arms to get their attention.

Celia shook her head, put two fingers in her mouth, and whistled loud enough to dim a police whistle. Instant silence. She nodded toward Roger, her grin daring him to beat that.

"Thank you, Miss Celia. Let's bow our heads and thank our heavenly Father for all the good He has given us." He waited a moment. "Father God, we thank You for this warm place, all the food You have provided, and those who have come to serve. Thank You for our guests and those who live here, as we all learn of You and Your love. Thank You for Your Word and for Your Son, in whose precious name of Jesus we pray. Amen."

"Dinner is served." Hope stood at the beginning of the serving line. "Line starts here. There's plenty of food, so no rush."

Two hours later the food was gone, but for what Clarice set aside for Annie and friends. While some people had left, others were sitting around the tables visiting—street people, residents, former residents, family, friends, volunteers, it didn't matter. Raving about the dinner, complaining about the government, catching up on old news. Children played in the play area; several checkerboards came out; two old men played dominoes and taught some younger folks the intricacies of the game.

"This is what J House is all about." Roger slipped his arms around his wife's waist.

"If only we could keep it this way." Hope leaned back into the protection of his arms.

"I know." He kissed the back of her neck. "I'm taking Julia and Clarice down to feed Annie et al."

"They're not 'et al.'" She dug an elbow into his ribs with only enough force to make her point.

They listened to the phone ring, started toward it, and knew someone had already picked up the receiver. A few moments later a shocked-looking Julia came out of the office.

"That was Cyndy. She said she almost came to the dinner, but then something scared her." Tears trickled down Julia's face. "I talked with my granddaughter. On Thanksgiving. She said not to worry. Ha. But at least I heard her voice." She stepped into the circle of arms, and the three of them hugged.

In a bit she blew out one breath and then another, shaking her head in wonderment. "Well, let's go feed Angel Annie."

"You know what her real street name is?"

"I do, but I'm not going to push that one on Clarice. If she thinks Annie is an angel, so do I."

"You came back." Annie took the foam containers Clarice handed her.

"I told you I would." Clarice returned to the car for a carton of hot coffee.

"Dint you bring nothin' stronger?" The man next to her took his package with a gruff "Thanks."

"Sorry, strongest we have." Roger passed out two more boxes. "You ever decide you want off the streets, you can find me at J House, and I'll see how I can help."

"That's for women."

"On the inside, but you never know where help will come from anyway, or for whom."

Clarice knelt in front of Annie. "I'll see you again."

"Don't need to." But even in the shadows, Clarice recognized the grimace for what it was—a smile.

"What a day." Clarice leaned against the car seat as the three of them drove back to J House.

"Amen to that."

"Did you call Andy?" Julia asked from the backseat.

"No, but we can do that when we get back."

True to their decision, as soon as they got back to J House, Julia and Clarice grabbed Hope's arm and pulled her into the office to use the speakerphone so they could all talk. "Happy Thanksgiving. We missed you," they chorused when Andy answered the phone.

"Me too." Her laugh wore a patina of tears.

"So what did you do to celebrate?"

"I read a book. That's what I did most of the day. The fog kept my parents and the kids from coming, and Martin wanted to stay in bed and watch football on TV, so I turned on the fireplace and read. What a treat."

"Did you have turkey and the trimmings?"

"Yep. How was it there?" Andy squealed when Julia said she'd talked with Cyndy. And laughed at some of their other stories. "Wish I could have come."

"Next year."

"Perhaps. And if the kids are here, they can come help too."

"Tell Martin we're praying for him." They said their good-byes, and Clarice pressed the Disconnect button.

"I think she was pretty down today." Julia leaned back in the office chair and rubbed her upper arms. "I think it's time we work on Martin."

Clarice held both thumbs up. The grin they all shared boded interesting times ahead for Martin Taylor.

"And J House."

Chapter Forty-One

Hope

"I had a weird dream last night."

"Must not have been bad, if you didn't wake me." Roger sat down on the edge of the bed, first cup of coffee for the day in his hands. The fragrance of it made her groan.

"Not *the* nightmare. I was at an auction and bidding on something. No idea what, but I woke up with an incredible idea." Hope paused and patted back a yawn. "Do you believe that sometimes dreams give us instructions?"

"Well, they did so in the Bible, so that is good enough for me." He shrugged and rotated his shoulders, tipping his head side to side to stretch his neck.

"Hurting?"

"Not bad. So what's your great idea?"

"That we set up an auction for the property—for J House."

"As in big crowd, auctioneer, that kind of thing?" He looked over his shoulder at her, eyebrows nearly meeting and his mouth sideways. "You've got to be kidding. That wouldn't work. I'd bid a thousand."

"No, you nut." She thumped him on the shoulder nearest her.

"You're gonna spill my coffee."

"I'm thinking we invite a special group, all those people who've contacted us with possible offers."

"You want them to duke it out?"

"No, I want us to all work together to see if we can help each other out."

"At an auction? Honey, that dream must have scrambled your brains."

"Knock it off, Hotshot, and help me think."

"I can't. I haven't had breakfast yet. My brain doesn't work when my stomach is empty."

She gave him a gentle push. "Go eat while I shower. Big things ahead." Her mind continued leapfrogging from idea to idea while she soaped and rinsed. How could this be a win-win situation for everyone? If she and Roger didn't want to be in the Tenderloin, where did they want to be? *Right here, this is where I want to be.* The little voice popped up whenever she gave it a moment. Or it could steal a moment. First things first: make a brainstorming list, call and talk to Peter, go looking for other areas to move to, not specific buildings. *An auction. Big Dad, are You sure You want us to go this way?*

As soon as she was dressed, she opened her Bible. *"I know the plans I have for you, plans to prosper you and not to harm you."* In all their praying, there had not been any indication anywhere that He wanted them to close the shelter, but since He'd not sent a retrofit savior, the only alternative was to relocate. So He had to have a place in mind. But knowing the way He worked, He wouldn't show it to them until the last minute. She liked the line, *God is slow, but He is never late.* That sure applied here. And what about the Saturday Market? Surely He had a plan for that too.

"Breakfast's ready."

"Thanks." She took her pen and pad along with her. After grace she studied the lists. "You want to hear what's at the top of the list?"

"Sure." He passed her the buttered toast.

"Make lists of all I know or think about this auction."

"Sounds good." He nodded.

"Call Peter."

"Yes." He glanced at her plate. "Your eggs are getting cold."

She ate a couple of bites. "Number three is look for an area where we might like to be. Other than right here. We probably should drive by that apartment building in the Tenderloin."

He shuddered. "You won't like it."

"I'm trying to be grateful in all ways. Better any roof over our heads than closing the doors."

"I stand rebuked. You're handling this better than me."

Hope sighed. "Oh, how I wish that were true. But if we can't count on Big Dad now, when can we?"

"You want me to what?" Peter stared at her, only his one finger tapping on the pad of paper in front of him. "Why don't you just dictate the letter to Clarice while I try to assimilate what I think you said."

"Okay." Hope slit her eyes, the better to think. "Dear Blank." She nodded to Peter. "You have to fill in the blanks."

"Fine."

"I am calling a meeting of all those parties still interested in purchasing Casa de Jesús." She paused. "Okay, back up and change 'still interested' to 'who have shown interest.'"

Clarice nodded.

Peter was nodding by the time Hope had composed her idea for the letter. "This is far out, but what I've noticed is that God works way outside the box, and perhaps He has given you an outside-the-box idea. Let me see if I have this clear. The potential buyers are to bring any properties they have access to that might work for your new place to the table along with their offers on this place?" She nodded as he continued. "And be prepared to be creative."

"Yes, that last is most important."

"Do you have a date in mind?"

"Yes, but before I tell you, do you think that if this deal goes through, the building department will allow us to stay here until we can complete the transfer?"

"All we can do is try."

"You're looking a bit shell-shocked, my friend." Roger leaned back in his chair, arms across his chest, but the grin said he was enjoying Peter's confusion. "Now you know how I've felt all day."

"If you two are done commiserating, I say we do this thing in two weeks. I want it all done before Christmas."

"Two weeks!" Roger and Peter wore the same looks of astonishment and snapped out the same words.

Hope shook her head. "You know Big Dad delights in last-minute answers. Far as I can see, we are about down to last-minute. I do not want to see a Condemned sign on the barred door. So the meeting is scheduled for the fifteenth. You want it here or at your office?"

"My office."

"You are still shaking your head. See now, all you have to do is pretty that letter up with all your legalese and send it out."

"I can't believe this."

"You want me to type this up?" Clarice held up her pad.

"Yes, please. I'll take it with me."

"Hard copy and disc?"

"Yes." When Clarice left, Peter turned to Hope. "You have a real jewel there."

"And the beauty of it, she wants to stay on."

A short time later, after Peter left with the promise to have this in the hands of the potential buyers by the morning, Hope drank half a glass of water without stopping. "I'm calling the Girl Squad for another prayer session. You have anything you want covered?"

"Just the usual. I'll be ready in about ten minutes for a drive to look at other areas." Roger slapped his thigh. "Come on Adolph, let's get you a quick run."

Hope dialed Peter's number. "Give Peter a message for me, please, Wendy. Tell him to add a P.S. to the letter. 'Be prepared to finalize a deal at that time.'" Wendy repeated back what Hope had said. "That's right, thanks."

"Hey, Clarice, do you know how to send out group messages to our e-mail group? I need to ask them all to pray for us for the next two weeks, that Big Dad will have His way."

"That's all you want to say?"

"Pretty much."

"You're not going to tell them what's going on?'

"Nope. Tell Julia we'll be back in time for the training session tonight. I don't have anything else on the calendar, do I?"

"No, nothing written down."

"I'm going to clue Celia in, and then we're out of here. Oh, and call Andy and Julia to see if they can meet here tomorrow morning."

"I will."

"So what do you think?" Hope asked Celia after explaining what had gone on.

"I think Big Dad come through on this one. And when He does, I don't never doubt again."

Hope puffed out her cheeks on an exhale. "Me either. Pray hard."

Chapter Forty-Two

Andy

Andy stared at the calendar she'd just flipped over. December 1. What a difference a week could make. Martin's entire attitude had changed, all because he'd stopped taking the pain pills. Well, that probably wasn't the only reason. It might have had a little something to do with changes she'd made as well—changes she hadn't been capable of making until the Girl Squad had prayed for her.

First, she stopped feeling sorry for herself. So what that it had been a lousy Thanksgiving? Thanksgiving was just a day. Martin was her life.

The physical therapist had come the day after Thanksgiving and started Martin on an exercise program.

Friday, Andy called Martin's doctor, told him he'd stopped taking the pain pills, and asked if he could attend church on Sunday. Because of the physical therapist's report, he agreed.

Just getting out of the house had given Andy a much-needed lift. Having Martin by her side boosted her even higher.

Outside J House, before the service, Martin shook hands and personally thanked Hope, Roger, Clarice, and Julia for the help and support they'd given him and Andy these last three weeks. On the way in, he discreetly put a check in the donation box, then led her to seats near the front and sat down next to Celia.

Andy introduced him to Celia, and before the service started, she overheard Martin ask Celia about her long fingernails. How could she function with them? Celia laughed and said, "All the better to scratch yourself with," and demonstrated by poking a nail into her neon-blue hair and scratching her scalp. Andy gently elbowed Martin. She didn't know whether to be embarrassed or glad he'd struck up a conversation with a stranger. Celia didn't seem the least bit offended, but Andy knew Celia had seen and heard it all. Besides, anyone who dressed like Celia was just begging for attention. And Martin had given it to her.

Andy was glad to see Hope come to the lectern. Not for the first time, she thought Hope didn't look like any pastor she'd ever seen before with her orangy hair, her slightly exotic features, and now her protruding belly. Hope reminded the congregation that fear was not of God, that worry was not of God, and… Andy couldn't remember the third point, but the main point had been, "Our loving duty is to praise Him for everything. The good, the bad, everything."

That afternoon Andy sat down at her computer and waited for the messages to download. As much as she'd enjoyed Hope's sermon, she took issue with praising God for everything that came by. She could praise Him for healing Martin, but not for Martin's getting sick. She could praise Him for giving her such wonderful children, but not for the fog and weather that had kept her kids away. She could praise Him for the abundance in her life, but not for Martin's being a workaholic.

The end of the sermon echoed in her ears. "If you don't know how to praise Him, you must learn." A children's song that she'd learned long ago danced through her head. She sang the words. "Praise Him, praise Him, all ye little children, God is love, God is love." Maybe if she sang the words long enough, she would be able to accept them.

"Did you say something?" Martin called from the bottom of the stairs. He'd been in the living room all afternoon working on his computer, trying to catch up. Earlier in the week, his secretary had brought over some paperwork for him to go through, and later today his boss would be making a visit.

"I was just singing," she called back. Then in a whisper she added, "Thank You, Father, that Martin is feeling better." It was easy to praise the positive things. "Do you need anything?"

"No. I'm just going to take Fluffy out for a walk. He really wants to see those parrots, and so do I."

"Okay," she called back, then in a whisper, "Thank You for giving us Fluffy." At length, she opened her e-mail program. It wasn't just any e-mail program. This one was a fancy one that let her add smiley faces, animal pictures, and almost any kind of clip art. But best of all, she could make her own e-mail stationery. Consequently, every e-mail she sent had a soft-focus background picture of Lavender Meadows or closeups of lavender stems or bouquets of lavender.

The first few e-mails were from her Medford friends, filling her in on their Thanksgivings. A couple were spam, which she blocked so they couldn't e-mail her again. Like it would really do any good; for every one she blocked, two came in its place. She often thought she would like to meet the people who sent her those porno e-mails and give them a piece of her mind.

She clicked on an e-mail from her mom. There wasn't any message, but the paperclip in the corner told her there was an attachment. She clicked on that and waited.

The attachment hadn't even finished opening when the phone rang. Andy could see by the LED display that it was her mother.

"Hi, Mom. What a coincidence. I'm just this second downloading the picture you sent. What's up?" The picture came onto the screen. It looked to be a plot of land. They talked in general about how Martin was, their Thanksgivings, and the kids. "What's this picture?" she asked at the first conversation break.

"It's the McCauley farm. They're moving to Ohio to take care of their aging parents. Fred McCauley walked over this morning and told me that he wanted to check with us before he listed the farm with a Realtor. He thought we might be interested in buying it so we could expand."

Andy nearly dropped the phone. Of course she'd thought about expanding Lavender Meadows, but not beyond the few unplanted acres they had left, since that was all they had. Just last week, however, Shari had put together some projections for Lavender Meadows' growth. Andy hadn't had time to study them yet, but she had printed them out and left them in her ever-growing pile of to-dos.

"What did you tell him?"

"That I'd call you."

"How many acres is it?"

"Thirty."

Andy was afraid to ask how much. She knew what property was going for in and around Lavender Meadows, so she knew approximately what the land was worth. "We don't have any money to buy it, Mom. We'd have to take out a loan for the down and…"

"No, we wouldn't," her mother interrupted. "He said he doesn't need a down, that he'd be willing to carry the paper himself for fifteen years."

"How much is he asking?"

"One hundred thousand."

"That's crazy. It's worth a lot more than that."

"Yes, it is, but he's willing to sell it to you for that price, because most of the land isn't buildable and because he doesn't want anybody tearing down the old house. He remembers when you rallied to save the Jessop place and thought maybe you'd do the same for his old family home." Alice rattled off the rest of the details, and when she finished, she said, "I know that this isn't the best time to lay this on you, honey, but I didn't have any choice."

Andy put her hand over her mouth and stared at the picture on her screen. The price and the terms were beyond belief. Surely, the property was worth two or three times that amount, even though they couldn't use it for housing construction. She remembered the house. It had been built in the 1880s. It was a rare old gem, and it would indeed be tragic to lose it to some tract-house developer.

"Mom, do you know what having that thirty acres would mean? We could more than double our fields."

"It would also mean we'd have to hire more people, not just to plant the lavender, but to care for it, to harvest it, and to ship the final products. One thing, though, that old house is real close to the main road. We could spruce it up a bit inside and outside and use it as a retail store."

Andy gasped. Flashes of varying shades of lavender paint and white gingerbread trim danced like breeze-nodding blossoms through her head. "That's a great idea. Mom, you're a genius! Let me talk to Martin, and I'll call you back."

Andy dug Shari's market projections out of her pile, sat down with a cup of tea, and studied them.

Martin and Fluffy came back, and both of them went to get a drink, Fluffy to his bowl and Martin to the small fridge she kept in her spare bedroom/office.

"What are you doing?" he asked between swallows.

It had been three weeks since she'd said anything about the business to Martin. And it had been three weeks since she'd seen any signs of jealousy. That his mind had been on other things—like staying alive—might have had something to do with it.

"I'm looking at the sales figures for the last quarter and the sales projections for Lavender Meadows," she said, ignoring the jolt of fear that hit her between the eyes. The last thing she wanted to do was put him in a bad mood.

"Who put them together for you?"

"Shari."

"Our neighbor, Shari?"

"That's the one. She's the employee I told you I'd hired."

"So what's it look like?"

"See for yourself." She handed him the papers. *Okay, God. I need You right now. Really need You. Things have been going so well this last week. He's been just like my old Martin, and I want him to stay that way.* As he read, Andy watched his facial expressions and sipped her tea. An eyebrow rose, then he frowned, then both eyebrows rose. She was just about to tear the papers out of his hands when he set them down on the desk.

"It looks to me like you can afford to either hire Shari full-time or hire someone else part-time. Either way, it means—" The doorbell rang. "That's probably my boss. I'll get it." He started for the door.

Andy listened to Martin greet Brad Grandolay and heard their footsteps as they went up the stairs to the living room. While Martin hadn't said anything about her being around while they talked, she didn't think either of them would be comfortable with her nearby, so she went back to work.

She spent the next hour alternately thinking about what Martin had said, wondering what he would have said if the doorbell hadn't rung, and trying to analyze Shari's figures. To Martin the sales figures meant she could afford more help, which would free her up to spend more time in San Francisco with him. But to her, they meant the business was growing faster than any of them had realized and that they would have to plant the rest of the acreage this spring or turn down orders for lack of product. Planting the rest of the acreage would barely yield enough lavender to keep up with current orders. And what with the online catalog business growing…

It was dark by the time Andy went back upstairs. Martin's boss was gone, and Martin and Fluffy were sitting on the sofa staring out the windows at the lights.

"Don't you want some light on in here?" she asked, heading for the switch. When Martin didn't answer, she thought he must be deep in concentration. "I'm fixing salmon for dinner." Martin loved salmon and usually made some comment to that effect, but not this night. "Martin, are you all right? Do you have pain?"

He turned and looked at her over his shoulder. "I'm fine. I'm just sitting here thinking, that's all. Salmon sounds good."

Andy decided two could play at the thinking game. She had every bit as much to think about as Martin. A half hour later, when she put dinner on the table, she'd made her decision. She wanted those thirty acres. Now that she'd had a taste of success, she wanted more. In that way, she supposed she was a lot like Martin. Hopefully, she would never get so involved with her work as to exclude the people most important her: her family. *Thank You, Lord for this opportunity. Now how do I tell Martin?*

Chapter Forty-Three

Julia

"I've got a surprise for you all as soon as we finish working on your résumés." Julia smiled at their groans. Tonight they had ten girls, several of whom were ready to send out their résumés. She had a list of places for them to send to, knowing that the first time out would most likely be practice.

Fawna burst through the door. "I did it. I got a job."

"With Peter's chef?"

"Yes! No more fast food." She pumped the air with a fist clenching a paper. "I am now an assistant chef."

The others all clapped and cheered, squealed, ran up and hugged Fawna, and then all of them were in a circle, arms over shoulders, doing a kick dance around the ring. Once around and Clarice stopped, patting her chest.

"I never did a dance like that before."

"You kick pretty good for someone your age." Celia fanned her heaving bosom.

"Okay, back to résumés." Julia raised her voice, then repeated her message louder.

"Slave driver." A couple muttered but flashed her grins as they took their places again.

"Where's Hope?" someone asked.

"She supposed to be lying down. Had a big day."

"She's right here. What's the hoopla about?" Hope strolled through the door.

"I got the job!" Fawna rushed over to Hope and showed her the paper. "See, it says so right here. I'm their new assistant chef. Starting tomorrow."

"Tomorrow." Celia groaned. "Now I'll have to cook again."

"And redo the schedule." Hope hugged Fawna and patted Celia on the back. "Everyone's gotten so spoiled with you doing most of the cooking. Fawna, you are on your way. Way to go!" They swapped high-fives.

"Okay, back to work, celebration is now on hold until we finish here."

An hour later, with résumés critiqued, rewritten, read aloud, and cheered, Julia stood in front of them again and nodded. "Good job, girls. You're dismissed."

"What's our surprise?" someone called.

"Surprise, did anyone ever mention a surprise?" She glanced around the eager faces.

"The boxes are in the office. We'll need help getting them." Celia and Clarice headed for the office. Two girls leaped up and followed them.

"What's in them?"

"I'm not telling." Clarice leaned over to help pick one up.

"Huh-uh, hefting boxes is for young backs." Celia bumped her away with one hip. "You lead the way." She started to pick up the box, grunted, and motioned for one of the girls. "Get the other side."

"I'll get it, Mrs. C," Tasha said when Clarice tried to help again.

"Do you mind if I carry the box cutter?" Her question made the others giggle.

All the girls gathered around as they set the boxes up on one of the tables. Clarice cut open the boxes, and a sigh of delight ran from girl to woman at the sight of all the clothes and accessories.

"Okay, let's lay things out according to sizes." Hope held up a jacket. "Good interviewing stuff here. Size 10."

"Brand-new?"

"This would fit you."

The next half hour, giggles, "ooh's," "aah's," and holding things up to say, "How does this look?" and "Whatja think?" bubbled and snapped, a girl party like none of them had ever had before.

Hope finally raised her hands. "Here's the way I see it. Let's pick out the best outfits for interviewing, in a range of sizes, and keep those in the closet in the office. You wear what fits you for your interviews, make sure they're clean, and then hang them back up for the next one. When the rest are here, everyone can choose one thing. How does that sound?" She glanced to the others for approval.

Some of the girls drifted away, but some stayed to help, hanging skirts, jackets, shirts, and pants on hangers, then hauling it all into the closet in the office, where others had been pulling the office supplies out and stacking the boxes in a corner.

The door opened, and Hope looked up. "Hi, can I help you?" She caught her breath. "Cyndy?"

The girl nodded. "Is my grandma here?"

Chapter Forty-Four

Now that Andy was fairly sure she wanted the property in Medford, how should she tell Martin? Before she opened her mouth and said all the wrong things, she decided to get some advice on what to say and how to proceed.

The next morning, she told Martin she had to go to J House for a couple of hours but would be back before lunch. He still hadn't said much since after his boss left. Was he feeling overwhelmed by all the work he had to do? Had his boss said something to tick him off? Or had he started taking those pain pills again?

She clicked her left turn signal to turn into the parking lot of J House. She had to wait for a black Lincoln Town Car to drive by before she could complete her turn. As it passed, she caught a glimpse of three men. Recognizing the front-seat passenger as Martin's boss, Brad, she waved. Evidently he didn't see her, because he didn't wave back. Either that, or he was intentionally ignoring her.

As always, J House was an anthill of activity. "Good morning, Celia. It's hard to believe you're still picking veggies in December."

"They grow year 'round here if you keep plantin'." Celia pulled a carrot, wiped it off on her pant leg, and handed it to Andy, top and all. "Could use a washin'." She uprooted another carrot for Adolph, who was sitting next to her, one paw raised. "Dumb dog. Likes carrots. If I don't watch him, he pulls his own."

"My dog at home likes carrots," Andy said, fighting a jolt of homesickness at the thought of Comet. "She likes Jell-O, too. You should see her try to eat it."

Celia shook her head. "Did you hear all the news?"

"No. Tell me."

"Fawna got a job over at the lawyer fella's building, being the assistant to the chef. And..." Celia paused for dramatic effect. "Julia's granddaughter showed up last night."

"Thank You, Jesus," Andy said in a whoosh. "That's wonderful news. Thanks." She opened the door and went inside. She couldn't wait to see Julia and tell her how happy she was for her. She followed the sounds of conversation to find Julia, Clarice, and Hope in the kitchen. Andy gave Julia a big hug. "Celia told me the news. You must be overjoyed."

"I'm still in a state of shock."

"Did she go back to the hotel with you last night?"

Julia nodded. "She took a shower, washed her hair, and crashed on the couch. When I got up this morning, she was gone."

"Oh no."

"It's okay. She left me a note saying she'd be back this afternoon." Julia raked her hand through her hair. "Why now?" she wondered out loud.

"Maybe because we've been praying so hard," Clarice said, pouring tea into mugs for all of them.

Julia heaved a sigh. "I'm singing thank-yous, but let me tell you, I have no faith that if she does show up this afternoon, she'll stay around."

Hope smiled. "It's a good thing we don't have to have faith in each other. Only in Big Dad."

"True, but how many people would call this a coincidence?" Julia asked.

"As far as I can see, there are no coincidences; there are only God-incidences." Hope sipped her tea. "Let's talk about the things we need to pray for. Clarice?"

Caught off guard, she hesitated before speaking. "First and fore-most, for the future of J House."

"Thanks and true, but what about for you?" Hope asked.

"I'm off the prayer list. It looks like I'll be getting my Social Security checks and maybe even part of Herbert's. That's all I need."

"That's not all you need," Andy said. "If you plan on living here, you're going to need a lot more than Social Security checks. We'd better pray that you get everything back."

Clarice laughed. "That's okay with me."

"Julia?" Hope prompted.

"Just that Cyndy comes back...and stays."

"Andy?"

Andy told them how much better everything had been between her and Martin since their last prayer meeting. "Getting all that off my chest did me a world of good. So I'd like for everyone to pray that it continues. But before we pray, I need to ask your opinion on some-thing." She told them her situation in as few words as possible. "I want to pray for help in telling Martin that I want to go home and that I want him to come with me. I thought I'd wait until after we get there to tell him about the property. I need to walk the land. It has to feel a certain way..." She waved her hand in front of her face, as if to say that she knew she was being silly.

Julia stretched out her arm and pretended to be holding some-thing in her fist. "We understand, Scarlett. We surely do understand."

Andy burst out laughing.

Hope set her mug on the counter. "My prayers are for the coming auction—that God brings about some kind of miracle so we have a new home for J House. And if, at the same time, we need a new vision for our work, that He will please show us what He wants."

"It's not like we're asking for much, is it? Clarice studied the tea in her mug. "I think it's easier to pray for world peace."

"So let us pray," Hope said. "And let's remember that He is right here with His arms around us."

After the prayers, the Girl Squad talked at length about how Andy should talk to Martin in a positive way. It was Julia who suggested that she start off by telling him she was going back to Medford—in the kindest possible way—but also in a way that didn't ask permission. She gave a couple of examples, which Andy committed to memory.

On her way home, she called Martin's doctor and got an okay for him to travel.

Martin was sitting at the kitchen table, staring at his computer screen, when she went up the stairs.

"Hi, honey. What are you doing?"

"Just fooling around on the Internet."

She put her purse away and sat down across from him. "Martin, something concerns me."

He watched her, seeming a bit wary, but nodded.

Here we go. "You seem different since Brad was here. Is everything all right?"

He half shrugged.

"Do you miss going into the office?"

"Not really. I didn't do it long enough to get accustomed to it."

"Do you miss traveling?"

"No, not at all." He closed down his computer.

Was he closing the door on talking to her, too? She waited for him to get up, but when he didn't, she took that as a sign to continue.

"Martin, Mom called yesterday. I need to go home for a week or so. I have things there that need my attention. I called your doctor, and he said you can go with me as long as we go by car, bus, or train. He doesn't want you flying yet, or driving." She leaned forward. "If you don't want to go, I'll understand, and I'll find someone to look in on you. Maybe someone from J House, or a home nurse." His brows drew together in a frown. "I have to be back here before the fifteenth. That's the day J House goes up for auction, and Hope needs my support." She reached across the table and took his hand. "I'd love it if you'd go to Medford with me."

The corners of his mouth turned up in a half smile. "It would be nice to get out of here," he said, to her great surprise. "I think I now know how a caged animal feels. Maybe we could stop at Granzella's on the way and get real hamburgers and milk shakes. You know that place in Willows we liked so much."

She raised her eyebrows.

"Oh, all right. You can have the hamburger and milk shake, and I'll eat a salad."

She couldn't believe her ears. He was not only saying he would go, he was saying he'd enjoy going. "I'm sure we could," she said, wanting to keep him excited. "It's normally about an eight-hour drive, maybe ten with walk stops. We could drive it in one day, or spend the night in Dunsmuir. Might be fun to stay in one of the cabooses there."

"What about Fluffy?"

Andy had forgotten about Fluffy. "I'll ask Julia to pet-sit. I'm sure she'd be delighted to get out of that hotel for a few days and enjoy the comforts of a home."

For nearly an hour after that, in answer to Martin's questions, Andy talked about the Girl Squad and what had brought each of them to J House. Martin seemed truly surprised when she told him that Julia was a family-law attorney and that Clarice had been a wealthy woman before Gregor had fleeced her out of her money.

She told him about Hope and Roger, their history, their present, and about their coming miracle baby. By the time she finished, he knew nearly as much about J House and the women who worked there as she did.

"They're like a second family," she told him. "I was wrong in thinking there wasn't anything about San Francisco that I'd like. I love J House. And I love the Girl Squad and Celia."

"Celia of the two-inch-long-frosted-purple fingernails?"

"That's the one. She's a mainstay at J House."

"Home, sweet home." Andy drove up the long dirt drive and mentally kissed every row of lavender and blooming chrysanthemums they passed. It felt like she'd been gone for years rather than weeks. Everything looked exactly the same, wonderfully the same. *I praise You, Lord, for making such a beautiful place.* These days she worked really hard at remembering to praise God not only for the good things, but the bad things, everything—just like Hope preached.

"I'd almost forgotten how beautiful it is," Martin said, turning to give her a smile.

"I don't think I could ever forget."

It was barely noon when they pulled up to their house. Comet came from behind the house barking. When Martin opened the door and got out, the Border collie started yipping with excitement.

"Hey there, you," Martin said, patting the dog's head.

"I think she's missed you."

Martin laughed. "Yeah, I guess so. Good girl. Good girl. I missed you too."

Andy searched the yard and saw Chai Lai watching her from her chair on the front porch. Unlike Comet, Chai Lai was far too refined to come running. Instead, she got up, yawned, stretched, then jumped down to sit on the step and wait for Andy to come to her.

"Hello there, sweet cat," Andy said as she picked her up. "Did you miss me?" Tears filled Andy's eyes when the cat touched her face ever so lightly with her paw.

"Hey, Mom!" Andy called when she saw her mother coming toward her. "You look great."

Alice held her arms open to her daughter. "Oh, honey, I'm so glad you're home." Andy went into her arms and hugged her mother tightly. "You, too, Martin," Alice said, waving Martin over and taking him into her embrace as well. "You gave us all quite a scare."

"Where's Dad?"

"Walking the fields."

"Why?"

"Because that's what he likes to do. He loves those plants as much as you do. They're his babies." She took Andy's hand. "Go on now. You two get settled. I'm going to fix us a nice salad for lunch. Be at the house at one."

Andy nodded, then watched her mother walk away, as graceful as ever.

Martin opened the trunk and took out two small suitcases. They'd just packed enough for the night they'd spent on the road, since they both still had clothes here. "I'll take these in," he said, pulling up the handles and wheeling them to the front entry.

Andy stopped in the middle of her family room. She'd never been away from Lavender Meadows more than a few days, so coming home felt extra comforting. She gave it the once-over like a nosy visitor, checking, inspecting, and criticizing. This piece of furniture was out of date, that doodad didn't fit the décor, the edge of the chair cushion was frayed.

For all its many flaws, it was home, and she wouldn't change a thing. She loved it just the way it was. She let out a sigh at the thought of having to leave it again. How long before she would be back this time?

Not long, she promised herself. Christmas was coming. Once Martin was back to work, she could come back here to work.

"I'll take those," she told Martin, indicating the suitcases. "Why don't you take a nap until lunch? I'll bet you're tired."

"Sounds good," he said. "I could use one."

She unpacked slowly and let herself enjoy putting each item away in its proper place. By the time she was done, it was almost one. She turned to find Martin watching her.

"I forgot how comfortable this bed is. I slept like a baby."

"Good, but you'd better rise and shine. We don't want to be late for lunch. You know how grumpy Dad gets if he has to wait."

"Yeah, I know."

The way he said it, she knew he was referring to a time, prior to their getting married, when he'd shown up for dinner at her parents' house fifteen minutes late. Her dad had sat him down and given him a lecture about manners and had embarrassed her to tears.

Since then, Martin had never been late. Nor early either. He'd always been right on time.

They sat around an old-fashioned farm table—a solid piece of oak two inches thick. It had come from a tree near the front of the property, struck down by lightning over eighty years ago. The table had been the center of family life for three generations, and now was Alice's one prized possession.

Over coffee and Alice's famed apple crisp, Walt asked about Martin's heart attack.

Martin gave them the details as he knew them. "I guess I'm lucky to have survived." He turned toward Andy. "I shouldn't have kept my condition from you. I'm sorry. I was wrong not to have told you."

His admission took Andy by surprise. His gaze met hers across the table. "You saved my life. I don't have the words to tell you how grateful I am."

Andy couldn't have forced words past the lump in her throat if she'd tried. So she nodded and sniffed. *Thank you, Jesus. Praise be to God—I mean You, Big Dad.*

Walt cleared his throat. "Ya darn fool. You shoulda told her."

"Walter!" Alice scolded. "You hush now. It's none of your business. You didn't tell me when you fell in the creek and hurt your back."

He ducked his chin and studied the coffee left in his cup. "That's different."

Alice shook her head. "No, it isn't."

Andy interrupted before her parents could take their bantering to the next level. "The doctor put Martin on an exercise regimen and told him he'll have to make some lifestyle changes."

"What kind of changes?" Walt wanted to know.

Andy was all ears. She wanted to know too, because whatever he did usually affected her.

"Some of the changes were made *for* me. I won't be traveling any more, and—"

Andy cut in. "I thought you still had some training to do."

He shook his head. "Not anymore. When I had the heart attack, they put someone else on it."

Andy started to open her mouth and say something about not being indispensable, but she stopped herself. If she was reading his expression right, he already knew. *A miracle, Lord. Thank You, thank You, thank You.*

"So what's this new job of yours all about? Andy tells me you have a big fancy office and a secretary…"

Andy thought Martin looked almost embarrassed. Didn't he know she talked to her parents about him and his job? Didn't he know she was proud of his accomplishments?

"They made me senior vice president of national sales. I have twelve men under me, doing what I've been doing all these years— traveling from city to city, from company to company." He looked down at his plate. "If my boss has his way, I'll have twelve more by the middle of February."

Andy's jaw dropped. "Honey, you didn't tell me that."

"I didn't know until the other day when Brad came to the house."

She eyed him with concern. "That's twice as much responsibility as you have now. Will you have an assistant to share the load?"

"No." He took a bite of his dessert. "This is great. Just what the doctor ordered."

The conversation veered away from Martin to Andy. She told her parents about J House and the Girl Squad. "I have to be back in San Francisco on the fourteenth for the auction."

"Oh, that reminds me," Martin said, stopping the conversation. He turned to Andy. "That day Brad was at the house, I told him about J House." At Andy's perplexed expression, he added, "AES is looking to diversify its holdings. Brad told me he'd take a look at the place and see if it had any potential."

Today was one surprise after another with Martin. What would he tell her next?

"I saw Brad and two other men the other day when I went to J House. I was waiting to make the turn, and he passed me in a black Lincoln. I recognized him and waved, but either he didn't see me or he was ignoring me."

"They were probably scoping out the place."

"What would they do with it if they bought it?"

"Condos, maybe. I'm not involved in that facet of the company."

"Will they be at the auction?"

"I don't know. I'm just the messenger."

Andy sat back in her chair and nodded, but all the while her thoughts went reeling off in various directions. *Martin is only the messenger.* Something, she wasn't sure what, was happening here. *What are we doing, Lord? What are You trying to tell me?*

Later that afternoon, while Martin was checking with his secretary, Andy and her parents walked over to Mr. McCauley's farm and got a quick tour of the house and the more recently built detached garage.

"If you decide to take it," Mr. McCauley said, "then part of the deal is that you don't tear down the house. The house has history, know what I mean? Your grandfather and the people who built it were probably friends. Or enemies. Who knows?" He turned and pointed to the front porch. "They don't make fretwork like that anymore. It's a lost art."

Andy agreed. "It's a beautiful house," she said, looking at it and thinking how cute it would look painted in shades of lavender, the fretwork white. She could just see a cottage-style sign out front near the road that said "Lavender Meadows."

While her parents and the McCauleys talked, Andy walked over to the small garden next to the house. Remnants of spring and summer vegetables lay forgotten. She bent down and scooped up a handful of dirt and rubbed it between her thumb and her fingers. Then she brought it close and smelled it. There was nothing like the smell of good, rich soil.

Later that afternoon, Andy, her parents, and Shari met in the office. Shari said she was willing to work thirty hours a week and that she had a niece with bookkeeping experience who was looking to work part-time while her son was in school. Shari pointed out that between the two of them, with Alice, Walt, and Andy, they should be able to take Lavender Meadows into the next year and beyond without any problems.

They were well into their discussion when Martin walked in. "Don't let me interrupt you," he said, sitting down at the worktable.

Andy felt a little uncomfortable with him there but didn't dare ask him to leave. This was the part she'd been working up to—buying the McCauley farm. The trip here and the property were the two things she had gone to the Girl Squad for help with. "We were just talking about the future of Lavender Meadows," she said. "Based on Shari's sales report, the business is growing at such a rate that if we don't plant more lavender fields this spring, we'll have to turn away orders and limit our growth."

"Well, what's the problem? You've still got a few acres left to plant."

Walt stood up, walked over to the window, and rattled off how many rows could be planted times how many plants times how much yield. "We'll be good for another year, and that's without any more large contracts." He turned around and looked at Andy. "We *could* buy harvested lavender from another grower. 'Course it might not be as good as ours, and…"

"And it will cut down on the profit margin," Shari pointed out. "I've already looked into it." She smiled.

"Wow. Aren't you the one?" Andy teased.

"Yeah. I took a few business courses in college."

"A few?"

"Well, it was my major, but…you know."

"You never told me that," Andy said.

"You never asked."

They continued their discussion, switching to the new accounts, the online catalog, the classes, and the from-home sales. Though they hadn't finished the Christmas season, Shari had estimated sales based on what had already come in, calculated the expenses, and guess-timated the year's profit at $130,000.

Andy blinked. "Are you sure that isn't the gross?"

Shari gave her a long-suffering look. "I'm very sure. Business is booming around here. You've just been so busy doing other things, you haven't noticed. We've been pushed to the limit to keep up with the orders."

Martin got up. "May I see this guess-timate of yours?"

Shari handed it to him, then looked at Andy with a question in her eyes.

Andy held her breath while he perused it. Her heart had taken up a new position in her throat when she said, "So what do you think, honey?" Those were the magic words the Girl Squad had suggested. Give the problem to him, had been Julia's suggestion. And now she was. "We could use some input from a disinterested party."

"I'm not disinterested." Martin shook his head. "Shari, don't you think this sales guess-timate is too high?"

"I'd say it's on the conservative side." Shari picked up a stack of Internet orders. "These just came in today. Thirty-five hundred dollars' worth. It's just a darn good thing Andy took the profit from the first Nordstrom order and put in right back into stock."

Martin's wrinkled forehead cleared. "It looks to me like you need to expand your operation here. Can you buy or lease some acreage somewhere?"

Andy blinked and nodded, but inside she was dancing and singing. *Thank you, Girl Squad. Thank You, God, for…everything.*

Chapter Forty-Five

Hope

"I think I'm going to be sick."

"Not the baby. Hope, are you all right?" Roger stopped in the midst of pulling on his pants and turned to her.

"Just this auction today. I know I'm supposed to be letting God do the whole thing, but He's been so silent. What if…?" It was hard to believe it was already December 15. She rubbed her forehead and sighed loud enough to make Adolph come to the bed and stare at her. His tail wagged, and he whined, low in his throat. One black paw came up on the bed. "Sorry." She stroked his soft head and the paw.

"Huh-uh, don't go there. We agreed to leave this in His hands, and there is nothing we can do about it anyway, so leave it there."

"Sometimes that is easier said than done."

"I know. You want your coffee in here?"

"No, I'll get my shower and dressed for the day. This should be a power suit day, but my power suit no longer fits around my middle."

"Might there be something in those clothes from Macy's?"

"Good suggestion, mon. I'll ask Celia to look."

"I'll ask her, and you get in the shower."

When Hope returned to the bedroom, three black skirts of various sizes and lengths lay on her bed. The note said, *Wear your tan blazer and that black turtleneck. You don't button the jacket anyway.*

Hope smiled. No matter how outrageously Celia dressed herself, she had excellent taste for others when it came to clothes.

Two hours later they stopped at the door to Peter's office. "Big Dad, please."

"Lord, You know our needs, and this is Your gig. Show 'em who You are." Roger hugged his wife one more time and pushed open the door.

Four hours later, the door closed behind the bidders. Peter stared from the papers in his hand to Hope and Roger. "Do you feel as shell-shocked as I do?"

They nodded. Hope looked around the board room, half expecting it to be destroyed by the whirlwind that had gone through. Chairs should be turned over, papers scattered, and windows broken, but instead the lights reflected peacefully in the long, polished-to-glass table. The chairs were all pushed back in. The cart with ice water, coffee, and tea had been trundled out by one of the assistants.

"This hardly seems possible." Peter shook his head again.

"Sure beats the apartment house in the Tenderloin." Hope blew out a breath. "Thank You again, Big Dad. We all saw You in action today, that was for sure."

"And the warehouse in South SanFran. Although it's true, either of those could have worked too." Roger took a swig from his glass of ice water. "Here I came all prepared to do battle…"

"Me too."

"And God took care of the whole thing. Even to the inspection report on our new house."

"Something." Hope screwed her face in thought. "AES, the name sounds familiar."

"You saw it on the papers, dear."

"No, from somewhere else. Hmm. It'll come to me. What a party we can have when we tell everyone the decisions are all made. All their prayers are answered." She sat down and fanned herself with a paper from the table. "I still wish we could stay where we are, but since God engineered this, He has a purpose. Two houses, eh." She threw her hands in the air. "Shout to the Lord, all the earth, let us sing!"

"I'll have all the papers ready for signing by Friday. The title to the house is already researched and clear. You could start fixing that house up next week."

"I'll put out the word. We need volunteers big time. Wall strippers, painters, carpenters, anyone can find something to do there. Since AES is taking care of the new roof, electrical, and plumbing, we can't do much until they are done." Roger looked directly at Peter. "Send us your bill."

"Can't. God stamped it Paid in Full."

"Peter, you…"

"Can if I want. This is my business. Bye." He ushered them out the door.

Hope gave Peter a hug and took her husband by the arm. "Let's go tell the others. The Girl Squad has been praying all this time."

"Good news," Hope said into her cell phone. "Turn the prayers to praise." She clicked off the phone before Celia could do more than scream.

A short time later, Hope stood in the common room at J House, her nonstop grin making the others giggle and cheer. "J House has been sold to a company called AES, right here in the city." She swapped an incandescent smile with Roger.

Andy nearly jumped out of her chair. "Hey, that's Martin's company. He told them about J House."

"Give him a big thank-you."

"How much did we get?" one of the others called.

Roger looked to his wife and wiggled an eyebrow. "One-point-five million dollars."

"But that's ridiculous." Andy's chair took a backward leap. "This property is worth much more than that, two, three times at least."

"That's highway robbery…" Clarice sat back and crossed her arms. "I hate people getting fleeced."

"Roger, quit teasing them." She waved her arms to get quiet again. "Wait a minute here. We are also getting a huge Victorian house out in the Western Addition, along with the vacant lot next to it. There is an empty house next door that we can purchase at a greatly reduced price. AES will provide the new roof, rewiring, and plumbing."

"What about the Saturday Market?"

"We'll use the vacant lot and most likely close off the side street for a few hours. We'll be able to expand and include new vendors because of the extra space."

"When do we have to move?"

"Tomorrow, if they had their way, but most likely by the first of January, if they can get those repairs done by then. We cannot inhabit the house until it meets codes, and they understand that."

"That's impossible."

"Well, who would have thought what we have going now would ever be possible?" Roger looked from face to face. "Let's go look at our new home."

"Put the phone on answering machine, 'cause we're going to see our new home." Hope shook her head when the others peppered her with questions. "Who's here in case of emergency?"

They left Alphi's mother in charge and headed out the door to pile into the van.

Hope read the directions to the area called the Western Addition, where old Victorian houses in various stages of restoration and disrepair lined the streets. Roger finally stopped the van in front of a three-story building with a two-story addition on the back, and a garage on the back corner of the lot. The house next door wasn't as large but looked to be in a little better shape. The vacant lot needed major cleanup.

"That's ours, that's really ours?" Celia leaped out of the van and ran up the cracked concrete walk. "Hey, it even has a basement. Three stories tall and a basement. And look at all the room for my garden, and a real play area for the little ones."

"Lotta work to be done." Andy waited on the sidewalk for the rest of them to get out of the van. "But the inspector says it is sound?"

"Have the paper right here." Hope walked up the sidewalk to the other house. "You know, if Clarice wants to live in the main house, we could take over one floor here for our home. What do you think?"

"I think we need to go ahead with an offer on this one, too, and put that money God is sending us right back into the hopper."

Julia stared from house to house. "I am really having a hard time believing this. My attorney side is warring with my faith side, like this is too good to be true." She held up a hand, traffic-cop style. "I know, I read the papers, but…"

"It turned out the way I hoped, a win-win deal for everyone. Brad Grandolay said the rent on those condos they'll build in our building would be four thousand or so a month. Can you believe that?"

"I can. Remember, I was in the housing market recently. Mrs. Getz gave us a gift, or we wouldn't have our house." Andy stepped around a hole in the stairs and crossed the front porch to look in a window. "I can't wait to see this all cleaned up. Count me in."

"Me too." Julia joined her. "I always dreamed of fixing up an old house like this."

"Painting these in true Victorian style will make them lovely, refurbished dowagers."

"What kinda word is that?" Celia turned from looking in the other window. "When can we get keys to go inside?"

"We're meeting them here tomorrow, but final keys won't be available until all the papers are filed."

"Weeks?"

"No, Brad said hopefully one week. He wants us out of Casa de Jesús as fast as we want out."

Andy shook her head. "If I hadn't seen this happen, I would never trust that title could go through that fast. But then ours did, in less than two weeks, so…"

"So God has been at work."

Andy fumbled in her purse for her ringing cell phone. "Hi Martin. We're over at the new J House." Andy listened a moment and answered. "Sure, I'll stop and get some. We'll be on our way home pretty quick."

"We need to be getting back anyway." Roger called to the others, and they loaded back into the van. "I need to send out a help call for volunteers. This is going to be one busy time."

"Yeah, and get ready for Christmas." Hope started to laugh. "Hang on for the ride, folks. Who knows what Big Dad is going to do next?"

Chapter Forty-Six

Hope

"Cyndy, darling, why are you crying?" Julia braced herself as her granddaughter threw herself into her grandma's arms.

"She's been waitin' for you to get back." Alphi's mom, Patricia, formerly Trish, turned and spoke so only Hope would hear. "Cried most of the time but wouldn't say nothin' to me."

Hope watched as Julia comforted her granddaughter, both of them crying. She pulled some tissues from the resident tissue box on the front desk and crossed the room to hand them out. "You want to go back in the other room so you can talk easier?"

"Thanks." Julia kept her arm around Cyndy as they followed Hope. "Is there anything I can do?"

"Please, Grandma, I want to go home. He'll find me if we stay here."

Julia looked at Hope over Cyndy's head, tears still flowing. They sank onto the couch. When Hope started to leave, Julia beckoned her to stay.

Big Dad, I can sure see that this is not good news. Please help my sister here.

While Cyndy lay against Julia's shoulder as if she had nothing left to hold herself upright with, Julia mopped her face again. "May I tell Hope?"

Cyndy nodded, a barely-moving-the-head nod.

"Cyndy went to the free clinic because she thought she had the flu and wasn't getting any better. They said her blood test showed hepatitis."

"Oh, dear God above." Hope closed her eyes and melted into the wing chair. "And you just learned this?"

Cyndy nodded.

"Child, I hate to ask you this, but how long since you've turned tricks?"

"Week or two. Gave blood two weeks ago and nothing showed." Tears continued to trickle down her face, leaving black mascara tracks. She looked like someone had slugged her in both eyes, they were so swollen.

She could be prosecuted for endangerment, transmitting an infectious disease.

Hope left off the thought. "Do you know the names of the johns?"

Cyndy shook her head. "King will kill me if he finds out."

"You've been back with him?"

Cyndy nodded this time.

"Does he know where Julia is staying?" Hope asked the girl.

"Don't think so."

"I'm calling the airlines to see when we can get out." Julia sighed and sent Hope a pleading look. "If Clarice would like to…"

"If Clarice would like to what?" Clarice walked into the office, back from checking on the girls preparing dinner.

"Stay in my room at the residential hotel. I'm not taking all my things. We'll just leave now."

"You mean give up my cot?" Clarice smiled at her friend. "Sure, thank you for the offer. I can catch the bus back here every morning like you've been doing."

"What can we do to help you?" Roger asked.

"A ride would be good."

"You have it. I'll be ready whenever you are." He knelt in front of Cyndy. "If we can get King on dealing, will you testify?"

Panic made her shudder, but staring into his eyes, she finally nodded.

He patted her knee. "Good girl."

Hope handed Julia the phone and the phone book. "You want something to drink? Have you eaten?" At the girl's shrug, Hope poured her a glass of orange juice and put crackers and cheese on a plate. "This will help tide you over until..." *Until what? Oh, Lord, while she'd be safer back there, I want Julia here. I am so selfish, I know. Keep them safe. Above all, keep them safe.*

Julia stopped dialing and set the phone down. "We'll be back, my friend. Hopefully in time for Christmas, or at least to help you move." She dialed again, and after making her arrangements, she turned to Roger. "We'll be on the red-eye at ten. I'll go get some things together. Clarice, you want to come with me now?"

"Give me ten minutes?"

"Sure."

"Fine, I'll have the van ready at the side door. Even if King has someone watching J House, we'll get Cyndy out of here safely."

"Thanks for your prayers. I'll see you soon." Julia hugged her friends and, taking her granddaughter's arm, headed to the door.

The next day, Andy read an e-mail from her mother asking when she was coming home again. While the number of corporate orders had slowed, there were plenty of personal orders, and those took more time in the long run. She and Martin had discussed where and how they were going to spend Christmas and agreed that since Thanksgiving had been such a bust, they would celebrate Christmas in Medford. They planned to fly home on the twenty-second.

She took her mother's message in hand and went to talk with

Martin. The thought of going home earlier thrilled her to the tips of her toes.

"So what do you think?" she asked after laying it all out for him.

"I think we should stay with our original plans." He checked his calendar. "I have a doctor's appointment next Tuesday. And the company Christmas dinner is this Thursday."

"You feel up to going?"

"For a while, at least. I'll just take it easy."

Andy felt her resentment rising. *But what about all the work to be done on the new J House?* The thought dropped her mouth open. She'd be bailing out on the Girl Squad. And all the getting ready for Christmas. Julia had already left, and whether she'd be back in time to help was pretty doubtful.

Martin stared at the calendar. "I'd really like you to be here for the company Christmas dinner."

"All right. I can leave on Friday then, and you can fly up after your appointment. AES is pretty much closed between Christmas and New Year's anyway, isn't it?"

He nodded. "If the doctor will let me fly."

"Well, if not, you can take the train. He said your heart was doing great. There doesn't seem to be any residual damage."

"You're probably right."

I refuse to borrow trouble. I'll send Camden down for him if I have to. "Thank you, Martin." She nibbled on her bottom lip. "You will be all right here by yourself, won't you?" She flashed through a list of her to-dos. "Oh, and don't worry about Fluffy. Clarice is looking forward to taking care of him. She's hoping she'll get to see the parrots while she is here." *Not that I haven't been hoping for that since we moved in, and so far, nada.*

∽∾

Andy let her gaze drift lovingly around the family room of their Medford home. The stockings she'd made those years ago, hanging on the mantel, the manger scene with the stable frame that Cam had built in wood shop, her quilted Christmas banner hanging on the wall, the tree lights twinkling in the corner. Every ornament brought back memories. She hadn't put a tree up in the living room this year, but the eight-foot pine her father had cut and delivered made the whole house smell like Christmas. A continuous whirlwind was a kind description of the last few days. If she thought about it, exhaustion nearly swamped her. Along with signing the papers on the McCauley farm and dealing with lavender orders and decorating, she'd even managed to bake three different kinds of cookies: krumkake, the buttery, paper-thin cones that Bria loved; Cam's Rice Krispy bars; and thumbprints rolled in chopped walnuts for Morgan. Martin's favorite divinity filled its usual Christmas can.

The busier she was, the less time she had for missing Martin.

Chai Lai leaped into her lap after dozing along with Comet on the rug in front of the fireplace.

"You're as glad I'm home as I am, aren't you?" Andy stroked her fur, and the cat's engine chugged into full purr. "But you know it's not the same. I want Martin here. Wednesday can't come soon enough."

Comet came over and laid her muzzle on Andy's knee. The dog hadn't left her side since she came home.

The phone rang, so she set the cat down in the warm seat of the chair and answered it.

"Hi there. Can you come pick me up?"

"Martin, where are you?"

"At the airport."

"Here?" Her tone flew higher, her grin nearly splitting her face.

"Would be a long drive to SFO, now wouldn't it?"

"You came early."

"I changed my appointment."

Martin never changed appointments. "The doctor said?"

"I could fly, I can go back to work after the first of the year, and would you quit asking me questions and come and get me?"

He was teasing. She laughed and bit her lip. "I'll be right there."

She threw the switch that turned off the tree lights, made sure the screen banked the fire, grabbed her coat and bag, and flew out the door. "Martin's home. Martin's home. Just us before the kids arrive." Her words caught her by surprise.

Camden had flown into Seattle and was driving down with Bria and Morgan, all scheduled to arrive sometime on the twenty-third. Everyone would be home for Christmas. "Thank You, Father. Thank You!" She shouted out the words. If some other driver thought she was nuts, so be it.

When she reached the airport, Martin was already standing at the curb with two huge suitcases waiting for her.

She leaped out of the car and threw her arms around him. "Merry Christmas." The kiss he gave her warmed her clear to her toes, already plenty warm in fur-lined boots.

"Merry Christmas." He cupped his hands along her jaw line. "That house was miserable without you there."

"Really?" She kissed him on the chin. "Welcome home." She pulled away, slowly, watching his eyes. A smile crinkled the edges. "Here, I'll get the bags." She popped the rear door open, and together they lifted the bags in. "You're not supposed to be lifting heavy things."

"I didn't. We did."

He filled her in on all the news of AES, said Clarice and Fluffy became instant friends… "That cat doesn't know a stranger."

"Neither does Clarice."

"Roger dropped by a couple of times. You didn't sic him on me, did you?"

"No, I think he enjoys talking with you."

"He's a good friend. Wish I could help with the moving, but I'm sure there'll be other things I can do later."

Andy bit her tongue to keep from shouting praises aloud, although she was singing inside. Instead, she said calmly, "Good. God sure worked some miracles there." She reached over and took his hand. "I'm so glad you are here."

"Me too."

Comet greeted him like her long-lost best friend, dancing in the frosty air, yipping, and even a getting out a bark or two.

"She's been so happy with me back." Andy slid his suitcases out on the ground. "What all did you pack?"

"I went shopping online early this year and had given them that address."

"I bought everyone gift certificates. They'll have to do their own shopping, other than the little stuff I've been picking up."

He stopped just inside the doorway, clicked on the lights for the tree, and nodded. "You did it, made it be Christmas here, but then I knew you would."

"Thank you. I could sleep for a week."

"Andy, we need to talk."

"I know." *I know what you are going to say. Please don't say it now. Can't it wait until after Christmas?*

Love him and accept him for who he is. The voice sounded firm, as if not brooking any argument.

Are you going to trust Me?

Yes, Lord, I trust You.

"You want some eggnog or spiced cider?"

"Cider." He leaned over and picked up Chai Lai, petting Comet, who had glued herself to his ankle. "I'll throw some more wood on the fire."

Andy poured the cider she'd made earlier into two mugs, set cinnamon sticks in them, and set them in the microwave. While the cider heated, she fixed a plate of cookies. "You had dinner?"

"Yes, at the airport." He dusted off his hands and settled back in his chair. "Ah, this feels so good."

Then let's stay here. Or... And this was what she wanted the most.

She set a tray on the hassock and handed him his cider, the cookie plate in her other hand.

"Thanks." He sipped and ate one cookie in two bites. "Did you have a good drive up here?"

"Sure. The roads were clear in the mountains. There was plenty of snow, good thing. We need a heavy snowpack to refill Lake Shasta."

"I've been thinking."

"Me too."

"I really missed you." Martin held her gaze, steady and warm.

"Me too."

"So here's what I'm proposing. I turned in my resignation."

Her heart skipped a beat. "What? Martin, are you serious?"

"I am. I saw how important your business is, and its growth potential. I'm hoping you can put a fairly good salesman to use."

Andy left her chair and knelt by his. "Martin, darling, what brought this about?"

"The meeting with Brad. When he said twelve more people on my team, I could feel my whole body clench. All I could think was more hours, more travel, more everything. When the doctor said 'Change your life,' I thought I couldn't do that, but somehow God made me see what is really important. You. You and me." He traced her jaw with a gentle fingertip. "I don't want us to be apart for long times again. I used to think that was okay, but not anymore. I guess this heart attack made me stop and think. And then when that house felt so empty without you... Our marriage is more important to me than anything else." His voice caught, and he cleared his throat and blinked several times.

Andy laid her cheek on his hand. "Oh, Martin, what can I say? I used to like being here alone, my lavender and all the busy things I did, but not anymore. No matter how busy I stayed, this house is lonely without you, and talking on the phone or e-mail just isn't enough."

He stroked her hair and along her chin. "You didn't answer my question."

"What?"

"About putting a pretty good salesman to use—if you want to build more business, that is."

Andy grinned up at him, then tilted her head, watching him from the side of her eye. "Can you plant lavender, answer the phones, fill orders?"

He sighed, a pretend sigh, she could tell by the light in his eyes. "If I must."

"Till fields, move sprinklers..."

"I thought that was your father's province."

"Learn the properties of the different lavenders, practice your French, take your wife to France..."

"I'll do my best. You drive a hard bargain. However, I must inform you that I will not be available for work until the first of March, and I really had hoped for some vacation time with my favorite woman before I start my new position. Oh, I forgot to ask, do I get paid vacation and shares in the company?" He kissed her on the tip of her nose; then his lips found hers. "I love you, Andrea Taylor."

A bit later, Andy looked up into her husband's face, where the firelight flickered and love glowed. "What about our house in San Francisco?"

"Well, we need to live there until I leave the company, and then

I was thinking that if Julia comes back by then, perhaps she'd like to lease it from us."

"What a good idea. She'd love having Fluffy. I don't think he'd do well here. Chai Lai wouldn't like him."

"And I thought we might take Comet along. She just might like the city. There are plenty of places to walk her."

"Martin, you mean it?" Comet heard her name and raised her head, staring at him.

Martin leaned over and patted her. "Other people have dogs in the city, so why not us? After all, it won't be for long."

"More cider?"

"Sure." He smiled at her, an older version of the smile that used to set her heart to fluttering. It still did. "There's a package for you. J House fudge. Roger brought it over. He's a good guy."

"Yes, he is."

"I told him I'd like to help on the restoration of that old house. Several of the AES employees are planning to volunteer."

"Really?"

"Hope said to tell you to hurry back. She's missing the Girl Squad."

"Me too. We'll be there after January first." She leaned against his arm. "Funny, I never dreamed I'd be looking forward to going back."

That night in bed in her black nightie, Andy let her thoughts rove. God had answered so many of their prayers in such interesting ways. She'd always thought that home was here in Medford, but home was really where she and Martin were together. And if God could put together friends like the Girl Squad once, wouldn't he do so again? Of course, He could keep the group together, even across lots of miles. After all, planes flew back and forth every day. Hmm. Something to talk to Hope about.

Epilogue

April 1

"We ready?" Celia shouted.

"Yes!" The response chorused from vendors, those on the street blocked off by traffic barricades and those on the once-vacant lot, which now wore the lawn and sculpted look of a minipark. Customers lined the sidewalks, waiting for the ribbon cutting. City officials, Social Services representatives, folks who'd been blessed by J House, AES employees, and all the friends of J House mingled outside the perimeter ropes.

The Girl Squad stood with arms around one another as Roger handed Alphi the huge scissors. The press and a local television station had their cameras, audiotape recorders, and camcorders running.

Roger raised his arms for silence and beckoned to his wife. Hope handed her baby to Andy and stepped forward to take the mike.

"Let's pray." She waited a moment for silence, started, then cleared her throat. "Father God, our Big Dad, we thank You and praise You for all the work You've done to bring this day into being. Only You could have worked this all out…" A heartfelt "amen" came from someone in the crowd. "We dedicate this place to be used for Your glory and to share the love You so freely give each of us, to those who need it. May all who shop here, live here, and worship here feel Your unending love and presence. We thank You and praise You for all who gave of their time and goods to make this happen. And everyone said…"

"Amen!" The word was a resounding shout.

"Alphi, cut that ribbon."

He grinned up at her and closed the handles of the scissors so the huge blue ribbon fell into two pieces.

Roger took the mike. "Welcome, everyone, shop away, and join us for the barbeque provided by AES and our friends." He turned and gave his wife a smacking kiss, to the delight of the throng.

Hope and Roger shook hands with those around them, while the rest of the Girl Squad gathered around Andy and Amadea Faith Benson.

"That is the most beautiful baby I've ever seen," murmured Clarice.

"You say that every time you see her." Julia gave her friend a hug.

Andy juggled the infant in her bright yellow-and-white matching dress, hat, and booties. "Hey, baby girl, you are one loved child."

Amadea Faith stretched her arms and made baby noises without even opening her eyes, then settled back into her nap. Dark curls peeped out from under the rim of her bonnet.

"Your mama named you one pretty name."

"It means 'loved of God.' " Clarice touched the tiny hand with a gentle finger. "She is so precious. Hope says that since all the grandparents are gone, I get to be the official grandma."

"Good thing." Julia glanced around at the crowds. "Can you believe how many showed up?"

"Elephant ears, get your elephant ears over here." Celia could be heard above the piping flute and the guitarist, the laughter and the buying and the selling. Groups stood around visiting, and a roving man with a camcorder took some footage of the baby.

"Let's go sit on the back porch in the shade so we can visit," Andy said, nodding toward the house, now painted a blue gray, with white and navy trim, and a touch of lavender.

"I'll tell Hope." Clarice set off.

Julia and Andy waved and paused to chat with people they knew.

"Not a good day for selling scarves and things, eh, Starshine?" Andy smiled at the woman, who smiled back, showing off her new dental work.

"Some celebration anyway. Look around—old folks, new ones. This move is a great thing." Starshine reached for a package on the table. "Give this to Hope, will you?"

"Sure, you knit something for the baby."

"Of course." She motioned to the fine needles she had inserted in a skein of soft baby yarn. "You have no idea how many baby things I've sold. Hadn't thought of that before."

"You and I need to talk. I'm thinking some of your scarves and hats might do well in my Lavender Meadows catalogue. You willing?"

"Does San Francisco get fog?"

"Good. See you later." She and Julia made their way to the porch, where they could see over the long tables where people were already eating.

"That was a good thing." Julia nodded. "Here, let me hold her." Andy handed her the baby.

"I remember when Cyndy was this small. So hard to believe."

"They sure grow up fast."

Clarice came up the steps with three elephant ears in their flat containers. "Celia sent these over. Said we all needed a treat."

"Bless that woman." Andy took hers and broke off a bite. "You know I'd never had an elephant ear until I visited the market that first time."

"You'd been deprived." Julia held hers carefully, so as not to drop sugar and cinnamon on the sleeping baby. "Clarice, I got another letter yesterday. The court said that all of your property will be held until after the trial. Sorry."

"No problem, long as it is all safe." She eyed the rings on her fingers. "I'm kinda getting used to these. And every time I look at them I think, *He won't be seeing diamonds for a long time.* The jerk."

The three chuckled together.

"Can a man join you, or is this a hen party?" Martin held out a cardboard carton with containers of coffee. "I came bearing gifts."

"Bless you, of course you can join us." Clarice took one of the proffered cups and lifted it in salute. "Smart man."

That late afternoon, back at their house, which would soon be Julia's, Andy and Martin sat in chairs out on the deck in front of the loft.

"This was such a good idea." Andy leaned back so she could look up in the treetops. "I feel like we have a tree house here." Martin had the deck built one time she was gone to surprise her.

"They should be coming."

"Who?"

"They come about five or so."

"Who?"

"Wait and see."

"Martin." Andy shook her head. "You have been so secretive, what's going on?"

"Just wait." He poured her another glass of cranberry punch. Comet lay at his feet, her tail brushing the redwood decking.

Andy closed her eyes, enjoying the rustle of the leaves in the slight breeze. "What's that noise?"

"Here they come." He leaned forward, scoping the sky. Comet sat up.

A squawking and shrieking noise came closer. One bright green bird with a red head fluttered around and landed on the bird feeder, eyeing the humans and the dog, before picking up a sunflower seed.

"One of the parrots. Martin, you…" Andy stared at the bird, her smile growing wider as several brilliantly colored birds joined the first and fought over the other feeders lining the deck rail. Even while they ate, the raucous calling and castigating continued.

"They usually come at this time. That's why I was in such a hurry to get back here."

"And you never told me."

"I wanted to surprise you, so I've been making sure they have lots of food here. Julia's been keeping the watch too."

"I got to see the parrots. J House and the Saturday Market are a going concern. The baby is an absolute doll. And you, Martin, what an incredible thing to do." She laughed as one bird hung upside down. "What kind are they?"

"Cherry-headed conures. I was so afraid they wouldn't come today. They don't all the time."

"And tomorrow we head home."

"Right. But this will be our other home." They had kept the loft for themselves and leased the rest of the house to Julia.

Andy watched the squabbling birds and chuckled again. "Thank you, Martin. For everything." *And to quote a friend of mine, Big Dad, thank You for being our real home.*

About the Author

LAURAINE SNELLING is a member of the more-than-two-million-books-in-print club, but then, she was a mother of three teenagers with a dream to write "horse books for kids." Her Norwegian heritage spurred her to craft *An Untamed Land,* volume one of the Red River of the North family saga, which, due to reader demand, spun off Return to Red River, a trilogy following more of the Bjorklund family. Three more historical sets have followed, one set during the Civil War that traces the journey of a young woman leading thoroughbreds across the country to safety and a new series called Dakotah Treasures that follows the birth of the town of Medora, North Dakota.

Writing about real issues within a compelling story is a hallmark of Lauraine's style, shown in her contemporary romances and women's fiction, which have probed the issues of forgiveness, loss, domestic violence, and cancer. *The Healing Quilt* explores the relationship of four diverse women who come together to supply their community with a much needed mammogram machine. In *The Way of Women,* three families cope with the aftermath of a volcanic eruption.

All told, she has had over fifty books published—she thinks. She's not sure. She'd rather write them than count them. Lauraine's work has been translated into Norwegian, Danish, and German, as well as produced as books on tape.

Awards have followed Lauraine's dedication to telling a good story: the Silver Angel Award for *An Untamed Land* and a Romance Writers of America Golden Heart for *Song of Laughter.*

Helping others reach their writing dream is the reason Lauraine teaches both at writer's conferences across the country and at her home in the California Tehachapi Mountains. She mentors others through book doctoring and with her humorous and playful Writing Great Fiction tape set. Lauraine also produces material on query letters and other aspects of the writing process.

Her readers clamor for more books more often, and Lauraine would like to comply, if only her ever-growing flower gardens didn't call quite so loudly over the soothing rush of the water fountains in her backyard, or if the hummingbirds weren't quite so entertaining. Lauraine and her husband, Wayne, have two grown sons, a cockatiel named Bidley, a basset hound named Chewie, and a possible Rummikub addiction.